Praise for

WHAT SHE LEFT

"In *What She Left*, T. R. Richmond leads the reader down a dark and twisty path of suspense and intrigue. This gripping and stylishly written novel left me chilled to the bone and captivated me from beginning to end."

—Heather Gudenkauf, *New York Times* bestselling author of *The Weight of Silence*

"An extraordinary and bold creation." —*The Guardian* (UK)

"This is how books should be written: full of trust and respect for the reader, allowing you to follow the darker paths and investigate on your own. A book of immense accomplishment, thrilling and clever."

—Elizabeth Haynes, *New York Times* bestselling author of *Human Remains*

"Strikingly modern." —*The Sunday Times* (UK)

"*What She Left* is bold and inventive storytelling. The reader becomes the investigator, sorting through diary entries, letters, tweets, and emails to discover the truth beneath the tales of an entire cast of potentially unreliable narrators. This is not only a clever thriller but an insightful exploration of identity and the personae we create in the social-media era."

—Alafair Burke, *New York Times* bestselling author of *The Ex*

"Thought-provoking." —*Fort Worth Star-Telegram*

"A deliciously modern take on the psychological thriller. A shifting, mesmerizing, mysterious story. Very well written and intelligently realized, occupying a territory halfway between literary novel and thriller. A memorable debut." —*The Daily Telegraph* (UK)

"A classic whodunit, given a modern twist." —*The Huffington Post*

WHAT SHE LEFT

T. R. Richmond

SIMON & SCHUSTER PAPERBACKS
New York London Toronto Sydney New Delhi

Simon & Schuster Paperbacks
An Imprint of Simon & Schuster, Inc.
1230 Avenue of the Americas
New York, NY 10020

This book is a work of fiction. Any references to historical events, real people, or real places are used fictitiously. Other names, characters, places, and events are products of the author's imagination, and any resemblance to actual events or places or persons, living or dead, is entirely coincidental.

Originally published in 2015 in Great Britain by Penguin Books

First Simon & Schuster trade paperback edition November 2016

Interior design by Lewelin Polanco

Manufactured in the United States of America

10 9 8 7 6 5 4 3 2 1

The Library of Congress has cataloged the hardcover edition as follows:

Richmond, T. R.
What she left : a novel / T. R. Richmond. — First Simon & Schuster hardcover edition.
pages cm
1. College teachers—Fiction. 2. Women college students—Fiction. I. Title.
PS3618.E5728W53 2015
813'.6—dc23

2015004385

ISBN 978-1-4767-7384-1
ISBN 978-1-4767-7390-2 (pbk)
ISBN 978-1-4767-7391-9 (ebook)

To Isabel. For everything.

Dedication in *What She Left* by Professor J. F. H. Cooke, published September 2013

To Alice Salmon (July 7, 1986–February 5, 2012) and Felicity Cooke (October 16, 1951–).

Without the former, this book would have been nothing; without the latter, so would I.

PROLOGUE

Article in the Arts Council magazine,
The Operative Word, 2001

What's in a name? That's the question we asked teenagers to answer in 1,000 words for this year's New Talent competition. Here's the winning entry from fifteen-year-old Alice Salmon.

My name is Alice.

Could leave it there. I know what I mean by that. I'm me, Alice Salmon. Tall, average-looking, big feet, hair that goes wavy at the mere mention of water, a bit of a worry bear. A massive music fan, a proper bookworm, loves being outdoors, though dies at the sight of a spider.

Mostly it's Alice, people call me, although occasionally I'm Al or Aly or Lissa, the last one of which for the record I hate. When I was a kid I used to have squillions of nicknames like Ali Baba and Ice and, my favorite of all, especially when my dad called me it, Ace.

My uncle calls me Celia, which is an anagram of Alice, although I get the word "anagram" muddled up with "anachronism." "That's what I am," my dad always says if anyone says "anachronism," although the word "dad" is actually a palindrome. I learnt that yesterday.

I like knowing this stuff, even if my best friend Megan says I sound as if I've swallowed a dictionary. It's not that I like showing off, but you've got to if you're going to study English. If I get the grades, I'd love to go to Exeter or Liverpool, but as long as it's a long way from Corby I don't mind, although wherever you go, there are probably people trying to get away from there. I'll be honest, I can't wait to move out; my mum's constantly poking her nose into my business. She reckons it's because she cares, but it's not fair it's me who suffers because she's paranoid. I obviously put that last line in after she read this and she'll never see it because I'm bound not to win.

Maybe what's in my name is the music I like (have listened to "Dancing in the Moonlight" about 400 times today) or the TV I watch (you're looking at the world's biggest *Dawson* fan) or my friends or the diary I keep? Maybe it's the bits of all of that stuff I can remember, which isn't much because my memory's lousy.

Perhaps it's my family? My mum and dad and brother who used to called me "a lice" or "Mice" or "Malice" as if it was the funniest joke ever cracked in the history of the world. Maybe it'll be my kids, not that I'm going to have any, no thank you: all that yuck and puke and poo. I haven't even got a boyfriend, although if Mr. DiCaprio is reading this, I am free on Friday . . .

"You'll change your mind," Mum says about the babies, but she said that about asparagus and I haven't.

Perhaps it's the things I plan to do, like travel, or the nicest thing I've already done, which hands down was that day's volunteering at the deaf place (can you see my halo shining?), or possibly the worst (no way am I fessing up to that!).

I could tell you about my best day ever. That's a toughie; maybe it was when Meg and I went to see Enrique Iglesias or I met J. K. Rowling or my gramps took me on that surprise birthday picnic, but the thing about "ever" is that it only takes you up to now, and tomorrow can be better, so I ought to talk about "so far" rather than "ever."

There again, sometimes you can explain what an object is by pretending not to talk about it (I've just googled that: it's "apophasis"), so maybe what's in my name are the things I could be doing instead of this, like my maths homework or taking Mr. Woof for a walk.

I used to wish more famous people were called Alice. Not,

like, mega-famous, because then whenever anyone said it, it would be them who everyone thought of—like if you're called Britney or Cherie—but semi-famous. There's Alice Cooper, but he's a man and that's not even his real name. There's *Alice in Wonderland*, too, which used to get quoted at me a lot, stuff like being curiouser and curiouser, though my favorite line was always the one about not being able to explain yourself because it's not actually yourself you see, even if I never understood it.

I suppose I am what I'm writing here, too, which might be rubbish. I asked my mum to read this—only to check the spelling—and she said it was great, even if the first and last lines did make me sound like an alcoholic, but that's just how she interpreted it.

Mum said there were a few bits I should reconsider, but there's no point submitting it if it's lies, although I did agree to knock out the textspeak and swearwords and there were lots of them in the first draft (this is the seventh!). I also use too many brackets and exclamation marks but they're staying in, otherwise (again) this wouldn't be me.

"At times it terrifies me how much we are alike," Mum said after she read it. Well, she's not the only one. Some days, even though she tries to hide it, she mopes around the house like the world's about to end. (Yes, this line went in after she vetted it, too—talk about the thought police!)

Dad reckons I must have been dropped on my head as a baby, because me and him have hardly anything in common, although we both love salmon, which is funny, because you could say that makes us cannibals.

My name is Alice Salmon. Five words out of my 1,000. I hope I'm more than 200 times those five words. Even if not now, I hope one day I will be.

I will finish this now and stand up and ask myself who I am. I do that a lot. I'll look in the mirror. Reassure myself, scare myself, like myself, hate myself.

My name is Alice Salmon.

PART ONE

Something Passing Stopped

Southampton StudentNet online forum,
February 5, 2012

Topic: Accident

Anyone know what's going on down by the river? Police and ambulances all over the place.

Posted by Simon A, 8:07 a.m.

It's true. Place crawling with cops. Johnny R's out rowing and reckons the whole bank's sealed off.

Posted by Ash, 8:41 a.m.

Hope there hasn't been an accident. That weir has always been a deathtrap. Uni should have fenced it off properly years ago. Dog drowned there only last month.

Posted by Clare Bear, 8:48 a.m.

Deathtrap maybe, but you'd have to be messing around or pretty damn unlucky to fall in the water over those railings.

Posted by Woodsy, 9:20 a.m.

It's a homeless bloke apparently.

Posted by Rebecca the biologist, 9:54 a.m.

Says on Twitter it was some lad at a stag party climbing the bridge for a bet. Hit his head on the way down so was unconscious. I used to fish that bit of the river . . . It's bitterly cold in winter. Few seconds in there and you'd have hypothermia, no question. The currents are crazy. You'd be swept out into deep water unless you're a mega strong swimmer.

Posted by Graeme, 10:14 a.m.

Used to be suicide hotspot that bridge. Seriously.

Posted by 1992, 10:20 a.m.

You bunch of coffin-chasers ought to zip it—imagine how their family would feel reading this shite.

Posted by Jacko, 10:40 a.m.

Their family are hardly going to be on here are they? Only saddos like you and me, Jacko, who don't have a real life!

Posted by Mazda Man, 10:51 a.m.

My brother's a fireman and he reckons it was an ex-student—girl called Alice Samson.

Posted by Gap Year Globetrotter, 10:58 a.m.

Was a girl in my brother's year called Alice Salmon. Top lass by all accounts.

Posted by Harriet Stevens, 11:15 a.m.

Lots of Alice Salmons on Facebook. Only one seems to have been at uni here. Nothing new on her wall since yesterday afternoon when she wrote "Can't wait for night out tonight in Flames." Was she still living in Southampton then?

Posted by KatyPerryfan, 12:01 p.m.

OMG. Just been told about Alice Salmon. Didn't even know her and devastated. She didn't have kids did she? Please someone tell me this ISN'T true.

Posted by Orphan Annie, 12:49 p.m.

Police literally swarming area now. Why so many? Was it not an accident?

Posted by Simon A, 1:05 p.m.

Afternoon, all. I was in her year if it is "the" Alice Salmon. She lived in Portswood then Polygon in her final year. She works in the media in London, although she never struck me as a media type.

Posted by Gareth1, 1:23 p.m.

Alice the Fish, we called her! Can't believe this is true. What about a Facebook tribute page?

Posted by Eddie, 1:52 p.m.

Aren't fish supposed to be able to swim?

Posted by Smithy, 1:57 p.m.

F**k off Smithy, this isn't the time. Tw*t.

Posted by Linz, 1:58 p.m.

Wasn't she dating some bloke from Southampton? She was the one with the freckles, right? Wore a lot of hats?

Posted by Not so plain jane, 2:09 p.m.

The university will put out an official statement on this subject shortly so until then it's inappropriate for this site to host any comments and I am suspending this thread forthwith.

Posted by StudentNet Forum Administrator, 2:26 p.m.

Letter sent by Professor Jeremy Cooke, *February 6, 2012*

My dear Larry,

I overheard the news. *Overheard* it, can you believe, in the faculty room of all places. You overhear that one of your colleagues has had a minor prang in their new car or that Tesco are planning a new superstore on the ring road or that your MP has lost his seat in a by-election, but not a death.

It was this morning and I was engrossed in the *Times* crossword. "Christian name for a code, nine letters," I muttered. "Seven down."

No one responded. I had the purgatory of three hours of lectures with first years in prospect. Around me, conversations carried on as before.

"What about that dead former student then?" Harris piped up. Silence while everyone waited on his next proclamation. The little upstart always knew how to work an audience. "It was all over the TV yesterday. Drowned in the river."

It had passed me by. There again, I often can't bring myself to watch the news; so much of it is uninformed, sensationalist rubbish and so depressingly predictable. I thought evolution was supposed to make us more civilized. Besides, I'd been double-digging the garden.

"*Points South* reckons she was a strong swimmer, too," someone chipped in.

"Yes, but *Points South* also reckons global warming isn't happening!" someone else replied.

Nothing like a death to spark some life into the faculty room conversation. I wondered if they'd react similarly when I go.

"I used to teach her," one of the English lot said. "It was the Salmon girl."

I felt my grasp on the newspaper weaken. Oh God. Not Alice. No, not Alice, please, anyone but my Alice.

"Very keen on Plath—predictably," she added. "Nice girl. Bright."

More voices. A dog walker spotted her; thought she was a bin bag initially. One theory gaining credence was that she was on a hen weekend and a few of them had been fooling around in a dinghy.

"The Alice Salmon who left in 2007?" I inquired as nonchalantly as I could.

"The very one," Harris said.

"Alice, Alice, who the fuck is Alice?" one of the postgrads laughed, clearly an in-joke.

This doesn't concern you, Jeremy, I told myself. *Not anymore. Concentrate on the crossword. Go and teach that bovine-like herd of freshers about cross-cultural diversity in kin relationships. Go to your hospital appointment, then go home and cook that bass.* Trouble was, Larry, an image of Alice had lodged in my brain. I tried to picture her serene and at rest, as Ophelia in the Millais painting, floating faceup, her dress dancing in the eddies and whorls. Except the river Dane isn't the clear cool spring of John Everett Millais's imagination; it's dirty and treacherous and full of debris and rats. In the time it took me to not manage another three crossword clues—I used to finish it over a cup of coffee, but I appear to be losing information these days—she'd become a different person to the one I remembered: now she played tennis at county level, had a real temper on her and spoke French—spoke it like a native. None of it true as far as I was concerned.

"By all accounts, she was quite a hottie," one of the new chaps said.

"For Chrissake," I blurted out, "listen to yourselves—you're like vultures."

"Don't give yourself a heart attack, old boy," he quipped.

Someone quoted the gag about how your hair and fingernails carry on growing after you die but the phone calls taper off, which sent the conversation off on a tangent: the health service, the Leveson media ethics inquiry, the latest round of pay negotiations, the situation in Syria. I remembered her graduation. It didn't raise any eyebrows, me attending. Why would it? I was a respected member of the faculty. Part of the establishment; one of the fixtures and fittings. I merely went to wish the class of 2007 bon voyage; to see them safely off into the big wide world. I'd stood quietly at the back—my epitaph, if ever there was one—and watched Alice, all grown up and leaving. She looked exquisite in a mortarboard and gown. I would have loved to have seen her mother there, too, but either I missed her or she avoided me. Elizabeth. The poor woman. How would she have heard the news? Presumably from the police; surely they'd have gone to her house rather than telephoning. God knows what it would do to her; she was a fragile soul at the best of times. I remembered what she looked like when she cried. Her mother, I'm talking about now, not Alice. The peculiar machinery of her grief: the way her face changed shape, the way her whole body did. I dropped the paper. Felt close to tears, and I can't have cried for twenty-five years.

"Endeavour," Harris called across the room. "Christian name for a code. Endeavour—it was Inspector Morse's first name."

He was right. The smart-arse, he was right.

Apologies for unburdening on you again, Larry, but you're the one person with whom I can be honest. Merely taking out my pen (a handwritten letter, what lovely dinosaurs we are) and beginning with my standard salutation brings so much comfort. There's no need for formalities, no withholding; I can truly be myself. I appreciate I don't need to ask you to refrain from mentioning this to anyone, as there will inevitably be repercussions at this end.

She didn't deserve to die, Larry.

Yours as ever,
Jeremy

Alice Salmon's Twitter biography,
November 8, 2011

Occasional tweeter, frequent shopper. Opinions (mostly) my own. Handle with care. If found, return to sender. Meanwhile, mine's a skinny frothy latte . . .

Extract from Alice Salmon's diary,
August 6, 2004, age 18

Wish I had normal parents.

Mum even barged into my room earlier and plonked herself down on the bed to have a go at me. "How are you feeling?" she asked.

The last thing I needed was a lecture. The room was all wobbly. "Stop being a control freak," I told her.

"I'm only concerned."

I love her loads, but if she loved me as much as she claims, then she'd give me a break.

"Bad things happen when you're that drunk," she said, stroking my forehead.

That was her all over, assuming life is a series of disasters waiting to happen. Well, it might have been for her but it won't be for me. "Bad things happen when you're sober," I replied enigmatically.

"For once, listen to me, Alice!"

That was libelous, too, because I spent most of my life doing that—I had no choice. "I can't wait to move out," I said. I'm counting down the days. The end of September and Southampton here I come. Mum was adamant I shouldn't go there, banged on about how it was nuts to turn a place down at Oxford. That was so typical of my mother—quick enough to dole out advice as long as it doesn't impact on her. As long as I become the vision of me she has in her head: the hardworking grade A student who gets a nice husband and 2.4 kids or becomes a teetotal nun. Well, no way was I going to Oxford with a bunch of toffs. She's also now insisting I'm home before midnight next Friday and out of the blue yesterday announced she wasn't sure about me going to V. "Maybe you ought to drink. It might make you less boring," I said.

She began picking up my clothes off the floor, hunched over like an old granny, frantically tossing them in the washing basket. She was in a right strop.

"For God's sake, leave my stuff alone! You're always on my case."

She did that thing then when she bites her lip and looks all deflated like a balloon at the end of a party. "Well, I'm sorry for being concerned about my daughter's welfare. I'm sorry for loving you!"

"I didn't mean that, I meant—"

"What exactly *did* you mean?"

"You're just so sanctimonious," I said, deploying my current favorite word. I used to include a new word in every diary entry when I was a kid, ideally making them many-syllabled or erudite (that may have even been one), complicated commendations that would have impressed anyone who stumbled across my scribblings, not that I let anyone within a mile of them. All the old diary stuff's gone—burnt—and this, dear reader, is the eighteen-plus edition! This is the bits of me people don't see. Like the black-box recorder in an airplane. I might as well write this stuff down, because no one round here listens to me; I might as well be invisible.

Mum says she'll miss me like crazy after I fly the nest and it makes me imagine myself as a baby bird, a big ugly one like an ostrich or a stork, not an elegant graceful one, and remembering that when she was in my bedroom made me want to take back the last few minutes. "Why *don't* you drink?" I asked.

"It's a long story," she said. "It's complicated."

But even that annoyed me. *I* was the one with the complicated life. All she had to do was go to her stupid job in the building society wearing an "Elizabeth Salmon, Mortgage Adviser" badge and either give money to people who couldn't afford to borrow it or not give it to those who could. She never talks about her academic career, but it must have been a million times more interesting than working on a shitty high street. I imagined V again—the texts arriving from Meg, the photos of Pink and Kings of Leon onstage between all the outstretched arms in the sunshine—and felt a burn of anger. "You're just jealous," I said.

"Of what, exactly?"

"The fact that I've got a life. It's like a graveyard round here."

A bit later I went down to the kitchen and Mum was stacking the dishwasher. I put some toast on. "How are you feeling now?" she asked. "We could go for a walk later if you fancy it. Fresh air helps."

I munched my toast. It tasted of nothing but made me feel sick.

"That stuff you said, Alice . . . you don't really think that's the case, do you?"

Right then I couldn't recall exactly what I *had* said. A motor had been turning in me: that thing that made me say what I shouldn't, do what I shouldn't, and now I felt shit—hungover shit but shit-shit, too; just plain bad. I put my hand on the sleeve of her faded pink dressing gown (Dad bought it for her one birthday—I helped him choose it; OK, I chose it *for* him) and felt ashamed. I gave her a big hug and cried a bit and she hung on.

"There, there, sweetie," she said, rubbing my back. "Let it all out. There's no harm done. Parents have to let their kids grow, but they also have to let them go. You'll understand that one day."

I pulled a face.

"That's all for the future," she said. "You've got a lot to fit in before then. There's university, for starters. Imagine, both my babies away at uni."

We don't see much of Robbie now he's at Durham. He's been in Australia this summer, the lucky sod; I get pictures of beaches and messages like "How's Corby, loser?"

The Robster reckons all I do is doss around because it's only the party stories he hears, but that's about a hundredth—OK, a tenth!—of my life. There's the running and the piles of schoolwork and the volunteering at that shelter for the homeless, plus I've had TWO jobs—admittedly that doesn't make me Oprah Winfrey or Anita Roddick, but I've been waitressing in a bistro and doing shifts in the leisure center.

"Sorry about earlier," I said. "I'm so stupid."

"You're your mother's daughter all right."

We did a bit of surfing then, reading the National Union of Students' site and other uni-related ones to check what I was supposed to be taking (the list gets longer by the day!) and studying the pictures of girls playing hockey or wandering in twos and threes between brick buildings with books under their arms or holding their mortarboards in the air. It all felt unreal. Soon I'm going to move out.

"You'll be fine, sweetie," Mum said, reading my mind. "You'll be absolutely fine."

Maybe this, I thought, sitting at the kitchen table, *is nostalgia: the swoosh of the dishwasher, the smell of the pine floor, the click of the boiler. Maybe this will be what I'll come to remember, come to miss.* Mr. Woof came up and nuzzled into my lap.

"What does it make you feel like, drinking?" Mum asked.

I nearly said "Awful," but I recalled the night before. The Peppers were playing and one of the guys was dancing on a table and I'd had a huge gulp of punch, tasted the pineapple, and it had struck me how brilliant it would be if life could stay exactly like this forever. "Guess it makes me feel kind of better," I said. "Not like I am—not like Alice."

"Sweetheart," she said, "it's an illusion. How you feel when you're full of gin is not real."

"Hate gin," I said.

"Wish *I* had," she said, half smiling. "*This* is real. The morning after, the regret, the shame, us arguing, that's the worst—although we'll put it right. We'll always put it right, you and me." She was running her hand through my hair how she used to when I was a little girl. "Look how beautiful you are," she said.

"I hate arguing with you," I said.

"Me too."

"You're the best mum I've got by far!" I said, laughing, wiping snot from my nose.

"And you're the best daughter I've got by far."

Letter sent by Professor Jeremy Cooke,
February 7, 2012

Larry,

Two letters in two days; this must be a record—certainly as regards our recent correspondence.

It's appalling the way a death brings out the worst in people. The students have been positively feasting on this Alice business despite none of the current crop actually having known her. As you can imagine, the campus rumor mill has gone into overdrive—it's replaced the Arctic weather as the main topic of conversation. The students have taken to their phones, laptops and iPads to trade theories. They shake their heads and nod enthusiastically in the canteen and in lecture halls and stand around, stamping the snow off their feet, gossiping in chilly huddles in the quad outside my office. There I go again, old chap, referring to it as a quad—that ostentatious habit I cultivated when I fostered pretensions of

Oxbridge; it's actually a concrete space through which the students shuffle directionless, an apt metaphor for their futures if ever there was one.

I'd cycled back to my office from the faculty room on Monday, eschewing my lecturing duties by feigning sickness (an irony there) and searched for Alice online. There were lots of Alice Salmons, but I soon found the one in question. Social media was awash with it; who says you can't teach an old dog new tricks, eh, Larry? This is how news works these days: a giant, grotesque game of Chinese whispers. Titbits of gossip, fag ends of conversations, nuggets of recycled information overheard between four down and nineteen across. But such tosh: she wasn't a bubbly blonde, she wasn't a feminist crusader, she wasn't Fleet Street's finest. It was all so damn reductive. I saw her variously described as happy-go-lucky, perfect, irresponsible, unlucky, stupid, fit, fat, gorgeous, a one-in-a-million.

"No," I heard myself muttering. *"Stop it."*

Perhaps this is how youngsters grieve nowadays? That shrink I had a brief flirtation with many years ago (it would have been shortly after I knew Alice's mother, as you may recall) used to say that pain had to go somewhere.

I read everything about her and by her I could find. "Your with the angels," someone had written on her Facebook page, and it gave me a little stab of sadness. At least get your damn spelling right. I cut and pasted it all onto my desktop and experienced a rare sense of satisfaction, of calm. There. I had a little bit of her. It struck me that if I'd discovered all this after a few minutes, how much I could learn if I delved deeper. I'd like to hope we're all more than the sum of our parts. Even me. A sixty-four-year-old academic whose place in the world has never felt entirely set.

I've just reread this dispatch; I did it out loud because I like to get a measure of cadence. Something too awful about the sound of one's own utterances, though; it's like hearing someone else. The tired, treacly public school vowels; not even a trace of Edinburgh. Strange that that's me, my voice. *Old Cookie.* Is that what the students have had to listen to all these years, poor blighters? I've been trying to recall Alice's voice. An accent that was hard to place. Socially mobile parents. A grammar school inflection. Shot through with laughter. Where's it gone, the voice that once said to me, Why *do* you treat me as if I'm special?

I can hardly contact Elizabeth, but I could go to her friends and colleagues. I could go to the brother. I found him on his firm's website along with a potted biography and a black-and-white photo. Robert. He doesn't look much like his sister or his mother. It wasn't hard to track down her friends, either. They work in marketing and property and finance; a few have young families, little Sophies and Georges. The children Alice will never get to have. One by one, I contacted them. "We haven't met," my communications began, "but we have something in common . . ."

To research, to record, to collate—yes, this is the role of the anthropologist. Larry, might it not bring her family some comfort—happiness, even—if I could pull together some such information? Breathe a flutter of life back into her? Make her dance once more, because she always was a dancer. She must have got that from her mother: Elizabeth loved to dance.

It would be grand to hear your take on this. Despite your credentials, you've always been far more grounded than me, always been regarded as—a ghastly phrase, admittedly—a man of the people, even if I have viewed you exclusively as mine. You've been the one person to whom I've been able to turn. "Inspiration" is an overused word, but that's what you've been to me. You've never judged me. I'll never be able to repay you, although I have this week made provision for your children in my will.

Ah, the delicious indulgence of writing longhand. As a child, it used to worry me that my handwriting kept changing style: I feared I'd never be an adult until it stayed constant. That would then be me: formed. How do people develop that sense of self nowadays, when all they write on is keyboards? I'm determined to continue corresponding with you in this way. It's one of our traditions, one of our secrets. One of our many.

You won't be surprised to hear this Alice news has hit me hard. I'm not going to pretend it hasn't; why would I? Whoever else we've duped, we've never lied to each other. That was our pact: no lies. In a world where secrets were omnipresent, our honesty has been one of life's few constants. You're like a compass bearing for me.

"Partners in crime," you once joked.

I've dragged all the information into a "Save Alice" folder. Calling it that made me chuckle; naming a piece of work has always been one of my favorite parts. The first reply from one of her friends came within ten minutes.

Forget Ophelia, it's Alice Salmon I'm going to paint.

Blog post by Megan Parker,
February 6, 2012, 10:01 p.m.

Bought a card but what do you say? How can a card offer even a teensy grain of comfort? Alice is dead. My best friend Alice is dead. Never known anyone my age who's died before. So unjust so unfair so unreal—like being told there's a giraffe in the garden. Can't stop crying. How can you be gone? How can you die when other people go on living? Breathing and eating and walking around, murderers and rapists and scum like that? There's no justice when someone as wonderful as you can die. You're not gone for a day or a week or a month or even a whole summer like when you worked at the holiday resort but forever. Not letting myself dwell on how that might feel or how long that might last.

Couldn't face being on my own so came home to my mum and dad's. Dad reckons there'll have to be a postmortem because there always is when someone dies unexpectedly. "That poor girl, having to go through that as well," he said.

Where are you? Where have they taken you? I know some places you're not—you're not on top of that hill in the Lake District with me and Chloe and Lauren, us with our hands on the elevation marker.

You're not in that Thai restaurant we always used to go to on Clapham High Street (a restaurant, *get us,* Alice, haven't we got all adult?!). You're not in the minibus on that hockey club tour singing along to "Amarillo." There'll be so many places you're not now. There it is again, the giraffe in the garden: that you're *not*. But when I look out there's nothing, just the rusty swing that me and you used to play on, telling each other secrets and making plans for when we grew up and you've only got to do a few of them, just as you were getting the hang of life, you crazy silly girl, it's snapped shut around you. It's not fair, but when I used to say that to you, you replied that the world wasn't fair, it was full of injustice, and if people simply opened their eyes they'd see.

I posted the card to your mum and dad. A stupid card with a pink flower on the front and "With deepest sympathy" underneath. Seems surreal that it's *you* we've got deepest sympathy over. They'll miss you so very much. Robbie will, too. Wish I knew what you'd want me to do about Luke as well—whether to hate him or not, because a bit of me is certain you'd have got back together.

We've been friends since we were five. Stuck together through thick and thin . . . you always used to joke that you were the thick one and I was the thin one . . . and school and rubbish boyfriends, and we even got to go to uni together and not because we were scaredy-cats but because Southampton was such a great place and it was fab having you there, even though you were far more in with the in-crowd than I ever was!

Who's going to keep me on the straight and narrow and tell me I'm weird for having a thing about older men?! You joked we were a right pair of hopeless cases, didn't you? You going through what you were with Luke, and me holding out for George Clooney but prepared to accept Harrison Ford at a push.

"Anyone who's anyone dies at twenty-seven," you said after Amy Winehouse OD'd, but you only said it to spark a debate. You used to do that a lot, and you didn't even make it to twenty-seven. "Dies"—that's a horrible word, a hateful word. There are all sorts of theories flying around, but why were you by the river in the first place? You hated water.

Alice, babe, hope you don't mind me putting this stuff on the blog. You'd have probably done the same. "Get it out," you used to say. "Spit out the pain. Throw it all back at the world."

Spoke to Chloe and Lauren earlier. Didn't talk much; we just cried. Rang your mum and dad, too, but they were on voice-mail. We'll all have to be strong for them now: your lovely dad with his mad sweaters and that way he has of saying "Al-ice," pausing between the "Al" and the "ice" as if he's asking a question, and your mum, your gorgeous mum, a one-woman dynamo, who you're an absolute spitting image of and take after in so many ways, but you won't take after anyone any more. It's stopped, you have, a line's been drawn under you, the last page in your book, and there's a huge hole where you and that laugh and that AWFUL taste in music and those OUTRAGEOUS leggings should be.

I've just rung your mobile because I wanted to hear your voice. *Not here. Obviously. Would love to talk to you though so pleeeeease leave me a lovely message and we'll chat very soon . . .*

My mum's come in and said we have to remember the good times, because that's how people live on. I looked over her shoulder at the rusty swing. "There's a giraffe in the garden," I said.

She must have thought I was mad.

A light has gone out. Love you, Alice Palace . . .

Article in *Anthropology à la Mode*, *August 2013*

"Why I Exhumed the Past"

Professor Jeremy Cooke has gone from unknown academic to household name in twelve months. In this personal piece, he candidly explains how the discovery of a body sparked his "research" and changed his life forever.

It was hardly a Eureka moment, although possibly as close to one as I was ever going to get.

I'd been in the library and had seen a student scrawl his initials in the condensation on the window. *RP*. Robert Pearce, I think his name was, although that's immaterial. I'd been transfixed by the letters and, after he'd left, had found myself inserting an "I" between them. One of the librarians smiled awkwardly at me. *Old Cookie,* she was probably thinking, *he's an odd one.* I sat down in the student's vacated, still-warm seat. It stayed for hours, the RIP, so I did, too. I must have dozed off and, when I woke, it was gone. RP—RIP—had been there, then not there. That was when it struck me. How each of us does this every day: leaves a trail, an imprint, a mark. Our mark. Might it be possible, I pondered, to reconstruct a life out of such fragments? To reassemble a person, piece them back together from such soluble shards? Because I had the perfect opportunity. A life—actually, *a death*—on my very own doorstep. There, right under my nose. Alice Salmon.

It was definitely, to use the modern parlance, "a moment." Seeing that geographer finger his initials in the condensation and feeling the quick, unfamiliar, arresting joy of a new idea. It had been a few days earlier that Alice, as one account euphemistically put it, "went in the water." It had been, a coroner was later to conclude, between midnight and 2 a.m. on February 5, 2012. But it had been eight years earlier, the autumn of 2004, when she'd first come here. Of course to the world at large—and indeed me initially—she was just another fresher then, one of thousands I've seen over the decades. I recall spotting her a few times early in that term: tallish, long hair, striking.

Much has inevitably recently been made of our "connection," but regardless of that she was perfect for my purposes on so many levels. Not just because of how she died, more because of when she lived. The way we communicate has changed more in the past twenty-five years—in one lifetime—than it did in the previous thousand. The Internet has rewritten the rulebook. Her generation has seen that change, has *been* that change.

Naturally, I had no idea where it would lead, but I wasn't allowing for the law of unintended consequences. As far as I was concerned, it was going to be a straightforward, hopefully illuminating piece of work, admittedly one that would require sensitivity. It wasn't so much a case of attempting to prove a thesis; I merely sought to map a life. Hers. Yes, because of our "association," but more because she was like the rest of us: complicated, fascinating, unique, human.

"Isn't it all a bit lowbrow?" one or two of my colleagues enquired.

But bugger them. For once I went with my heart. I wanted to see how much of that dear, beautiful girl was left behind, what remained. After all, it wasn't until relatively recently—it's worth reminding ourselves that, in evolutionary terms, almost everything is relatively recently—that, unless you were a nobleman or a royal, your life and death would pass unrecorded. Beyond your immediate family and perhaps a small peer group, *unnoticed*. You'd be remembered briefly by those surviving you, but beyond that, *nothing*.

It wasn't exactly "research" I embarked upon, not in the traditional sense. That's too grandiose a description and alludes to a more methodical approach than I was able—or inclined—to apply. "Obsession" was a word others were quick to use, and perhaps there was some verisimilitude in that. To ape the Scout movement's motto, I've done my best.

My "findings" are all in my book. Some light editing has been necessary to avoid ambiguity, but I'm confident that what's left is representative, if not entirely comprehensive. I hope it does her some sort of justice and, more critically, that it *brings* justice. Because that is my sincere wish: that the contents are treated as evidence.

Twenty-five, she was—poor, precious little thing—when she went in the water.

Perverse, how the world often only takes an interest in you after you're gone, but 'twas ever thus.

Ironic that it's resulted in me becoming a minor celebrity. All my work on ethnolinguistics and the Sami languages passed without notice, other than among a small circle of academics. I was suddenly in demand. Sky News sent cars to my house at ungodly hours to whisk me to studios where young blond women dabbed makeup on my cheeks so the cameras would "love me." Their questions frequently referred to a "journey": hers, mine, theirs, everyone seems to be on one these days. Anthropologist. They all clung to that word. It was as if it gave them authority, authenticity. *We've got an anthropologist: a real, live one, here in the studio*. Soon it wasn't even solely my area of expertise I was in demand to pontificate about; I found myself called upon to discuss all manner of current affairs. Afghanistan. Abortion. The new iPhone. Even once, on Channel 5, our obsession with daytime TV—an irony that was clearly lost on the producer.

In the face of this newfound currency, my paymasters were conflicted: I brought kudos to their establishment, but the Alice affair was a mixed blessing, with reporters descending on the faculty as they have my home.

Nowadays that's how I'm introduced. The Alice Salmon anthropologist. The man who unearthed the truth about the river Dane girl. Once, heaven help us, the boffin-turned-sleuth. Alice and I have become a corollary of each other. A footnote in each other's stories. Although we always would have been that anyway.

An early proof of the book is on my desk: Alice's face peering out at me from the cover. Should you choose to read it, by the time you turn the final page you'll know the truth about Alice Salmon. I'm wary of deeming every word strictly true because those whose lives she touched are inherently subjective: layered with love or, as I was to discover, in some instances hate.

On the whole, people have been remarkably helpful, even when I explained their contributions could end up in the public domain. I was clear from day one: there was to be no sanitization.

It was going to be the lot, however shaming or shocking; an approach, incidentally, I steadfastly extended to myself.

Given the territory I was in, it was inevitable that I would meet some opposition, but I couldn't have predicted the reaction from some quarters: that sabotage attempts would be made on my work, that my reputation would be systematically tarnished, my wife targeted. They called me sacrilegious, branded me a pervert, accused me of trying to dig up the dead. But we Homo sapiens have a duty to do that. If we didn't, we wouldn't know about Tutankhamun or Machu Picchu. Without that probing sense of curiosity, without constantly looking over our shoulder, we wouldn't know about the cave paintings at Lascaux, wouldn't be able to stand there and stare at those magnificent running Paleolithic bulls, marvel at the sheer damn *wonder* of them coming alive in front of us, now and 17,000 years ago. I hope I still have time to see them again one last time. I'm looking forward to the next chapter in my life, even if it will be a short one.

I'm wary of slipping into lecturer mode, but what we call "communication" today—speech—actually originated about 100,000 years ago. Nonverbal means evolving into verbal ones. Writing was a seismic step: it gave us the ability to record, to remember. It speeded the spread of knowledge. It was both evolution and it quickened evolution. It's what sets humans apart, defining how we live and who we are. Alice was a brilliant communicator. I was determined to let her speak for herself. As one of my former colleagues put it with uncharacteristic sagacity: *Let her be her own story.*

I like to think, as well, that I'm a better man than before all this began. I'm definitely less pompous, although perhaps assuming one is so marks the height of pomposity.

When I run my finger across the cover of the book, I resist my natural inclination to conclude that it, like any book, is inadequate—pages, ink cast into shapes, the white fading to yellow, the paper crumbling and disintegrating. A life span of its own. I remind myself of its power, its potential. That justice will follow. It must.

I remind myself as well that human beings I've never met—who I can't even visualize—will cradle this paltry offering in the palms of their hands. (I'm no technophobe, but am of the generation that envisages it as a tangible, corporeal object rather than an electronic one.) That I'll be heard, that I'll speak to strangers, and my words will connect, like sinewy tissue between us. Perhaps it's absolution I'm seeking. Atonement. Forgiveness. Of course, there's one person in this whole sorry saga who I'll never, ever forgive.

Possibly there was a little truth in those comments, after all. About why I chose the girl I did; why I wanted—needed—to put her back together again. To make her live. Because that's what we all crave, isn't it? To feel we're important, that we're desired, that we've been noticed. That we've made a difference. That we're missed. That each of us is remembered. To feel, as my colleagues in her old department might say, *blessed* on this earth.

But more than that. More than that and less than that.

Simply, that each of us is *loved*.

Alice Salmon, RIP.

- What She Left *by Professor Jeremy Cooke is published next month by Prion Press, priced £9.99.* Anthropology à la Mode *readers can get a discount if they order a copy via the number on p. 76.*

Alice Salmon's "Favorite Quotations," Facebook profile, ***November 3, 2011***

"Grammar is the difference between knowing your shit and knowing you're shit."

Anon.

"Be the heroine of your life, not the victim."

Nora Ephron

"The truth hurts for a little while, but lies hurt forever."

Anon.

"We've all heard that a million monkeys banging on a million typewriters will eventually reproduce the entire works of Shakespeare. Now, thanks to the Internet, we know this is not true."

Robert Wilensky

"Youth is a dream, a form of chemical madness."

F. Scott Fitzgerald

Notes made by Luke Addison on his laptop, *February 8, 2012*

You never knew I was going to propose, did you? Well, add it to the list of things I never told you. The night you confronted me about Prague—the night you said we had to take a break from each other—I had a ring in my pocket. Been planning it for weeks. Was going to tell you the next morning to pack an overnight bag; we'd walk to the station, go to Gatwick, then Rome. It was all booked.

"Luke, I'm going to ask you a question and I need you to answer honestly," you'd said before I had a chance. "Can you promise me you'll do that?"

"Course," I'd replied. I was picturing your face: how you'd look when I explained you didn't need to go to work on Monday, how I'd cleared it with your boss, it was all sorted. It was delicious: knowing that the eighteen months we'd been together was only the beginning. Yes, we might have been a bit young—no one ties the knot until at least their late twenties these days—but why wait? You weren't the only one who could be impulsive.

"That rugby weekend you went on in Prague—did you sleep with someone?"

The air went out of the room. I sat down on the end of your bed and felt the jeweler's box in my pocket, a rigid square weight. I couldn't lie, not to you. "Al, it was nothing."

"Who was she?" you asked, a flat, resigned tone to your voice.

It had been seven weeks after we'd met. I'd known exactly how long it was because I'd decided if it was less than two months I'd keep quiet, if it was more then I'd confess. "It doesn't matter who she was."

"It matters to me," you bit back. "Believe me, right now it matters to both of us."

"It was a girl on a hen weekend. I was drunk."

"Why didn't you tell me?" Another new tone to your voice: hard, unyielding.

"I was scared you'd dump me." I fingered the ring in my pocket. Thought: *Should I just do it?* Never mind waiting until we're in the restaurant in the Campo de' Fiori—I'd picked it because it was famous for its prosciutto and that was your favorite; the table was booked; I'd even tipped off the maître d'. Just do it. Prove how much I loved you, prove that what happened seven weeks after we met was no more than a girl whose name I could barely remember on a weekend I could barely remember. But you started crying and when I reached out you batted away my hands and slumped down on the side of your bed so we were at right angles. Flashes of Prague had come back to me: the Irish bar, her and her friends on the table next to us, a cobbled street in the half-light—it was nearly four in the morning—turning left towards my hotel and her with me, that girl from Dartford or was it Dartmouth? Jen—no, not Jen, *Gill*. It had all felt so far away from my real life. "It meant nothing," I repeated, twisting round and taking your hand. I watched you crying, the miniature Christmas tree flashing on the chest of drawers over your shoulder. More of the Prague trip had come back to me: the smell of wet cobbles, the *rohlík* signs in bakers' windows, how it had felt like the end of an era. I knew you were the one, Al, even seven weeks after meeting you I did, but I knew as well that you'd mean an end to the me I'd got used to—the lads' trips abroad, the 4 a.m. finishes to drinking sessions, the random encounters in bars—and I wasn't sorry; I'd miss that, but I had you now and that would be better. Already then I loved you, Alice, but it was as if I had to say good-bye to the old me first, send that person out with a bang. One last, huge blowout.

"I think you should go now," you said.

I visualized our plane taking off for Rome and the two empty seats, yours a window because you loved the view.

"You don't get to have your cake and eat it, Luke. Life's not like that."

"Fucking Adam," I said. "The gobshite."

"Secrets rarely stay secret." You wiped your eyes. You'd loved the last eighteen months, you said. But we were in our mid-twenties now and relationships were too important to risk getting wrong. "We need to work out how we feel about each other."

"I know how I feel," I said. "I love you." I wasn't going to let this happen, not again, not with you. I'd wondered again about pulling out the ring. Saying: *Look*. But it was all wrong; I'd made it all wrong. Plus your mind was made up.

"Well, I don't," you said. "Right now, I don't know whether I love you. Or I do, but I don't know if I love you enough."

"I'm the same person I always was," I said.

"No—no you're not." You were close to losing your temper; I'd only ever seen that once before, when you'd seen that man on a bus slapping a little boy.

"I've never claimed to be an angel."

"Don't you dare try to make this my fault, Luke."

"It was only seven weeks after we'd met, for God's sake! We weren't even referring to each other as boyfriend and girlfriend by that stage."

"Go, please, just go. I can't be with you for a while."

"We're not splitting up, are we? We're not."

"I want us to take a break. No texting, no emailing, no nothing."

In other circumstances, I'd have picked you up on that—laughed, said, " 'No nothing'—that's a double negative; that means I can," but tears were streaming down your face. It was only a fortnight to Christmas.

"No contact for two months," you said.

It seemed an odd, arbitrary too-long length of time, but it struck me as better than the alternative—nothing *but* weekends like Prague for the rest of my life.

"Now get out of my flat."

You used to be scathing about people with complicated love lives. It's very simple, you said, you either love someone or you don't. But I turned you into one of those people. That was my gift to you and now you're dead. You've been dead for three days and it's impossible, Al. Sleeping. Getting up, eating, showering, shaving, sitting on a Tube, answering the phone. It's meaningless. You told me you once had a spell feeling like that when you were a teenager and I never understood, but now I do. Finally, *finally,* now it's too late, I get a little sense of what it might have been like for you, what it might have been like to have been you, Alice Louise Salmon, the girl I met on Friday, May 7, 2010—see, I *do* remember our anniversary—in Covent Garden. You'd come and stood next to me—my animal magnetism, I later joked. You got served before me and I'd said, "There's a woman with bar presence," and quick as a flash you'd replied, "There's a man who looks as if he's trying to jump the queue!"

I couldn't live with you alive and us apart, and now I can't live with you dead and us apart.

I was never one for writing stuff down, but you said if no one ever did, how would we share and learn and get better. So here I am, writing what I'm feeling, like you used to—like you said could make all the difference.

You want me to be honest, Al? OK, well, here's honest. I got in a fight—two fights. You never knew about the second one because it was last Sunday, the day after you died, but you knew all about the first one because it was with you.

Email sent by Elizabeth Salmon,
March 3, 2012

From: Elizabeth_salmon101@hotmail.com

To: jfhcooke@gmail.com

Subject: Stay Away

Jeremy,

I can't believe I'm contacting you after all these years. I vowed I'd have nothing more to do with you—seems whoever determines our fate had a different plan. Let's skip the pleasantries. What the hell's going on? I hear you're gathering information about Alice. God only knows why. They tell me it's for some sort of research project. Frankly I don't care, whatever it is you need to quit it now.

My son, he works for a firm of solicitors, he drafted you a letter. I told him I'd posted it, but threw it in the bin. It was full of legalese, highlighting how much we would appreciate privacy, asking that you desist from any such work forthwith and including a veiled reference to possible legal action. I know you better than that. I'm warning you.

They say it's a scrapbook you're compiling. Well, put this in your scrapbook. *I'm proud of my daughter*. I don't give a damn what anyone says: I'm proud that she grabbed life by the scruff of the neck and lived it. I don't care where I am, sometimes I find myself shouting it: *Alice Salmon was my daughter.* I go into her room and tell her clothes and her CDs and her pink polka-dot piggy bank. I say good night and good morning and that I love her and that she may have done something silly or stupid but we don't hold it against her, course we don't; all we do is miss her. None of us are completely in control of our destinies and when it comes to silly or stupid I'm hardly one to preach, now, am I?

You always were prone to misinterpreting situations, so be in no doubt here: the sole reason for this email is to tell you to quit whatever bizarre and macabre exercise it is you've embarked on. I'm not even going to get into discussing the email you sent me just before she died. Sentimental, inexpedient and offensive.

They say God looks after drunks and little children. Well, where was God on February 5, Jem? If you're such a smart man, you answer me that. Actually, no, don't—don't even reply, just leave me and what's left of my family alone. Do that for me and, if not for me, then do it for Alice.

Elizabeth

Extract from Alice Salmon's diary, *November 25, 2005, age 19*

"Hello, Miss Perspective," the guy from the marketing course said as we left the lecture hall.

I was impressed he'd remembered my words.

"I'm Ben," he said, putting his hand out. "Fancy a drink?"

I hesitated, not because I didn't fancy him but because I didn't get asked out that often. "Well?" he said. "How about if we're something passing stopped?"

It was what I'd blurted a few minutes before in the talk when we'd been asked what made a good photo. "Very funny," I said, realizing it sounded like I thought he was taking the piss when what was actually zinging round my head was how I did, did, did want to hang out with him a bit. I was well up for it: nice men had been in distinctly short supply in the first year.

"Come on," he said, "I'm buying. Well, technically the bank of Mummy and Daddy is, but it all goes down the same way."

We filed across the car park and down the alley shortcut along the river to the high street. He was a third-year, one of the cool party crowd you'd spot rolling through town in fancy dress or clutching traffic cones or giving each other piggybacks. In the pub he bought us a pint of cider each, and he had a vodka Red Bull, too.

"Bit full-on, isn't it?" I said.

He ignored that and said: "That talk was shite. I've googled that bloke and he's hardly Henri Cartier-Bresson—it's mostly weddings and christenings he does."

"Nothing wrong with taking pictures of happy occasions. Suppose you only take pictures of war zones, then, do you?" I was still buzzing from the seminar. Bandying around words like "perspective" and "personality," it was why I'd wanted to come to uni. That and for this: meeting new people. I could feel the cider working in me, too, making me warm and cozy.

"No fucking chance. I'm not going to risk getting my arse shot off."

Perhaps, I thought, taking another long, slow mouthful of drink and watching him do the same, *some of his confidence will rub off on me.*

"Is that what you're going to do when you graduate?" he asked. "Be a photographer?"

"I wish, but I'm totally crap at the technical stuff. By the time I've worked out the ISO, the shot's gone. I'd be a rubbish paparazzo!"

"I'd rather be a garbage man than a pap. Actually, scratch that—garbage men have to get up early. I'd rather be a drug dealer. At least they contribute something to society!"

"What *are* you going to do?" I asked. A lot of third-years were already applying for jobs.

"God knows, I'm useless at most things." There was something childlike about him. "You?"

"I'd like to go into journalism. Along with the rest of the world."

"Tell me you're not going to work for *Heat*. Please tell me that."

"God, no, it'll be far more upmarket! The *Times Literary Supplement* at the very least."

We both took another sip. It was going down too well.

"I've always thought the media should confound stereotypes, but all they do is reinforce them," he said.

"Very profound," I told him, but was thinking: *Actually, it is.*

"Have you ever watched rolling news?" he went on. "I mean, actually sat and watched it. I do it a lot on account of being congenitally lazy and it's utter shite. Even the presenters are disinterested."

"Uninterested."

"What?"

"You mean 'uninterested,' not 'disinterested.' They mean different things. They're supposed to be disinterested because that means impartial, but what you're implying is that they don't give a toss."

"Fair enough," he said.

"What *are* you going to do, then?"

"Probably end up working for my father."

The way he said "father"—languidly, contemptuously—made me conclude it would be a reluctant choice, but possibly his only option. It struck me I wasn't sure I'd like this guy if I got to know him. "And what does he do, your father?"

"Insurance."

"Work in a call center, does he?"

"Very funny. Actually, he insures ships."

"Am I supposed to be impressed?"

"You can be whatever you like. We should celebrate."

"Celebrate what?"

"Whatever you fancy. I'll drink belatedly to Charles and Camilla getting hitched, if you need a reason."

"I'm a republican."

"There's a surprise! How about me having negotiated an extension for my patenting and intellectual property assignment? Making it through a talk by a man who reckons he's Robert Capa? Being here, in Southampton? Me and you having met each other—yes, that's the best reason of the lot."

I liked the way he was sitting, half turned towards me, one leg folded up under him, his left arm along the back of the sofa behind me. The way he used his hands, too; he was so animated.

"I'm fucked. I haven't eaten today. For the record, I'm not suggesting we do," he said, then after a pause: "*Eat*, I mean, not fuck. Although you know . . ."

"You should be so lucky," I said. His comment had moved our conversation on to a new plane, one where a different outcome was possible. *You could sleep with this man, Alice.* The thought billowed past me and he went back to the bar.

"Here was me thinking you were going to whisk me off for a romantic meal," I said as he plonked two more ciders and two more shorts down on the table.

"Eating's cheating," he said. "I took a punt, got us gins, doubles. You know I said I'm useless at most stuff? Well, there's one thing I'm not," he said, disappearing to the toilets. When he came back he was smiling. "There, that's one of the things I can do well!"

"What, weeing?"

"No, what I did after I did that." He tapped the end of his nose. "Now how about a snog?" He leant in to me and we kissed. He's not your type, I thought as I saw the woody freckled heft of his forearm. It occurred to me I'd never worked out what my type was.

"Enough about me. What does your father do?" he asked.

"He runs his own planning consultancy," I said, then thought, *Bollocks to that old bollocks, I don't need the approval of this boy.* "Or he did, but that went belly-up. Dad's a heating engineer."

"I'm sorry to hear that," he said.

"What, that the business went tits up or that he's a heating engineer?" Something was driving me to needle him; he was provoking a mix of contempt and attraction I'd never felt before. Another couple of drinks and I might be able to do the same as him: say anything and get away with it. "Let's get drunk on the shipping magnate!" I said.

It wasn't long before he was back at the bar. Tall, a good three inches taller than me, and I'm five nine, and he'd clearly been working out, too. He returned with champagne.

"I'm still not impressed."

"You won't be wanting any, then!" he said, pouring two glasses.

Life could surprise you sometimes, a Tuesday afternoon and fizz in a pub with hardly anyone else around and this new man, Ben—I'd always liked that name—with the amazing eyes. I watched the bubbles and the word "decadent" swam into my head.

"I liked it, what you were saying about photos earlier," he said. "What that guy was banging on about, about his job being to catalogue rather than influence history—that was pretentious bullshit, but what you said was real."

"Seriously, what *are* you going to do after you leave Southampton?" I asked, suddenly intimidated by where this was heading.

"As little as possible. Maybe work in a bar." We kissed again. "You . . . are . . . amazing."

"Bet you say that to all the girls."

"Course I do, but I don't mean it with them. I mean it with you, Miss Something Passing Stopped. Don't move a muscle: back in two shakes of a toad's tit," he said, disappearing to the toilet again.

I felt a wave of dizziness and decided I ought to go, that I was close to the point of no return, not a point that I *couldn't* get back from—but how I did would be out of my hands. I did this periodically: it was like watching myself crossing a line.

"You want a bit?" he asked when he returned.

"No."

"Come on, live a little, let your hair down."

He touched my hair and I wondered what cocaine would be like, what it would make me feel like, what it would make me *be* like—just more of me, or a different person? Green Day's "Holiday" started playing and it struck me that I hadn't done so bad. I felt a little surge of pleasure at being me. There were bubbles in my nose and I even felt a bloom of fondness towards a previous me: the girl in the gray-and-yellow school uniform who'd shout "I hate it all" through her bedroom door with the Boyzone poster on it.

"I've always fancied you something rotten," Ben said.

"What do you mean, *always*? You haven't known me always."

"I've known you for at least an hour. That's long enough."

"Long enough for what?"

He put his hand on my leg and I touched it: hot, fleshy, bony. He squeezed in and I slid into him as his weight pressed down on the sofa. "It's nice to meet you, Miss Something Passing Stopped," he said.

The seminar guy had asked what a photograph actually *was* and when no one had answered he asked me—the young lady at the front with the purple scarf—and I'd gone red and blurted out, "A fragment, a bit like freezing time," and he said, "Very poetic," and would I like to elaborate, which was when I said, "Like something passing stopped."

"Shall we go back to my place?" Ben asked.

"For coffee?"

"That as well."

For one instant I nearly walked away, but the champagne goodness was pinging around me, and no way was I going back to my house. Six of us shared it and it was a dump, and if the others were out I'd be home alone, and I'd been in *my* room earlier and it was back. *IT.* The bad stuff—the feeling miserable and wound up, not sleeping, when a battered corkboard on the wall could almost make you blub. I'd never given it the satisfaction of a name. IT would do.

Ben put his hand on my thigh. *Alice, this is so very unlike you,* I thought. I *never* sleep with men on first dates. I saw us reflected in the full-length mirror, intertwined on the brown sofa with a row of empty glasses on the low wooden table. "Shall we go now?"

"Yes," I answered as casually as I could, but it came out self-conscious and like the old me—but he didn't know the old me, and it occurred to me that maybe if I'd tried some cocaine, I wouldn't be that me.

"I want to sleep with you," he whispered in my ear as we stood up. I felt a million miles from the girl back in Corby who'd wondered how she'd touch a man and how she'd be afterwards, if she'd look different or be different, even if it was only to the people who knew her best, Mum and Dad (not Robbie; that numpty wouldn't have noticed if I'd grown an extra leg!). "There's plenty more booze back at my place. Plenty more of everything," he said, touching his nose.

"I'm a good girl," I laughed.

His place was cold and a pigsty and we drank white wine then vodka and he played Eminem and when the neighbors banged on the wall he banged back. Later, he sprinkled cocaine on the coffee table and did what they do in films, cutting and scraping it with a credit card. Then he rolled up a note and sharply inhaled and I watched the white powder race up into his nose.

"Your turn," he said.

"Not too much," I said, feeling suddenly more sober, then drunkenness crashed back over me.

"You'll like it, I can tell."

"I'm scared," I slurred.

He told me not to be a baby, then "Don't worry, it's fine, it's absolutely fine," and the way he said "absolutely" had that same languid slow-motion quality about it, except everything did now: the way his hands worked, the shadows of the leaves from the tree outside patterning the wall—even the music was slightly warped.

I leant forward and thought: *A new you starts today, Alice.* But I can't have been too wedded to the old one because it didn't stop me. I felt a clean, shocking rush as I sniffed it—sniffed it all in as I'd seen in the films and it felt immediately better, everything did.

"Good?" he asked.

"Good."

And one of us said something about shipping magnates and fridge magnets and we laughed and poured red wine—I didn't know we were on the red—and I thought I'll have to be careful with this stuff: I could get to like it rather too much.

Then this morning as we lay in his bed he said: "This is what I call *freezing time.*"

It had snowed and his heating was on the blink. Images of last night flashed into my head: him nibbling my ear, whispering I was beautiful; his shoulder blades: big boney lumps. He made tea and we read the papers and he announced he was off home today for the weekend—back to Bucks or Berks, I didn't catch which, for his brother's twenty-first. A marquee job. "Going to be a monster night," he said.

"What was last night, then?"

"That was a mere prelude."

But you never sleep with people on first dates, Alice, I thought.

Never stopped me last night.

You never do cocaine.

Ditto.

I hadn't been sure whether I should go or stay to try to salvage something, find in him one trait I adored beyond how fit he was. Everyone has that.

"Seriously, thanks for your company last night," he said.

There, maybe that was it, that comment: he so meant it. And he did that a lot, I'd noticed, starting sentences with "seriously." I thought, *In a few years' time you'll be in a suit in some swanky office and we won't be students anymore.* I tried to commit this room to memory. The wine bottle with a candle in it, the dead spider plant, the ripped-off MEN AT WORK road sign propped between the wardrobe and the wall. I knew I might well not see him again, or I was bound to, but maybe not in *this* way. He'd become the bloke I'd got off with after the photography talk, someone the girls teased me about, Mr. Marketing Man or Mr. Something Passing Stopped.

"Is this what we're going to be, then," he asked. "Fuck buddies?"

I'd laughed when I'd heard that expression on an old episode of *Sex and the City,* but now it seemed brutal and less than what this was. He reached under the bed and pulled out a tray with more cocaine on it. "Time for a top-up," he said.

I started collecting up my clothes and dressing. Can it really only have been a couple of years ago that I'd genuinely believed that sleeping with someone was such a massive deal? I felt a little ache for that me. At the very least, I would have liked to have remembered whether I'd taken my own clothes off or if he had.

"Seriously, don't go. I'll be lonely if you go."

He did a line, then prepared another one and smiled at me.

"Everything OK?" Mum had asked the morning after I first slept with Josh. She knew he was staying; she and Dad liked him. Better the devil you know, was Mum's view. They're all devils, Dad reckoned. The few months we were dating, he and Dad would shake hands when they saw each other—the two men in my life. Ask each other: How's school? How's work? Did you see the Man U game? *Men are so similar and yet so different,* I'd thought, watching them one day: their incompatible shapes—Josh skinny—nice skinny—and Dad rounder. It had crossed my mind that this must be adulthood: my first boyfriend. "Never let anyone treat you as if you're less than precious," Dad had said, but now Ben, Ben with his cloying aftershave and his pink-flecked skin from where he'd shaved, was doing precisely that.

I sat down on the edge of his bed. My head thumped. I recalled the assignment that was already three days overdue that I had to finish today and the shiny, spacious silence of the library. Looked at the cocaine, at Ben, then back at the cocaine; maybe I was still a bit tipsy. I thought: *Mum and Dad would be horrified, but it's no big deal and I've already done it once*—it was last night when I crossed a line (no pun intended); now would just be *again*. It occurred to me what the word of my next diary entry would be. It was a no-brainer: "coke."

"That's my girl," Ben said as I angled my head downwards.

It felt so good I could have cried.

PART TWO

No Word for What We Are

Letter sent by Professor Jeremy Cooke,
February 17, 2012

Good afternoon, Larry,

I used to think I'd live to a ripe old age. Was convinced I'd be one of those old boys who shuffles along the high street in a cap and coat regardless of the weather. Who loses track of time and looks suddenly and startled at his watch, then mutters. Who, when he tries to speed up, resembles some mechanical object put together wrongly. Who doesn't notice blobs of snot on his nose, spittle on his chin; has a vacant wateriness in his eyes and steadies himself on tables and chairs as if against an increasingly fast-spinning, ever-more-incomprehensible world. But obviously not. It's a spot on my prostate: a hard, cancerous spot. The doctor and I traded best- and worst-case scenarios, and hearing him articulate words with which I either wasn't familiar or had certainly never associated with myself—"biopsy" and "metastasis" and "finasteride"—I decided to get flowers for Fliss on the way home: a huge bouquet with asters and iris and baby's breath. Maybe cook a roast: pork, that's always been her favorite. This last bout of appointments have made me realize quite how lucky I've been to have had her by my side all these years. She knows, of course, but you should, too.

I wanted to spend my retirement pottering. Pottering around the garden with my trowel, around antique shops in Winchester, around the house with my coffee cup that says: *World's Grumpiest Man.* I rather fancied temporarily discounting my fossil fuel concerns and buying an old sports car, tinkering under the bonnet. Was going to get a pair of overalls—not sure I've ever had overalls—and would have left oily fingerprints on the kettle. Even, God forbid, if I'd ended up in a home, lined up along a wall with the other inmates as if we were waiting for a firing squad or sitting in circles, turning over cards above carpets chosen to conceal "accidents'—even that, reduced, childlike, embarrassingly charged with sexual ambition, even that would have been better than what I am facing: the nothingness.

I suppose I shouldn't complain: I'll still get to see well over twice as much life as Alice did. But it'll take some processing nonetheless. I rather thought dying was something that happened to other people, like arguing in public or bankruptcy. All these millions of years of evolution and we've never fixed the inescapability of this particular defect of being human, have we?

"Sounds like there's some displacement going on here," Fliss had said softly, when I'd informed her of my plan to "catalogue a deceased ex-student."

It's certainly proving a diversion, filling the gaps into which fear would otherwise rush. In fact, it's positively flooding in—Alice's past, served up in photos, emails, texts, Twitter exchanges, anecdotes, even some half-baked theories, one purporting she was a heroin user. To think we used to be no more than a few formal records, papery and objective: a birth certificate, a driver's license, a wedding certificate, a death certificate. Now we're in a thousand places: disparate but complete, ephemeral yet permanent, digital but real. This huge repository of information *out there*. God, it's impossible to have secrets anymore. We'd have never slipped under the radar if we'd been born forty years later, old boy, that's for sure.

A few individuals have even arrived in person, too, reaching into their short memories or scruffy pockets and prompting me to instinctively take up my notebook or Dictaphone. Capturing these details, it's becoming compulsive.

"Are you the Alice man?" one young lady asked this morning, employing a sobriquet I didn't dislike. She held out her mobile like a supplicant. "It's only a text, but it's the last one we swapped."

Flicking through what I've collected earlier, I pondered: *What actually* is *this?* This photo from a friend of Alice beside a tent on a school camping trip. This picture of her on a trip to the Brontë Parsonage—"Poor residents of Haworth didn't know what had hit them," the accompanying email said. This note from a couple who lived next door to her when she was a kid and "used to see her bouncing up and down on her trampoline over the fence."

"Sounds a bit like a belated obituary," Fliss had said.

"Indeed it is," I'd replied, picturing the paucity of mine: a few paragraphs in the university journal, a couple of column inches in one of the broadsheets.

I'm dying, Larry. There, I've said it. It took a while, but I can now. Not in a philosophy undergrad "We're *all* dying" sort of way, but actually, *literally*. Nothing imminent. I'll see next Christmas, the one after, probably the one after that, too. Me all over, isn't it? I can't even die dramatically.

I wonder what it's actually like, the point of demise. Where it'll be. How it'll feel. One's wife beside one's bed, clenched held hands—or conceivably that's merely the sanitized TV version. Perhaps I'll never know it's happened. Or worse, I will—but it'll be ambiguous and confused: some complicated transition to . . . to where? Another thing us so-called smart scientists have never been able to figure out. I have no intention of going gracefully into that good night. It's time to be honest, to set the record straight. About Alice, about me, about everything.

Not sure how they'd have been at your university, but some of the faculty here are jolly sniffy. "How's *Project Salmon* progressing?" one inquired this morning, barely concealing his disdain. But sod the lot of them. I've spent a lifetime seeking the approbation of my peers when they only follow your ideas to steal them or rejoice in their shortcomings. God, how did I ever enjoy the company of these people? They're like foxes sniffing each other's arseholes.

I doubt our news, however grave, gains much prominence in your corner of the globe, but it's not inconceivable that you'll have picked up parts of this story independently. The media here are gorging on it and they're ignorant of the half of it. At least for now. Forgive me if I omit any facts in my recounting, but I will do my best to be comprehensive and equitable. Never trust the teller: Trust the tale—that's what Lawrence said. Well, you may have to bear with me, because my grasp on detail isn't what it was. I've never lied to you, not wittingly, but I expect I'll be tempted over the coming weeks and months. I shall resist: even the less flattering bits, and, jeepers, there's enough of those. Untruths, infidelities, obsessions, subterfuge—where do I begin?

I'll have to be careful, given when the last time I saw Alice was, but I have to do this. Indubitably, as a portrayal of Alice it can't be infinite in its reach, but one is mindful of the Japanese term *kintsugi*—the celebration of the break, of the flaw, the put-back-together version becoming part of the history of the object. And as swan songs go, there could be worse.

Then this morning this girl in my office, cradling her phone in her hand as if it was a historical artifact. Megan, her name was: a pretty little thing who worked in PR. "I loved her," she said.

I couldn't think of anything other than what it would feel like to have her hands—the red nails—on me, on my papery and pale skin. "Do you not still?" I asked. "Do you not *still* love her?" Strange, how we grapple with tenses. Loved. Love. Knew, know. Wanted, want. Friends of ours—I refer to them as "friends," but we've long since fallen out of touch—lost one of their boys as a teenager. One of the questions afterwards they found hardest to cope with—perhaps they still do—is one of the simplest: How many children have you got?

"I love her," she said.

"I know, sweetheart," I said, reaching out.

She shrank back as if there was nothing more repulsive in the whole world than an old man. "How? How do you know?"

"Because I do, too."

Article on *Nationalgazette.co.uk* website,
February 6, 2012

"Tragic Girl Dies Near Bridge She Battled to Close"

A young woman has died near a bridge she campaigned to close.

The body of 25-year-old reporter Alice Salmon is believed to have been discovered in a canal in Southampton early yesterday morning (Sunday).

Sources say Salmon, who had studied in the Hampshire city, but more recently lived in London, was back there on a weekend visit.

The police are staying tight-lipped, but the theory that's emerging locally is that the keen festival-goer got separated from her friends and was heading across the bridge after a long day of celebration.

In a cruel twist of fate, her first job on a local paper in the south-coast resort saw her lobby for better safety at the exact location where she is thought to have plunged to her icy death.

In one article she'd dubbed the bridge, which is 25 feet above the water and a popular pedestrian route, "an accident waiting to happen," and called on the authorities to erect higher fences along it. "The question shouldn't be how much would it cost—the question should be what might the cost be of *not* doing it," the extrovert Salmon wrote in the *Southampton Messenger*.

Former colleagues will remember her as a fearless campaigner on crime—a passion she developed with her "Catch the Night Stalker" campaign, which led directly to the conviction of a man who had violently assaulted an 82-year-old great-grandmother.

Social-media websites were soon awash with theories. One Twitter user said the bridge was "the ideal spot for summer drunk-diving." Another, who purportedly knew the victim, claimed she had a "complicated love life."

Her parents declined to comment when the *National Gazette* contacted them, but a neighbor is reported as having said they're "literally in pieces."

Also look out for:

Youngster Set for England Football Debut
Outrage at Government Plans for Budget U-turn
Car Factory Crisis Sparks Redundancy Fears

Notes made by Luke Addison on his laptop,
February 9, 2012

When I said I got in a fight, Al, that's not right and I have to get this right. I didn't get in a fight, I *started* one. This poor bloke hadn't done anything wrong but I took a swing and then we were rolling around on the floor and he was massive—that was why I'd picked him—and he was on top of me and his fist was smashing into my face. "Hit me again, you bastard!" I was screaming, every punch a brilliant flash of pain, momentarily pummeling out the previous twenty-four hours from my head. As soon as it stopped, you rushed into the void and my face is a right mess but he walked away without a scratch, not that I was trying to hurt him; there's enough pain in the world without twats like me doling out more, like we're spreading confetti at a wedding.

It had been in some shitty pub by Waterloo. I'd just got back from Southampton. My head was all over the place. Had grabbed a pint and been in the beer garden when the call had come from your brother. "Where are you?" he'd asked.

I didn't tell him—course I didn't. What was I going to say? *Just arrived back in London, having followed your sister to Southampton*. Merely replied as casually as I could: "Out."

He knew we were having time apart. He'd never liked me—never said as much, but it had been obvious. "I've got some terrible news," he'd said, and it didn't sound as if it was the first time he'd said it. I could hardly hear him; the beer garden was standing room only. I did hear how it was impossible to take in, precise details weren't yet clear, the night before, utterly unreal, your parents were in bits . . . I'd stood there pulling the chalky smoke of a spliff as deep into me as I could, feeling the wheezy rush, a gang of feral teenagers circling me. But they didn't have the faintest comprehension of how incapable they were of hurting me, them or their mates inside. I was dead myself. "Run along home now or I'll put this glass in your face," I said to one. It was a wild, rocking feeling: the Stella, the weed, the need in me rising incrementally to douse one fire of pain with another.

Later, a text from your mum saying, "Come and see us." Then, later still, when I was suffocating under the guilt, a massive bloke at the bar. Me thinking: *He'll do.*

Those two months we were apart, Al, I did what we agreed: I got my head straight and worked out what I wanted. Not that I needed to: I knew—it was *you*. I'd worked hard, saved a load of dosh, even viewed a few flats for us. I didn't see anyone else, but did you? Who the fuck was this Ben you'd been swapping messages with on Twitter? You were clearly hiding something from me when we were arguing last weekend. It cuts both ways, Alice. It was *our* future, not solely yours, *ours*. And now you're dead and whoever he is you're not seeing him anymore, are you? Any more than you're not seeing me, and that's what jealousy does to you, that's what happens when you're in love, and I was in love with you, Al. Prague was nothing—it was a girl from a place beginning with a "D" that I couldn't even remember the name of in a grotty hotel room. We barely exchanged more than a few dozen words, then as she was collecting up her stuff to go she'd said: "You're in love, aren't you?"

"What makes you say that?" I'd asked.

"Because I'm not and when you're not you notice it in other people."

I was half expecting her to come out with some quote—you *so* would have done in a situation like that—explaining exactly what she was getting at, but the woman who wasn't you merely wiped either a tear or some mascara off the side of her eye and let herself out of my room.

But all this isn't because of her, it's because of *me*. I have to write that.

"If no one ever wrote anything down, we wouldn't have Jane Austen, and imagine a life without her," you said on one of our first dates. I'd been stumped for a reply so stayed schtum because I didn't want to appear a philistine, although you soon rumbled me on that one!

Lives are like that world-record domino attempt I saw on TV when I was a kid: one thing out of place changes everything that comes afterwards. If it hadn't been for Prague, you might not have been in Southampton, or even if you had, you might not have been so drunk or might not have gone down by the river and I certainly wouldn't have been down there with you. Or maybe you'd have texted me during the evening and I'd have realized you were wasted because of your dodgy punctuation and it would have been like a phosphorus flare and I'd have replied, "Babe, be careful" or "Go back to your friends." Usually when you were pissed I could get through to you, though sometimes it was as if you were behind a pane of glass.

You used to say I was a fun drunk, a funny drunk, but I'm a messed-up drunk, a scared drunk, an angry drunk, and my face is a right mess, but why shouldn't other people see what I've done to myself, what you've done to me—to us? I used to imagine what our kids would look like, whether they'd get my nose and your freckles, my chin and your hair, my ears and your dimples—I used to put that picture of our future together in my head—but you smashed it to pieces when what I did in Prague was only seven measly weeks in; we weren't even a fucking item.

Strange how being punched was the first time I'd felt even remotely human for almost two months. Since you said, "I want us to take a break." Since you'd said, "No nothing."

Strange as well that the police aren't asking more questions—that they're not more suspicious. All they're doing is appealing for witnesses, especially those who were with you in the run-up to Saturday night. Suppose a drunk girl dying isn't so unusual. Every minute of every day someone's dying.

"I understand you were having time apart," one policewoman asked me. "That must have been difficult. Had you and Alice argued?"

I laughed at that one, laughed out loud in her clever, smug, probing little face.

Extract from Alice Salmon's diary,
December 3, 2006, age 20

Paris, I'm only in Paris!

I hadn't spoken to Ben for weeks, but he called on Wednesday and asked if I fancied a weekend away, his treat.

"I'm busy," I said. "Working on my dissertation."

"How about if I said you'd need your passport?"

There's no word for what we are. We're not dating, but we do stuff together. We're not boyfriend and girlfriend, but we intermittently act like it. Sort of. It had been the same ever since I'd met him at that photography talk. And here we are in Paris.

"It's a bit small," he said about the *Mona Lisa.*

"Yes, but look at those eyes. She wouldn't take any shit."

I had to explain that the *Venus de Milo* was Aphrodite, but his only comment was it was a shame they couldn't be arsed to finish it. Then, when I'd cracked up, he said: "See, told you a break from your thesis would do you good. How's it coming along, the dreaded *feces*?"

"Dreadfully. Feels like I'm drowning. Why, you offering to help?"

"I'd rather stamp on my own testicles!"

We've been up the Eiffel Tower, where Ben gleefully informed me that if you dropped an apple off the top it would kill someone at the bottom, then visited the bridge with all the padlocks on, the Pont des Arts (see, I knew all those boring French lessons would come in handy one day!). "Couples put them here, then throw the key in the river to demonstrate their commitment to each other," I said. "They say if lovers kiss here, they'll be together forever."

He looked nervous. "Don't get any funny ideas, Fish Face."

It tugged at me again, the unsatisfactory sense of what me and this man were. "Friends with benefits," he'd once described us as. But I'm going to be twenty-one soon; he already is. A year or so ago, when we'd first met, fine, but I'm not going to be pissed around now. "We could do this stuff more often," I said. "Like, be a proper couple."

"It works for me as it is."

Meg reckons he's a complete idiot, but she doesn't—sick buckets at the ready—see the side of him that I do. Like when he appears on the doorstep with flowers, or introduces me to people as Miss Something Passing Stopped. "It wouldn't be so terrible, would it, dating like normal people?"

"Thought you hated normal?"

"I'm not advocating settling down and buying a caravan. I'm merely suggesting we could see a bit more of each other. It might be fun."

"You know me, Fish, I'm not after anything heavy." He stared down into the water. "I like as and when."

We'd had a brilliant day and now I knew this conversation would eat away at me. Even if we changed the subject—and of course we'd change the subject—it would be there. "You are allowed to change," I said, forcing a smile.

"Don't spoil this weekend," he said.

"Don't make me, then."

Screw you, Ben, I thought. I'm worth more than as and when. I ran my hand along the padlocks and it occurred to me that maybe it would be here—on the Pont des Arts, the lights of the Eiffel Tower twinkling in the distance, in Europe's most romantic city—where our so-called relationship would end.

Then again, I'd thought that before.

I shouldn't have come to Paris.

It's one of the stupidest things I've ever done. I should have stayed at home and plowed on with my dissertation (no debate what this diary entry's word is going to be—dissertation!). Dr. Edwards, my tutor, says I could be on course for a first, reckons I've got—and I quote—"an extremely mature appreciation of Austen's work." "You're a sensitive reader, Alice," he told me. "You've also self-evidently got a soft spot for doomed heroines."

None of his encouragement stops me getting stressed-out. It wouldn't be so bad if it was going to disappear once I've handed it in, either, but then there'll be job hunting. (It's all right for Ben, because you don't need a job if Mummy and Daddy are bankrolling you.) Sometimes it feels as if I'm simply not smart enough to keep up. I mean, I might get ten or eleven questions right on *Mastermind,* but I'll only get four or five on *University Challenge.* If I was an electrical appliance—an iPod or a washing machine—they'd have put a product recall out on me and I'd get taken back and fixed; but you can't do that with humans, and if you look at who made me—certainly Mum—she's just as bad, although if I ask her what she was like when she was my age, she clams up. "It's not about waiting for the storm to pass," she once said. "It's about learning to dance in the rain."

I used to be convinced that keeping this diary was a pressure valve, but it doesn't help, any more than expanding your vocabulary helps, because you can be as articulate as Stephen Fry and all it means is that you've got more ways (a veritable cornucopia!) to describe how shit you feel. Not one of those words he spouts on *QI* can make *IT* go away. All they do is give it a new form, a new shape, a new sound.

There is one way to make the stress go away, of course. Earlier I looked towards the hotel-room bathroom and recalled another bathroom a few years ago, quietly opening the medicine cabinet, and taking out the contents—the plasters, the eyedrops, the nail scissors, the acetaminophen—and putting them on the side of the bath then sliding them into a nice line like I was moving my token on a monopoly board (I was always the Scottie dog).

I shivered and picked up my phone. Ben had supposedly nipped out for ciggies but he was probably in a bar. *Come back,* I texted him. Last night was how it always was after our conversation on the bridge. We didn't resolve anything. Nothing changed. I frantically called him.

"*Alice,*" he answered, as if he was expecting someone else.

I had a vision of him leaning on a bridge, tilting his head upwards, blowing out smoke and thinking of me, and I felt a bit like a character in a book but couldn't decide what I'd be: flawed and tragic or ballsy and not about to take any shit. "Where are you?"

"Buying apples!"

"I'm serious. Where are you?"

"Out."

He was slurring. I decided this definitely couldn't go on. It was over and realizing I'd be the one who'd end up in tears made me hate him a tiny bit.

"Actually, I've been getting you a present," he said. "Got you a surprise."

Half an hour later, another text: *That present I told you about, you've gotta model it for me when I get back.*

I felt a little thrill, or maybe the bloom of shame.

"Are you my Aphrodite?" he asked later as we drank the wine he'd ordered on room service.

It's true: I do have a soft spot for the doomed heroine.

On the train home I was trying to work on my dissertation, but abandoned that and watched the countryside whiz by and switched to my diary.

When I was twelve or fifteen or seventeen, this wasn't how I'd have imagined I'd be at twenty—on the Eurostar, having spent a weekend in Paris with a man who couldn't bring himself to utter the word "girlfriend."

Ben was out for the count. So trusting, so vulnerable, his mop of blond hair and those perfect white teeth. He probably wouldn't budge until we got to Waterloo, then he'd wake, startled, stretch, reach up for his rucksack, and then we'd head to Southampton and he'd go to ground for a few days, then maybe a text, something silly about this weekend—Nina Simone in that brasserie or the *Venus de Milo* or the apples. Yes, he'll like that, he'll remember that: that you can kill someone by dropping an apple on them from the top of the Eiffel Tower.

He won't get a reply, though.

"We've got to stick together," he once said, flushed with panic after I'd shouted at him. "Besides," he'd added, the old confidence flooding back into him, "you can't dump me because we're not actually dating!"

There'd been a longer gap after that exchange than usual: months instead of weeks. But I still let it happen again: the end of an evening, the bit when the band finishes or you're standing next to someone in the student union or the point in a house party when there's two of you left in the kitchen—a heavy inevitability about it, me and him. That's me all over, doing stuff even if every bone in my body is screaming (can bones scream?) *don't.* Getting into debt. Telling my landlord he was a parasite. Getting wasted at the anthropology department Christmas party in the first year. Part of me is glad I can't remember more of that, but a bigger part *needs* to. All I've got are flashes. Anchovy canapés. Chatter about some discovery in Indonesia, a hobbit thing. Cold wine ("Not terrible," Professor Cooke had said, although he'd have preferred a red, spouting names and grape varieties that might as well have been a foreign language to me). Then later trying to read a plaque on the wall and the letters swimming out of focus. Laughing, and Old Cookie saying: "Time we got you out of here, young lady."

Ben twisted in his seat and asked sleepily, "Where are we?"

It made me sad that we wouldn't be able to reminisce about this weekend together. We'd be remembering the same thing, but from different perspectives.

Dr. Edwards is forever banging on about perspective. "Whose eyes are you looking through?" he asks. "Who's the narrator in this story? Who's the hero?"

Ben came to, yawned and rubbed his face, and for an instant I wavered.

Too late, I thought.

"We're all the heroes of our own stories," Dr. Edwards once said.

"Or heroines," I responded. "Don't forget the heroines. After all, for much of history, Anonymous was a woman."

"Very true. A bastardization of a Woolf quote, I believe."

It had been a lightbulb moment. In my story it was me. Always me.

"We could get bagels," Ben said and I thought: *You idiot, we could have got bagels, but you've blown it. No second chances. Or rather, you've had about six second chances. No seventh second chance.*

He didn't have a clue what he had coming. I almost felt sorry for him.

Email sent by Professor Jeremy Cooke,
March 4, 2012

From: jfhcooke@gmail.com

To: Elizabeth_salmon101@hotmail.com

Subject: Stay Away

Dear Elizabeth,

I'm immeasurably sorry about Alice. It'll mean nothing to inform you of that, but I am. One's forever talking about the power of words yet they seem woefully inadequate at instances like this. I debated whether to send you a condolence card, but concluded it would be safer not to, especially after my ill-judged earlier email. Apologies if that was insensitive.

I can understand why you're so protective of Alice—what parent wouldn't be?—but perhaps I should explain precisely about my "research." I view it more as tribute than obituary; it certainly isn't about exposing her foibles because we all have enough of those. You know me, Liz: I'm interested in people, people in all their brilliant

Technicolor detail. And they don't come much more brilliant or Technicolor than Alice.

Quasi-academic endeavors are like a life. They're hard to judge partway through; you have to view the end results, but can you not draw reassurance from how many of Alice's friends and colleagues are coming forward to help? You also have my word I'd never treat her memory with anything but respect.

I should stress this is a personal project, not one conducted under the university's auspices. Frankly, I'm sick of academia: its snobbery and small-mindedness. Of course, I say I eschew the word "research," but I can't *not* be an academic, any more than you can't *not* work in a building society or your husband can't not be a heating engineer or your son can't not be a lawyer. See what I mean about our traces? A brief foray into the Internet has revealed some of *yours*.

I see your son's got two children—gosh, Liz: you, a grandmother!—and a partnership in such a reputable firm is a huge achievement for a man of his age. I probably shouldn't refer to him as "young," but you get to an age when virtually everyone seems exactly that—except one's peers, of course, who start falling off their perches with alarming alacrity. Funerals are the only occasion I have any contact with most of my contemporaries these days. Two of the bloody things I've been to this year and it's only March. I'm jolly proficient at them: the walk, the handshakes, the awkward first lines, even the hugs—and as you know I've never been a hugger. I know sodding "Abide with Me" by heart.

Could we get together for coffee or something stronger? We could meet somewhere "neutral" if this place harbors ghosts for you. I could share some of my—again, forgive the insensitive word—"findings."

If you'd like my view, it's that Alice—the real Alice, the one I've come to only properly know over these past few weeks—was very different to the one most people encountered. Deeper, more complex. She's extraordinarily similar to you.

How have *you* been, Liz? I gather you stayed in Corby. No doubt Southampton seems a lifetime ago now. I never escaped; I'm even in the same bloody office. It's my birthday soon, a big one: sixty-five.

Guess that'll make you fifty-four. I'm not in great health, but Fliss is taking me out for dinner: a country-house hotel in the New Forest. They do some great Italian reds and the venison is spectacular. We go there every year, sit at the same table. I like tradition.

No one calls me Jem these days.

Yours,
Jem

Blog post by Megan Parker,
February 8, 2012, 9:30 p.m.

This might be a massive mistake, but sometimes you've got to go with your heart. "Publish and be damned," that's what Alice used to say.

She was one of the decent journalists, one who tried to make a difference. She didn't do stories about the Kardashians or Katy Perry's new dog or print pictures of celebrities with sweat rings under their arms or stumbling out of nightclubs and was as appalled by the phone-hacking stuff as the rest of us. But she could spend weeks going after someone who'd swindled an old lady out of her savings or a dodgy builder who'd done a bunk halfway through an extension, leaving a family in the lurch. So I'm going to take a leaf out of her book. Besides, it's not as if it can make the situation any worse.

"Sometimes you get an answer without knowing what the question was," Alice said once. "You've simply got to put it out there."

I found it in a box of items her mum gave me that she couldn't bear to sort through. It was mundane stuff—old copies of *Cosmo*, a load of H&M receipts, a printed JustGiving page for a sponsored run Alice was planning, a "save the date" card for a wedding in the autumn, plus some work stuff—but buried among it was a sheet of A4 paper with a Post-it stuck on it which said in Alice's handwriting: *Received on December 21, 2011.*

I've sat here for two hours grappling with whether to make this blog post live.

Publish and be damned.

REMEMBER ME LITTLE MISS LOCK UP THE CRIMINALS? MADE YOU FEEL GOOD DID IT? GETTING PEOPLE ARRESTED SO WE CAN ALL SLEEP AT NIGHT. GOING ROUND CALLING MEN MONSTERS. WELL YOU OUGHT TO BE CAREFUL OR YOU'LL GET YOUR OWN MONSTER. HOW'D YOU LIKE THAT? A CHRISTMAS MONSTER! YOU AFRAID OF MONSTERS? WHO DO YOU THINK YOU ARE YOU STUCK UP BITCH? YOU AND YOUR CAMPAIGN YOU KNOW NOTHING ABOUT ME. YOU DON'T SCARE ME. DO I SCARE YOU? HOW DO YOU SLEEP? TOO MUCH GOOD BEHAVIOR, TIME FOR BAD. PREFER OLDER WOMEN BUT YOU'LL DO. FROM A FREEMAN

Comment left on the above blog post:

You're as much of a WHORE as your friend. How do YOU sleep at night Megan Parker?

A FREEMAN

Q & A with Alice Salmon in autumn 2005 issue of Southampton University student magazine, *Voice*

Q: Why did you choose your course?

A: A teacher once told me that school can make us fall in love with an author, but uni helps us understand *why* we're in a relationship with them. I wanted to find out how a virtual recluse like Emily Brontë could have so much to say, so young. It wasn't as if she'd traveled or even had the Internet. All that wisdom, cultivated in a tiny corner of a windswept Yorkshire moor. Actually, I'll have to remember that line, it sounds dead good: *cultivated in a tiny corner of a windswept Yorkshire moor*!

Q: Are you dating?

A: No, but I'm open to offers. Not that I have time for men!

Q: Glass half full or glass half empty?

A: Half full, definitely. But I'll have a top-up if you're buying. A mojito, please.

Q: Favorite place?

A: Southampton. Specifically, Flames on Wednesday nights. Otherwise, anywhere that involves hiking boots.

Q: Who inspires you?

A: The people in New Orleans for rebuilding after Hurricane Katrina. I watched a clip of a lady getting winched out of a flooded house and having to leave her dog behind—she put food down knowing she was leaving the poor thing to die. OK, it's not a person, but I was in floods of tears.

Q: Politics?

A: Plenty, but it's mostly inconsistent and contradictory. Student loans suck, though!

Q: What are you going to do when you grow up?

A: Am never going to, so can't answer that! Seriously, would like to say secure world peace, abolish poverty and lobby for equality, but I'll probably end up unemployed or a permanent intern. And that's assuming I even get my degree; right now I'm overdue with an assignment.

Q: Describe yourself in three words.

A: Late, loyal, hard-working. (I figure "hard-working" is hyphenated so only counts as one.)

Q: What would you change about yourself if you had a magic wand?

A: My feet, my hair, my shoulders . . . how long have you got?

Q: What makes you angry?

A: All the usual things. Injustice. Violence. Selfishness. Myself. Plus cold coffee. I can't stand cold coffee.

Q: Most treasured possessions?

A: My iPod and my family and friends. Not necessarily in that order . . .

Q: Best bit of advice you've ever been given?

A: Luck is believing you're lucky. Someone famous said that; can't recall who.

Q: If you won £1 million on the lottery, what would you spend it on?

A: Do lecturers take bribes?

Q: Biggest achievement?

A: Winning a writing competition when I was fifteen.

Q: Biggest regret?

A: *Je ne regrette rien.* Or actually I do, but if I told you I'd then have to kill you . . .

Q: Finally, tell us a secret about yourself.

A: When I was a child I'd pretend to be someone entirely different to strangers, make up new names and construct a whole new background and identity for myself.

Want to feature in this slot? You won't get any dosh, but you will get to see your words appear in Southampton's most exciting zine and you'll get your fifteen minutes (well, fifteen questions) of fame.

Email sent by Elizabeth Salmon,
March 18, 2012

From: Elizabeth_salmon101@hotmail.com

To: jfhcooke@gmail.com

Subject: Stay Away

Same old Jem, you haven't changed a bit, have you? *Your* work, *your* birthday, *your* wine—this isn't about *you*. Don't treat me like one of your students. Am I supposed to be impressed that you looked us up on the Internet? It's hardly a revelation that we're all there, you included. Some things haven't changed. The undergrads clearly still regard you as detached and conceited. The breakthrough with your phonology research obviously eluded you. Ditto the once-talked-about Order of the British Empire award. Not nice to see your shortcomings in black-and-white in front of you, is it? Sounds to me as if it's *your* life not Alice's that's in need of some reconstruction. Are you happy? How's your marriage? Does your lack of children prey on your mind? See, having your existence held under a microscope is not pleasant, is it? I wouldn't normally dream of asking such questions, but that's what you're doing with Alice; you're the one who's put us in this situation. We all have parts of ourselves we'd prefer to keep private. Isn't one postmortem enough? You quit this now . . . please . . . none of your fancy highbrow explanations or justifications but stop.

I bet you've never had anyone knock on your door asking for a quote about a dead relative, have you? David and I have. Journalists call it the death knock. They used to come for pictures, but nowadays they rip those off the Internet so it's quotes they're scavenging for. A few weeks into her first job, Alice was told to death knock the mother of a boy who'd been killed in a hit-and-run. She refused. Can you imagine—fresh out of college, barely learnt where the kettle is, standing up to an editor? She told him that wasn't why she went into journalism. It didn't poison her against her choice of career but she never did do a death knock.

So sick of reading rubbish about my daughter. She's in danger of sinking under the sheer weight of it. We're well aware of the facts. She had 210 mg of alcohol in her bloodstream.

Which bit of the word "accident" do these bloodsuckers not understand?

Here's an irony for you. Alice nearly didn't go to Southampton at all; she was offered a place at Oxford. Merton. Of course I championed the merits of that location—anywhere but Southampton was fine as far as I was concerned—but she preferred somewhere "real." I'm glad I got away from your city. Academia was a horrible, tribal existence. A small world, too, and I was tainted.

She's not some sort of join-the-dots exercise, Jem, some dusty archaeological artifact for you to brush off and exhibit. She isn't *yours*. Enough people have raked over her life. Hunt someone else and leave our Alice alone. Don't do what you always did—run away with an idea, confuse facts with fiction, warp the world to fit *your* reality. No, I most certainly won't be joining you for a drink—I quit a long time ago and I can't imagine my husband being exactly enamored by the prospect of us meeting in a social capacity. He's a sensitive man, so I haven't mentioned us emailing; please have the decency to treat this contact in confidence.

Was going to make another point, but lost my thread . . . don't bother replying—unless that is you've worked out how to bring the dead back to life and I'm assuming even an esteemed anthropologist like you hasn't quite managed that yet.

I'll ask you once more nicely. Whatever you're doing, stop. I'll beg if I have to. I miss my baby girl so very much, Jem.

Liz

Statement issued by solicitor acting on behalf of Holly Dickens, Sarah Hoskings and Lauren Nugent, ***February 6, 2012, 10:00 a.m.***

Alice Salmon was a kind, generous, and wonderfully warm human being and it's incomprehensible that she's been taken from us.

She was bright, beautiful and popular, and we'll always count ourselves lucky to have been among her many friends. We feel an immense weight of grief, but our sadness and loss is dwarfed by that felt by her family. We can't begin to comprehend the pain they must be experiencing. Our hearts go out to them.

As has been widely commented, the three of us spent the

early and middle part of the evening of Saturday the fourth of February with Alice in Southampton city center. Obviously we have cooperated with the authorities in every way we can, and will continue to do so. We are confident—and sincerely hope—that they will soon configure the tragic chain of events that immediately preceded Alice's death. This won't bring her back, but may offer a fragment of comfort to her family. Regrettably, we are unable to shed any light on Alice's movements or whereabouts after about 10 p.m.

It's torture to think of what our friend might have done or where she might have gone in the few short hours between then and her death. We'll regret not taking better care of her, and not preventing what came next, for the rest of our lives. For that, we are truly sorry.

We collectively feel the way we can now show most respect to Alice is to not fuel the fire of speculation. For this reason, we have elected to not speak publicly about her. Indeed, the police have recommended we adopt this course of action. Meanwhile, we would urge everyone to respect the Salmon family's right to privacy.

Letter sent by Professor Jeremy Cooke,
May 30, 2012

I've had rather a shock, Larry.

Some raggedy urchin barged into my office this morning and announced: "You're the bloke who's bringing the dead girl back to life, aren't you?"

"I wouldn't exactly describe it like that," I replied.

He slapped a rucksack down on my desk, pulled out a CD, a pair of trainers, a mug, and an earring.

"What the hell—"

"I come bearing gifts," he said. "These are Alice's."

"You stole these?"

"That's one way of putting it. Not that she gave a toss about me, but I was mad about her and seeing as we weren't going to get it together I decided to at least nab a few reminders!"

"If this is genuine, you should give it to Liz. Elizabeth Salmon, her mother."

"It's genuine all right."

"Who are you? What's your name?"

"That's not relevant."

"It's important—for completeness, for my records."

"Put me down as an interested party," he said. "Yes, a very interested one. I knew them all," he said. "Her and her crowd—I was at the heart of it."

"You were a fellow student?"

"Yes, former housemate, too. We shared a gaff in the second year. An insider, me, buddy."

"So the pair of you were close?"

"Proper close." He held his hand up and crossed his fingers. "Was like that with her, her mates, her fellas, the lot. Give you full chapter and verse I can, for a price!"

He extracted a white T-shirt from the rucksack and unfurled it; it said on the front: *If they don't have chocolate in heaven, I ain't going.* He held it to his nose, breathed in deeply, deliriously. "I've got all sorts. It's like treasure."

"Is that hers? Why have you got that?"

"It was a big house; six of us shared it. Shit got lost. Shit got mis-laid. Sadly," he said, grinning wolfishly, "she was one miss I didn't lay! Actually, it was easy: she was forever losing stuff. I took things cos they made me feel closer to her. I'm not stupid—I did it bit by bit. You ought to be careful what you're doing: it's like messing with a Ouija board."

"It's hardly that."

"Is she going to get a plaque?"

"Universities aren't too keen on advertising former students who die in questionable circumstances."

"They must hate what you're doing, then, dude; you're making her famous." He gazed off absentmindedly. "She was mega-fit."

It used to pain me to think of the men in her life. The first few months she was here, I was angry at every fresher boy I saw—the prospect of them with their rucksacks and badges and toothy smiles potentially getting *their* hands on her. You'll well remember my preoccupations back then, Larry. One day I spotted her coming out of halls. Actually, I'd asked a warden where she was rooming—D3, Bates Hall—and waited for her. I almost reached out. Would that have been so very terrible, when I was padding along behind her, to have stretched out and put my hand on her shoulder or touched the small of her back? Taken her hand, maybe?

"Want to see one of my favorite items in the collection?" he asked. He held out a pair of purple knickers.

"You sick bastard."

"Now, now, no need to be like that. We've got a lot in common, you and me. Besides, I'd give them back, but she hasn't got a lot of use for knickers where she is now, has she?"

You weren't unaware of the charms of the younger woman yourself, were you, Larry? The smell of perfume, you once said with that poetic sensibility of yours, was like Handel at his best. Sometimes you became dizzy, you once confessed, watching the students from *your* office window, even if it was a scientific objectivity with which you made such observations. I liked to think of us as aesthetes. Spend long enough on a campus, too, and even the ugliest, most socially inept men (naturally I'm referring to myself; you're neither) find themselves presented with certain "opportunities."

"What are you planning to do with this stuff you're collecting, anyway?" the boy asked. He looked around as if he was expecting to see a box marked "SALMON, A." "Sounds like a giant jigsaw—wonder what it'll look like when it's done. I reckon she did herself in. That must have crossed your mind, the old hara-kiri."

I recalled the sharp, sterile smell of my specialist's room, how I'd reacted abrasively to his diagnostic ambiguity. "I'm not paying you all this money for best guesses," I'd snapped as he added to my burgeoning case notes on his computer.

The boy in my office and I sat in silence for a few seconds; then, infuriated by his manner I said: "Do you know what that expression actually means?"

"Yes, course—top yourself."

"No, how it *literally* translates?"

He looked at me vacantly.

"It's Japanese; it means 'stomach cut.'"

The boy didn't reply. *How terrible to be inarticulate,* I thought. *To never be heard.* Perhaps that's why we write. Why Alice kept a diary. She put it beautifully once: said it wasn't about standing up and shouting, "Look at me!"—more about standing in the crowd and shouting, "Listen to us!"

"'Seppuku' is the more formal word for it," I said. "That's the written form, but 'hara-kiri' is more commonly used in speech."

"Whatever. What I asked was if your little investigation was looking into that."

"No," I said, but the notion had been on a loop in my mind. The desperate and the displaced had always been drawn to that stretch of river—I'd occasionally sat there myself—but it was clear-cut as far as the police are concerned: she was drunk, she slipped, she drowned.

"Why's everyone always nice about people when they're dead? She was a right head case when she was alive."

I fondled the stone paperweight on my desk. A present from Elizabeth, my sole memento. No photos, no letters (we never dared), just this one precious dense gray object, smaller than a baby's head, smaller than a fist. That whole period of my life reduced to this: a lump of chert from Chesil Beach and our memories, the vestiges of chemical reactions in the sappy, subjective 1.5 kg of jelly-like gray matter we call our brains.

He stood up, sauntered around my office, ran his finger along the spines of a few books. Professor John Winter's *Man to Man,* Margaret Monahan's *Where the Body Becomes the Brain,* Guy Turner's *Painting the Past.*

"Don't touch those," I snapped.

"Who writes this stuff?"

"Among others, me. At least, I've *contributed* to a few."

"Always the bridesmaid, hey?" he said, with surprising perceptiveness.

A lecturer falls for a student—it's such a colossal cliché, isn't it. But that day I was trailing her, my heart beat faster, my teeth gritted, my fists clenched. It was like I was an undergraduate again myself. She appeared nervous, fresher-nervous, but she laughed a lot and the ones who are quick to laugh are always all right. I wish I could laugh more. Remember that statistician with the penchant for pink gin and boys I told you about who used to room near me? He once accused me of being a "dry old stick." I took it as a compliment: I was honing my too-intelligent-to-find-funny-what-the-rest-of-the-world-finds-funny demeanor and considered it a necessary attribute for the original thinking I was intending to do. I got damn good at it; shame the same can't be said of the original thinking.

"For God's sake, put them away," I said, nodding at the underwear. "Whoever's they are."

"Oh, they're Alice's all right. You're welcome to keep them," he said. "Call it a token of my goodwill, a gift, although there's no such thing as a free lunch, is there, Prof?" He reclined in the chair and draped the underwear over the lamp on the table next to him. "Unrequited love is a bummer, isn't it?"

On the wall, a photo of my wife. One of Milly, a Labrador of ours back in the 1990s. A black-and-white picture of me with my mother. What did he know, that boy in the photo, of the things he'd go on to do, to become? He was grinning, but even then it was an apprehensive grin. Bet it never once crossed that boy's mind that it might come to an end, his life, this thing that woke him up in the morning, that made him press wild flowers between the fragile pages of his grandfather's Bible, made him stare wide-eyed at atlases and into microscopes. How could he have imagined the moment of its coming, the first true sight of mortality? A doctor's words: *The tests have thrown up some results that we need to address.*

He poked at the stack of books on to which the knickers had fallen. "Wow, these are sick."

Not sure whether that expression will have reached you, Larry, but I gather it means "good." Not sure, either, if I ever will get to visit your great country now. People in my condition probably shouldn't fly; I doubt it's advisable for them to be that far from home and their doctors and tablets and treatments. This, I'm learning, is how illness works: one by one taking away your constituent components. The ability to travel, one's sex drive, one's sense of purpose. It's like randomly taking figures out of equations or unpicking a molecular model until you're left with something that doesn't work, that doesn't even remotely resemble you.

"These books, this office—you're like something from a movie. You're great."

"I'll take that as a compliment."

"Take it how you want, but we need to talk about the letter."

"What letter?"

I noticed his forearms: completely covered in tattoos, reds and greens and blues and yellows. "I take it you're aware there's nothing original in what you've done there," I said, captivated. "Humans have marked their bodies for thousands of years. Ötzi had them."

"Who?"

"The Iceman. The Stone Age cadaver we unearthed in 1991. He was over five thousand years old."

"Holy shit," he said.

There was no "we" about that discovery, I thought. Yet again, I'd been a bystander. "He had brown eyes, he was blood group O, he was forty-five years old when he died—when he was murdered; we've even established what his final meal was: chamois. Speculation is that his tattoos were an attempt at pain relief; the poor chap had arthritis."

"You are one yourself," he said.

"One what?"

"You say humans have marked *their* bodies, but that's a weird way of putting it. You ought to say *our* bodies, because you are one: a human. But enough of that crap; what are we going to do about the letter, Mr. Iceman?"

"What letter?"

"Don't play the innocent. *Your* letter. You're a local celebrity, dude. Imagine the shitstorm there'd be if the media turned on you. They'd savage you—you *and* your missus."

He delved into the rucksack, extracted a carefully folded piece of paper, and slid it halfway across the desk, keeping his hand on the top. I recognized my handwriting and my heart did a little flip. "Sweet Alice," it began.

"Get out or I'll throw you out," I said, anger seizing me. It was reminiscent of when I was in my fifties or maybe my forties. I actually *felt* something. I fondled the paperweight and the most peculiar question unfurled in front of me: What would it be like to bring it down on his head? Make him go away, shut him up, make him know what it's like to be mortal, finite. I rubbed my face, composed myself. "She made people feel different about themselves," I said. "She touched people."

"She didn't touch *me*. Maybe she did you? Maybe you did her? What's the matter? You look like you've seen a ghost!"

Larry, it's all so complicated. We know it's complicated, but it's even *more* complicated than it otherwise might have been.

This little yob's theory about suicide—I've been testing it, as I have all the others. My task is to assemble intelligence from the madness, shape order from chaos. It's a calling in which I've been rather immersed; hence, incidentally, the disgracefully long gap since my last communication. You will make allowances for me, won't you? Because I'll endeavor to paint out the patterns, but my cognitive abilities aren't what they were. A fresh day and new details filter to the crown of my mind, take precedence—chunks of past illuminated in the alternately faithful and foggy terrain of recall. But I'll endeavor to demonstrate fidelity to the facts, however gory and salacious. It's all there, locked away in the heads and hearts of a handful of us, primed for the extraction. My job is to dive into detail, verify, authenticate, substantiate, separate fact from fable: lies, love, grudges, adultery, betrayal, murder.

I sat there trying to breathe. Trying to breathe life back into more than one corpse.

There it was, conspicuous and incontrovertible, the billet-doux and the revelations therein: trumpeting a bitter cocktail of protectiveness and, well, something much more unchaste.

Jesus, what have I done?

Yours as ever,
Jeremy

Article on *Southern Eye* website,
December 7, 2012

First Cop on Scene of Salmon Death Quits Force After "Beyond the Grave" Calls

The ex-cop who was first on the scene after Alice Salmon died has spoken for the first time of his harrowing experience.

Brave Mike Barclay has told *Southern Eye* how the episode, which refuses to leave the headlines nearly a year on, contributed to him quitting the force after nearly three decades' service.

The official investigation remains open, but the former law enforcer said his first reaction was that the incident could have been "sexually motivated" because "her top was torn and hitched up."

It was immediately apparent to the dad of three that he was dealing with a corpse, so he made no attempt to fish her out of the river Dane—instead calling for backup. "I was prepared to walk alongside her if she floated downstream, but she was tangled in reeds," he said. "The guy who'd called 999 was sitting on the ground in shock, repeating over and over how he'd found her like this.

"My sergeant arrived and took charge, then the whole world and his dog was there—CID, CSI, the bronze inspector, the boys with their scuba kit, the works. What was vital was sealing the area—the footpath, the steps, the bridge; basically the priority was scene preservation and stopping members of the public contaminating evidence."

The postmortem concluded the cause of death was drowning, with the coroner subsequently reporting Salmon to have alcohol and cocaine in her bloodstream. Returning an "open" verdict, he also recorded "abrasions and cuts on her face, grazes on her knees and a large recently sustained bruise on her right shoulder."

"Even in the poor light and at a distance, I could make out injuries on her face," Barclay said. "I'd have hazarded a guess at blunt-force trauma—it was like she'd been punched."

He was particularly distressed by hearing Salmon's mobile. "It was in the mud beside the water and it kept ringing. Whoever was calling was entirely in the dark about the news that was on its way to them," he said.

"If you do thirty years in this job you get desensitized, but my youngest daughter is in her twenties, so it got to me."

Barclay admitted to still having flashbacks, often triggered by the "sonar" ringtone that had been on Salmon's phone.

He concluded: "You have to deal with all sorts in the police service, but that case affected me in a way others haven't. It was my granddaughter's birthday party the next day, and when she blew out the candles on the cake, I made a wish, too."

Review by Alice Salmon in the Southampton music magazine *STUNT*, 2005

The Dynamite Men are a band to watch.

They burst onto the stage at the Pump House full of swagger and style and performed a sixty-minute set of hugely entertaining songs to a packed student audience.

Always a popular venue, it was standing room only, with the 200-strong audience having flocked to see this local trio.

First a confession: your reviewer has a vested interest. I once met the lead singer in a bar on East Street and was as awe-struck as a fourteen-year-old groupie. His real name, *STUNT* can reveal, is Jack Symonds and he's nineteen and comes from the Hampton and is a modern-day Lord Byron, disheveled and dishy with his curly dark locks, skinny jeans and brooding stage presence.

For an hour, the world slowed down. Money worries, exam stress and fascist landlords all receded as the world was stripped down to music that filled the room and filled our hearts. They sang of relationships, with the wistful and profound "Morning, Morning," which laments "waking up with a strange woman. I rolled over and saw her face. She wasn't smiling." Then there was the melancholy "Away," which speaks of the trials and tribulations of leaving home—that instant when "we see what's over our shoulder as smaller, but we're taller, so we stand up proud and walk on." But the lyrics aren't without humor. They explore what it is like to be penniless with the hilarious and clearly autobiographical "67p." Another of my favorites was "You Kill Me," a hymn to an unnamed first love (lucky girl!), someone who "broke my heart and didn't as much as blink."

There were lots of influences at work here. The Libertines, Oasis, even a bit of Amy. But they've merged all these into a unique sound. The sound of the Dynamite Men.

My favorite song was "Hit," a searing analysis of addiction, which saw a tortured Jack alone on the stage, describing with pitch-perfect accuracy the clarifying, soothing and emboldening sensation drugs can bring. "My turn in the toilet, my turn for a tablet, like breathing in pollen or swallowing a sparkling fish . . ."

Course, he wasn't entirely alone—he had bandmates Callum Jones (19) and Eddy Cox (20). They're school friends, so he said at one point, drawn together by the power of music to change the world. "We thought we had something to say!" he shouted.

We're listening, Jack. We're very much listening.

Music sources tell me there's a lot of luck in this business and right now that's all that's between the Dynamite Men and the big time. One nineteen-year-old maths student described it as the best gig he'd ever been to, and while I wouldn't necessarily agree—Pulp at the Apollo in Manchester takes that accolade as far as this reviewer's concerned—it came a close second.

It's easy to see why the Dynamite Men have already got a loyal following on the university circuit. Jack hung out with gig-goers in the bar afterwards. (You'll be pleased to hear your reviewer stayed with him until it closed—all in the name of research for *STUNT,* naturally!)

I felt privileged to have seen this band. It felt like watching music history. Like how it must have been the first time the Arctics performed. The sort of moment people are still talking about in years to come. The night the Dynamite Men first played the Pump House. They will continue to make explosions. They will continue to make noise. This is one band destined to make a very big bang.

I'll definitely be going to every one of their gigs from now on. (Student loan? What student loan?) Uni work can wait. Music like this can't. Besides, as Babyshambles put it, *Fuck Forever*.

Blog post by Megan Parker,
February 12, 2012, 9:30 p.m.

I've checked Alice's direct messages on Twitter. Glad to see you never took my advice and changed your password, Salmonette . . . you must have used the same one for every single site you ever registered for!

I found this exchange on January 15. Obviously I've mentioned it to the police, but a fat lot of good that's done. Publish and be damned, hey, Alice?

From @FreemanisFree: Haven't forgotten about you my little freedom fighter.
From @AliceSalmon1: Who is this?
From @FreemanisFree: Patience patience little Miss Criminal Catcher. All in good time.
From @AliceSalmon1: You don't scare me.
From @FreemanisFree: Feeling's mutual.
From @AliceSalmon1: Who are you or haven't you got the balls to tell me?
From @FreemanisFree: Oh I got balls enough, wanna see them?
From @AliceSalmon1: You're pathetic.
From @FreemanisFree: Your dead.
From @AliceSalmon1: Stop tweeting me or I'll report it to the police.
From @FreemanisFree: Like your new purpel hat. Would like to fuck you.
From @AliceSalmon1: Go to hell. And learn to spell while you're there.

Texts exchanged between Gemma Rayner and Alice Salmon, *December 14, 2011*

GR: Soz to hear re you and Luke—fancy a run to take yr mind off it?
AS: Can't, ankle knackered.
GR: Sports injury?
AS: UDI!
GR: Sustained?
AS: At Meg's the other day. Disagreement between me and the stairs! I blame wonky banister!
GR: Lightweight x

AS: Will ring u, be lovely to catch up. Need to hear about your flat hunting. Maybe could manage a gentle run in Battersea Park at w/e? x

---

Letter sent by Professor Jeremy Cooke,
June 10, 2012

My dear Larry,

That lad with the tattoos came back today. I stopped by my office to wade perfunctorily through some funding documents I'd been neglecting and there he was, sitting inside, bold as brass, as if envisaging my arrival. "You," I said.

"Hello, Iceman," he replied. "I figured you'd like to see your letter again."

He retrieved it from his rucksack. "Not sure why I kept it. Maybe it struck a chord with me. Discovering someone else had a thing about Alice, too, was, well, weird. It prompted a pretty full-on spell of nicking her stuff. A psychologist would have a field day with that, wouldn't they? Probably reckon I was upping my game to see off the competition!"

I should have anticipated the document making a reappearance, Larry, but I'd assumed it wouldn't have survived—lost or become indecipherable or moldered to zero: it was only paper, after all.

"Love this city, love being at uni here—even if some freakoid did shove a note under my door in freshers week professing their love for me," she'd confided in me once, when she joined me in my office for a soupçon of alcohol after our annual departmental bash.

"How unsettling," I'd replied, feigning ignorance. "Moths attracted to your bright light?"

"Flies round shit, more like," she'd said.

The boy in my office said: "You'd have to be a right screwup to write this."

The loop of a *B*. The high, sharp point of a capital *A*. Mine, all mine.

"She decided it was a practical joke, but I can spot a sicko when I see one. What do you reckon, Iceman? What's your sicko radar like? Practical joke or nutter? My money's on the latter—where's yours? Come on, where's *your money*?"

He was toying with me. "I need your name," I said.

"They call me Mocksy." He fondled my note; he'd no right to dredge it up. Another word I recognized, a turn of phrase, the construction of a sentence. In the right hands, linguistics is like a mini-DNA profile, as reliable as any identity parade. I looked around. My degree certificate, a faded photograph of me with a minor minister, a cutting from a magazine headlined "Cooke Closes on Breakthrough," referring to some ultimately futile strand of research.

"Instead of a signature, there's a question mark. What a wack job! A question mark and a kiss—it's the sort of thing a kid would do."

I stared down at the *X*. Those two crossed strokes. The twenty-fourth letter of the alphabet, a signifier of ten, an unknown variable, the first letter of the Greek word for Christ. A kiss. "You stay away from me and you stay away from Alice Salmon's memory, you hear."

"Why?" he asked. "*You're* not."

We both gazed down at the single sheet of paper. A previous piece of me, toxic, precious. "Sweet Alice, don't be afraid," it began.

"Five hundred quid," he said.

I've lost track of the number of occasions upon which I've unburdened on you, Larry. But I had—I have—so very few confidants. All those pages we devoted to Descartes and Thomas Aquinas must have paled into insignificance against the space I filled ruminating on Alice in 2004 and, prior to that, back in the early 1980s, my marital indiscretion. Remember how I begged you to visit? To make a mercy mission, like some lumbering Saint Bernard bearing brandy and sage advice? We could have gone to the Crown; could have holed up in the back bar and other patrons wouldn't have been able to work out whether we were perfect strangers or the most intimate of friends, and swapped stories over a pint of the awful, nutty, frothy mouthwash they call beer.

"Five hundred quid," the boy with tattoos repeated. "Or Mr. and Mrs. Salmon get to see a copy of this."

He held it back out and the faintest of smiles broke on the corner of his mouth. I saw another word and it gave me a pinch of melancholy for when I'd been learning to spell: the sense of infinite possibility, the first occasion upon which I'd grasped the concept that our understanding of the world—the world itself, therefore—was dependent on the words we had to explain it.

It's as vivid now as ever how I'd crept into Bates Hall: its cold stairwells, echoey corridors and frayed carpets. It reminded me of Warwick. The smell of stale food, chili con carne; the Proustian section of my brain was in overdrive. *You're not an undistinguished, inconsequential scholar,* I thought as I'd hunted for her room. She had one of those name tags on her door, the sort children do. If she'd opened it, who knows what I'd have done. Said hello? Inquired how she was settling in? Pushed my way in? I'd stridden along the corridor, my brain spinning: *Don't open the door, open the door, don't open the door, open the door.* It seemed critical that it didn't go unsaid how exquisite she was. Her having absolutely no idea, of course, merely made her *more* so. She was a carbon copy of her mother.

God, how I adore women. I've worshipped the shape of their necks, the color of their lips, the smell of their hair. *I want them all, each and every last damn one of them,* I recall once writing to you. It hasn't, as you know, been exclusively *women* I've found myself drawn towards—many is the occasion I've recounted my handful of encounters with fellow male undergraduates at Warwick. Why is it that when I recall those quick and largely unsatisfactory trysts, it's with a sense of shame? Hundreds of species of animals have been shown to be homosexual, yet only one—*us*—displays homophobia. I guess any one of those men could have set me on a different course. Instead I buried it away, that part of me, if indeed it *was* a part of me, the portion that had taken me to public parks and strangers' rooms festooned with the memorabilia of public schools, mostly slightly less minor than mine. It's irrelevant now. I've made my choices.

I'd phrased the letter in a way that I'd hoped wouldn't scare Alice. Astounding how it's possible to say so much and so little in nine sentences. I cogitated as I wrote it: *Am I having a breakdown?* I've often grappled with what that would feel like. It's probably not as dramatic as one imagines: a series of tiny, imperceptible and individually invisible steps. But I didn't care. I'd have been noticed, been heard, been felt. *Me.* Old Cookie. Even if she went public, they'd never twig it was me, and besides, it wasn't as if my career was going anywhere. Shortly before, I'd been passed over for the departmental headship in favor of a boy from Imperial. "It's not that we don't recognize your contribution," I was informed patronizingly. "Rather that the role requires a different skill set to yours."

Fliss could tell something was amiss. "You seem preoccupied," she said the night I wrote my epistle. I'd stumbled on an Attenborough documentary that temporarily satiated us, then we went up and she read a South Downs flora and fauna book and I flicked absentmindedly through mine on the last days of the Iroquoian, and within a few minutes she was snoring and I crept down to my study and dug out my fountain pen.

Fliss reckoned my affair—sorry to keep bouncing around in history, old boy, but that's how our memories work—made us stronger, but it tore chunks out of us. Trouble is, it's human nature to look after Number One. We all need to be convinced we're the most important being on earth; it's a prerequisite of evolution. Is that a very pessimistic prognosis—a symptom possibly of never having children, as you did? They say having them teaches you to put someone else before yourself. Sure, I've made sacrifices. Jesus, watching one's mother slowly die involves plenty of those—my father and I had severed all contact long before that vicious old bastard snuffed it—but if you'd have said, "Her life or yours?" how would I have responded? How would any of us?

Yes, I have been drinking, but only a little winter warmer. The Balvenie single malt Fliss and I have been saving for a special occasion. Trouble is, I never seemed to have one. I've spent my whole life doing that, Larry. *Waiting.*

Maybe the day I sneaked into Bates Hall was a special occasion? Feeling alive, vital, what it is to be a human being, a *man*. I hadn't felt like that—like this—for years. Sometimes we're more than science, aren't we? More than my anthropology or your genetics. We confound logic.

That's when we're at our best, at our most beautiful. Our most dangerous, too.

"Would you say I'm a good person?" I asked the boys in my office this morning, the one sitting opposite me with tattoos and the apprehensive-looking one in the picture on the wall.

"It wasn't a good person who wrote this," one of them replied. "Now where's my fucking five hundred quid?"

Ten minutes later I was standing with him at an ATM.

Yours as ever,
Jeremy

Extract from Alice Salmon's diary,
August 5, 2007, age 21

I'd barely finished my cheesecake and Dad was up on his feet, tapping his glass. "Your attention, please, for just a few moments. It only feels like yesterday Lizzie was rushed to hospital—and when I say rushed, I *mean* rushed. Our beautiful daughter was nearly born on the A427!"

My parents had booked this amazing restaurant for my twenty-first lunch—one of those places that's so popular it's got a waiting list, hence the late celebration! Eighteen of us, rellies, godparents and family friends, the ones I used to call uncles and aunties even though they weren't. I went for the Scottish smoked salmon (my cannibal tendencies!), which was yummy, although I'd have been tempted by the scallops and lobster with ginger if I wasn't a wuss when it came to shellfish. It had turned into a double celebration because I'd only gone and been offered a job. Yes, move over Kate Adie, you're looking at *Southampton Messenger* junior reporter Alice Salmon, start date September 10.

"We're all very proud of Alice," Dad said. "She's even got an upper-division honors, despite being adamant that she'd flunk all her courses."

He claimed afterwards it was an impromptu speech, but no way

José was it, him cracking all those gags like how it was Gordon Brown's first coup as PM to get me to pay some tax. He was quite the raconteur.

"I understand the real birthday bash is taking place next weekend in Southampton—somewhere called Flames," Dad said, and I got a pinch of sadness that he couldn't picture it, its alcoves and wood, its bright dance floor and dark corners—*the* place to go, we'd been told in freshers' week—when I'd had so many brilliant nights out there. "Men of Southampton, watch out," he added, which Aunty Bev obviously assumed was code for "sex," because she made a beeline for me straight afterwards and interrogated me about my love life (she is the God-squad side of the family).

"You look beautiful, Ace," Dad said, which set me off blubbing, and then he said he couldn't conceive anyone else in the world as his daughter ("Couldn't *conceive* it, hey?" Robbie yelled . . . one Peter Kay DVD and he reckons he's a stand-up) and how I'd done them proud, which made me feel guilty because I've actually done zilch. Then when he said the stuff about us being such a close family I was so upset, because it made me think, *there's so much you don't know about me,* and I had the urge to share the other stuff with him: how I'd never felt quite good enough, as if it was all one big act, which was why drink was so amazing: it made me feel the same size as everyone else, drink and a few lines (although I'm going to quit all that, because it's about my career now), but I'd like Dad to realize, because otherwise he's only seeing half of me.

"I can't believe that the tiny ball of screaming gorgeousness that Lizzie nearly gave birth to on the side of the highway twenty-one years ago has gone on to become this . . . this slightly bigger ball of screaming gorgeousness!"

And when he quoted his one bit of Latin, *tempus fugit,* Mum piped up and said, "Come on, Dave. I said I'd let a fire alarm off if you went over the five-minute mark."

"Thank you, Alice," he said. "Just . . . thank you."

I went round the table and gave him a hug and wondered if he could smell the wine and the coke oozing through my skin as if my insides couldn't take it anymore, and he felt the same as he always did: big and solid and soft and like my dad.

After we'd managed to get Dad to sit back down, I did the hostess bit, catching up with all my guests.

"You've grown up," Grampy Mullens said when I got to him.

"I feel very old."

"You wait till you're my age, then you'll feel old." A waitress brought him half a pint of beer. "Being an old duffer does have its advantages," he said, winking. He asked me to sit with him, maneuvered a chair round with a struggle, then talked about my gran, how she would have loved today; it had been three years but he still missed her every day, and what a stunner she'd been when they were "courting," picking her up in his Ford Anglia, all dolled up like Elizabeth Taylor, with her long hair and bobby socks. He's like this—he can have these amazing bouts of lucidity (that's going to be my word of this diary entry) when everything that made him *him* is still there, but then he'll have spells when it's gone and he'll call me "Liz" and Mum "Alice" and Robbie "David." "How much do you and your mum talk?" he asked suddenly. "Not chitchat, but properly talk?"

"We do a bit," I told him.

"Secrets always come out in the end, even if it takes decades. You beat them by making them come out on your own terms." He'd lost me, but he did a lot. It used to annoy me, but Mum said I had to cut him some slack, because when you're old your brain stops working in a linear way. "I've never known anyone as proud as that lass, but talk to her, listen to her."

We watched Mum wandering from table to table, catching up with friends. "Remember when you used to come over and walk Chip?" Grampy asked, and I wondered if today was one of those days when his brain wasn't working in a linear way.

"Course I do. That was one cool dog!" Rob and I would go over to his place to exercise him and when we came back Grampy would be watching through the window, waiting, and Chip would curl up by his feet and he'd pat his head and say, "Good lad, good lad, good lad."

One afternoon when I was in the sixth form he'd handed me a brown envelope. Insisted I *took* it. "You enjoy yourself at the university, girl," he'd said, and later, when I was paying my rent or buying books, I'd tell myself it was the Grampy Mullens money, but when I bought booze or ciggies, that was the student loan.

He loved hearing stories about uni because it was so alien to him, so I recounted a few now: the all-nighter I'd pulled to get my dissertation done, the git of a landlord who ran off with our deposit and the weird bloke with the tattoos we shared a house with.

"I need you to make me a promise about your mum," he said, going off on another tangent. "That you'll look after her for me when I'm gone."

"She's tough as old boots," I said, using one of his expressions.

"She's not as stout as she pretends. You're the same. Ask her about Southampton, about her time there. Ask her, because she needs you to understand, but wait until I'm gone, princess, because she swore me to secrecy!"

"What are you two whispering about?" Mum asked, bundling over. "You look like you're plotting."

"Talking about you, not to you," Grampy said, winking at me. Then, when she'd gone, he smiled mischievously and cracked one of our in-jokes. "Have I ever told you I left school at fifteen?"

It was one of his good days. A linear day.

"Hey, Fish Face," a voice piped up when I went to the restroom.

His glassy eyes reminded me of Grampy's, but the cause was different: Ben was wasted. "What are *you* doing here?"

"Figured I'd pay you a visit. You not going to invite me in to meet your family?"

"How did you know we were here?"

"It wasn't difficult, Lissa. You've been talking about nothing else on Facebook all week. Fancy a smoke?"

It was like the old days, except we had to go outside to smoke now, and this wasn't a student haunt and only one of us was hammered. I was careful to stand out of view of the restaurant, because I'd never exactly shared with Mum and Dad my penchant for the occasional cigarette and explaining Ben to them wouldn't be easy, especially to Dad.

"You got a job, then."

"Yes. It's not exactly *The New York Times,* but it's a start. Not a crappy internship, either."

"Plus you get to stay on in the Hampton," Ben said.

"That's probably a mistake. You can't pretend you're a student forever." I explained how it was going to be good-bye, Polygon, hello, Highfield, and that I'd be moving into a new flat the next week: sixty quid a month more, but there'd only be three of us. "I'm a young professional now, after all."

"Glad one of us is," he said. "This is going to sound weird, Lissa, but I'm . . . I'm proud of you; it sounds brilliant."

I was convinced I'd blown it, because I'd gone into what Mum called chatterbox mode at the interview—gabbling about how I fancied doing big-picture stuff, like the Madeleine McCann disappearance and the Virginia Tech shooting and liked reviewing music and was definitely up for crime reporting, because there were too many scumbags on the loose, and I'd been positive I'd cocked up, but the editor had nodded and said, "We've got more than our fair share of scumbags in this city."

I wondered what she'd be like, this new me. The one who'd wear her hair up, have a desk in an open-plan office, attend council meetings and court hearings, scribbling away in the shorthand I'd promised to learn by Christmas. I might not necessarily have liked the old Alice—rather, the young Alice—but I'd got used to her: the one who often didn't surface till ten, who did assignments in the early hours, poring over online discussions about Plath and scribbling notes in the margins of books; the one who loved fishbowls in bars on Bedford Place and hockey club weekends away and even, now he was in the past, this guy. It gave me a stab of sadness that it was over—the mornings drinking tea on scruffy sofas passing night-before phone photos around, segueing (maybe that should be my word for this entry!) into afternoons in the library and evenings on beanbags watching *Lost* and *Deal or No Deal,* the days and weeks bending into each other until, *bam,* my dissertation! "I can't believe you've gatecrashed my lunch. Have you got no shame?"

"No," Ben said. He smiled and it all came back: him dressed as Superman, the evening we first did coke, us in Paris. It was all so simple then—nothing but lectures and nights out and the flutter of excitement when he'd asked if I fancied coming away, no strings attached, but that I'd need a passport. Then I'd recalled how I'd launched into him on Platform 6 of Waterloo station.

"Are you dumping me?" he'd asked incredulously.

"Yes."

"Whore," he'd said, and stormed off.

And remembering that he could call me that gave me a spasm of anger, but it was over six months ago, it was history and I'd moved on. "I worked out what it was about you," I said.

"What, that makes me irresistible?"

"No, that makes you impossible." I felt like Grampy on one of his lucid days. Stuff made sense. "It's the way you never see beyond the present. This constant searching for gratification; it's like a baby, it's like an animal."

"Which is it?"

"Which is what?"

"You can't have it both ways—I'm either like a baby or an animal."

"Don't be a dick."

"How about if we split the difference—say I'm a baby animal? Fuck's sake, Lissa, give me a break, I've come all this way to wish you a happy birthday."

It was very him—traveling from Southampton to Corby on a whim. I could picture him stuck in that shithole of a student house. What used to be carefree would soon be embarrassing, sad. Eventually, having exhausted all his options, he'd creep back to his parents' place in London, the Georgian pad with the huge hall and the chandelier, sparkling like hundreds of earrings. It was true, but doling out a character assassination made me feel older than ever, and I wasn't sure I liked it.

"Remind me why I ever hung around with you."

"Because I'm gorgeous."

"Scratch the surface and I bet you're still the same ginormous cock."

"I've got a ginormous *what?*"

"See, it's impossible to have an adult conversation with you."

"Fuck adult, Lissa. Let's get drunk. Let's go on somewhere. It'll be like an after-party!"

I recalled what Grampy had said before he got on to all that weird stuff about Mum, about how I should live every day as if it was my last. Once I started work it would be all sparkling water and gym visits and early nights. I saw the room we'd eaten in—empty now, the tables getting cleared—and tried to visualize the next family gathering. I watched Mum helping Grampy into the car, lifting his legs in, then handing him his stick. Probably his funeral.

"Why not," I said to Ben. "You're only young once."

Alice Salmon's "Summer 2011" Spotify playlist,
August 30, 2011

Post Break-Up Sex	**The Vaccines**
Skinny Love	**Bon Iver**
Tonight's the Kind of Night	**Noah and the Whale**
Sex on Fire	**Kings of Leon**
Someone Like You	**Adele**
That's Not My Name	**The Ting Tings**
Just for Tonight	**One Night Only**
Sigh No More	**Mumford & Sons**
Your Song	**Ellie Goulding**
Mr. Brightside	**The Killers**
Dog Days Are Over	**Florence and the Machine**
Last Request	**Paolo Nutini**
Sweet Disposition	**The Temper Trap**
Just the Way You Are	**Bruno Mars**
The A Team	**Ed Sheeran**
The Edge of Glory	**Lady Gaga**
Sleeping to Dream	**Jason Mraz**

Email sent by Professor Jeremy Cooke, *March 22, 2012*

From: jfhcooke@gmail.com

To: Elizabeth_salmon101@hotmail.com

Subject: Stay Away

Dear Liz,

You may find this hard to believe, but I enjoyed reading your email; I found it extremely stimulating. Listen to me, one sentence in and I'm already sounding like a lecturer marking an assignment. Old habits die hard. Thank you, as well, for deeming me "accomplished"; I'd have preferred "great," but one takes compliments where one can.

Do you recall the cricket pitches? Houses now. The faculty room, too? The one half-decent room on campus and they appropriated it for a management suite; a bit of oak paneling and a few stone mullions evidently sufficiently encouraged potential investors to part with their money to relegate us foot soldiers to a ghastly breeze-block bunker. Do you remember those things? Because right now remembering seems very important to me. I've got a few issues with the old prostate, you see. Typical me—I can't even get ill in an original place.

I've been trying to pinpoint when we last spoke properly. We bumped into each other once in the early 1990s, didn't we, when you had Alice with you? I'd been in Corby for a conference and had visited your road out of curiosity. I had to wait awhile to spot you.

"Alice," you'd said, remaining remarkably composed when I'd blundered up to you, "this is an acquaintance of Mummy's called Dr. Cooke. Say hello to Dr. Cooke, Alice."

I put out my hand and she shook it nonchalantly. "I was a colleague of your mother's at the university a long time ago," I informed her, as if a little girl would have had any comprehension of what a colleague or a university or indeed a long time ago was. "You're a big girl, aren't you?" I said. I hadn't had much experience of children, of how to speak their language. A language all of its own: a subset of ours.

"I'm nearly seven," she said.

I recognized you in her voice.

"I'm having a birthday party on Sunday and there's going to be jelly," the child said.

Funny how that sticks in my mind all these years later. That there would be jelly.

"Will you be coming to my party?"

"Dr. Cooke's a bit busy on Sunday," you interjected.

"It's wonderful to see you, Liz. How have you been?"

You bit your lip, your eyes burnt, you rested your hand on the top of your daughter's head, gently turned her away and whispered: "It's a bit late to be asking now."

"But . . . but—"

"But nothing. How I am has got precisely zero to do with you."

Alice picked up on your tone, because she squirmed out from under your reach, spun round. "Doctors make you better," she said.

"Dr. Cooke's a different kind of doctor, sweetie," you told her. "He works with people who lived long before any of us were born."

"Wouldn't they be dead, then?"

"Very prescient, young lady," I said.

A car pulled into the drive. "Daddy, Daddy, Daddy!" she screamed, bolting from your grasp.

"Have you got a family?" you asked.

"No. We never did. A blessing that passed us by," I said, deploying the phrase Fliss and I defaulted to. It could have been either of us, I'd not infrequently remind my wife, to which she'd respond, "But it *wasn't* either of us; it was me."

"*You* did, I see," I said.

"Yes," you said. "We've got a boy as well."

"Bully for you," I snapped, remembering the slow, sinking dread, the tests, the theories, the statistics. They loved a probability, those doctors.

I hovered on the pavement, examined the man in your life. Hefty. Not un-handsome. Your age. Remembered those few months we'd spent together almost ten years before. He gave us a nonchalant wave, as if I was asking directions, began unloading provisions from the boot, and I felt a swift urge to walk up to him and say: I know things about your wife that you don't.

So Alice turned down Oxford? Well, I never. I imagine that sparked some discussion in your household. I got the grades but flunked the interview. They obviously detected in me even at that tender age what I was destined to become: good on paper. As a PhD, I was informed that, to be truly brilliant, academics needed soul.

Could I not persuade you to change your mind about that drink, Liz? I could show you the mementos of Alice I'm gathering. Heaven only knows what the university's "technology support" department must suspect I'm up to; my email hasn't been so busy for years. My favorite photograph thus far is of her climbing on the statue outside the biology labs. It's a constant battle, keeping the students off that ghastly piece of "art," but you can't herd them. She's got her arms round his bronze neck and is sticking her tongue out at him. Hurrah for Alice, I say, poking fun at the blighter—derivative plagiarist that he was.

Liz, can I ask you a question? How was she at the time of her passing? In her final days, was she in good spirits? Only—and forgive me for raising this—much of what I've read alludes to her state of mind.

What is it they say about journalism being the first draft of history? I wonder if that's what our correspondence is. The first draft of something. These words, the sentences they make, the sentiments they convey. The truths—or otherwise—we trade. Because nothing is entirely objective and facts are slippery little buggers. We're better equipped to communicate than any organism that's ever existed, but arguably we're not a whole lot better at it than we were 40,000 years ago when the Neanderthals reached out and stenciled their hands in the El Castillo caves. Every day we fail to communicate. We speak in riddles or half-truths or worse. Every day we pass up on that wonderful, beautiful chance to reach out into the darkness and connect. Still, the only way we've got of making sense of the madness is through these crazy, silly, magical, maddening little things we choose to call "words." They're all we've got.

I would have asked about how you were after we went our separate ways, I so nearly did on so many occasions, but I had no idea how you'd react or whether those around you were aware of your situation. I was sick with worry.

Naturally I'll treat your email in confidence. I, too, may have omitted to mention our correspondence to Fliss. Secrets, eh—aren't we're a right pair?

I would very much like to see you, even if it is our coda.

Yours,
Jem

Editorial column by *Southampton Messenger* chief reporter Alice Salmon,
September 14, 2008

"Southampton Residents Can Sleep Safer Tonight"

Liam Bardsley, the man who attacked an 82-year-old great-grandmother, was sentenced to four years in prison this week.

This monster targeted as many as forty homes in our area during a burglary spree lasting over a year.

He left a trail of victims in his wake—including courageous octogenarian Dot Walker, who confronted the 36-year-old when she was woken by "movement" in her kitchen. He knocked her to the ground and hit her, according to the prosecution, "at least five times in the face" before fleeing the scene. He was described in court as "an inhuman creature who showed no mercy."

He belongs behind bars. Why, then, we all want to know, has he only been imprisoned for four years? Taking into account so-called "good behavior," he could be back out on our streets in less than two.

Readers who responded to our "Catch the Night Stalker" campaign should feel proud of the part they played in sending this animal to jail. Without you bravely coming forward, we would never have been able to compile so much evidence against Bardsley—evidence that the police described as "vital" in assembling their case.

The photo we published with the family's approval of Dot after the horrific attack sparked a flood of calls to the police helpline (many of you also contacted the *Messenger* direct).

The four-year jail term he received for burglary and grievous bodily harm should have been much longer. Even twice that would be too short for a man prepared to tell an old lady that he "would gut her if she as much as whimpered."

We are today calling on the government to instigate tougher sentences for violent crimes against the elderly and are working with local MPs who have vowed to take the matter up in Parliament.

The last word must go to Dot, one of the bravest women we've ever had the privilege to meet—in many respects a typical pensioner, in others utterly unique.

Hearing about what happened in Court D of Southampton Crown Court this week, she said: "I only hope no one else will have to go through what I have."

When asked for her reaction to her attacker's sentence, she replied with wisdom, dignity and compassion: "He'll get his reckoning when he comes before his maker."

Do you have information about a crime? Ring Alice Salmon in confidence on the number at the top of page 7.

Notes made by Luke Addison on his laptop,
February 14, 2012

Your mum and dad's house was the last place in the world I wanted to be, but I couldn't *not* go. That would have merely aroused suspicion.

"You look like you've been in the wars," your mum said when I arrived. I spun her some line about a mountain-bike accident, but fessed up later to having been in a fight.

"Expect we'll all do a few things we're not proud of before we're through," she'd said. "Sorry about all these wretched questions the police are asking, but it's their job. We all need the same thing, sweetheart—the truth." And the word "sweetheart" clawed at me because I could imagine her calling you it and I was never close to my mum.

"You meant so much to her," she said, giving me an impromptu hug. Her hair against my face was the nearest I'd ever get to you.

Secrets, Al. So many secrets.

"You do realize Alice and I weren't together," I admitted. "We were having some issues." It would have appeared odd not to have mentioned it. They'd have wondered why.

"Of course I do. We're a close family. Our daughter talks to us. *Talked.*"

"I'd understand if you'd rather me not come to the funeral," I said, half hoping she'd seize on that.

"No, we want you there, or *I* certainly do. I'm working on the principle that the pair of you would have made up sooner or later. David's got a rather different view, of course."

It was odd being in that house, the house we'd been in so many times, the house that I'd been initially nervous of visiting; I needn't have been, your parents were fantastic, plying me full of booze even if it was some awful pale ale and stressing they wouldn't consider me the slightest bit rude if I took myself off to the conservatory and buried myself in the Sunday papers.

The house where we'd dog-sat, had a bath together, where you'd showed me your old school blazer and I'd joked about you wearing it for me and you'd called me a perv and we'd maneuvered into your single bed at two in the afternoon, you diligently turned your toy rabbit away, that was such a you thing to do, and afterwards lay staring up through the skylight at the clouds scudding across the blue.

The house was full of people who loved you, your name on every breath, in every sentence, in every room. They all did a double take when they saw my face. Your mum had put her arm round me and took me into the garden at one point; all those people and she found time for *me,* and I explained how much I hated myself. "Don't," she said. "Don't." I might have been different—*better*—if I'd had parents like yours. I'd felt a surge of warmth towards her, that she might not despise me for what I'd done. Later, I went to your dad, in the garage chipping away at a piece of wood on his workbench, and said: "Thanks for having me here."

"You've got my wife to thank for that. If it was down to me, I'd have put you through that window." He gazed at a small discolored square of glass. "Why couldn't you have kept your damn stupid prick in your trousers?"

He'll never forgive me; you can't blame him. I'll never forgive myself. Not that he knows the half of it. No one does.

He planed at the wood; shavings fell to the floor and layered up around his shoes. "Twenty-five," he said. "What sort of age is that? Answer me, you stupid little bastard." He raised his fist and I'd thought, *Hit me. Hit me as that man in the pub had. It might do us both some good.* But his arm slumped down and he made a noise like a wounded animal. "How could you do this to my baby?"

Can't believe they'd even want me at your funeral; wasn't as if we were related, not as if I'm next of kin, not as if we were *married.* That's another thing you don't know, Al. I was going to propose a second time. The morning you went to Southampton. We'd been apart for almost the two months you'd insisted on by then. No contact—they were the rules, *your* rules—but I was going to surprise you. Apologize, explain, make you see sense. You'd have been stunned—but in a good way, I reckon. I'd realized over those two months how there was one special person for everyone and you were mine, Alice Louise Salmon. Forget the trip to Rome. I was going to do it there and then on your doorstep. But Soph answered the door and claimed you weren't in.

"Where's she gone?"

"Southampton."

It filled me with despair, the possibility of a whole life of us not knowing where the other one was. *I must find you,* I'd thought. *I must find my Alice and propose.* Soph eyed me suspiciously.

I wasn't sure how much you'd have told her; I certainly hadn't broadcast what was going on. "Can I go up to her room?"

"No."

"She's in there, isn't she?" I said, the possibility of you being with another man stretching out in me. "Who's she got in there?" You'd been adamant that there wasn't anyone else involved when you'd given me the heave-ho, when we'd last been in your room and you were crying and the mini–Christmas tree was flickering and I was shaking you—I'm sorry, I couldn't help it. I lost it, that's how much I loved you. You promised there wasn't, but how was I to know what to believe? "I'm not pissing around here, Soph—who she's with?"

"Ask her yourself if you're that desperate. *Oh, no, she's not talking to you, is she?*"

"I'm sorry," I said, trying another tack. "I miss her. You've got to help me. Please."

"You've only just missed her," Soph said, returning indoors.

The idea flashed into my head: *Go to Southampton.* I'd taken out my phone. Alice S you'd been initially, because Alice Kemp was already in there; but once we were officially boyfriend and girlfriend I changed you to Alice and her to Alice K, and then once we'd been dating awhile you became Al. I texted you. *Our two months is nearly up. It's killing me not seeing you. Have something important to say.*

I'd stayed for an hour at your mum and dad's, which was the minimum I thought I could get away with, but I had to get back to this, this table, this beer. Images of you keep bursting up in front of me—you on the London Eye; you drinking champagne at ten in the morning the day Kate and Wills got hitched; you instructing a man on the Tube to shift his fat arse to let a pregnant woman sit down; you dancing in the kitchen at that party in Peckham; you looking like a startled deer when you spotted me by the river on that Saturday, your voice, your smell—you, washed away now, washed away in that cold water with all our secrets.

Now I'm not feeling anything other than pissed and stoned, and when I've finished these cans and this joint I certainly won't be seeing your face looking up at me, hurt and terrified, from the edge of your bed or from the table we never got to sit at in the Campo de' Fiori or that black water; I'll be sitting in my kitchen and even the anger will have gone: there'll just be the drone of the TV, the dull throb from the wounds on my face and the intermittent echo of a man sobbing in the room.

I'd stood for ages outside your flat. Soph kept peeking out of the window to check if I'd gone. You didn't reply to my text. I turned towards the train station. *You like surprises,* I'd thought. *I'll give you a fucking surprise.*

Blog post by Megan Parker,
March 20, 2012, 6:35 p.m.

I've been talking to one of the lecturers at Southampton about you, Alice.

I didn't remember him from when we were students, his name's Professor Cooke, but apparently he's been there since about 1820 and reckons the two of you crossed paths briefly. He's had this incredibly cool idea to make a kind of collage about you. Often it's just me and him chatting but other times it's actual real research, contacting people and verifying dates and precising stuff you wrote or said or did. Mum reckons it's good that I'm channeling my grief positively, even though you'd say that was more of her yin and yang nonsense.

I felt a bit like a traitor at first because it's so personal, but we have to speak up and drown out all the ill-informed, spiteful and stupid stuff that's been said about you. "We're the guardians of Alice's memory now she can't stick up for herself," he says and he's not wrong. You always maintained you fancied being in a book, didn't you, and that's what this could be—the book of you.

He said I shouldn't write too much about me or him on the blog, because it's *you* this is about, not us, and for it to truly work we have to be observers, objective rather than subjective, but I always—I've visited him about ten times already—ask how can I be objective when you were my best friend?

I can't believe I'm telling him half the stuff I am, TBH, but you can open up to a stranger in ways you can't to someone you're close to.

He reminds me of some character from a TV sitcom—the socially inept "uncle" figure. His students probably hate him but he's made for Radio 4. You'd love his office, Alice, every inch of every wall is covered with books, there are *thousands*. In fact, you'd absolutely adore Jeremy because he's one of those ultra-clever people who's been to some totally incredible places. Gawd, I sound like a schoolgirl with a crush, don't I?

Jeremy—if you're reading this, which you might well be because you congratulated me on my blog, welcome to a very exclusive club. BTW . . . you're one of only about six people who *do* read it. You can't hold any of this against me because your "hypothesis" is that the truth has to trump everything else. ☺

Listen to me, Alice Palace. Joking when you're dead and it's only been seven weeks. I asked Jeremy if that made me a bad person and he said if the worst thing I'd ever done was laugh at happy memories, then I hadn't done too terribly.

You'd like the way he always puts stuff in a historical context, Lissa. "How's history going to change the fact that my best friend's dead?" I asked one time and had a real wobble, so he gave me a hug—he's not a big man but he *seems* it, maybe that's what presence is?—and said that I should be proud to have had you as my bestie. I'd taught him that word, even made him say "chillax." You'd have found it hilarious. He said he'd try it on his students or his specialist—and that's right, isn't it? I was, I am, your bestie and always will be.

He's certainly interested in the threats you were receiving and says they're one thing I definitely did do right putting on my blog; it's inevitable there would have been those who were aggrieved and had grudges against you given the nature of your work. He says I ought to be careful talking to the media, though, because they've got their own agenda, but I'm streetwise to their tricks and how *I* come across is irrelevant—all that's important is that the facts are heard.

Mostly why I'm enjoying seeing him is because it's another excuse to think about you. I do all the time, hon, but it's like we have periods set aside—quality time Jeremy jokingly refers to it as—when we can concentrate exclusively on you. I do have a confession. Some of our get-togethers have basically turned into career counseling for me. You used to tell me I should jack in PR and go back into higher education, and these sessions—I stayed again last night until nearly midnight—are reminding me how fantastic learning is, even if a lot of what we're doing isn't so much learning, it's *remembering*.

I'm also conscious I shouldn't write too much because everything on the Internet's part of your CV now; it's never completely gone even if you delete it; it's still in people's feeds and caches and Google can still sense it even though it's not there, like how amputees can still feel their toes itching even after their leg has gone.

He asks me a lot about your funeral, Alice . . . sorry for ballsing my reading up . . . and when I gave your mum a cuddle she said, "Meg, how am I going to do this?" and I said, "You will because you want it to be a celebration of her life," and she said, "Not today, I mean the rest of my life."

Jeremy said he'd seen the hearse arriving: he didn't go in but had been keen to quietly pay his respects, and I mentioned how you used to say going in a church brought you out in a rash and he said he avoided them as a rule. Then he lost his train of thought and explained about these incredible sky burials in Tibet where they dismember the deceased—it's done by someone known as a *rogyapa*, or body breaker—and put the remains out for the birds of prey. It's called *jhator*, which means giving alms to the birds.

I didn't say a word to Luke at your funeral because he headed off straight after and he was majorly out of order turning up reeking of booze . . . I don't care if Luke is reading this, you wouldn't want me to lie, and the truth, like Jeremy says, is what matters now. He says it doesn't matter how I remember you, as long as I do. "Who's going to remember *me*?" he keeps saying, making me promise, absolutely promise, I won't get to his age and have regrets. Then when I explain about how many of our friends have promised to live better, fuller, *bigger* lives because of what happened to you, he says, "That's beautiful—that's the spirit. You go out there and grab it, young lady, go and grab life."

"*Carpe diem,*" I said once, using one of your favorite expressions, as if that would impress him, then shared more stories about us. Once I get started, it positively pours out, and he can barely keep up, sitting scribbling away and the diddy red light on his Dictaphone flashing.

"Daughters," he merely says. "Daughters!"

Comments left on the above blog post:

I do indeed read this, young lady. A sitcom character, eh? More Geoffrey Palmer than Victor Meldrew, I trust.

Jeremy "Silver Surfer" Cooke

You can't go round accusing people of stuff like that, Meg, you're out of order. For your information I wasn't drunk at the funeral. I'd had one pint. I'm like the rest of us, trying to hold it together. Besides, you seem to be conveniently forgetting it was Alice who split up with me, not the other way round, and I wasn't seeing someone else!

Luke

No one's interested in your stupid scrapbook shit and your dumb theories about a girl who drowned because she was PISSED out of her head. You need to be careful you and that old prick of a professor.

A FREEMAN

Texts exchanged between Gavin Mockler and Alice Salmon, *March 16, 2006*

GM: Hey Alice hows yr nite? LOL
AS: Whozat?
GM: Your fave housemate.
AS: Ace thanx, whole crowd here. We're in Corrigan's.
GM: That an invite?
AS: Moved on now. What you up to?
GM: Just chillin playing Warcraft.
GM: Corrigans is shit IMHO run by fascists.
GM: Liked talking to you in lounge last night calmed me down. Youre better than rest of them.
AS: No probs, just a chat, tho, yeah . . . BTW Spam Sam says if you're not out tonight you can tidy the house!
AS: Stop playing with yourself!
AS: Soz that last text was Ben. He stole my phone.
GM: RAOFLMAO—not!!! You cud do so much better than Ben Finch.
GM We're like creatures of the night us night owls.

Email sent by Elizabeth Salmon, *April 3, 2012*

From: Elizabeth_salmon101@hotmail.com

To: jfhcooke@gmail.com

Subject: Stay Away

How do I think things were in her final days and hours? Her state of mind, her whereabouts, her conversations, I go over it constantly in my head. My husband, he says I'm going in circles, but it's not like I can be any *more* hurt. Why was she down by the water? Was she that drunk? Was she that miserable? Who was she with? That missing segment between her getting separated from her friends and ending up in the river, it's torture to me. Then however frustrated and furious I get reading all the nonsense, the more I get exposed to it because all it does is drive me to seek out more information.

I used to believe in fate, but now I have faith in zip, other than the marginally consoling possibilities of facts. I hoard them, because I'm terrified I might forget her, Jem, might wake up one day and not be able to remember the detail of my daughter. Wake up one day and that she'll be gone all over again.

So I'm asking you for something I never thought I would—help. Help me answer my questions, help me find Alice. You owe me that. Jem, what the *hell* were you doing *emailing me*? She saw your email in my inbox; she saw it on the day she died. That would have been enough to send anyone into a tailspin.

Sometimes I despise Dave because he *let* this happen, but it's me who didn't prevent it. What did I give her that helped? Proper lessons like the ones they dished out with sugary simplicity on those shows she devoured like *The O.C.* and *Dawson's Creek,* advice to equip her emotionally to deal with the shit that's thrown at you. I passed on nothing except perhaps a love of Sylvia Plath; can't believe I introduced my daughter to her work when I understood only too well it could snag like a hook in your skin. A love of Plath and the hair I once pretentiously described in a poem as like a raven's wing (I'd clearly read that somewhere), plus of course a desire to periodically tell the world to go fuck itself. Those things and our intonation, our cadence, even how we wrote, that was me in her and her in me.

Why didn't I ever speak to her about it, Jem? It wasn't as if I wasn't aware this ran like a black streak through us Mullens women, the thing that visited her in the night and made her talk to foxes, the thing that I never had a name for but she called *IT*, the thing she put in big letters—IT—because small ones were insufficient. I used to reckon Plath was right, but she was so grotesquely wrong we should take her off the syllabus, not because we should control what people read like in *1984*, but because there's nothing beautiful about death or convincing teenage girls there is.

Alice didn't take her own life. She couldn't, she wouldn't.

I was in love with you. At least, a version of you—whether it was one that existed or one I'd constructed in my head is open to debate. It would be disingenuous to claim there weren't moments that in other circumstances could have morphed into fond memories, but they're largely lost now, tangled in the woody knot of what came after we split up. It's that which mostly remains: the anguished soul-searching of what came next (you have no idea, believe me). I recall one argument particularly vividly. "You mean Fliss," I'd shouted, because your inability to utter her name was driving me insane. "If you can sleep with me, you can at least say her name."

"Being married, it's complicated," you muttered. "You wouldn't understand."

"Don't patronize me," I spat. "I'm not some love-struck teenager." But that was how I was behaving. I'd waited for an hour outside your office and, when you had shown up spouting some rubbish about a meeting having run late, I'd exploded. "I'm not going to become one of those women who's permanently *grateful,* Jem. Grateful for a phone call, for an evening out, for a morning when I wake up and you're actually still in the bed. I don't have to do this. I'm young, I'm not unattractive."

Your response? "How about we sort all this out over a drink?"

Along with dispensing compliments, that was your modus operandi: priming me with gin. Filling me so full of its warming magic that I forgot or didn't care, didn't kick up a fuss, didn't scream, because we couldn't have that, could we, a scene? Wring the last ounce of fun out of me, then scuttle back to your wife. I loathed you for making me the sort of person I hated (for your information, I'd never been with a married man before—or indeed since), but I loathed myself more for letting it happen. I started to cry. "This is a joke," I'd said.

You moved towards me, puce with anger. "If it's all such a joke, why aren't you laughing, then?"

I was constantly scared during that period, but right then I had a visceral, physical fear. I could smell your breath: stale coffee and onions.

"Well," you said, squeezing my wrist. "Go on, laugh, then."

"You've never made me laugh," I said. "You buy me meals, you take me to not especially good hotels, you buy me clothes I don't need and jewelry that is the antithesis of my taste and then you go home to Fliss and probably fuck her, too, because you're so insecure."

You raised your hand—and admittedly I'd been drinking and my head was all over the place—but what I saw was a claw coming up at me—seriously, it was like an animal's claw. "It's over!" I screamed.

And here we are all these years on, back in touch. Can't believe I've written so much. Cathartic, I suppose. You're water under the bridge now, but you have a responsibility. You have power: divest it wisely. I've confided in you, Jem, so don't let me down.

For your "records," I'm attaching a few sections of her diary, plus one of my favorite photos. It's her and Rob on a beach, abroad, so it must have been before Dave's business hit the rocks. Look at her—staring out at the sea as if she could swim that blue with a few bold strokes, wade through it, walk on it. There's not a cloud in the sky. It's the sort of day you remember from childhood but never know whether it actually happened or if it's a trick your memory plays on you: ice creams and sandcastles and dozing in cars and being carried up to bed. The sort of day everyone should be able to remember, but a lot of kids never have. We really tried to give our kids days when it was sea and sky.

You're right, words so frequently do fall short. I'm sorry to hear you're ill. I can't say I'll pray for you, but you have my best wishes. When I visualize you, it's in an ivy-clad office, sipping Earl Grey and listening to cricket. Is that how it is?

You're right—we are indeed a right pair with our secrets.

I *would* like to see you again.

Yours,

Liz

Transcript of voice-mail message received by Professor Jeremy Cooke,
May 24, 2012, 1:22 a.m.

I know where you live, Mr. Hotshot Professor . . . Could track you down as easily as order a pizza . . . You better leave her alone . . . none of your business . . . Wouldn't be so keen to dig up the past then, would you, Mr. Anthroporologic? [sic] . . . She died . . . [indistinguishable word] . . . dead . . . gone . . . Which bit of that can't you grasp? She [indistinguishable words] bridge. [Indistinguishable words]. Should be ashamed, ashamed . . . No more opening old wounds, no more . . . [indistinguishable words] loved Alice. Watch yourself, old man, because bad things happen, accidents happen.

PART THREE

Life's Like Scrabble

Texts exchanged,
May 13, 2010

Between Luke Addison and Alice Salmon

10:06 a.m.

L: Thanks for a gr8 night, Alice, but feeling the burn now! How r u?

A: Who is this???

L: V funny! It's the guy you got drunk.

A: Was you who got *me* drunk—and on a school night. You're a bad man, Mr. Addison!

L: Don't normally drink, made exception for you!

A: Heroic exception!

L: That's me all over—a hero! Sorry about the White Hart, BTW. Didn't know it had become Balham's worst pub.

A: So it *was* a first date then?

L: No comment. ☺

3:42 p.m.

A: How's yr hangover?

L: It's a good one! Yours?

A: Self-medicating with tea, am drinking it by the bucket. How's the rest of your day?

L: Been in world's most boring meeting. Given any thought to Saturday?

A: Cinema?

L: Season of Swedish retrospectives on at Picturehouse . . .

A: On reflection, am washing my hair . . .

L: *The Road*? It's got Viggo Mortensen in it.

A: Was just trying to impress you when I mentioned that. Much rather see *Shrek Forever After.*

L: Ditto. Could eat beforehand in new tapas place on Clapham High Street? Tequila doesn't count as booze if it's with tapas!

A: Am cheap tequila date ☺

L: Will remember that ☺

8:02 p.m.

A: Flatmate's opened bottle of wine, so having one glass. Where are you?

L: Went to gym earlier to shake off last of hangover, now back in pub.

A: It's Thursday!

L: Thursday's the new Friday!

A: Aren't your friends grumpy with you for ignoring them?

L: Am outside having a smoke. Besides, they're not *mate*-mates. Rather be texting you.

11:41 p.m.

L: You still up?

A: Reading in bed. Where are you?

L: Walking home. Massively enjoyed last night Alice.

A: So you said!

L: Wanted to say it again.

A: Me too. Laughed more than I have in ages.

L: WITH not AT hopefully.

A: Both! Turning phone off now—need my beauty sleep. Text me tomorrow, got a long day so need distractions.

L: Available all day for distraction services!

A: Thanks x

Between Charlie Moore and Luke Addison

6:20 p.m.

C: How was last night?

L: Mental.

C: What, your date???

L: No, for a change! She was the business.

C: Seal the deal?

L: She went home m8.

C: You're kidding?

L: No. Trying not to balls this one up.

C: *Tastes vomit*

L: Cock.

C: Which one was this anyway?

L: Met her last weekend in Porterhouse, tall, dark hair, freckles, bit off the wall but gorgeous.

C: *More vomit*

L: Bigger cock!

C: That's what the ladies say! You seeing her again?

L: Too right—Saturday. Food then flicks.

C: Too keen!

L: But am keen.

C: Irrelevant. Don't let her see that. We need to do beers to plan Prague—will email you. Gonna be a messy one.

L: What goes on tour . . .

Extract from Alice Salmon's diary,
February 19, 2009, age 22

It's eighteen minutes past four and I can't sleep.

A new city, a new job, new flatmates. It's like freshers' week all over again. I've decided life's one giant game of snakes and ladders: get to the top of one ladder, then, *bam,* down a snake you go!

Nights feel most like the snakes. Should make a rule: no entries after 11 p.m.

That fox is outside. He always hangs around. A boy fox, I reckon, big but raggedy like a doll. Must be very lonely out there among the bins and the buses, and how much would he like even just once to feel grass under his paws? Hope he finds a girl. Or sounds like he's already found more than one, the plaaaaayer.

How can I feel this lonely when there are seven million people in London? I watch them on trains—in their skinny jeans and big glasses, reading the *Metro* and texting, tinny traces of Dizzee Rascal or Kaiser Chiefs escaping from their earphones—and imagine their existences unfolding alongside mine. Listen to their conversations and try to piece together whole lives from overheard fragments.

"You overanalyze stuff," Meg said once, and perhaps this is what she means. Watching a fox in the garden—rather, the stamp-sized square of concrete we share with the possibly pregnant lady downstairs, Maybe Baby, and the Polish family upstairs we call "When's garbage?" because that's as far as their conversation with us has gone.

Am I not too old to feel like this, to still surprise myself? To catch myself in the mirror and think: *Alice, WTF?* All those promises I made myself as a starry-eyed teenager—to never touch drugs, never get in debt, never let anyone down. Life overtakes you. Never imagined I'd get a tattoo and, OK, it's discreet, but it's still a tattoo and my parents would go ballistic if they saw it. Vowed never to let myself get messed around by a man, too, but here I am, still swapping texts with Ben. He even gate-crashed my twenty-first lunch in Corby.

"You seeing anyone these days?" he'd asked uninterestedly after breezing in.

"No. You?"

"Nothing serious." It all had a certain reassuring familiarity. "Remember when we stood on the Pont des Arts?" The way he pronounced it sounded very French. "That was special."

"I'm not going to spend the night with you."

"We'll see."

"I mean it."

"You were quick enough to let me buy you a drink."

"Don't spoil it, Ben. Let's end today on good terms. Let's prove we can do that."

He put his hand on my knee. "I'm still mad about you."

"You're not. You're mad about the idea of me. In practice, you can't cope with a girlfriend. And take your hand off me, too."

It was like a game of pontoon where he kept on twisting: that was him all over, keeping on twisting even though he knew he'd bust, because he always did. A bit of me felt ashamed that I'd fallen for him; Meg always said he was a dick.

He'd moved his hand up my leg. "What have we got here? You like that, don't you?"

"Get your hand off me."

"You're a prick-tease, Lissa, that's what you are."

I slapped him. Once, quick and hard across the face, and it was the first time I'd ever slapped anyone and immediately felt compelled to ask if he was all right. A red mark began blooming on his left cheek. "She loves me really," he laughed to a man on a nearby table. "I will sleep with you again," he said to me. "If not tonight, one day."

I left him in the bar.

This flat, I shouldn't complain. I'm lucky to have it. Had a good feeling about it as soon as I saw it on Gumtree.

"The room catches the sun—in the evening it shines right in," the ad had said, and three hours later I was having coffee with Alex and Soph.

"We'd like someone we can get on with," he said.

"But, failing that, we'll settle for someone who's not a serial killer," she added.

They showed me the room and the sun was shining right in. "When can I move in?" I asked.

It isn't shining in now.

He's still out there, that fox. Rusty, I'm going to call him. Little Rusty. I'm going to make him my word of this diary entry. I'd put food out, but

Soph reckons he'll have fleas and could bite, so sorry, little man, you're on your own; we'll have to just talk for now.

I look myself up and down in the mirror. Still as alien to myself as when I was a teenager: this thing I carry around, that carries me around, this body. I touch my hair, my face, my hips. Trace the tiny scar line on my wrist. It scares me: what she, that woman I'm looking at, is capable of.

Thing is, it's not solely in bad ways I surprise myself. Wouldn't have imagined in a million years I'd have it in me to sit in court when I was in Southampton and watch that animal I helped bring to trial for assaulting the old lady get sentenced and not flinch even when he blew me a kiss. Then there was the course after I'd started work when I had to give the presentation to all the bosses and I didn't get my words garbled ("Engage brain before mouth, salmon fry," Dad used to tell me), didn't even need my crib cards, and when I'd finished they'd all clapped; seriously, they all clapped and not piss-taking, either.

I'm probably being a drama queen. That's what Dad used to call me, and then later when I loved to dance he'd say I was more of a dancing queen than a drama queen and I loved dancing for him and I still love dancing now, I love it, love it, love it!

It's no big deal. Lots of people don't sleep—Mum included. I know because she told me once. She said when she was young she had spells when it all felt pointless: too little, too much, too overwhelming. "You will talk to me, if you ever feel like that?" she'd asked. "Promise you'll talk to me, Alice."

You've got to look at your monsters, she always says.

I'm lucky. I don't have many monsters. One, perhaps, that I've never dared properly look at. Old Cookie.

"I met an old friend of yours," I'd said, fishing for information, the next occasion I rang Mum after the anthropology party. "A Professor Cooke. What's he like?"

"He's bad news, Alice, that's what he is," she'd replied.

I'd largely managed to avoid him for the next three years, despite his periodic, clumsy attempts to ingratiate himself with me. Once, crazily, buzzing and bold after a night dancing in the Union, I took a detour and walked past his office; curiosity made me—the urge to know what happened gradually growing stronger than the desperation to forget, a propelling impulse to shout the odds at the old bastard. He was at his desk, gawking vacantly out of the window, like how Mr. Woof used to at the back door when he was waiting to be taken out for a walk. I almost tapped on the glass to check he hadn't died. Then I recalled his hands, and ran again . . .

Twenty to six. The toilet's just flushed. Alex will leave for work at ten to seven and Soph will go to the gym. Weird how I know their routines: these strangers who a ten-minute walk to a station brought together. They know I block the hall up with my bike and like to eat late, but they don't know that when the world is asleep Rusty and I are friends. Alex will have toast, Soph a black coffee, our three lives crossing briefly in the kitchen. "Have a good one," we'll say. "See you tonight." I won't mention I've been awake half the night; Soph won't mention another day's swung by with her barely eating; Alex won't mention he's still crazy about his ex. But I know, because our Venn diagrams overlapped here: Flat 8, 25 Bedlington Road, Balham SW12. The prospect of one day falling out of touch with them gives me a sinking dread.

But tonight it's dinner after work with the team. In some warm restaurant on the South Bank, the click of chopsticks, the ebb and flow of conversation about Boris Bikes and Heath Ledger, the jokes about Wayne and Coleen or Russell Brand and Jonathan Ross; in that bubble of laughter, this will be a mere memory.

A quick bath, a cup of tea, a glance at the headlines on my phone—they reckon the snow we had was the worst for twenty years—and she'll be here, the me who'll be on the South Bank in twelve hours, a mere half a day away, laughing, the life and soul of the party, the me in the mask.

Being single rocks, but it'll be shit to never have anyone and I sure have a knack for telling men who want to keep it no big deal that I need more, or men who want to get serious that we should take it easy (not that there's been too many of those: basically only Josh, and we were only sixth-formers). Always seem to get relationships the wrong way round, like I'm seeing the world through a mirror.

Were you awake at ten to four this morning? Did you look down at the garden and feel dizzy? Did you whisper to Rusty?

Tell me about those moments you have, you and only you.

Who are you?

Who am *I*?

Letter sent by Professor Jeremy Cooke,
June 20, 2012

My dear Larry,

You'll never guess where I found myself last night. A police station! The chap on the front desk, who was about fourteen, quickly concluded the voice-mail messages were a hoax. The whole situation was evidently a source of amusement to him. "What are you requesting, sir, round-the-clock protection?"

"They could be relevant to the Alice Salmon case," I said.

"Right, yes, that. Is that what this is to do with, *your research*?"

There'd been another piece on my work in a local paper; this one had got off to a promising start, dubbing it an "interesting insight into our collective modern memory," but then lost the thread and intimated it was me who'd discovered her body. I took out the photo of Alice I kept in my wallet, brandished it in front of him. "What if something bad *did* happen to Alice? Ask more questions, ask different ones. Re-piece her last moments back together."

"As I've explained, the investigation team would have done that, sir."

"But what if they missed something? They didn't know her."

"Let's not get carried away here, Mr. Cooke."

"It's *Professor*."

"We tend not to reopen black-and-white cases on the basis of a couple of rude voice-mail messages."

"It wasn't a couple, it was three, and they weren't rude, Kidson, they were threatening."

"It's *Inspector* Kidson," he corrected me. "If I had a pound for every time someone stood where you are, claiming there'd been a miscarriage of justice, I could have retired by now."

"You wouldn't be here if bad things never happened."

He looked at his watch. "Bad things keep me in a living, mate, but I can assure you the incident in question would have been thoroughly investigated."

It struck me that my downgrading from "sir" to "mate" signified the end of his patience. A couple of policemen shepherded an inebriated teenager through reception, hauling him along, his feet dragging behind him like a brush. It used to appall me, youngsters drinking themselves insensible, but now I can discern an uplifting quality in it. Bless them, they're convinced they invented the practice when the ancient Macedonians were at it in the fourth century BC. So raw and visceral, that display of vitality, that unashamed pursuit of gratification. I've never been averse to a tipple myself, but Elizabeth positively adored the stuff. She went at it with a primal need and it cut through her, made her uninhibited and terrifying. I'd try to contextualize it to her: explaining about Silenus and Dionysus or the Native American Indians fighting for firewater on the plains of Dakota, but she'd just drink and laugh and tell me to shut the fuck up—I adored that coarse streak in her—and drink more. She tells me she's quit now, which is no surprise. That was only going to end one of two ways.

"It makes me feel bigger," she once said. "It stops me feeling scared."

"We all need to feel a bit scared," I replied. Classic me: advocating inertia.

Wish I could stop feeling scared, Larry.

The fourteen-year-old policeman had a whispered exchange with a colleague, then said: "Why don't you go home to bed and get some rest, sir."

"I'm not ill," I said, and the irony of that proclamation hit me.

"Wasn't Miss Salmon drunk?" Kidson asked.

She'd been sitting with a stranger apparently; one chap I'd interviewed told me he saw the pair of them arguing, a real scorcher of a bust-up. Another claimed they'd been kissing. She knocked drinks over.

At one point she'd fallen over. She'd hugged everyone, cried. "Yes she was drunk, but that's not a crime."

"It is if *you're* like him," the policeman said, nodding at the spectacle unfolding before us.

It wasn't an implausible scenario. Luke Addison had told me he'd seen Alice drink herself unconscious on a few occasions. He'd got quite the shock when he'd come home from work and found me on his doorstep. "I'm looking for Alice Salmon," I said.

"She's dead," he fired back.

"I'm well aware of that, but I'm still interested in her. I'm interested in you, too."

"If only I'd been there, I could have protected her," he told me.

"You appear to have got your life back on track remarkably quickly," I'd said.

He gave me a long stare. *A temper,* I thought.

Outside the pub, rumor has it, Alice's group had gone in a chip shop, assuming she'd stay propped against the wall, but she must have got enough of a second wind to wander off unnoticed, with the speed and purpose drunks can muster, lurching, zigzagging, away from the city center and down towards the river. Frustratingly, they're staying steadfastly silent, the three girls she was supposedly with.

"Isn't it time to let this go, Professor?" the policeman asked. There was a new look of pity on his face and it occurred to me it was one I'd see increasingly frequently from now on.

"There's more than one way to die drunk," I informed him. "No wonder she had more success locking up the bad guys than you!" I'd read all about her campaigns to bring criminals to justice. Talk about a woman on a mission. "If Cameron's Big Society means anything," she'd argued in one editorial, "it's that justice is no longer exclusively the preserve of our police."

"I presume you are aware how many people hated her?" I asked Kidson.

"You said in the paper she was universally loved," he replied sarcastically.

"I said lots of things to them—they chose not to print them." There was a long wail from along the corridor, the drunk teenager presumably. "My point was that everyone who knew her loved her, but her job brought her into contact with plenty of people who didn't."

"I know the feeling," he said, glancing at his watch.

"There's more," I blurted. "When I got home yesterday, someone had been in my house."

"Was anything stolen?"

"No, but things had been moved, someone had switched on my computer."

"Was the computer actually taken?"

"No, but someone had used it. I could feel their presence."

Hard to tell whether his expression now was one of pity or if he was close to laughter. "Right," he said, "and was *anything* taken?"

"No, but someone had definitely been in the house. I'm very precise; things weren't as I'd left them. I keep getting this sense I'm being followed as well." I stopped short of full disclosure; what I didn't share was that I'd definitely seen the lad with tattoos around the campus, even in the hospital car park yesterday. He keeps appearing at my office, too, bearing items from his "Alice collection," like a cat bringing in a fresh kill. The last thing I needed was for the police to haul him in and have him blab about my letter (God, what if he knows about other stuff?), but I did need to inject some renewed urgency into their investigation. Alice may be enduring fodder for headline writers, but the police appear to be merely going through the motions.

"That Ben Finch, he was a twat," the little oik had proclaimed today. "Thought he was better than the rest of us. Banging on about his old school and the masters; why can't he have had *teachers* like the rest of us?"

"That's one of her former boyfriends, isn't it?" I'd asked him.

"In a manner of speaking. Right psycho he was; gave me a proper pasting once. Wouldn't stop booting me even when I was on the floor facedown."

"Why?"

"Because Ben Finch was a cruel bastard. Because them posh schools give you an evil streak. It's survival of the fittest in them places, kill or be killed."

"They can indeed engender some less-than-auspicious traits, but surely one wouldn't resort to such violence unprompted."

"Ask Alice. Or maybe not! The next morning, the smarmy bastard grinned at the mess my face was in and said, 'You ought to get that checked out, mate. Looks serious.' Then, when the girls were around, he took the piss more, said there'd obviously been a dispute in the gaming community!"

Clearly still fuming about the incident, despite so much time having passed, the lad had banged the desk agitatedly and declared: "I saw your wife in Waitrose."

"Stay away from her," I'd warned him.

"Five hundred quid" was all he'd responded.

Maybe my imagination is playing tricks on me, Larry. I haven't been sleeping. Fliss has been urging me to ease back on the old work a bit. She'd be rather less supportive if she realized that my muse's mother, the Elizabeth Salmon in the news, is the Elizabeth Mullens of old.

"Aren't some things better left unsaid?" she asked. "Perhaps some secrets are *meant* to go to the grave, Jeremy."

I didn't contest the point, but I disagree. I don't want secrets in my grave with me. I don't want things left unsaid. When it comes to Alice—Fliss, too—I want to replicate *our* relationship, yours and mine: the simple, salving clarity of it. Do you recall how we used to test our honesty pact, Larry? Pushing the boundaries in those letters. My spots, your eczema. My loathing of my father, your parents' poverty. My masturbation fantasies, you losing your virginity. It was like a game of cards: liberating, exhilarating. Except it wasn't cards we were playing with, it was ourselves (frequently literally at the time, grubby little savages that we were!). I looked forward to those letters with a charged sense of anticipation: reading them *and* writing them. I came to view moments of portent in my life—exam results, new digs, my marriage—almost not for themselves but for how I'd share them with you. You never called me Jeremy Cock like the other boys; never dubbed me "beak face" or "the mock jock" or "four eyes." All those leisure pursuits we shared—it was like we'd been separated at birth: philately and autograph collecting (signatures are very passé these days; it's pictures of celebrities on phones the youngsters collect) and obscure episodes of history, like when the Dutch sailed up the Medway and sacked our ships in Chatham in 1667. I remember thinking: *Finally, another boy like me.* It was the first time I hadn't felt completely alone on this planet.

CCTV had shown Alice moving a few yards, then stopping. Moving, then stopping; moving, then stopping. She was like a darted animal, lurching. Then, as the landlord of the last pub she'd been in told the media, she went "off radar" (he was also quick to point out she was well over the legal age to consume alcohol). She had bruises and scratches on her elbows and knees—consistent, according to the coroner, with "falling repeatedly to the ground in an advanced state of intoxication." UDIs—that's all they would have been, according to one of the students I'd interviewed. He'd had to explain. UDIs. *Unidentified drinking injuries.*

"I'm a taxpayer, do your damn job," I snapped at Kidson.

"Right, I've tried to be patient, but this conversation's over. If you feel like you're not being taken seriously, then you're at liberty to make a complaint."

"I demand that you write down what I've told you!" I shouted, and heard myself as others must: pompous, patronizing, superior. Old Cookie. "At least, make a record of it in your book." I leant across, seized his hand and pen and forced it down on to his pad. There was a little crack and he snatched it away.

"If you weren't a sad old man, I'd nick you for assaulting a police officer. Now, piss off back to whichever stone it was you crawled out from under."

All I want to do now is put my house in order, and with that in mind I have a confession: I may have neglected to give you full disclosure on one aspect of this. I've explained to you about my penchant for walking at night, haven't I? How it's a diversion and supplies the gentle exercise my specialist advocated. Well, I was taking one such constitutional in Southampton city center on February 4. Let's just say it had come to my attention that Alice was in the vicinity that evening.

Probably just as well Kidson and his cohorts hadn't done their job brilliantly or I might have some explaining to do.

When I'd eventually arrived home, Fliss—it was late but she'd stayed up; she was beside herself with worry—had inquired about my flushed, spooked demeanor: she was fearful it was some hitherto invisible symptom of my condition.

"If I give you this, will you stop following my wife?" I said this morning, handing over yet another envelope to the boy with tattoos. It's not the money, Larry, that's not important, but I have to protect Fliss.

"Ironic, isn't it, Iceman, how you're so determined to look after her when you're the one who's done stuff that could destroy her? Alice only had to share a house with me for a year, but your missus has had to do it with you since 1976."

It caught me off guard, him mentioning that year.

"It's written on the back," he said, winking. "The wedding photo on your bedside table."

I appear to have got myself into rather a pickle.

Yours as ever,
Jeremy

Email drafted, but not sent, by Alice Salmon,
December 10, 2004

I've really gone and done it this time, Mum. You hear about stuff like this and I prided myself I'd never let it happen to me, but now I have and how could I be so stupid?

"What do you make of our little gathering?" he'd inquired as we'd stood around in huddles forcing conversation. "We host this soiree on the same day every year; it's quite a tradition."

"I'd hate to see you lot when you're *not* having fun," I said, wine recklessness buoying me.

"I knew your mother," he said.

"Lucky you," I replied. The awareness swam past me. I was on my fourth glass.

"Your mother, how *is* she?"

What am I going to do? My memories are shattered . . . box files, a lamp with frilly tassels, him insisting I call him Jeremy rather than Professor Cooke, classical music. "Chin-chin," he'd said. "Bottoms up." I'm not even sure what I'm alleging. They'd assume I had a crush on him, like a few of the other students. He's famous. Should I confide in another lecturer? I took care of her, he'd probably claim. She rather overindulged. Another fresher who partook of a surfeit of booze. Silly girl.

Why am I even blaming myself? It's him who shouldn't have let the situation arise. But if I speak out, where will it end? What if I have to drop out of uni? They'd ask me questions and I won't have the replies: a stupid slapper who can't take her alcohol and who never learns. All that remains is his onion breath, his cracked laugh, starchy shirt, dry tanned skin, reptilian.

"Look at me," he'd said. "Focus."

And I'd hung on to him as the world swam. I'm scared, Mum.

I shouldn't have even been there. Keep the old duffer sweet, I'd decided when he'd proposed I join them for drinks, because a couple of his ex-students had ended up on the nationals and contacts like that are invaluable. He'd paraded me in front of a load of old crusties. "Remember this one's name," he'd said. "She'll be famous one day."

I'd prayed the ground would open up and swallow me.

"She's planning a career in the media."

"Haven't definitely made my mind up."

"A case of"—and he paused pretentiously—"'not knowing what you'll be but knowing yourself as you are.' Shakespeare," he added smugly.

"I do know! *Hamlet*. And you got it wrong. It's 'We know what we are, but know not what we may be.'"

"Touché," he said. "Chip off the old block, you are."

The waitresses kept topping up my glass, and the cloying sense of apprehension that typically seized me in situations like that evaporated. It was like slipping out of a pair of heels at the end of the night.

"What is it they say?" I'd heard one of his colleagues snigger. "An A for a lay."

Why didn't I go to the union, Mum? Would have been safe there. I'd have stuck to lager, played pool, hung out with Meg and Holly and Jamie T. We'd have gone back to halls, had coffee, the lads carelessly tossing a rugby ball around, Usher or Kanye West getting played by "Doncaster Will."

His office was a cross between a study and a bedroom. "The outside world's a dangerous place when you're this drunk," he said. "But it's safe in here."

Him, helping me out of my skirt. "Your hair's like your mother's," he'd said.

The room was spinning, a sick feeling. "Rest now, little one," he'd said.

A blanket over me, get it off, too hot, can't breathe, suffocating, get it *off* me . . . I'm so ashamed, but it's him who should be: him, him, HIM. "Sleep tight," he'd said, "don't let the bedbugs bite."

Then waking on a sofa, my hand in his. "You were having nightmares," he'd said gently. "You were shouting in your sleep."

"Get away from me," I said, springing up.

Outside, normal sounds—the beep of a delivery lorry reversing, two lads play-fighting, a girl laughing. The previous few hours . . . shadows, shapes, fitful sleep, him helping me sip water, like you used to with medicine when I was small, informing me that I'd caused quite a stir at the reception but he wouldn't hold it against me, though I ought to be careful, not everyone was like him: girls in that condition "ended up in all manner of unpalatable predicaments."

I didn't have my top on, my skirt was in a rumpled pile on the floor. I felt sick, pushed him away, pulled my clothes on and ran.

You always said I could always confide in you, Mum, but I can't send you this . . .

Letter sent by Professor Jeremy Cooke,
June 25, 2012

Larry,

I can't get Alice and Liz out of my head. I even dreamed of them last night. Woke up and Fliss asked if I was OK; I'd been muttering in my sleep. I didn't tell her I'd been consumed by a vision of Liz's hair, that long, lustrous sweep. "It's like a mane," I distinctly recall saying to her one afternoon.

"Thanks very much," she laughed, "for comparing me to a horse."

We were on the bed in a cheap hotel beside the A36. Despite our disrobed state, there was no embarrassment or shame; that habitually came later. Margaret Thatcher's voice was coming out of a small black-and-white TV in the corner. The Falklands. Nineteen eighty-two. Fliss battered into my brain, but I pushed her back out, stroked Liz's face. "You make me feel incredible," I said to this woman who wasn't the one I'd married six years earlier, this latest addition to the teaching staff who I'd first seen waltzing across the quad—she didn't walk, she waltzed as if she was moving to music—a couple of months before. She smiled; her teeth stained from the not very good red. It occurred to me that this was the me I could have been: the type of man who pays cash for hotel rooms in the afternoons. *I* am *that person,* I thought. "I've never felt like this before," I said.

"Me neither," she replied.

Larry, it's like a confessional, sharing this with you all over again. I was seeing myself anew: I wasn't deconstructing someone else's behavior or picking over the bones of someone else's existence; I was living for the moment, in the present, not some era thousands of years ago. I touched her black hair, each strand a package of DNA. *Forget DNA,* I thought stroking it. *This is her,* this *is Liz.* It felt like everything was changing: politics, rules, society. Maybe this shrill grocer's daughter was right: anything *was* possible.

"Aren't we the odd couple?" she asked playfully. "Well, my darling artifact?" She never tired of teasing me about how I was nearly eleven years her senior.

I reached out and she made a little noise and it brought to mind a sound Fliss made.

Stop thinking, I thought, *Stop damn well* thinking.

"Do you never get scared?" she asked afterwards—Liz did.

"I'm rarely anything else," I replied. There were lots of obtuse questions and cryptic answers, but that was the second occasion she'd asked me that particular one. It had come up the previous night as well as we'd dressed for dinner.

She lit a cigarette, inquired if I'd like one, and it gave me a rush of gloom: that she didn't know whether I smoked. She could have been being ironic, I suppose. "I'm trying to quit," she said, exhaling a thin trail of smoke.

You simply have no idea *that I don't smoke,* I'd thought. *You have no idea that I don't smoke, any more than you have no idea that I'd like to establish an orchid greenhouse or can't abide over-hot climates*—the fortnight Fliss and I had in Leukaspis was purgatory—or, for that matter, that I am mildly allergic to shellfish. We lay on the bed and I checked my watch: Fliss and I were attending a faculty function that evening.

"I'm serious," she said. "Do you never wake up petrified?"

"Of what?"

"Of where you might end up?"

Pale sunlight filtered through the drawn curtains. "I'll probably end up in the same office I am now, just arthritic and curmudgeonly."

Men hit a point, my PhD tutor once told me with what at the time even *I* considered to be near-crushing pessimism, when all they can do is try to fuck their way out of it. It won't work, he informed me, but you'll try all the same. Is that what I was attempting to do with Liz? I didn't know if I was going to leave Fliss; if I *could* leave her. Hard to believe now for such a premeditated man that I didn't have a plan. All I had was fear: fear that this could be my last chance to get whatever it was that was beyond my imagination. I'd whistled past eighteen and twenty-one and thirty, oblivious to those milestones, preoccupied with my scientific ambitions, but by then I'd have been rapidly approaching thirty-five and the landmark chafed at my consciousness. Halfway to my threescore and ten. Fear of another complexion, too. What if this was just the start, if there'd be more Elizabeths? I'd hoped she'd pick up on my answer, say: Curmudgeonly? Don't you mean *more* curmudgeonly? Because then we'd laugh and that would draw an end to that particular, pernicious conversational thread. But instead she watched the cold flickering and faraway images of dead Argentinians laid out in a line in a hole in the ground and asked: "Do you think we're fated to be together? Destined to keep coming back to each other, whoever we end up with? That happens." When I failed to respond, she said: "At least I *know* I don't know my own mind. You're one of the cleverest men I've ever met, but somehow you're one of the most . . . hopeless."

"I'm not convinced I'm suited to polygamy," I replied obtusely.

"There's such a thing as polyandry, too."

This felt like safer ground. "Indeed," I replied. "Masai women, among many others, practice it—a perfectly logical adaptation to high mortality rates among infants and warriors."

"You can't blame the women for keeping their options open," she said, the half smile on her face disappearing, "if their men are as rubbish as ours."

It occurred to me this conversation wasn't theoretical at all: it was about us.

I wondered if having sex again would help. Earlier, it had dawned on me it was like the law of diminishing marginal returns: sleeping with someone other than one's wife wasn't as bad after you'd already done it once. *Even now,* I'd thought, naked with a near stranger in a hotel, *I can't* not *be me*: dull, pedantic, academic.

A child began crying in another room and we sat. I knew, even then, that in the months and years to come I'd tell myself that we'd both been adults, that no one had forced her to do this, any of it, that it took two to tango. It was a central tenet of one of my first-year lectures: individual accountability. Along the corridor that child's cry reached a crescendo and then stopped. "I wonder if that's a little boy or a little girl," I said, but she wasn't listening. *I've changed you,* I thought. Whatever you might have been when you first waltzed across the quad, now you're a woman who sneaks into hotel rooms with a married man, then puts the same underwear back on and checks out, just as I'd made my wife someone who left me food in the warming oven of the AGA cooker and didn't probe too closely when I was "away with work"—as she'd been under the impression I had been more frequently this summer.

Liz stretched across me to grab the wineglass on the bedside cabinet, downed the contents, then took up the unburnt inch of her cigarette and sucked on it. A plume of ash fell on my leg. "For God's sake, Elizabeth," I snapped. "Be careful."

"Yes, we'd hate anyone to get hurt here, wouldn't we?" She laughed: hurt, hollow, the genesis of hate. "Don't *you* want children one day?"

"Ah, yes, that. Them." Fliss and I had pretty much given up on a family by that stage, despite us being poked and prodded by a small army of medical professionals. Some of the old rancor swelled up in me; it made me want to tell Liz how degrading it had been, how emasculating: how the human race would have become extinct if it had been left to couples like my wife and me.

"Maybe we're simply not destined to have a baby," Fliss had said. "Maybe it's going to be just you and me."

I'd balked at the prospect of that "not." "Don't say that," I'd retorted. "We'll keep trying until it happens."

"Maybe it's just not in God's plan for us. Besides, that wouldn't be so awful, would it, if it *was* just the two of us?"

Liz said: "Because I do want kids. Ideally one of each, but mainly a girl. That's unusual, isn't it? It's boys that women are supposed to want." She was off again. She could be like this, tumbling from optimism to despair in the time it took her to smoke a cigarette.

The news had left the Falklands for Washington and that garish, glorified actor Reagan on his pet subject, the so-called nuclear deterrent. I said: "Some people might argue the world's sufficiently dangerous that you're doing the next generation a favor by not bringing them into it."

"What if my daughter inherits all my bad traits and none of my good ones?" she asked.

"You haven't got any bad ones."

She merely snorted at that. "If I have a baby girl—*when* I have a baby girl—I'll be terrified she'll be too much like me, poor lamb."

I touched her skin, her soft, thin skin, and it occurred to me that maybe it would be with this woman that I have the son I'd always so wished for.

"Well?" she said. "You haven't answered my question. Do you never get scared?"

"Never mind being an academic—you could be a journalist," I said, reaching out again for her hair.

"You're insatiable," she said.

"Hardly."

"What *are* you, then?" she said. "What are *we*?"

I should have known that was the beginning of the end.

Alice Salmon's "To Read in 2012" Kindle collection

Trespass—Rose Tremain
How to Be a Woman—Caitlin Moran
Cranford—Elizabeth Gaskell
The Time Traveler's Wife—Audrey Niffenegger
The Brightest Star in the Sky—Marian Keyes
The Snowman—Jo Nesbø
Gone with the Wind—Margaret Mitchell
Cold Comfort Farm—Stella Gibbons
Fifty Shades of Grey—E. L. James
Eat, Pray, Love—Elizabeth Gilbert
The Help—Kathryn Stockett
The House of Mirth—Edith Wharton

Article on *Southampton Star* website, *March 15, 2012*

Alice Best Friend Reveals Dead Flowers Threat

The best friend of body-in-the-river-girl Alice Salmon has thrown fresh controversy on the case by revealing Salmon received a "death threat" just days ahead of her February death.

Speaking exclusively to the *Star,* Megan Parker claimed previously reported threats were "merely the tip of the iceberg" and said the 25-year-old had been "living in fear" after flowers had been left on her doorstep with a "sinister" note.

This latest explosive revelation is set to raise further questions about the final hours of journalist Salmon, whose body was discovered in a city-center river, leaving the authorities baffled as to the exact events surrounding the incident.

Parker said: "Alice confided in me about how she'd come home one night to find a bouquet of dead flowers, with a note pinned to them saying 'You next.' "

One suggestion is that the incident could have been connected with Salmon's work as an anti-crime journalist, which helped to bring high-profile prosecutions against more than one south-coast criminal.

"She'd been getting threats for ages," added Cheltenham-based Parker. "She used to go out on these crazy long walks on Clapham Common—I was constantly warning her how dangerous it was, doing that at night—but she'd even stopped that because she was convinced she was being followed.

"I only wish she'd gone to the police, but she made me promise to keep it a secret. She reckoned even sharing it with me could have put me in danger. She was the bravest woman I've ever met."

Parker, who's considering closing her social-media accounts for fear of recriminations over her connections with the crime-buster, said she was speaking out now as a mark of respect for her friend.

She said the tragedy had left her "inconsolable," but played down rumors of a spat among Salmon's friends. "In our own separate ways, we all feel some accountability. I was well aware she hadn't been happy for the last couple of months and stood by and watched her spiraling downhill. I'll never forgive myself for that.

"There are a lot of crazy allegations being bandied around, but ultimately this may have simply been a terrible accident. She'd made a lot of enemies, but it would be conjecture to assume that they had any bearing on all this. We may have to accept that we'll never piece together the chain of events that led to Alice's death."

In an article for leading women's magazine *Azure* as recently as last October, Salmon herself disclosed a feeling of "watching life through a pane of thick glass" and detailed how she "simply wasn't designed for it."

Hampshire Police confirmed this morning that they were keeping an "open mind" on the case. "It's a live investigation with multiple lines of inquiry," a spokesman said. "Meanwhile, we have assigned the Salmons a family liaison officer and once again extend our sympathies to the family and friends of Miss Salmon."

The case continues to grip the public's imagination, and these latest revelations, following feverish media coverage, will inevitably put it back in the spotlight.

"It wouldn't surprise me one little bit if some scumbag she'd banged up went after her," one *Star* reader commented on our Facebook page. "Crime is rife in all our cities . . . Salmon took a few big scalps and villains can't be seen to let journalists take liberties."

The photograph on this article was replaced on March 16. The original showed Megan Parker, Alice Salmon and a third woman identified in the caption as "ill-fated Salmon's friend Kirsty Blake." Ms.

Blake has asked us to make clear she was not the person in the picture and asked us to remove it, which we were pleased to do.

Email received by Alice Salmon from editor of *Azure* magazine, *November 2, 2010*

Hi Alice,

Thank you for your idea, which I read with interest. It was swirling around my head on the train on this morning's commute and that's typically a good barometer of a piece's potential strength! We'd need you to major on the personal element in terms of how diary-keeping helped you address some of your teenage issues, but use the proposed national diary archive as a nice topical hook. Let's grab a few minutes on the phone to nail a detailed brief.

Call me.
Olivia x

PS: "An antidote to life"—I *adore* that line. Is that yours or a quote from somewhere?

Blog post by Megan Parker, *March 27, 2012, 7:13 p.m.*

"Megan Parker, best friend."

At least they introduced me correctly, Alice, although it went rapidly downhill. Maybe I was naive, like those idiots who go on *Big Brother* convinced they'll be portrayed flatteringly.

"Best friends have such a special bond," the journalist had said when she contacted me via LinkedIn. "Doing an interview would be a chance to explain why she was so important to you."

To avoid any curveballs, I inquired what her first question would be before the cameras rolled.

"That's easy. It'll be: Describe Alice."

She was true to her word on that one.

"Kind," I said. "Beautiful. Talented."

The journalist, Arabella, nodded encouragingly and the camera twitched in the corner of my eye. She'd insisted we do this by the river. "It'll help put your comments in context," she told me. "It'll help make it feel more real to viewers."

"Can you give me an example of those things, Megan?"

She'd used my name a lot, to reassure me we were friends, on the same side, Team Alice. I'm fully au fait with all the devices and tricks journos use; that's what working in PR does for you.

I recounted the tale of you traveling halfway across Southampton on a mercy mission once when I was laid up with flu, then said there'd never been a dull moment when you were around: you were a total live wire. Cue enthusiastic nodding: I was delivering.

"Megan, how did you feel when you heard your best friend had died?"

You would have chuckled at that one. Clichéd, you'd have said.

"Shattered," I said. "Numb. I still am. I've never been without her before. We were besties, even when we were small."

We were standing at the spot where—depending on who you listen to—you entered the water.

"Tell us about that—about when you were small."

I bumbled that one a bit, managing to claim we'd met when we were five and then six. Stupidly, I hadn't done any planning, preferring to speak from the heart.

"Any particular memories from when you were that age you'd like to share with viewers?"

I gave her lots, but none made the final edit. They were cut—probably by an intern or media studies graduate, a whiz with Final Cut Pro, desperate to produce a hard-hitting piece of work for their portfolio. There was no room for that sort of color; they had a very specific angle in mind.

The journalist smiled, a practiced, well-worn maneuver. "What's your take on what might have occurred that night?"

What I should have said was it wasn't my place to speculate and that we'd be better placed to respond once the facts had come to light, and that for now, out of respect for your family, we should hold off conjecture. But what I said—and it was stupid, I'm not unaware of that, but being by the river had upset me and this woman had thrown me off-kilter—was: "I wished she hadn't drunk as much."

"Was she very drunk?"

"I wasn't there."

"Is there a lesson in this for other young women drinking on nights out? For us all, perhaps?"

I broke down and felt the forensic heat of the camera. They left that in—of course they left that in. Nothing like a few tears to serve up with the microwave meals and cups of tea, as long as they're someone else's.

"Was Alice popular?"

"Massively," I said. "Everyone loved her. But me most."

"You've spoken of her receiving threats."

"I loved her so much."

"This must be devastating for her friends. Her boyfriend, especially—did she have a boyfriend?"

I hesitated, praying she'd throw me a lifeline. She could have said: I gather she was a fan of *My Big Fat Gypsy Wedding*, or: She was planning a sponsored half marathon, I believe?—but she'd picked up a scent. "She did have a boyfriend?"

As if she wasn't perfectly well aware of that fact. She'd have done her research, watched other clips, read up on today's subject: Alice Salmon.

"Yes, sort of." What I should have done was sworn: I'd been taught in a media class that if an interview's going badly wrong, swear, because then they'll then be forced to cut it.

"I heard she was about to get married."

"Was she?" I asked, dumbfounded.

I should have done this interview in the days following your death rather than seven weeks afterwards. They'd have been more respectful then. It was a tragedy then, nothing more. Now, the "Isn't it awful she's dead?" angle had been done. They were after a new hook; in editorial meetings they'd have discussed how they could "take the story on" and some bright spark would have mentioned there was a lot of chatter on the Internet about threats, about how drunk she was, about a rift with her boyfriend. What is it they say? *If it bleeds, it leads.* This wasn't the sort of journo you were. "We haven't heard much from her friends—she must have had a best friend, get her best friend," the news editor would have said.

So they got me.

"I hear she was quite a complicated individual," the interviewer said.

I was a breath away from shouting, *What the hell is that supposed to mean?* But I was desperate to make it right, to leave everyone with the right impression of you, to make you proud of me for having put myself in front of a camera when I hated the limelight. So I said yes, a woman of many sides, hidden depths, not without contradictions, and with every answer you slipped a fraction further from me.

"I'm interested in what her boyfriend Luke is like," she said.

"He's a good actor," I said, and immediately regretted it.

"Really?"

"No comment," I said.

The cameras switched off, they un-miked me. "Thanks, hon," Arabella said. "You were perfect."

"Is that it? There's other stuff I'd like to share."

"Another time, sweetie."

I knew how it worked. They'd pack up their kit, grab lunch on the hoof and head back to the studio. She'd make a diary note to revisit the topic when they were next covering binge drinking or if there's a heat wave this summer and they're doing a slot on the dangers of swimming. Possibly a year on; yes, that's always an easy story: the anniversary angle.

"Are you proud of what you do?" I asked, and any sympathy she might have had over how I was edited dissipated.

Her colleague informed me the segment would "probably" make the six o'clock show, but that depended on whether something "bigger" happened between now and then. "With a bit of luck, it'll air at nine as well," she said.

I rang your parents, explained there'd be more on the news tonight, and apologized.

Predictably, the report ended with the shot of me looking wistfully across the water. In the end it went out at six and nine and then again at ten. I'd obviously cried enough.

Extract from Alice Salmon's diary,
May 20, 2010, age 23

"What's he like?"

"Nice."

"Is that the best you can do? Nice. You're a journalist, woman!"

"OK, extremely nice."

Meg was in town for a meeting, so we were grabbing a pizza. Chief subject of conversation: Luke.

We'd had exchanges like this since we first got interested in boys. Sometimes her asking the questions, sometimes me. I showed her his Facebook avatar. "Looks a bit like David Tennant, wouldn't you say? Without the spaceship, obviously."

"Is he keen? How often does he text? Once a day or more than once a day?"

"More. Five, six times . . . sometimes more."

"Oh my God, he's a psychopath!"

As if on cue, a text landed. We both laughed. I explained he works in software—not the geeky end; he does project management, people management—and how he comes across as a bit of a lad on first impressions: he'd turned up for our second date with a black eye from rugby, but that was all show. "He's a fantastic listener, too."

"Remind me, how many times exactly have you seen him?" Meg asked. "You sound as if you've known him forever."

"Twice. Three times if you count when we met."

Luke reckons it was me who started chatting to him in the Porterhouse, but it was definitely the other way round. "I'm hoping you'll give me your number," he'd said, and I'd had to call it out three times because it was so noisy. He'd dialed it on his phone, pressed ring and I saw my phone light up briefly in my handbag. "There," he said. "Got you now."

For our first date we went for drinks in Clapham Junction and Balham, then last weekend we went to the cinema because that's second-date law. At one point he referred to a skiing holiday and said "we," but that needn't necessarily have meant a woman; that could have been friends. Then he just out and said he'd been seeing someone, Amy, last year and asked when I last dated.

"I'm practically a nun," I told him.

"My last relationship didn't exactly end brilliantly," he said.

"They never do," I replied, recalling how I'd dumped Ben with a flush of shame. But everything before now is irrelevant; it's history. Yes, it had got pretty bad last year—I'd ended up going to the doctor and, because I've been prescribed antidepressants before, he asked the mandatory "How do you feel?" question, but it's a nothing question; journalists and TV presenters use it all the time. It's lazy. Then, when I said "Fine, mostly," he suggested I make another appointment. And when I walked back out through the waiting room I saw young mums and figured maybe that wouldn't ever be me, and geriatric grannies and figured that also probably wouldn't ever be me, and there was a screen explaining how they're giving out fewer antibiotics, because they've handed them out so liberally we're all going to die through lack of resistance, and I half considered going back and telling the doctor that that's what it was like, that sometimes it felt as if I had a lack of resistance to the entire world. But erasing the past, it's as easy as rolling your finger over the wheel on the mouse, block-highlighting emails and hitting Delete. Gone. Sitting in the cinema with Luke—we ended up opting for *Robin Hood*—I'd realized this could be a fresh start. I'm seeing him tomorrow, too. The theater, daaaarhhhling. It's lovely, this sense of anticipation, optimism. I'm happy. And please note: No artificial substances were used in the making of this diary entry!

Going home from the Porterhouse, I'd looked at his number and wondered how long it would stay in my phone: whether it would merely be a "recent," moving down until it dropped off the bottom or if I'd save it into contacts. Contemplated if it would become one I'd eventually know off by heart. *Stop it, Alice,* I'd told myself. *Don't get carried away. You're building yourself up for a fall.*

Because pretty much the only thing I've been certain of up to now is that being me isn't enough. Like, I've always wanted to run a marathon, but the other week standing outside Balham Bowls Club, I thought: *This is the me I want to be,* the one who'd just been passed her third glass of wine and was puffing on a Marlboro Light. *Sod training for a marathon,* I'd thought, *you're only young once. Life's like Scrabble: you shouldn't save your good letters; you've got to use them as soon as you get them.* But on the train heading home from Covent Garden, it felt enough.

Maybe you've come along just in time, Luke.

Everything's changing. I'm getting a promotion at work. I'll be a senior reporter, no less. I like my job. I like the person I am there and, yes, I might have to interview crazies and listen to psychos protest their innocence, but I get to meet incredible kids who've got cerebral palsy but are still determined to go to uni, or lovely old ladies reunited with long-lost relatives after half a century. I've got the hang of this career business, just as I got the hang of being a student, the niceties and nuances of my profession: the intros and paras and bylines, the news in briefs and double-page spreads. Our language.

Everyone's changing. Meg's determined to quit PR and considering returning to full-time education, Alex has got a new girlfriend, Soph's got a new boyfriend, Robbie's landed himself a partnership. Even my little fox buddy Rusty has disappeared. I kid myself he's moved on, but he's probably dead. He had fun while it lasted. He gathered his rosebuds. Where have I heard that expression before? That'll niggle at me now, like a word on the tip of my tongue.

I finish my camomile tea. That girl Luke mentioned he was seeing last year—I wonder if he meant he was seeing her during last year, or had been seeing her for longer and it only ended last year. The former, I hope.

Dating—that can be my word for this diary entry. Yes, that sounds good. Dating.

There is some truth in what Meg said. I do feel as if I've known Luke forever.

Notes made by Luke Addison on his laptop,
February 26, 2012

It was never my plan to confront you by the river.

I'd been trying to get you on your own all evening, watched you in every pub you went in, but you were never *not* with someone. I'd nearly had an opportunity when you went to the loo in one, but you started gassing to some old boy. God knows who he was. He stood out like a sore thumb in a tweed jacket; maybe he owned the place.

Initially I'd searched all over; then it had dawned on me. Facebook and Twitter. "Started working on tomorrow's hangover," you'd tweeted at 4:12 p.m. "Nando's it is, then," at 5:20. "Soton rocks," at 6:12. I'd flicked back through earlier tweets. 1:41: "Do we ever really know anyone?" 1:51: "Going to get blitzed."

You did a double take when you eventually saw me. It was as if you didn't trust your own eyes. "Luke," you said. "*Luke*."

"Hey, Al. Surprise! Came to see you."

"Don't want to be seen."

We were by the river and you were on a bench. "You're like buses," you said, and laughed, but it wasn't a happy laugh.

"You're drunk."

"Who are you, my dad?"

It was dark, and a few flakes of snow began to fall. "Look: snow," you said, except it sounded like "lukesnow." "It's a long way down when you fall, isn't it?" you said, taking a swig from a can of gin and tonic. You started sobbing and I reckoned your drink could have been spiked and the notion of you, my beautiful Al, out there drunk with men prepared to do that to you and all because of me made me furious. All it would have taken would have been for you to have stood a few feet further along the bar in the Porterhouse, a thirty-second delay on the Victoria line, my four thirty meeting running on by a few minutes: a colleague asking one more question under "any other business." Any of these and you wouldn't have ended up with me. "Been trying to call you all evening," I said.

You started frantically patting your jeans pockets. "Lost my phone."

"No you haven't, sweetheart, it's here." I picked it off the ground and handed it to you. It must have clicked on when it hit the ground, because music was playing: one of your favorite bands, The xx. "You look cold," I said.

"Cold hands, warm heart."

Your face was red, hair all over the place: it reminded me of you after sex. Maybe sleeping with you would fix this—breaking ourselves down into random parts; then when we came back together we might be different and I might not be such a dick. I reached out to take your hand but you pushed me way. "Who'd have thunk it, huh, my mum!"

"What are you on about, Al?"

I got an image of her, pouring coffee and inquiring about my job. "Bet she was gorgeous a few years ago," I'd said after we'd been introduced, "definite MILF," and you'd said, "Oi, enough of that," then that she still was. Gorgeous, that is, not MILF!

"What about the lemmings?" you said. "You never replied to the lemmings email."

Course I hadn't: I hadn't seen it at that point. You were talking gibberish as far as I was concerned and frustration fired up in me. "Me and you, Al," I said. "It was going to be me and you against the world."

"Me and you and a girl in Prague!"

Mention of that place was like a fresh blast of cold air.

"Why can't I stop feeling like this?" you said.

"Like what?"

"Like *me.*" Except it sounded a bit like "smee."

There were wet patches on your shoulders; I'd have given you my coat if I'd had one. "There's nothing wrong with you. You're perfect."

"Perfect people don't end up here."

I saw an ice cream hut, steps down to the water, the bridge. *We're both seeing the same things,* I thought, *but it doesn't help.* "Being on your own is shit."

"Being with someone shit's shitter. You don't get to choose which bits of me you like and which you don't. That isn't how it works. I'm not some sort of pick-and-mix. You should care about me whatever; you said you *would.*"

"I do."

"You do when it suits you, when it's easy, but what about when it's hard? Because that's what counts. Asked you to give me more time; why'd you ignore that?"

I wondered how we'd remember this. Piecing big nights out together had been a regular morning-after occupation for us, and I loved those nights, but recently the ones I'd liked best were the quiet ones, the ones when we were sober, when it was just us. I recalled watching you undress one night shortly after we'd met, seeing you taking off your makeup, and how it had come to me as a revelation: I didn't *have* to be a shit boyfriend. "I do love you," I said.

"Do you never want to swim away from it all, Luke? Because I do. I don't know who I am anymore."

"You're Alice."

"Good one," you said, as if I'd cracked a joke. Then: "Who is that? Who is Alice?"

A police car went by and it was as if the noise of the siren opened up a hole in the seal around us and another wave of drunkenness crashed over you. "Want my friends," you said. "Want to go home. Where is home?"

"Balham," I said. "You live in Balham."

"Not there," you said. You shivered and put your arms round yourself, rubbed yourself. Tiny arms, bones with a thin covering of flesh. "Don't sleep. Winds on snow."

"What are you on about, Al?"

"Am wrong," you said. "'S diamond on the snow. Gotta get it right."

An ambulance raced by, lights and sirens on.

"Someone's evening's ended badly," you said.

You'd often do this—have moments of near sobriety in drunkenness, as if you were coming up for air. You brushed a few flecks of snow off your lap and it occurred to me you must have bought these jeans since I'd last seen you. What else had happened in those eight weeks? This is how it happens, how couples split up: they simply *let* it happen, and I thought, *Fuck it, why not? There's probably never a perfect—or rather, entirely wrong—time,* and dropped onto my knees. "You're the one, Alice," I said.

But you must have thought I'd slipped, because you burst out laughing. "Stand up, man," you said. "Man up, man!"

I pulled myself up, anger suddenly punching through me. I tried to control my breathing, made myself stare at the plaque on the bench, something about a dead woman. *How she'd often sit here and watch the world flow by.* You lit a cigarette, had two long drags and blew the smoke up in my face.

"Don't make me hate you," I said, which wasn't what I'd planned.

You had another swig of drink, another drag.

"Don't fuck with me," I said.

"You're the one who fucked around."

"Once, Alice, once. Since when did *once* constitute fucking around?"

"Once more than I cheated on you. I'm more shat upon than shitting," you declared, laughing. "That's Lear. Sort of."

A group of men bowled by in the distance singing. "Why can't you all stop following me?"

I wondered if you meant that guy you'd been flirting with in All Bar One. You were virtually on his lap. I'd stared in through the glass, the way we had at those sharks in the aquarium, and had to stop myself charging in. Maybe there was some history there: you hooking up with an old flame, getting back at me for Prague. I deserved it. Jealousy's like grief: it multiplies up and out, spreading hate and hurt, but all I want is to go back to how it was. You, coming round for *Live at the Apollo*. I'll even let you watch *Wallander*. Coming and complaining about the piles of dishes and the three-day-old pizza boxes, running back to my room from the shower, shivering and dripping water, then saying it wouldn't be massive and it might not be the poshest burb—it might end up being Tooting or Brixton or Elephant—but we could just about afford to rent our *own* flat if we pooled resources.

"Was honest about how I feel," you said. "Love's not like a tap: you can't simply turn it off. Wasn't it enough for you—me baring my heart and soul in an email? Can't believe you ignored it."

"You look like you need a hug."

"I do, but not from you, not now."

A nugget of resentment formed in me. I was on repeat, destined to keep messing up like some awful *Groundhog Day* parody. *I'm twenty-seven,* I thought. *I'm too old for this.*

"Remember when we went skinny-dipping?" you said. "Let's do it now."

"Don't be ridiculous, it's snowing."

"You're the ridiculous one, shagging around."

That nugget of resentment hardened, so I tried to count to ten before speaking, heard water tumbling over the weir in the distance; but at about six I heard myself say: "Look at the state you're in. You're an embarrassment."

"You're no better. We're as bad as each other. You, me, even my mum."

The urge filled me to get wasted. I'd had six or seven pints, but all I felt was half—half-sober, half-drunk, half-empty, half-full, half-what-we-had-been. I needed to get so shit-faced I wouldn't even know how much I was messing up. "Can I have some of that?" I asked, nodding at the can.

"'S gone," you said. "All gone."

This wasn't how it was supposed to be. I was going to propose and I wasn't planning to hurt you—I'd done that enough—but I could feel anger mushrooming in me, musty and sour and spiteful. A new feeling that wasn't love: barbed and uncontainable. "Come back to my hotel."

"Rather sleep on this bench."

You focused dejectedly on the dead-woman plaque, then squinted at my trousers. "They your keys or you just glad to see me?" you asked, giggling.

I cast my eyes down to the outline of a small jeweler's box. I'd even got proposing wrong. You'd made me get it wrong. I'd pictured myself sharing the news with Charlie, putting a brave face on it. Texting him from the hotel bar or the train tomorrow. "Back on the horse, mate. You've got your wingman back. Beers Friday?" I couldn't discern whether what I felt was elation or despair. I took out the box, hurled it into the river and it made a plink.

"What was that?" you inquired indifferently.

"History, that's what it was—which is what you're going to be soon."

"Very profound," you said, and maybe if you hadn't laughed

I wouldn't have done what I did next, but right then—hair in your face, the half-smoked, gone-out cigarette by your feet—you were the one person I hated more than myself. I had to break it—had to break us—so completely we couldn't hurt either of us any longer. "That girl in Prague, she was gorgeous," I said, and recalled with a bright clarity how I'd been before you: on my own, nothing to lose, no one to care about, no one to let down, no one to be let down by. "The sex was dynamite. I might as well be dead as in bed with you. You might as well be dead as in bed with me."

"Funny you should say that."

You sucked futilely at the empty can. I reached out and there was a rip. Saw your black frilly bra, the one I'd bought you for Valentine's Day. Needed to pull you so close it would drown it all out, or push you so far away I'd never see you again. Yes, that was it, no one to hurt, no one to hurt me. I could live like that. I could survive. I had to live like that to survive—shepherding girls I'd met on Saturday nights to the front door on Sunday mornings, kissing them on the cheek and saying "I will" when they inquired casually if I was going to call, then texting Charlie, Mr. Single, saying, "Mate, I pulled an uber-hot chick last night!" Only had the confidence to talk to you the night we met because I had nothing to lose and I'd been so glad I'd left all that shit, that me, behind; but now I'd go back to it and I'd cope and it couldn't be any worse than this, but I needed you gone first, erased. Right then I loathed you, Al, for making me think there was an alternative. I saw the bridge with its trusses and cantilevers, and recalled I'd once set my heart on being an architect. Another abandoned dream. "Come back with me, please," I said. One final pathetic effort.

You tilted your head upwards. "Least Ben's honest about how shit he is."

I ignored that, whoever the fuck Ben might have been, and for a second had a handle on it, me after you. How this would become a memory—how Amy had, or Laura or Pippa. A fleeting, foggy sense of me looking back on you in a year or two or five; yes, with a twinge of regret, but as a memory. I'd view you as a stepping-stone on the way to her—whoever *she* was, my next girlfriend. Maybe it—tonight, this—would become an in-joke of ours, me and her: how I'd once fought with a woman on a bench by a river in the snow. How I'd once followed a girl to Southampton like a muppet. Dated a journalist. We'd laugh, initially awkwardly but gradually less so, about it, you, us, just as now you and I laugh—laughed—about me and Amy splitting up over a lamb shank or Laura telling me at a bus stop in Neasden that I was emotionally stunted. I hated losing Amy, hated losing Laura, hated losing you. When was this going to end? "I love you, Al," I said again, and you weren't the only one who was crying. "I won't let you leave me."

But you sprung up and when I grabbed you, you were wet from the snow and small; you always maintained you were big—Shrek-like, you claimed—but I felt twice the size of you, three times, ten times, and furious that I couldn't protect something this fragile, this beautiful.

"Why does everyone want to put their hands on me? I can't bear it."

When you started screaming I put my hand over your mouth, because if someone had heard, they'd have been convinced I was attacking you. I could feel your breath, your lips, your teeth, your nostrils, your neck. Over your shoulder there was the faint glow of a cigarette in the distance on the other side of the river.

"Can't breathe," you squealed.

"Stop shouting, then."

"Help, help, someone help me."

"Shhh . . . I'm trying to help you."

"You're hurting me."

"You can throw yourself off that bridge for all I care," I said, tightening my grip.

You craned your head sideways so you had it in view, but I didn't let go. I saw your cleavage, and had a vision of you on the bed with no clothes on and lust tugged at me, like a fish on a line. I put my other arm out, but you swiped it away, so I grabbed at you; I had to hang on, had to keep you, so I could explain, the realization dawning on me that what I had in my grasp was a handful of your hair.

"Get off me!" you screamed.

Comments left on Alice Salmon's leaving card from the *Southampton Messenger*, *November 20, 2009*

We'll miss you and your laughter but not your minging trainers on the radiators!

Amanda

It was inevitable that someone with your talent would get poached* sooner or later. It's a great opportunity and one you couldn't say no to. Our loss is London's gain. Thanks for all your hard work and enthusiasm. Maybe we can lure you back one day?

Mark

*Poached Salmon, geddit?!

We've summoned Rentokil to disassemble your desk. Warned them to expect rats!

Barbara S.

Remember the successes like the "night stalker" campaign? You put one of Southampton's most dangerous men behind bars and you should be proud of that. All the best.

Bev

Next stop, the *New York Times*, via a short spell in Balham!
Gavin

PS: If Cazza claims your leaving present was her idea she's lying. It was mine.

Go, Fish Face, go. If you leave your iPod behind, don't worry, no one will claim it. Thankfully your taste in books is better than your taste in music. Thanks for the reading recommendations and thanks for the memories.
Bella

Sob! You've been like a big sister to me, does that make you sound old?? Learnt so much from you and you've been a brill shoulder to cry on. Have adored every minute of working with you. Tweet me, Miss S!
Ali xxx

It's already passed into legend—the day the new girl stood up to Sexist Sexton and refused to do a Death Knock.
Gavin

Hope you like the Kindle. It's the new DX one with the big screen! You've got absolutely no excuse not to read Kafka now!
Cazza

PS: Gav's talking out of his posterior!

Who's going to make the tea now, even if you did insist on having yours so strong you could stand the spoon up in it? Enjoy the big smoke. V jealous! When can we come and visit? Two sugars please.
Phil

Friday nights in Flames won't be the same without you. Make sure you come back and see us. Make mine a double :)

Juliet

Good luck.

From Anthony Stanhope

You've done your best to play it cool, Miss Salmon, but I have it on good authority that you're crazy about me so let me know when you're ready for that date!

A man like me won't hang around for ever!

Big Tom

Journalist extraordinaire, queen of bakers, runner, charity worker, champion of the dispossessed, tequila enthusiast, brilliant friend. Is there anything you can't do? Watch out, men of London.

Loads of love and big hugs, Michelle X

Letter sent by Professor Jeremy Cooke,
June 29, 2012

My dear Larry,

I went to the river after I'd been to the police station. To the spot where a procession of TV presenters had stood, as if their geographical proximity gave them some unique insight. "It was here," they'd say in hushed, authoritative tones, "that a promising young life was cut short. Here, at this normally peaceful and tranquil spot, that a young woman died tragically. Here, where an otherwise normal Saturday night out—the sort that thousands enjoy every weekend—reached its horrific conclusion." They focused almost exclusively on this stretch, titillated viewers with uncorroborated details about the strength of the current on February 5 (medium to fast), how much she weighed (purportedly anything between 9 stone 4 and 10 stone 5) and what she was wearing (jeans, a purple silky top and boots . . . that they were knee-length, black, from Topshop—one newscaster got very carried away with that particular kernel of detail).

The scene had been awash with flowers initially: an explosion of winter reds, pinks and yellows—the ideal backdrop for cameramen. When I visited, just the wilted remains of one small bouquet. There wasn't a soul around, it was after 1 a.m., and I'd knelt by the water, put my hand in, felt the rush of cold. Initial reports claimed it was a jogger who'd spotted her body, later revised to a dog walker. He'd been shocked when I got in touch, asked if I was official. Yes, I'd reassured him. I'd asked him questions as if I was entirely uninformed, but it seems so important: to fill in all the blanks. He'd thought she was a tree trunk, then it dawned on him they were clothes. "I couldn't take it in," he said, this man who I'd met in the Debenhams restaurant. "It was as if my brain wouldn't process it: a dead woman in the water." He didn't use the expression—it's actually one with which I've only recently become familiar—but what he'd seen had been the first-stage "immersion artifacts." Alice's skin, pimpled like a bad case of goose bumps (cutis anserina, the technical term is), the smooth softness swollen and wrinkled like a washerwoman's. Putting his coffee down, he'd said she'd had a stick in her hand. Apparently it's not unusual for objects to remain grasped after death, fixed by a cadaveric spasm. Left in the water longer, fish and other creatures would have nibbled Alice's flesh, lips and eyelids. The word for that was a new one on me: anthropophagy. Left longer still, she would have sunk before eventually resurfacing, bobbed back up by the gas produced by her body's bacteria. "Bloat and float," I saw that ghoulishly described as in one Internet chat room.

The man in Debenhams was petrified the police would arrest him: put two and two together and come up with five. "The council's replaced a lot of the fences near the bridge," he said.

I explained about Alice's newspaper campaign when she'd worked in the city. How strongly she'd felt about it; how her single-mindedness and tenaciousness had achieved results.

"They've been vandalized, but you'd have had to *want* to jump to get through," he said.

I'd had my suspicions at first, but I simply can't see it: her taking her own life. Not Alice. For every page in her diary she devoted to how bad she felt, there were two to how fantastic life was. She'd got through bad spells before. Liz, bless her, is vaulting from theory to theory. I expect she'll have crept up to the notion of suicide, edging out to it as one would a cliff, but she's steadfastly refusing to accept or even acknowledge its plausibility and my conclusions thus far bear that out: time and again that girl had soldiered on, beaten back the blackness, persevered, *lived.*

By the river, I'd put my hand back in, and there was a faint memory of being in a dinghy, leaning out the back, my hand trailing in the water. I dropped down onto my hands and knees. "Darling, where *are* you?" I found myself calling and saw my reflection—the half-moon glasses, the eyebrows, the wrinkles, the tufts of hair—then I was washed away. I wondered what it would have been like to have stepped in, to have followed her, to have gone after her. It's not the pain of illness that scares me, Larry; that's not so impossible. It's the prospect of decline I can't abide. The thought of Fliss having to watch it. As if I haven't hurt her enough.

"You're not escaping that easily," she said when I made a wisecrack about one final holiday to Switzerland. Her face had crumpled and she said that life was precious, it wasn't ours to take, and besides, she cherished every single second with me.

When the boy with tattoos had mentioned hara-kiri, I tied the little shit up in knots by outlining its literal translation. Explained how defeated samurai would restore their honor by disemboweling themselves, and the displacement was similar to lecturing; if you focused intently on detail, you didn't see what you were looking at, didn't feel anything; there was just the banking up of details and facts, the familiar architecture of knowledge. "Imagine a shame so great it compels a human being to take their own life," I'd said, and he did what he'd done previously: asked me why I talked about human beings as if they were a different species, as if I wasn't one of them. He'd asked for more money and I'd explained how the less noise samurai made after they'd sliced themselves open with their swords—their *wakizashi*—the braver they were.

Staring up at that bridge, I realized something, Larry. It was how utterly useless all this knowledge was. Were I to take up a knife, plunge it into the left side of my abdomen and draw the blade across to the right, then turn it upwards, would that knowledge stop the blood pooling around my feet? None of it meant a jot, any more than having learnt such words as "brachytherapy" and "zoledronic acid" could make my illness dissipate.

"There's nothing like cancer to expand your vocabulary," I'd said to Fliss, after one of my hospital visits.

"I love you," she said, and I'd decided: I'm going to tell you. When this is done, when I've gathered all the information about Alice I can, I'm going to tell you what she meant to me, her and her mother. I'm going to tell you and the whole world, because how will you believe I'm being honest about *anything*—how will you believe how much I love you—if I can't be honest about the positions they've variously occupied in the recesses of my heart?

"It's nice how you're putting this girl back together again," she once remarked as we were flicking through a slide show of photos of her on my laptop.

"You make her sound like Humpty Dumpy," I joked, recalling how all the king's horses and all the king's men couldn't manage it with that poor little fellow.

"Presumably you're not intending to publish any of it, though?" she'd asked.

Bless her, she had no idea.

I've worked out what this new feeling is that prompts me to say to the principal, "I'm doing this with or without your blessing," or to the chancellor, "I don't give a toss what your view is," or to our latest departmental recruit, a square-jawed, barrel-chested brute, "Are you as boring in the bedroom as you are in the laboratory?" I felt it after I had the first inkling of what it might be that sent me scuttling four times a night to the toilet. Again when I spotted the momentary flash of recognition in my doctor's eyes. Later still when the specialist uttered the word "terminal." I'll tell you what it is: it's a lack of fear. Finally, a complete and utter lack of fear.

"I'm not giving you any more money," I said to the tattooed boy. The faint sound of music had reached me from his earphones. *Perhaps this is what it'll be like after I'm dead,* I'd thought: *echoes of the world.* He'd reached down into his rucksack and I was expecting another Alice item, but he retrieved a glass figurine that should have been on the sideboard in our dining room. I'd bought it for Fliss for an anniversary, when we were in the old house.

"Fuck you," I heard myself saying.

He was momentarily dumbfounded. Why did I never stand up to bullies as a child, Larry? "I don't *care* what you do with the letter," I said. "I'll be dead before long. You've got another fifty years to live. Imagine that: another half century of being you. That must be torture. You've got more to hide than me, more to lose. You'll not get another penny out of me."

He always locked the door behind him, but I'd wondered what our tableau would resemble if anyone had come in. A lecturer and one of his students? A scientist and one of his assistants? A father and his son—a young one, admittedly, perhaps from a second marriage who'd dropped by to say hi or extract some cash from his old dad?

"You only hate me because we're the same," he said. "You might dress it up, but you're the respectable face of what I am. You're me in a tweed jacket."

I laughed out loud at that one.

"Fuck you, Iceman," he said.

I wondered if I'd had a son whether we'd have ever spoken to each other like this—whether we'd have fought, got on, admired each other, trusted each other, loved each other. I went to grab the figurine and it tumbled to the floor, smashing. "I'm going to beat you to the truth," I said. "I'm going to put it all in a book, and you, you little shit, might even feature."

"Looks like Mr. and Mrs. Salmon are going to get a bit of new reading material, then!" he'd replied.

We're all going to get some reading material, if I get my way.

The coroner's verdict was tantamount to admitting we're stumped. White froth in her mouth and nose, fluid in her lungs, aquatic debris in her stomach—such observations would have suggested to those examining Alice that she drowned, that she was alive when she entered the water, but that doesn't explain what came before. Doesn't it strike you as ironic that, in a world where our every step is watched, monitored and filmed, she took her last few unseen? At least, by the wider world. Should someone be behind bars for this? There are those who would probably argue I should be for what I did that December evening in 2004, although that's another story.

When I'd visited the river after my session at the police station, I'd sat there until it got light, scanning the water and debris and the deep, fast-flowing inky-black water whipping by. And I watched Alice Salmon. I remembered my Humpty Dumpty book, its yellow cracked cover, touching the spine, feeling the story, feeling that baby egg himself.

"It's anthropomorphic," my father had said. "Do you remember what that means, Jeremy?"

For the life of me, I couldn't; all I wanted to do was to say the story out loud, for once to hear *him* say it out loud, the familiar reassuring shape of the rhymes. "We've been through this," he said tersely. "Will the taste of this help you remember?" he said, unbuckling his belt.

It's a single quatrain. But it doesn't mean a thing, being enlightened about its form. So what that I know that brittle, bulbous egg makes an appearance in *Through the Looking Glass,* discussing semantics with its protagonist, Alice. Wonder if *our* Alice ever read that book? She'd have loved the eponymous hero. I'll put you together again, dear sweet Alice, and when you're convoked in my book—when we're together in my book—maybe it'll be the right time for me to have a great fall.

Thing is, old chap, I saw her on the night she died. I didn't mention this to the police; they'd only get the wrong end of the stick. Not that anyone saw us when we'd talked, when we'd argued, but it would only fuel further speculation. I'd charted her movements on Twitter: a list of pub and bar names, pins in a map. It was on the aptly named Above Bar Street when I eventually caught up with her and heard laughter pealing from a huddle of smokers in a pub doorway. *I recognize that laugh,* I thought. Its pitch, its timbre. I turned and gawked. *I recognize that hair,* I thought. *Alice.*

"*You,*" she'd said, shocked, scared. A few minutes later, a slap across my face.

Why couldn't she have been wearing shoes, not boots, Larry? Then they wouldn't have dragged her down so much. There'd been marks on her face, the man in Debenhams had told me. Presumably, he said, from where the current had battered her against hard surfaces. That'll have been the steps, I thought. The swell of the water had bashed her repeatedly into those.

In my head, I replayed the scenario: her gliding downstream; yet I knew deep down she wouldn't have been like Ophelia because of another thing I've learnt. Bodies in water always float facedown.

Yours as ever,
Jeremy

Text from Elizabeth Salmon,
February 4, 2012, 1:27 p.m.

Alice, do me a favor, sweetheart: I can't open my email. Can you log in from your phone? Am at the garden center and need a voucher code. Will be on the email that arrived yesterday. Hope your weekend in Southampton goes well. Your father says don't drink too much. Love you x

---

Letter sent by Professor Jeremy Cooke,
July 3, 2012

Frankly it was the usual ghastly affair, Larry. Shallow, futile conversations. Professional point scoring. Anthropological one-upmanship. At least there was plenty of booze, which salved the pain.

We were at a gathering of scientists after a conference. Not creeping around in a tawdry hotel, not grabbing a half-hour assignation in my office with the blinds shut, not in my car by the side of the road in the New Forest. Liz and I were at a party. This is what she'd wanted. Us, out together, in public.

Every time the front door opened, I couldn't help checking who it was.

"Relax," she reassured me, "you're miles from home. We don't know anyone here. Besides, everyone's preoccupied with themselves—you've said as much yourself. It's human nature."

We stood in the kitchen. A few people were dancing to Abba in the living room. No one was my age; everyone was either in their twenties or over forty. Liz was wearing a black dress and the necklace I'd bought her; she looked divine. I was captivated by her neck on that particular night: the long, white curve of it, like a swan or an orchid's stem or a piece of ornamental blown glass. I felt like a character in a movie—Charlton Heston, say, or Gregory Peck.

A procession of men homed in on her. "Are you two together?" one asked brazenly.

"Well, I'm not her father, am I?" I snapped, jealousy spearing me. I put my arm round her, felt her small shoulders. "You look beautiful," I whispered.

I could feel the tension in her body. I should have anticipated this: there'd been silences over lunch when she'd poked at her mackerel, and when I'd inquired how her food was she'd merely replied, "Dry." Even attempts to pull the conversation back onto a more satisfactory plane by talking about a topic I knew—or guessed—would fascinate her: the raising of the *Mary Rose,* hauled from its ocean grave after 437 years, were unsuccessful.

"I can't go on like this," she said.

"This wine isn't up to much, I'll give you that."

"I need to feel I'm on a trajectory."

I waited for the moment to pass. When it didn't, I said: "Easy to tell you're in the English department. You'll be referring to our *arc* next!"

"Don't make fun of me," she said. "It's not unreasonable. What we're doing, it's all so shoddy and it's not fair on anyone, least of all Fliss."

My wife's name passed like a shadow across the room. The kids of whoever was hosting the bash—they'd been terrorizing guests all night—ran into the kitchen. Poor little wretches, their parents had made them dress up: ties and tank tops. These academics, they couldn't even leave their offspring out of their obsessions.

"Why is it men always think different rules apply to them?" Liz asked.

I waited, hoping it was a rhetorical question.

"Can't you see? If there is going to be an *us,* I want it to be something I can be proud of."

One of the children, a precocious little fellow—he reminded me of myself at that age—came over and introduced himself. His had been one of the names on my and Fliss's list, but we'd long since given up talking about names. We'd long since given up talking about children. I knew at home she'd be watching *The Two Ronnies,* laughing at the bit where they pretended to be newscasters, making coffee in the part where Ronnie Corbett told the shaggy-dog story.

"You're never going to leave your wife, are you?" Liz said when the child had wandered off.

"Steady on," I said. "We've only known each other for a few months."

"A few months, a few years—it makes no difference. You'll never leave her."

"Isn't loyalty a good trait?"

"Now's not the time for your facetiousness, Jem. We all need to be in control of our own destinies and I'm no more than a passenger in yours."

I glanced at my watch. She took a big swig of gin.

"Do you love me?" she asked.

"Wow, *there's* a question."

"Yes, there *is* a question—and now I want an answer."

"Us anthropologists struggle with that concept," I said. "It's generally accepted that love, specifically romantic love, evolved to focus one's mating energy on one partner, as that attachment enabled us to rear progeny as a team. An American's been doing some fascinating work in this field. This whole area of what love is *for* is very stimulating."

"I don't care about that. God knows why, but what I care about is *you*. I thought you cared about me." Liz sparked up another cigarette. Seemed like the only time she didn't smoke was when she was in flagrante or eating. I recalled how my wife and I had given up together shortly after we'd met.

"I might have not always made the best choices when it comes to men, but I'm not stupid," she said.

"I didn't say you were."

"So why are you treating me like I am?" She fixed the same stare on me I'd seen over the mackerel. I turned away: a hostess trolley, a caramel-colored sofa, a hi-fi system with records stacked against it. "That's you all over, Jem—you're full of opinions about everyone else, but ask you one damn simple question about yourself and you're floundering. I can't work out if I love you or hate you more. It's an easy one with myself—it's hate; hands down, it's hate every time."

"For God's sake, don't hate me," I said. "Don't hate yourself."

"I'll tell you what love's for—it's because without it we're just bodies banging against each other. Having an affair's bad enough, but it makes it worse somehow if it's just sex. It's more disrespectful."

"Disrespectful to whom?"

"Don't play the innocent. Your wife, for starters, or have you conveniently forgotten about her again?" She put her cigarette down. "I could have just about lived with what it would have done to Fliss if we were going to live happily ever after. If we're not, then you're merely treating me like . . . *like a lump of meat.* If we're not, then I'm acting like one."

"I read an interesting paper today on mitochondrial DNA," I said.

She started sobbing and it occurred to me how different Fliss looked when she cried: quieter, older, more composed. That moment—comparing these two women's pain—was the first time I'd ever known what it was like to properly despise myself. I reached out, traced the definition of her spine with my forefinger. "Liz, darling, don't be like this; don't cry."

"You've never treated me like I'm precious. You care more about people who lived thousands of years ago than you do me. Don't I matter?"

"Of course you do, you know you do."

"I don't; how would I? You never tell me. I feel so dreadfully *lost*."

Why do we all have to be so damn fragile, I'd thought, but I must have said it out loud because I heard a faint voice answer: "Fragile? Fragile? I'm positively robust compared to how I used to be."

Liz got drunk very quickly. She flirted with other men. She knocked some glasses over. When I tried to touch her, she said she couldn't do half a relationship.

We'd stood, Liz and I had, in front of the Titians and Caravaggios in the National; she'd said she didn't care who saw us, she didn't give a damn, life was too short. We'd had a weekend in Dorset, ambled along the shingle on Chesil Beach and listened to the waves. Driven to the sea at Beachy Head in my TR7, the car that Fliss joked was a symptom of an early midlife crisis, and we'd drunk champagne with the roof down in the salty breeze. Part of me had wanted to rush straight home and tell Fliss, tell her about how far you could see and the little lighthouse and the sheer vertiginous magnificence of that white drop. Rouse her gently from sleep—she'd been in bed by the time I got back from that particular "weekend symposium"—and say, "Fliss, Fliss, you'll never guess where I've been." It had been such an extraordinary day, it seemed only natural to share it with her. A bit of me had wanted to take her to the same spot so she, *Fliss,* could experience the same joy that Liz had, so I might see the same smile on her face—she smiled so rarely these days—as had burst on to Liz's. *One damn life simply isn't enough,* I thought, and the impossibility of the situation again winded me. *You've* let *yourself love two women, you stupid, selfish man.* The words of a master, history or classics, echoed around the room as if he'd been addressing a dog: "You've been a silly boy, Cooke, *silly*."

"Jeremy Cooke—well, I never!"

I wheeled round. Martin Collings. He'd worked with Fliss when she'd been at University College London. They'd kept in touch.

"Martin, how lovely to see you," I said, peering over his shoulder. Liz had gone to the lav. We'd been standing in the kitchen, hardly speaking;

neither of us wanted to bring the evening to a close—we were both separately terrified of what might come next.

"I've been positively atrocious," Martin said. "I haven't been in touch with Fliss for an aeon. Is she here?"

"No," I said. "She's not."

I scanned the room for Liz. She was drunk and had been gone for ages. *Please,* I thought, *please have walked out on me.*

"How's your work? You still preoccupied by the dead?"

Liz reemerged and stood next to me. She fell against me. There was nothing, no connection, no intimacy, just weight. "I love you and I hate you; either way you've blown it, you stupid prehistoric old relic!" She kissed me on the cheek. It was a good-bye kiss: tender and wet and cruel. I tried to catch Martin's eye; I could almost follow his train of thought, the apparatus of his mind going into overdrive.

Liz left the room and I made the hand gesture of someone drinking—as if to say, Haven't got the foggiest what that was about; ignore her, she's drunk. Neil Diamond started playing and she went, wobbling, into the living room as if drawn by the music, as if she'd remembered she'd left something in there.

"What are you playing at, Jeremy?" he asked.

"Playing at?"

The music stopped and then started again. REO Speedwagon. I heard Liz's laughter and I felt strangely calm: as if it was out of my hands now. *He'll tell Fliss and it'll be better than carrying this huge caliginous secret around.* But something made me persevere with the lie, the cliché. It was like a part I had to play.

"You're not thinking . . . Oh, how positively hilarious. She's my assistant, the latest recruit to the department. To be frank, though, she's got a bit of a problem with the old vino."

I visualized Fliss putting some food down for the dog, sliding the bolt across the back door and climbing the stairs to bed. "These infernal academic parties: you know what they're like—bound to drag on—so I'll probably stay away overnight," I'd told her.

"Don't bullshit me," Martin said. "I've known your wife for a long time; she deserves better than this."

Liz danced with the man whom I'd told I wasn't her father. *That's that, then,* I thought. *That's what an affair was like.*

"You utter shit, Jeremy," this friend of my wife said.

Much later—no one cared about drink-driving in those days: it was 1982—I crept in and patted Milly when she clambered out of her basket to greet me and whispered I'd missed her and bathed and slipped into bed and my wife whimpered something I couldn't make out: it might have been "Welcome home" or "Why didn't you phone?" or "I'm all alone." And I lay awake next to the woman who was unlike the one I'd spent the evening with in so many ways, but mostly for one reason: I was married to her. I didn't sleep. I waited for the phone to ring, waited for that sycophantic toad Collings to seal my fate. The phone never rang. *Maybe I've got away with it,* I thought, listening to my wife's gentle, catchy breathing.

How was I supposed to know what Liz was going to do nine days later, Larry? Should I have foreseen that? Stopped that? We weren't each other's problem anymore. When the news of it reached me, it came as every bit as much of a shock as when I heard Alice had died. A tentative knock on my study door, a colleague, one of the few who was aware of what was going on between myself and her, an expression midway between sympathy and contempt. "Jeremy, have you heard?"

Yours as ever,
Jeremy

Postcard sent by Alice Salmon,
August 17, 2009

Dear M & D,

Weather baking, hotel adequate, food dreadful. Lots of pool time and lots of cocktails. Not much sleep. Island beautiful (have insisted we do one "cultural" thing every day!). Look more like a lobster than a salmon! Lots of Germans, but you'll be pleased to hear I haven't mentioned the war once yet, Dad. Was it Fuerteventura we came to when I was a kid? The girls say hi.

Love you loads.
Ax

PS: Who says no one sends postcards these days?

Email sent by Elizabeth Salmon,
July 22, 2012

From: Elizabeth_salmon101@hotmail.com
To: jfhcooke@gmail.com
Subject: Tell me

Jem,

Attached is a scan of a note I received this morning along with some photocopies of your handwriting and an instruction to "compare the two." I need you to reassure me this note wasn't written by you because they are remarkably similar. She was eighteen, a fresher, her first time away from home—a note like this would have terrified any girl that age. The spidery writing would have totally freaked her out. If it wasn't for me, Dave would have buried you. Can't believe I let you inveigle your way back into my affections—my God, I sent you photographs of Alice as a child! Tell me I haven't been duped, Jem. Tell me it wasn't you who wrote this note. Whoever sent it to me said they had confronted you with it, reckoned you were "sweating like a pedophile in a Santa suit." I more nearly drank today than at any point since I quit. Bought a bottle of gin in Tesco and sat in the car park with it on my lap. All I'd wanted was to go to sleep and to wake up when this was all over. Nine days after you and I split up, I drank a whole bottle of the stuff. It's not without reason they call it "mother's ruin." It never goes away, that craving, it's like a dull pressure on the back of your brain. You assured me the police would eventually come up with answers about what happened to my baby, Jem, that's what you said, but they haven't . . . All they've done is fob me off and run into dead ends, and some of the avenues they've explored, frankly I despair . . . You once referred to the trail we all leave, the trace. For both our sakes, I hope this note isn't yours. God, who am I to get all sanctimonious?

Elizabeth

Opinion piece by Ali Manning on the *Daily Digest* website, *March 16, 2012*

My phone rang late last night and when the caller introduced herself as Holly Dickens it took me a second to twig. She was one of the girls with Alice Salmon on the night she died.

Readers may well be familiar with Alice's story. She's barely been out of the news since she drowned last month in Southampton. Tipsy, she had got separated from her friends, then is believed to have toppled into a river. The "could-have-happened-to-me" nature of the incident has made it a talking point across the nation.

Holly had got in touch because she was aware I'd worked with Alice in a previous job. She asked if we could speak confidentially; I agreed. We talked for over an hour, much of which she cried through. She spoke of her "unshakable guilt."

It's become a popular pastime for some commentators, blaming this young woman and her two pals, Sarah Hoskings and Lauren Nugent, for Alice's death. As if letting her slip out of sight for a few seconds was a crime. As if we haven't all been in that situation.

"How can it be that one minute you're getting ready for a night out with a friend and the next you're at her funeral?" she asked.

But I had no answers.

"Alice was sitting on a wall outside the chip shop," she told me. "One minute she was there, the next gone. We only turned our backs for a few seconds. I can't believe we lost her."

Between them, they then called her mobile eight times and eventually made the not-unreasonable assumption that Alice had made her own way back to the hotel.

"She was street-savvy; it never crossed my mind she was in danger, but with hindsight she was in a spaced-out mood all day and we should have checked because she was a bit tipsy. None of us can forgive ourselves."

I finished the conversation with Holly and remembered my and Alice's spell working together at the *Southampton Messenger*. Happy days.

A few seconds later, Holly rang again. "I wouldn't mind," she said, "if you did want to quote me. People need to understand we made a mistake that we'll regret for the rest of our lives but that we loved Alice."

These three girls have done nothing wrong. As if losing a friend isn't enough, they're also being lambasted for refusing to engage in tittle-tattle about Alice, having stoically stuck by their promise to not comment beyond their official statement. This dignified decision was eminently understandable. It was the product of a wish to respect Alice's family and it was also, let's not forget, taken on police advice, for fear doing so could inadvertently prejudice any subsequent prosecution.

I reminded Holly that she shouldn't blame herself and that what happened to her could have happened to anyone, that people in glass houses shouldn't throw stones, that there but for the grace of God go any one of us . . .

Also see:

WORDS: Premiership footballer's four-star hotel "orgy"
PHOTOS: So much for MP's brazen boast he'd "quit the fags"
VIDEO: Street gang strike at elderly cyclist

Feature written by Alice Salmon in *Azure* magazine, *October 20, 2011*

Everyone from Anne Frank to Bridget Jones has done it, but modern women are embracing the diary-keeping tradition. With a new initiative set to ensure the practice gets a fresh lease of life, Alice Salmon explains how it helped her survive a teenage crisis.

I prized one of Dad's razors out of the packet and slumped to the floor.

It was hot and a lawn mower was whirring in a neighbor's garden. It was pointless cutting that grass—it would only grow again. I was thirteen and that was how everything felt that summer—endless, futile, never changing or improving. I put my right hand to my left wrist and gave the razor a jangly jerk. For a few glorious, magical moments, it all disappeared—the exam stress, the 34 percent in Biology (I was clearly thick as well as ugly), even the bust-up I'd had with my best friend Meg, so typical of me, accusing her of hating me. Obscured by the urgent, bright inescapability of pain. Overtaken by a more startling revelation: blood.

Alice, you've cut yourself, I thought. *Look what Alice Salmon has done. Look what that silly girl's gone and done.*

"Daddy," I called out, but he wasn't home. No one was.

Robbie's radio was playing Britney's "Baby One More Time" and beyond it—behind it—that lawn mower. *Don't pass out,* I instructed myself. *DON'T. PASS. OUT.* It was a new, clean cut and it was a new, clean feeling. I heard Mr. Woof barking and fear ambushed me: What if it leaves a scar? Ever my father's daughter, I ran through the practical calculations: I'd wash the towel, get bangles, wear long sleeves. I couldn't have my parents finding out because I'd hate to upset them. More blood—more of my blood—came out. How near the surface it must have been. I held my wrist under the tap and the water eventually went clear, then I put two plasters on the wound in a cross. I put the towel through a hot wash and scrubbed the bathroom until there wasn't the faintest trace of my insides out.

When my mum saw the plaster and asked what on earth I'd done, I said I'd caught it on a nail walking home from school.

"My God, we should get that seen to; it might need a tetanus."

"It's nothing," I said.

Dad reckoned it was typical me, wrapping my arm up like I'd been at death's door over a scratch. "Always the drama queen," he said, "my Ace. And what's this I hear about you cleaning the bathroom, Salmon Fry? What on earth's got into you?"

"Where was the nail, Alice?" Mum asked when he'd left the room.

"On the way home from school."

"*Where* on the way home from school?" It was a tone I'd heard before. But I could be a convincing liar when I needed to be.

I put the date at the top of the page—August 13, 1999—and it all came tumbling out: initial random rubbish about the rich, vivid patterns of the seat covers on the bus, then more personal stuff. As I wrote, the pressure lifted.

It had been a month before then that I'd sat on the bathroom floor and now it was back, the feeling that I was watching life through a pane of thick glass and that, whatever was out there, I wasn't designed for it.

The feeling I got writing wasn't dissimilar to the one I'd had in the bathroom, except there wasn't blood on the floor: there were words on a screen. The cursor moved from left to right, dragging a trail of letters behind it, accumulating into sentences and paragraphs, of my making and yet independent of me. 682 words. 1,394. 2,611. That was my first diary entry and I soon became addicted to it. I wrote in free periods, on trains, buses, in front of *Pop Idol* and when I couldn't sleep. Later, in uni lecture halls and hunched over my desk at work, concealing my labors like a schoolgirl shielding an exam paper. I wrote on my laptop, in notebooks, on my phone, on scraps of newspapers, on the blank pages in the backs of novels. I wrote everywhere and saved my outpourings religiously: paper copies in boxes and digital ones on memory sticks. I used to imagine the house or flat burning, a dishy fireman holding me back, saying, "No, Alice, it's too dangerous," but me breaking free and darting selflessly into the flames to retrieve them. "Can't you see?" I'd cry out. "It's my diary, it's *me*."

If the urge to go back into the bathroom seized me—when what I later came to refer to as *IT* was pressing in on me—I'd open my laptop. Often I'd write in the night or in the deep gnawing trough of a hangover, but the compulsion could grip me without warning. Only later did I learn the expression "displacement." Learnt, as well, that alcohol and drugs had the same mitigating effect, but they weren't consequence-free. I'd see my reflection on the screen, let go, hang on, make some sense of the madness, my antidote to life, my stereo, then later my iPod, on shuffle, bouncing from Ricky Martin to Pink, or Robbie to The Peppers, or Steps to R. Kelly.

I realized no one would be interested in it and anyone reading it would be convinced I was delusional, but I didn't care. I could breathe.

When I was sixteen I lost my eyebrows in a fire.

I had to burn my diaries, you see, I simply *had* to. Like a shop closing-down sale, everything had to go.

I'd come home early from school and my mum had them spread open on my bedroom floor. "What are you doing? Why are you snooping through my stuff?" I interrupted her, being my usual unreasonable self.

"Baby, you never told me."

I'd been desperate for three years to tell her about the faint white lines on my left wrist—how they weren't in fact from a nail on a wall or a broken sash window, a fight with some glass that the glass had won—but now my head went to mush. "Get out."

"I'm your mum."

"*How dare you go through my stuff?*" I shrieked. "*This is private!*"

"There's so much of me in you," she said, and she might have glanced down at my wrist, but the stuff about that was in a leather-bound pad Aunty Anna had given me one Christmas and there was no sign of that. "I'm your mum," she repeated.

"Yes, *unfortunately,*" I said, the old urge galloping through me—to run and not stop until I'd got so far no one would recognize me and then I'd be a different me, unspoiled and cool. "I wish you were dead! I wish *I* was dead."

As soon as I'd got shot of her, I fired up my laptop and repeatedly hit Delete. Later, when Mum and Dad had gone out—she was reluctant to leave me, but I'd promised if she gave me an hour's peace we'd chat later—I gathered up my paper diaries and dumped them in the metal barrel Dad burnt garden rubbish in. Then I threw a load of petrol over the top from a can in the garage and *whoooosh,* it went up in a ginormous orange flame that took off my eyebrows in a rush of warmth and fear.

"*Burn!*" I screamed, ripping the pages out, feeding the flames. I felt nothing for the girl who'd written this rubbish. I was a new me.

It was my sixteenth birthday.

The day after I burnt my diaries, I went back into the garden. Charred scraps of paper had blown onto the lawn. A robin appeared on the edge of the birdbath. He flapped his wings, splashed. He was having the best time. It occurred to me that I'd like that—to be in water. Swimming. I'd always been rubbish at it, but it would feel lovely: the cool currents, me held up, buoyed, as if I weighed less than myself.

"It didn't all burn, love," Mum said later that afternoon. "I haven't read any, I swear, but I fetched it in because you might like to have it one day."

I'm twenty-four now and I still haven't told my mum about the diary entry I burnt from when I was thirteen called: *Why I went to the bathroom to let the pain out.* This article will force a conversation I've been delaying for almost a decade. Perhaps that's why I was so keen for it to be published. I'll ensure we have that conversation before she reads this piece—and she *will* read it because she reads everything I write, even the dull stuff about planning appeals and nightclub fights; she reads it meticulously. She's given up cutting them out—her scrapbook got too big—but she never fails to proclaim how wonderful they are and I never fail to get that warm, uplifting bloom: my mum's proud of me.

I wasn't trying to kill myself, I'll tell her first off; all I was trying to do was let the bad stuff out. I'll tell her, as well, that those feelings never disappear, but you learn coping mechanisms, and for me keeping a diary was the best. Because here's the strangest thing: Guess what I did after she'd given me the carrier bag containing the black and burnt fragments of me between thirteen and sixteen? I went upstairs, flicked open my laptop and began writing.

Alice Salmon, age sixteen, I began.

I wrote about how the charred paper had left soot on my fingertips and how I'd smelt it like a baby instinctively exploring the world. I wrote about the robin, how the red of his tiny chest wasn't exactly red—actually more ochre. How he'd ruffled his feathers and shook himself: his existence the most important thing in the world to him, the only thing in the world.

Sometimes it's easier to forget, but remembering is what makes us human. Diaries help us do that, leafing those layers of life into order and logic. Anne Frank and Oscar Wilde recognized that. Samuel Pepys did. Sylvia Plath. Even fictitious characters like Bridget Jones do. But most are kept by ordinary people like you and me, and it's our scribblings that a groundbreaking project aims to celebrate. The National Diary Archive plans to preserve our everyday observations. I might well hand over a copy of mine.

What I did wasn't unusual: statistics suggest that more than one in ten girls self-harm. I was one of the lucky ones: I got away with it, the small scar virtually invisible now, apparent only at certain angles and in certain lights and only then if you know where to look.

I don't hate the girl who did it: the one who used to stare at the scalpels in art classes or her dad's razors in the medicine cabinet and think it would be *so easy,* so easy to drag one of those along the inside of her arm, the little white wrist like the tummy of a fish—one straight line would do it, like she was doing up a zip or tearing pieces of bread to feed the ducks. Far from it. She's my secret.

"Are you ready, Alice?" Mum had called up when I was sixteen and a day.

"Surprised T.G.I. Friday is open on a Thursday," Dad said in the car, his "restaurant" joke.

I laughed and decided to hang on in there, to see how far I could get and where this thing, life, might take me. A levels next. Then university, the prospect remote and intriguing: parties, brainy debates, freedom—me, my very own Joey Potter from *Dawson's Creek.*

I even wrote that down like it mattered. Because it did. It does. It was a diary and I knew all the while I kept one there'd be no blood on the bathroom floor.

**More information is available at:*

www.youngminds.org.uk
www.selfharm.co.uk
www.mind.org.uk

Voice-mail message left by Alice Salmon for Megan Parker,
February 4, 2012, 1:44 p.m.

Fuck, Meg, call me urgently . . . Can't believe the email I've just seen . . . Call me, need to talk to you before I get hold of Mum . . . I only went into her email to find a voucher thing . . . It looks genuine but it can't be. It's too awful to contemplate. I know you're on a hill squillions of miles away but pick your phone up, please . . . I'm still on the train. Fuckety fuck. I'm going to get drunk tonight. Jesus, I can't cope with this. Am so out of my depth. Call me . . .

Letter sent by Professor Jeremy Cooke,
July 6, 2012

Dearest Larry,

You died in November, but I didn't hear until January. Transpires there'd been quite a few obituaries, but I avoid reading the newspapers: it's all feral youths running riot, superinjunctions and the double-dip recession. They called you "great," a "game-changer," a "man who redefined his field." Qualities they'll never attribute to me.

We've been acquainted for more than fifty years. "Anyone know what a pen-friend is?" my English master had asked. "Cooke, you're to be paired with a boy in Canada. Specifically, New Brunswick."

I pored for hours over my first communication to give the right impression. I even admitted—superciliousness disguised as humor you mistook for irony—I was disappointed not to have been conjoined with a Papua New Guinean headhunter.

Your reply began "Hiya Jeremy," a greeting that leapt out at me for its informality. "I'm Larry Gutenberg and I'm eleven years old and I'm a pupil at Adena Elementary School."

"I wish to be a great scientist," I informed you. It was a badge of honor that my letters were as free from spelling mistakes as yours. I used to imagine you reading them, nodding, impressed, thinking: *He's like me, this Cooke chap.*

"I was wondering whether I might be able to visit my chum Larry," I inquired of my father after we'd been corresponding for some months. "I'd be incredibly grateful."

"You two are like a pair of little homos," he said dismissively. I later learnt it was my mother, not he, who wanted children.

We wrote every quarter, through O and A levels. The swinging sixties might never have happened as far as I was concerned. "I'm going up to Warwick in the autumn," I informed you when I was in the upper sixth, aping the language of Oxbridge, and you never drew me up on that, despite presumably spotting my ruse.

Then there were your ideas. Already then they were arcing away from me. You were leaving me. It came to me as a revelation, in some ways a eureka moment, the instant when I felt: *This is as far as I can go.* By the time I was in my mid-twenties, I realized I was never going to be a truly phenomenal scientist.

While my research kept running into dead ends and cul-de-sacs—while I kept returning like some fated migratory animal to the point where I'd begun—your work attracted ever more plaudits. I witnessed your successes with an alien sensation: one almost entirely devoid of jealousy. I wanted to be there with you, to celebrate, to stand alongside you. You were the scientist I'd always wished I could be: intuitive, brilliant, fearless, alive. They even named a law after you. Gutenberg's theorem. When I heard the term uttered in revered, respectful tones, I felt like screaming: *He was mine long before the eponymous law. Mine, all mine.*

Then came 2004 and *The Genes Department*. The holy grail: a serious science book that flew off the shelves. As I turned the pages, swept along by your intoxicating currents of theory—as I was taken on those elaborate, delicious tangents—I felt a mounting sense of rage. Blind fury, in fact. Every damn page bathed in this white light. It was like I was holding the very essence of science in my hand. Bright and beautiful and simple, but new and incredible. Moment after moment of it. I'd have given my life for just one of those pages, one of those moments. Jealousy, hitherto so conspicuously absent, flooded into me. *You complete bastard,* I'd thought. It was like you'd been unfaithful to me. The one thing I always wanted to do, write a book, and you beat me to that.

I distinctly recall when I finished reading it. It was the afternoon of December 9, 2004. I know because it was the day of the annual anthropology party, and that bash is always on the first Thursday of December. Walking to it, my head full of vitriol, I'd bumped into Alice. *Well, well,* I'd thought. *What a coincidence. You.*

You never realized, Larry, but you were partly responsible for what transpired that night. You'd quoted the opening stanza from Robert Herrick's poem in your final chapter. *Gather ye rosebuds while ye may . . .* I'd interpreted it as I had so much of what you said: advice, instruction, gospel.

How do you feel about featuring in my Alice book, old chap? I'm immensely excited. Possible titles keep presenting themselves to me. *The Sum of the Parts* is my current favorite. It's a source of immense regret to me that you'll never read it.

Unlike the pyretic media coverage, my watchword shall be "balance." Jesus, the story is still front-page news as the public canters from theories of accident to suicide to worse. The more coverage it gets, the more coverage it gets. Our journalists do this: jump on isolated tragedies, treating them as talismanic of all the other similar such ones they don't have the time or space or budget to cover. Alice Salmon: the perils of a night out when you're twenty-something.

"I'm Larry Gutenberg's wife and I have bad news," the note from Marlene began. She only contacted me because she'd stumbled across our letters when sorting through your possessions, a task she'd put off until after Christmas. I can understand why you wouldn't have shared our correspondence with your wife. A man needs secrets, a sense that he's more than what those around him imagine.

Marlene says you finished your coffee, pulled on your favorite jacket, announced you were taking the dog out and never came back. I've tried to view it as a Captain Oates–like episode: in reality, you stumbled on the pavement and were dead by the time the ambulance arrived. Not a way for a man who had a theorem named after him to go. My friend, the great Larry Gutenberg.

You going off radar has floored me, old chap. That you could slip out of view, unnoticed. Remember how I used to badger you to write your autobiography? "Shucks," you'd said, "isn't the science enough?" Sooner or later someone was bound to write your biography. Wondered what they'd have said about us? I know what I would have. What I will say. Three words. *I love you.*

I'll treat you well in my book, Larry. I promise. I've arranged with Marlene to take possession of our correspondence—she sought approval from your sons first—and I rather fancy I'll be including it in my little tome. After all, I'm never more honest than I am with you, and we'd all benefit from a smidgen more honesty. No one more so than Alice.

Kids don't get to become pen-friends now, do they? The Internet's opened the globe up, taken away that mystique and intrigue. It's made everyone a potential pen-friend. Either that, or a stalker.

Yours as ever,
J

Email received by Alice Salmon,
February 4, 2012, 1:52 p.m.

Subject: Delivery Status Notification (Failure)

The email titled "You????" you attempted to send at 1:51 p.m. on February 4, 2012 failed to reach the chosen recipient—jfhcooke@tmail.com—because the destination mailbox is not recognized.

Please do not reply to this email as it is an automatically generated delivery status notification.

Voice-mail message left by Alice Salmon for Megan Parker, *February 4, 2012, 6:31 p.m.*

Left about twenty messages for my mum but can't talk to her now, not like this. Been drinking and bad Alice has come out to play . . . , old Alice. Wish I was on a hill in the Lake District with you guys, a long way away from all this shit . . . The evening's going tits up and talk about a rave from the grave, I could have sworn I spotted that freak Cooke earlier. He's either got a doppelgänger or I imagined it. My head's all over the place after seeing that email . . . It can't be, Meg, surely it can't. It's too gross to consider. It makes me want to puke; it's too yuck. "The days of us"—what the fuck does that even mean? Will ring Mum tomorrow; could be a sick hoax, I suppose. Maybe I should pretend I never saw it? Guess who texted me earlier too: Ben! Wish I was sober and could talk to you and listen to you. All I do is talk at you these days . . . So sorry for getting that drunk last time we saw each other; my ankle's still killing me! Am seeing Lukey Monday; def made my mind up about him. All clear . . . wine and lager clear! How long do voice-mail messages go on for, Parkster? Can talk for England, that's what you always say. Wonder where I got that from? Pick up pick up pick up pick up. Piiiiiiiiick up, Megan. Please. Am outside pub. All changed down here. Don't recognize this street. Can hear the river. Nothing's forever; we're all something passing stopped. This email to Mum—

PART FOUR

Translating the World

Post on Truth Speakers web forum by Lone Wolf, *June 21, 2012, 11:22 p.m.*

Here's a fact about little miss perfect Alice Salmon. All over the media she is but no one's mentioned she got her boyfriend to try to KILL me. His name was Ben Finch and he was a C**T. Sorry, I realize swearing's against forum rules, but it's the truth, plus I'm a moderator, so report me!

I tried spinning him a line about the photos he'd found of Alice in my room being for a night-school project but he totally flipped out. "She's mine," he was yelling as he stuck the boot in. "Mine mine mine." My face, my gut, my back, my bollocks, my kidneys—they taught him well at Eton or Harrow or whichever institution he was programmed in. Yes, that C**T knew where to kick all right!

She was different, though. Me and her we had a connection. We shared a dump of a house in the second year, 2 Caledonian Road, and we'd meet in the lounge in the night. "What's keeping you awake, Mocksy?" she'd ask and we'd confide in each other, and I could forgive her Ben Finch then. "We need to stick together," I said once and she didn't disagree.

"Dump him," I begged, the morning after he'd given me the pasting. "He'll do this to you one day." I showed her the bruises that had gone all purple, although they'd had a bit of help from me and a bicycle pump—well, I had to leave her in no doubt what sort of psycho Ben Finch was.

"What's wrong with me? I'm such an idiot," she said, then got defensive and full-on denied it was him, but he'd have sworn her to secrecy. Yes, that BULLY would have forced her to keep schtum because this would wreck his rep, good old Ben Finch, the life and soul of the party, prizes from the rowing club, destined for the board of Daddy's business.

"I don't care if it hurts if it makes you see sense," I told Alice. "Can I have a kiss?"

"You're such a freak, Mocksy," she said.

"I'll kiss you one day."

Then she went schizo. "I'm glad Ben did this," she said. "You deserved it. I asked him to warn you off."

See, the TRUTH will out if you push hard enough and her dying is justice because bad shit happens to bad people and she probably got off on it, picturing his size ten brogues stomping down on me.

I tried to sell a piece about her to the nationals after she snuffed it but they weren't interested, the idiots. Billed it as the real deal: all the goss from the man who knew her best. Student housemate, yes, virtually an ex-boyfriend, I said. Offered it to them all as an exclusive, but the tossers wouldn't recognize good writing if it bit them on the back of the hand. Once they read what I've got to say they'll come running, though.

After the Caledonian Road lot went out, I lay on Alice's bed and imagined her washing my wounds and they hurt but it was a nice hurt and it made me love her more so I added her mug with the elephant on it to the collection of her stuff stashed in my wardrobe—a scarf, a pen she'd chewed the top of, a bra. I pretended they were gifts from her.

"It got broken," I said to Alice when she inquired about her mug. It was no big deal; a lot got broken in Caledonian Road.

I've gone off topic because I began this thread to talk about an EVIL university professor. I've been doing research of my own, you see, and soon the individual in question will be brought to his knees. Justice is coming.

Extract from Alice Salmon's diary,
March 18, 2011, age 24

"What's the secret to a long marriage?" I asked. (Yes, yes, I appreciate it's a clichéd question, but readers would be interested.)

"Letting the other person think they're in charge," Queenie said.

"Agreeing," Alf added, grinning.

They'd shepherded me into the front room, brought tea and biscuits on a chintzy tray and passed me their "diamond wedding" album. "If we get to our sixty-fifth anniversary, we're going to the fun fair," Queenie said.

"The posh one at Thorpe Park," Alf said, hobbling off to let the dog out.

"I'll definitely come back and interview you after that," I told them.

"You'll have long since moved on by then, dear," she said. "Clever girl like you."

I've just been promoted. Chief reporter, no less. Whoop whoop!

They showed me their drawings of the South Downs. The painting pensioners. The green-fingered eighty-somethings. The love-struck octogenarians. This is how this job conditions your brain: sound bites.

"I've got a confession for you, Alice," Queenie said. "I rarely read newspapers. There's more truth in a decent novel."

I could almost hear the editor sneer: *How were the crumblies? Live out the interview, did they?* Juicier quotes, he'd be after. I inquired: "Have you got any advice for youngsters, Mrs. Stones?"

"Live every day as if it's your last," she said.

That's not a bad quote, I thought. But "depth and conflict," that was the editor's adage. "You must get on each other's nerves a teensy bit?" I said, aiming for that gray area fractionally beyond rhetorical.

"He can be a cantankerous old goat, but I wouldn't be without him." We watched Alf on the patio, waiting for the dog to wear itself out. "I expect you went to university, didn't you?" she said. "I wish I had. We didn't back then, particularly girls. If you need a line or two about regrets for your article, that's one."

"I studied English," I told her.

"That's what I'd have done." She shook her head fondly at her husband, maneuvering himself sideways down a patio step. "Soppy old bugger reckons I'll always be his princess."

Always won't go on forever, I could have said. But I'd learnt to expect this particular contradiction: how happy stories could make me sad.

"Presumably you're courting. What's he like, your young man?"

"He's called Luke."

"Luke, that's my grandson's name. Handsome, is he?"

I pulled out my phone, skipped to the photo of him on his bike outside the Houses of Parliament, and when I passed it to her she avoided touching the screen, as if she was fearful she'd smudge it.

"He's got a kind face. Handsome, mind."

The TV was on mute, *Radio Times* on the arm of the settee, *Poirot* circled in red.

"We lost a child," Queenie said, unprompted.

A life not without tragedy, I thought. *No, I will not go there.* I put my notebook down and she leafed through pictures of a boy, ten or eleven or twelve—kids that age all merge into one—and traced her finger round his black-and-white outline. "You can never have enough photographs, because this can be an unreliable tool," she said, tapping her head. She'd had her hair done—presumably for the interview, for me. It seemed so disrespectful, attempting to distill their lives into this one thing—an article, a diamond wedding, an article about a diamond wedding—because a life's not one thing, it can't be, it mustn't be. She said: "You get to a point where you forget what you've forgotten."

"I write stuff down in a diary."

"We all translate the world in different ways," she said. "I like photographs. Incidentally, can we get a copy of the ones the man takes later?"

He'd stand them in the doorway or persuade them to sit on the bench in the garden, holding hands or the picture of their dead son. He'd say "Smile" and "Lovely" and "That's perfect" and go back to the office and burn the shots of them onto a disc, correcting the colors and the exposures and balancing skin tones and erasing ugly details, then do his expenses and get a flyer to beat the traffic.

"He looks a nice lad, your Luke."

When he'd inquired about my day, I'd explained I'd met this incredibly sweet couple and they'd said he was handsome and referred to him as a lad. Tomorrow morning, at six forty, the alarm having gone off twice, I'd nudge him sleepily and say, "Come on, *lad,* shift yourself." Then later, when he makes me a playlist or buys flowers or leaves surprise parcels on the doorstep, chocolates or a soppy note, "You're a good lad."

"You love him, don't you?"

"It's early days yet."

"Don't be coy. You do, don't you? I'm eighty, I can tell."

There was grunting from the kitchen and a bowl clattering to the floor, where Alf was feeding the dog. I tried to visualize Luke old, but couldn't get beyond him in the fancy-dress outfit he'd worn to that party—the cardy with leather buttons, the stick, the flat cap. Perhaps he'd be *cantankerous*? It was an old person's sentiment, an old person's word (and definitely my word of this entry!).

"You'll probably live together before you get married, won't you, you and your Luke?"

"We've only been seeing each other a year," I said.

The term "housewife" skittered into view. Sod that. What about all the alternatives? Alice Salmon, investigative journalist. Editor. Music journo. Charity worker. Traveler. Famous novelist. Party animal. Fuckup. I said: "Maybe at some point in the future."

"Dear, the future isn't all that far away."

"I still haven't ruled out jacking it all in and doing a world tour," I said as a compromise. "Australia, Argentina, Thailand. I've always fancied Mexico. No one settles down until they're at *least* in their late twenties these days."

She spread out her family tree on the table: a patchwork of names and numbers and interconnected lines, grooving backwards, upwards, the dates increasingly remote, the names those in novels: Winston, Victoria, Ethel, Alfred. There, a bit up from the bottom—beneath them four children, seven grandchildren and two great-grandchildren—and connected by a single sharp line: Alfred Stones and Maud Walker.

"Maud's a pretty name," I said.

"I always fancied myself as more of a Rose. Can I give you a bit of advice? For you, not for your newspaper. Don't try to be everything. Your generation is lucky, but you have to pick your path." She touched a corner of her family tree. "For me, having my place on this feels comfortable."

What a peculiar job I have, paid to sip tea and pry into the hearts of strangers and capture the outpourings on a Dictaphone or in the shorthand I've got to 100 wpm.

"When I heard you were popping round to visit us, I worked out how many days sixty years is," Queenie said. "It's 21,900—excluding leap years. 'Where can we live but days?' Expect you're familiar with that poem, aren't you? It's Larkin."

"My mum likes him—or she likes to hate him."

"He was a foul specimen."

A hazy memory stirred in me. School, and Meg scribbling on the inside cover of my file. A clock on the wall, ten minutes till the end of the period. It was a Friday, as today was. *Days.* I saw myself at my desk in the office, Sky News on the TV on the wall above my head—coverage of the Fukushima meltdown on loop—glancing at that clock and rushing this piece so I could get away to meet Luke.

"There'll come a day when they don't wake us," Queenie said, pouring the last of the tea, bony marbles under the skin of her knuckles. "The days."

" 'Where can we live but days?' " I said, reciting two or three lines of the poem automatically.

Alf reappeared. "Feel free to portray me as a love rat," he said. "Just don't have us on a bloody journey. We're going to be on a proper one of those soon—the biggest one!"

I went back to the office and cobbled the story together, then wrote this. I needed to get the details down so I'd have something to remember when all I could do was remember, especially if you get less good at it, as Queenie maintains. I'd also like to have something to show a young me if she came knocking to ask about my life when I was eighty. I wasn't appalled at how the piece turned out. It did them about as much justice as you can in 500 words. I kept a few bits back—quotes I assumed they'd rather me not include, which I'm not sharing even here, and the aspects of me that I obviously saved for *here.* Like how Queenie had asked: "How do you feel when you're not with Luke?"

"As if something's missing," I'd replied. "As if a piece of *me* is missing."

Email sent by Professor Jeremy Cooke,
February 2, 2012

From: jfhcooke@gmail.com
To: Elizabeth_salmon101@hotmail.com
Subject: The days of us

Dear Elizabeth,

Long time no speak—or rather no "e-speak," as contemporary phraseology would have it. How the devil are you? It feels like an eternity since the days of us.

You'll be perplexed as to why the hell this old dinosaur is making contact. Well, I've picked up from the Internet that Alice may be back in this fine city for some sort of reunion this weekend and it's rather sent me diving headlong into the past, sentimental old buffoon that I am. Life's short, Liz, or it certainly is in my case—so why shouldn't I break cover?

I bear scant resemblance to the old me. In fact, with the exception of my regulation uniform of cords and tweed, you'd barely recognize me. Would I you? I've tried googling you with limited success, unlike Alice, who's virtually omnipresent online. A bad guitar player but a good cook of Italian food—that's the résumé she gave one site. I never realized she played the guitar.

I'm not expecting a visit—our contact was minimal when she was a student here—and, knowing her, she'll be constantly surrounded by a coterie of pals. I'm not unreservedly repugnant to former students, though; I do keep in touch with a few. Their motive may be that they've identified me as a prospective referee, but it allows me to feel my endeavors are not entirely wasted.

I wasn't entirely repugnant to you, Liz, was I? I do regard our spell together with great fondness. You were beautiful. You still are, I expect. I was in pieces after we went our separate ways, not least due to the circumstances, particularly vis-à-vis your actions.

I'm not anticipating a reply to this email—although one would be most welcome—but felt compelled to reach out. Metaphorically speaking, of course. Which, with hindsight, is how the majority of my existence has been. It's as if these last sixty years have been, not so much an act of living, but more an act of observing. We weren't metaphorical, though, were we? We were very real, very literal.

Apologies for the intrusion. It felt important to say I hadn't forgotten us. There's a curious sentiment. *Us*.

Yours,
Jem

Notes made by Luke Addison on his laptop,
March 7, 2012

I defy anyone not to have been creative with the truth given the circumstances.

I couldn't exactly tell the police the facts—that I'd yelled at you and grabbed your hair—could I? They'd never believe that was the extent of it.

There's another factor as well. Huge chunks of that night have disappeared. I simply can't recall them. That's how pissed I was. Yes, Officer, I did have her by the hair but I can assure you I wouldn't have subsequently hurt her, even though I can't actually remember. I might as well sign my own arrest warrant.

What I mustn't do—what I've promised you I won't do—is forget the bits of you I can remember. Your green eyes and the crow's feet you once claimed in a startled panic to have spotted. Stuff like that, it vanishes so quickly, and the rest of the world is dead set on making me forget. It wouldn't take much. My boss encouraging me to oversee a big project; it might be exactly what I need, to get my teeth into something concrete. The lads at the rugby club insisting I come over on Saturday for a run-out: it'll do me a power of good. Letting my colleagues persuade me to go to the Porterhouse for a quick one: Come on, it'll be a laugh, I deserve it, the whole team will be there—and three hours later another girl could be ringing me, so I've got *her* number in my phone and you'd be a former girlfriend, the one who died, the one I'd taken to Margate, the one I'd get over. No. No. NO.

I stand in Waterstones and leaf through books you loved. I listen to your summer 2011 playlist because that was the best summer *ever.* I go back to Southampton to immerse myself in your favorite city, back to the river, the scene of the crime, the place where we'd fought. I stare at photos of you on my phone as if you might materialize by magic if I can only concentrate enough.

At work I sit like a zombie and shrug when clients ask "Where are you on this, Luke?" Spreadsheets swim in front of me. Voices echo unanswered around meeting rooms. What are we forecasting for third-quarter profits? What will 2013 look like for our business? Where can we take out costs?

Colleagues reassure me it's normal, but covertly they love it: a story that's on the Internet in *their* very own office. A death, the whiff of a crime. I pass their desks and they frantically close browsers or snap shut their phones. You don't have to be a genius to establish the rest of those exchanges. He's holding up remarkably well. He's falling apart. He's almost *too* calm.

And now I'm writing this down, despite my natural comfort zone—as you so frequently pointed out—being diagrams and numbers. "Bet you'll put *this* in your diary, won't you?" I'd snapped by the river. "It's pathetic, the way you'll pour your heart out on a piece of paper."

"'S laptop," you'd said, and rage had boiled inside me.

You can forget pretty much anything. It's easy: you merely have to set your mind to it—block it out or keep replaying an alternate version so frequently that it becomes the reality. But I knew I'd never forget grabbing your hair.

"If you ever touch me like that again, I'll report you to the police," you'd said.

It had started to go curly where it was wet from the snow and the palm of my hand tingled from its touch.

Afterwards, I walked until I found a late bar and necked cider and stabbed at a jukebox and danced on my own and when two lads laughed I thought, *You know nothing about me or what I've done,* and I had whisky and woke at five a.m. on the floor of my hotel room, my arm up on the side of the bed like I was clinging to a shipwreck, sick on the carpet, flashbacks to the night before breaking into my consciousness like stones smashing glass. Then I'd sat on the floor in my boxer shorts and tried to piece together the previous few hours, as we'd done so often, and I cried like a baby.

I'd had a scalding shower, scrubbed myself: had to get what had happened off me, had to get *you* off me, then got a train back to Waterloo. Crossing the platform, scuttling past the WHSmith shop, the newspaper headlines jumped out at me—middle-class incomes under pressure, Facebook valued at £100 billion, the charges that might be brought as a result of the *Costa Concordia* disaster—it had winded me. What I'd done. I went to the nearest pub, bought a pint of Stella and a double vodka and Coke.

"I didn't kill her," I said to Charlie a few days later.

"Mate, no one suggested you did," he replied.

Bizarre that we weren't spotted by the river or caught on CCTV.

Last night I read it's vital that victims of crime cooperate to produce a photofit within twenty-four hours. Otherwise the impression they generate can diverge wildly from the reality. If the police don't solve a crime—especially a serious one—within twenty-four hours, the chances of doing so plummet, this article said.

In that beer garden in Waterloo, my phone rang, a number I didn't recognize. "It's Robert Salmon speaking. Where are you?" he asked. "Are you alone?"

That was when I started lying.

Later still—two Stellas and two double vodkas later—that massive man at the bar, me thinking: *You'll do.*

And now I'm staring at the email you sent me on Friday, February 3, the day before you died, marginally before our two months was up. I'd found it three weeks after you died in my junk folder, shunted there because of the attachment, which seemingly flagged it as a virus risk, sandwiched between spam from a man claiming to need urgent cash because he was stranded in the Philippines and one offering me affordable office supplies.

"*US*," you'd typed in the subject field, and my initial reaction had been: Why had Al emailed me about America? But then I'd recalled we'd talked about a holiday there—visiting Ground Zero, the Empire State, eating bagels, taking in a show on Broadway. Maybe head out to the West Coast. *Dawson's Creek, The O.C., 90210*. "The vicarious landscape of my childhood," you referred to it as. But you'd meant "*US*" as in me and you.

I count the days since you died. Thirty-two. 768 hours. A photofit now would bear a barely approximate resemblance.

The police, your family, your friends, that man in the pub, Megan, the contractor who I sat in a meeting room with today and complained about "under-delivery." Stupid, they are, all of them, ignorant and in the dark. It's me and you: we're the ones who know what happened. It's our secret.

"Hey Mr. L," your email began.

Extract from transcript of interview with Jessica Barnes conducted at Southampton Central police station led by Detective Superintendent Simon Ranger,
April 5, 2012, 5:20 p.m.

SR: To reiterate, you're not under arrest and are free to leave at any time, but please can you confirm your full name, age and address, and that you're happy for this interview to be recorded?

JB: Jessica Barnes. I'm nineteen and live at 74a Hartley Road. Yes.

SR: Jessica, can you explain what you did on the evening of Saturday, February 4?

JB: Me and a load of friends had a night out in town, seven or eight of us—do you need names?

SR: Not at this stage, but it would be helpful to hear which pubs you went to.

JB: We started off in the Rock and Revs, then went to the High Life and ended up in the Ruby Lounge. Went to Carly's Bar as well—oh, yes, and the New Inn.

SR: The Ruby Lounge is by the river, isn't it? Was there any reason you went there?

JB: It's a good place to end the night: they're open till two and it's proper buzzing.

SR: Towards the end of the evening, I gather you became separated from your friends. How did that arise?

JB: I'd had an argument with Mark.

SR: Mark?

JB: My boyfriend. He was out with his mates, so we'd arranged to meet up at the Ruby Lounge, but he was being a right douchebag, flirting with Lottie. No way was I going to stand around watching that, so I was out of there. Went along that shortcut path by the river; it brings you out by Hooper Road and I was going to get a night bus there.

SR: What time would this have been?

JB: No idea, was ages ago. Would have mentioned it before, but I thought nothing of it. Like, only heard about the drowned girl on the news this morning; was at my dad's and it was on the telly. I never watch news. Why should I if it doesn't affect me? Might have been about midnight.

SR: So this was when you saw a couple on a bench on the other side of the river?

JB: Yes, I told the policeman that earlier.

SR: It would be helpful if you could share your impression of what they were doing.

JB: It was a long way away and it was snowing and shit.

SR: How old would you guess they were?

JB: Older than me, maybe thirty.

SR: But presumably you could make out roughly what they were doing?

JB: They was definitely arguing, because I heard bits. I was there for a few minutes having a ciggie while I decided whether to go back to the Ruby Lounge and have it out with Mark. Is it that dead girl off the telly? It is, isn't it? I'll be devastated if it is.

SR: Until we establish more details, we'd prefer to keep her as "the girl on the bench." Can you describe either of them?

JB: He might have had a black shirt on—I was only there for a few minutes. Wasn't paying them no attention; my head was all over the place and none of my business was it? I wasn't going to go all emo. It's her, isn't it? They said she drowned. The students are right stuck-up wankers but she looked nice. Am I going to get into trouble? I haven't done anything wrong.

SR: No one's suggesting you have, Jessica. But an extremely serious incident did occur, which may or may not have involved one or both of the individuals you seemingly encountered. It would inform our investigation if you could recollect more of their exchange.

JB: They was miles away. The river's well wide there, so it was hard to make out, like, when you're on the phone and the signal's shit and you get bits and then nothing and then bits again. Think they was planning a weekend away, because I heard her mention Prague. I saw this thing about it on the telly; all the posh couples go there for breaks.

SR: What other snippets of their conversation did you pick up? Did you hear either of them refer to each other by name?

JB: Yes—she called him Luke.

SR: Are you positive about that?

JB: Yes, deffo, because my kid brother's been watching all the *Star Wars* films and he's been going round saying "Luke, I am your father," and that's what made me notice.

SR: Anything else?

JB: This'll sound nuts but she said something about lemmings.

SR: OK, let's try a different tack. How were they arguing? Would you say it was an *angry* argument?

JB: What other sort is there? Thing is, you know how some arguments you're constantly *on* it? Well, them two were worked up, then calm, then worked up, and there were bits when they were either not talking or whispering. Couple of points she gave him a right sledging and once he fell over, stumbled onto his knees. It was like he was begging. Might have slipped on the snow, I suppose.

SR: How drunk was the girl on the bench? Was she more or less drunk than you were?

JB: Less. No, more. She was just a drunk girl. It's her, isn't it? They said she was a crime buster for violence against women, is that right?

SR: Others in your situation might have called the police?

JB: Say I had called the old bill—sorry, *you lot*—what would I have said? I'd have gone, "There's two people on the other side of the river," and they'd have gone, "What are they doing?" and I'd have gone, "They're on a bench talking." They'd hardly have mobilized special branch, would they?

SR: Jessica, this isn't a joke. Someone's died.

JB: Sorry, but you're making out it's my fault and it's not. I'm not going to get in trouble, am I? I can't lose my job; I've got a baby. I'm sorry. I knew I should have rung 999 when he started pushing her around. They said on some Internet thing that she was pregnant—is that true?

SR: Pushing her around? Elaborate on that.

JB: After he'd fallen over she was cracking up and he got right in her face and put his arms round her, but not in a good way. I'm sorry, I'm sorry, please don't arrest me. I've got a baby . . .

Letter sent by Professor Jeremy Cooke,
July 9, 2012

Larry,

Remember I told you years ago about that shrink, the supercilious fellow with the Roman nose and birdlike shoulders? Well, I've been reexamining the notes I made from our meetings. He actually had the gall to accuse me of not liking him very much.

"Don't take it personally," was my riposte. "It's *people* I don't much like."

"Curious," he said, "to hear that from an anthropologist."

"To an anthropologist, existence *is* curious," I informed him. "Curious and baffling." It was like intellectual tennis. "Accept it," I said. "You're fundamentally incapable of mending me."

"It's not about mending you; it's about you acquiring a deeper understanding of yourself. How about you elaborate on why you've chosen to visit me, Jeremy?"

His repeated use of my first name irked me. After a pause, doubtlessly of exactly the length he'd have been taught at some second-rate polytechnic, he shrilled, "There are no incorrect answers here."

"There's not a huge amount else to do on Wednesday afternoons. The students play sport."

It was the second consecutive Wednesday I'd trooped like a battle-beaten soldier into this supposedly highly regarded and discreet practice in a residential suburb of Winchester, despite my opinion of shrinks being far from positive. I'd been taught to take an evidential-based approach and they're so bloody woolly. Not that she'd have cared, but Fliss was gloriously oblivious, as she had been to where I'd spent so many previous Wednesday afternoons when the students played sport: locked away in tawdry hotels with the latest recruit to the English faculty, Elizabeth Mullens.

He scratched his mangy beard, crossed and uncrossed his legs. Clearly gay. In the silence that ensued, it enveloped me again: that dense, cloudy anger at his probing and at me—for *needing* to be here with a diminutive forensic man approximately five years my junior with tiny round spectacles worn presumably in a bid to convey gravitas. "She thinks I'm playing squash," I said. "Fliss does. My wife."

"Why does she think that?"

"Because that's what I told her."

"Does she always think what you tell her?"

"Believe me, she hardly *ever* thinks what I tell her."

"Should she?"

"Of course not. She has her own mind."

"Does that worry you?"

"Not as much as the tyranny of Ayatollah Khomeini, or these bloody trade unions."

Even then, it dawned on me how redundant I was rendering the exchange. It had been the evening after the party when my wife had confronted me. She'd been washing up when I'd arrived home and when I'd said, "Hello, darling, how was your day?" she didn't turn round, as she didn't when I said, "You're up late," or "I'm off to bed, I'm bushed"; but when she finally did she was crying. "Martin rang," she said.

I froze.

"He mentioned he bumped into you yesterday evening—how *was* the party?"

I should have cut my losses there and then, Larry, and admitted it. That might have counted in my favor: mitigation. But I'd pressed on. "Boring. Typical academic get-together. You know what they're like."

"Actually, I don't. Explain to me."

"Pearce is still on the brink of resigning; Shields remains convinced he's about to get the call from Nobel; Mills is clinically incapable of having a seminal idea."

Some men cover their tracks naturally well; others teach themselves. I fell into neither camp; I sounded ridiculous—as if my wife had asked, "What shape is the earth?" and I'd responded "Cuboid." "Boring academics blowing smoke up each other's arses," I added.

"Boring academics from the English department?"

Behind me, a clicking from the AGA cooker, my wife's pride and joy.

"Yes."

"How's that new girl getting on?" she asked. "The one who was profiled in the newsletter: Liz Mullens?"

"Fine, I gather." The wooden table, the dog in her basket, a box of cereal and two bowls on the side, ready for the morning. As an environmental consultant, my wife frequently referred to the notion of "habitat." *This is mine,* I thought. *Ours*. Without this, without her, what would I be, what would I do?

"You promised you'd look after me forever."

Larry, that scruffy shrink, a budding Bolshevik if ever there was one, was relentless. "How about *I* get to ask *you* some questions?" I asked to interrupt the bombardment.

"We won't make much headway that way."

"Please, one."

"Ultimately it's your money."

I could have hugged him in that instant, my skinny adversary with the string of worthless letters after his name, because contempt wasn't a sentiment I was typically displayed, at least not to my face. "What *is* sex?"

"Right now, I'm sensing it's an area we should explore."

That response made me want to reach out and give his pigeon face a sharp slap, like I might a child who'd misbehaved, if we'd had one. "Exploring it's what's got me into trouble," I said.

"You can't blame sex. Whatever you've done, you've managed all by yourself."

After a slow intake of breath, he added: "You still haven't explained why you're here."

"Because it's like seeing a prostitute. There are no consequences: it's entirely transactional."

"There you go again, back to sex."

I loathed his relentless picking. But he was right: I was thirty-five years old and part of me was broken. Silence, and the specter of one of my greatest fears, inarticulacy, clung to me like wet fog.

"Would you like to share with me who she was?"

I hadn't at that point directly confessed to my infidelity, so he must have filled in the blanks. "Why, fancy giving her a call? You could hook up: she's not choosy!" I heard the petulance and spite, and cringed.

"Are you still in contact?"

"She threatened to put a carving knife between my shoulder blades if I ever went near her again."

It came back to me how I'd once dropped to my knees before Liz and she'd cradled my head in her hands as she might have a child's, or as if I were a piece of pottery she was shaping, and the sharp absence of her stung me: her taste, her smell, a coppery tang on my tongue, a low-down ache in the pit of my stomach, my balls. Bet you've never felt that, have you? I almost spat.

Fliss had recounted the details of her and Martin's conversation with a dispassionate disinterest, like she was relating a scene from a novel: Rushdie's *Midnight's Children,* perhaps, or the latest theory on one of the genus of flowers in which she specialized. "After he called, I had a rummage around in your jackets."

"You did *what*?" I said, my righteous indignation never sounding more ill-conceived.

She handed me a piece of paper, a restaurant receipt. Her lip quivered. "How *could* you?"

"How are you feeling?" my shrink asked.

Wet on my cheek; the sod, he'd made me shed a tear. "Well done, you've earned your money today. Damn perplexing behavior, the shedding of tears," I said, scrabbling into the familiar architecture of a debate, "the function of which remains the source of much contention in scientific circles."

"Throw me a bone here, Jeremy—one professional to another."

"I'm sick of feeling as if life's escaping me. Can you stop that, Dr. Richard Carter? Can you? Please."

"No," he said. "Only you can do that."

"No one's faithful these days," I said, aware it wasn't an entirely unfounded observation, because with the exception of brain-dead, cockless old stiffs like Devereux, the whole campus was at it. "It's the eighties: everyone's shagging everyone else."

"I can assure you they're not."

"Are you married?" I asked.

"No," he said.

"Never taken a wife, eh?" I heard myself, and it was with chagrin. The man who extolled the benefits of discussion and debate, who believed that the human species was set apart by a handful of attributes—one of the key ones of which was our ability to communicate—reduced to using that gift as a child would. She'd thrown a colander at me. Fliss had. Sounds amusing now—the sort of scene that might feature in one of those dreadful soap operas—but I can assure you it wasn't then. It had connected with my forehead and split the skin, freeing a sticky string of blood.

"Surely, intelligence," my shrink said, "is the ability to make yourself and those around you happy. You've clearly failed in that respect."

He had me; the little shit had me.

Nonchalantly, he added: "How is the woman who's not your wife dealing with the situation?"

"She tried to kill herself."

Twitter messages to @AliceSalmon1 from @FreemanisFree, ***between January 16 and January 27, 2012***

How's that walking of yours on the common?

The lord said justice is mine.

Enjoy your Italian meal last night?

Nice hairdryer you got for Christmas.

That picture of flowers on yr bedroom wall new?

Like to party, pretty girl?

Coming to get you.

Extract from transcript of interview with Luke Addison conducted at Southampton Central police station led by Detective Superintendent Simon Ranger,
April 6, 2012, 1:25 p.m.

LA: This is a joke; I was her boyfriend.

SR: Were you? Because we've been informed that the pair of you weren't actually an item at the time of her death.

LA: It's complicated.

SR: Explain to us how it was complicated. I gather yourself and Alice had separated.

LA: We were working through some issues, yes.

SR: Issues?

LA: I slept with someone else and Alice needed space to get her head round that.

SR: So she dumped you?

LA: No, we were having a break. But we were going to get back together—she was well up for that.

SR: I'm presuming she was the instigator of this break rather than you? Must have hit you pretty hard.

LA: I was gutted.

SR: How would you respond to the suggestion that you're a bit of a ladies' man?

LA: I loved Alice.

SR: Be that as it may, you're someone who likes to get his own way, are you not? Would you describe yourself as controlling?

LA: No, of course not.

SR: But you're a physically big man. What are you, six one, thirteen-plus stone? Loud, a handful, one of the boys, a man who likes a drink, never knew how a night out would end when Luke was around—these are ways you've been described. One of your colleagues dubbed you a bully.

LA: I was mad about her.

SR: Mad enough to push her in a river?

LA: Go screw yourself.

SR: Let's keep calm, shall we, sir?

LA: Would you be calm if you were me? My girlfriend's dead and you're treating me like I'm the one who pushed her off the bridge.

SR: Interesting choice of words. Unless I'm mistaken, no one's proved she was "pushed off the bridge," so why did you choose to phrase it like that?

LA: A figure of speech. I want to know what happened to Alice as much as anyone. There's a bridge, Alice ended up in the water: it's not rocket science to conclude there's a fair probability she fell off it.

SR: But you said "pushed," not "fell."

LA: You lot need to pull your heads out of the sand, do stop-and-searches or house-to-house inquiries. Widen the net, look further afield.

SR: Suit you, would it, if we focused further afield?

LA: This is fucking ridiculous.

SR: Please don't swear at me, Luke. Or are you prone to lashing out when you're provoked?

LA: Aren't we all?

SR: No, I'm a calm person. But I'm also a perplexed one, because twenty-four hours after Alice died you led us to believe you were alone in your flat on the night in question, and now it comes to light you were in Southampton.

LA: I've explained about that. I shouldn't have lied, but I was worried you wouldn't believe me. I knew you'd jump to the wrong conclusion.

SR: What conclusion should we have jumped to, Luke? See, there's another inconsistency. After you'd changed your story once and admitted you *were* in Southampton, you claimed your exchange with Alice by the river was—and I quote—"good-natured." Well, a witness has told us that you made serious threats against Alice.

LA: Witness? . . . What witness?

SR: One who observed your little contretemps. She purports you had Alice—and again, I quote—"round her neck."

At this point, the interviewee laughs.

LA: This is farcical. Have you never heard of the concept "innocent until proven guilty"?

SR: I wasn't aware I'd used the word "guilty." Interesting you choose to put that on the table. If you were me, how would you interpret these contradictions?

LA: I loved her.

SR: I'd rather you accounted for these inconsistencies. We also have it on reliable authority that you're a man with a temper, and it's not difficult to envisage how that temper might have been put under strain: emotions running high, throw some booze in the mix, the woman you were devoted to giving you the heave-ho. Make even me furious, that would.

LA: Find who did this, please.

SR: When we spoke to you forty-eight hours after Alice died, you had a black eye; and when I inquired how you came by it, you informed me it was playing squash. Do you wish to reconsider that?

LA: I don't remember.

SR: Let's try that answer again, shall we?

LA: Some bloke hit me in a bar.

SR: That's better: we're getting somewhere now. Did this "some bloke" hit you before or after Alice died?

LA: It was the next day. I was drunk. I'd just been informed Alice was dead.

SR: So you *do* drink a lot?

LA: I like to go out on Friday and Saturday nights.

SR: A binge drinker, then?

LA: No—a normal twenty-seven-year-old.

SR: Had you been drinking prior to confronting Alice by the river?

LA: No.

SR: That also intrigues me, because we've got a landlord prepared to go on record as serving you at least two pints of cider.

LA: It's none of your business, none of this is.

SR: The moment Alice died, it became my business. The night porter at the Premier Inn on Queen Street maintains you came in at ten to four. His word: *legless*. Luke, I've been doing this job a long time and there's an easy way and a hard way of us doing it, but we get to the same conclusion either way. I had a quick search back through our records: you were arrested for assault in 2002.

LA: I want a solicitor.

SR: Assault in a public house in Nantwich.

LA: No charges were ever brought.

SR: Scant consolation to the individual you gave a pasting to.

LA: I was seventeen; if you're going to dredge up that far back, we'd all have stuff we'd prefer to hide.

SR: Like Prague? Is that something you'd prefer to hide?

LA: Fuck you.

SR: Careful. That temper of yours could be a dangerous thing.

LA: I've got nothing more to say.

SR: Luke Addison, I'm arresting you on suspicion of the murder of Alice Salmon . . .

Voice-mail message left by Alice Salmon for David Salmon, *February 4, 2012, 5:09 p.m.*

Dad, it's me. Where's Mum? Why isn't she answering her phone? Get her to ring me; it's urgent. How's she been today? Has she been on her laptop? How you doing? I'm a bit squiffy. I'm in the Hampton for this reunion and been reminiscing about you blubbing when you drove me here for freshers' week, you old sop bag! When are we going to have one of your Sunday lunches, then go out with the dog? Miss you, Daddy. Sorry I haven't always been a brilliant daughter. You probably deserved better than me. For what it's worth, you're the best dad a girl could ever have. What was it you used to call me—your angel? I liked that. I best go, my battery's running low. Love you always.

Post on Truth Speakers web forum by Lone Wolf, *July 6, 2012, 10:50 p.m.*

If you could only expose something seriously bad by doing something a bit bad, would you? If it was the only way of uncovering a scandal in a drugs company or MI5? Or if you had to commit a burglary or a minor assault to expose a bigger crime like a murder or a rape? Most of us would, because powerful people shouldn't be allowed to get away with doing bad things.

Professor Cooke.

No one can touch me for sharing his name.

Professor Jeremy Frederick Harry Cooke. THE ICEMAN.

He wears a jacket and cords and me pointing out he's evil is not illegal. It's called freedom of speech and I didn't learn that from a shitty degree—it was Sports, Media and Culture I wasted three years on, well, not quite three because I saw the light and jacked it in early.

He can't touch me—no one can—which is ironic, because that's what he did to someone else!

Trust me, I might have been wrong about other stuff, but I'm right on this one and he needs to be EXPOSED. When I wield the sword of truth, you won't say I'm a joke and a nutter then, will you?

Now he's even putting his spin on it via a book. They say history gets written by the winners. Well, not anymore, we all write it. I said he couldn't use any of the stuff I'd shared because of copyright, but he said nothing's ever off the record, so here's a taste of your own medicine, smart-arse.

I'll be honest, I did have a financial "arrangement" with the Iceman. I even had a new tattoo to celebrate it, but he reneged on our deal. I wasn't being greedy, it just would have been nice not to have to worry about cash like Ben Finch doesn't have to—it's all right for him, living the life of Riley and convinced he got away with trying to MURDER me because of them pictures he found.

Nearly showed my favorite picture of Alice to her one night when we were sitting in the lounge in the second year talking about photography, the one of her in the park on a run stretching against a tree. Them nights, they were special, but plenty of Sunday afternoons we chatted, too. She'd be proper hungover then and on that battered sofa with the red rug over it, sipping tea out of her elephant mug. Her phone would be on the arm, messages flashing up on it, and I'd ask if she'd had a big night and she'd say how did you guess and I'd tell her I'd heard her stumbling in and she'd apologize and go all guilty and hesitate as if she was waiting for me to explain what she'd done.

We so had a connection until the PSYCHO Ben Finch turned her against me. I love how I'm free to say stuff like that here. I've posted 181 postings in the last three months. Two of the nationals have blocked me, but that's because they can't handle my comments and because they're controlled—they're as bad as North Korea. This is a world of citizen journalism, when the man in the street gets heard because the Internet's David's friend not Goliath's.

The press keeps people like me down and lets people like Ben

Finch and Alice Salmon and the Iceman prosper. But not anymore, justice is coming—Alice is dead, Ben Finch has gone off the rails and the Iceman is about to cop it because of what he did.

Have you guessed by now who he abused? WATCH THIS SPACE!!!

Column in the *Evening Echo*,
March 17, 2012

Greg Aston: The Hard-hitting Voice of Reason

It's a cliché to say you could leave your front door open in the old days, but we did care for each other more then. Mates, family, neighbors—they mattered when I was a lad. If there was a cold snap, we checked the old lady next door was fed and fine, rather than leaving her to freeze or starve. A posher paper than this might dub it a "moral compass," but it's simply recognizing what is and what isn't acceptable behavior.

Three women who don't have it are Holly Dickens, Sarah Hoskings and Lauren Nugent. They're the trio who embarked on a drinking spree with Alice Salmon the night she drowned. Half-cut, they allowed themselves to get separated from Alice and she ended up in the river.

One of them, Dickens, appealed for sympathy in an article yesterday in which she suggested they "lost" Alice—like she'd been a piece of luggage in an airport. The journalist merely endorsed her position by suggesting it could have happened to anyone.

Had this trio not been behaving in a socially irresponsible manner, it's unlikely they'd have let a friend wander off ("abandoned" is the word I'd use) and Alice Salmon would still be alive today.

"A bit tipsy," Dickens described their level of intoxication as.

Pie-eyed, more likely.

The three of them should be held to account for their behavior.

Their silence, meanwhile, has only served to create a vacuum into which misinformation has poured. Many turned to social media for answers, where Alice's final tweet simply said: "Say Hello, Wave Goodbye," which has been interpreted as a reference to lyrics in The Hoosiers' recent cover of the classic 1980s Soft Cell song.

Were I a cynical bloke, I could conclude that their motive for this silence is born not so much out of sensitivity for the Salmon family but from chagrin about their own behavior. No wonder they've dodged the spotlight. I'd be ashamed if I was them.

These women (I've seen them referred to as "girls," but they're not: my better half had had two kids by the time she was their age) are the products of the responsibility-dodging, gratification-seeking, binge-drinking "me generation." Indeed, Alice was a victim of it. We all have some responsibility for that.

We made drink-driving socially unacceptable. We made football hooliganism socially unacceptable. Now let's make binge drinking socially unacceptable. Let's end the culture that turns a blind eye to yobs—male and female—rolling and rampaging through our streets, fighting, spewing and lurching from one discount drinks emporium to another.

If any good can come out of this awful tragedy, it's that we might become less willing to let our cities be used as lethal weekend playgrounds.

Comments left on the above article:

True, buddy, how can you "lose" someone? She wasn't a set of keys or a mobile phone. What they did, it's like turning your back on a toddler—it's a definite no-no.

Monkey Blues

This vow of silence's a bit odd. If I'd been them I'd have spoken up sharpish to make doubly sure no one was pointing the finger at me.

Onlyme

Which bit of the word "grieving" do you bloodsuckers not comprehend?

Made in Bridlington

Hoosiers my arse, the David Gray version is the best cover of the song by a mile.

Mighty Mike

Talk about life imitating art . . . I read a piece that said Alice's favorite book was *The Secret History*. Well, in that a group of students at a prestigious American college go to ground after a death.

Hazel

Wouldn't you keep it zipped if your best mate had carked it? It's the only way they can honor her memory. We'd be quick enough to diss them if they were throwing themselves in front of a camera, plus it's so easy to inadvertently implicate yourself. This isn't a friggin' circus!!!

Junk collector

I was moved by their statement. They got it in the neck for it being too slick and for getting their solicitor to read it out, but I wouldn't have been able to face the cameras if it was only twenty-four hours since my BFF had died.

EmF

Letter sent by Professor Jeremy Cooke,
July 19, 2012

Dear Larry,

For the record, I persevered with Dr. Richard Carter.

"You clearly enjoy the company of women" was his opener to one session, "but let's explore how she, Liz, made you feel."

I'd felt myself crabbing from exclusively blocking and baiting this chap—we were like two out-of-condition shortsighted bantamweights—to a state that might have arguably been described as candor. "Alive," I said. "Transcendent, primal, glorious. Like a bastard. Like a man."

"What do *they* feel like, Jeremy?"

In our early exchanges, I might have responded with a snide "You'll never find out," but I offered up: "Like someone else."

"Is that good?"

"Richard, I'm an upper-middle-class, virtually middle-aged, white, Anglo-Saxon academic. My existence is predicated on convention, my job demands rationality and diligence. 'Meticulous' was how masters would describe me at school. The 'someone else' didn't have to abide by normal rules; he got to tear a near stranger's clothes off."

I'd lost a stone after Fliss left, and I'd never had weight to spare. She'd gone back to her parents in Lincoln. Everyone's at it now, a practice that took root in the 2000s, returning to the nest like thundering cuckoo chicks because their student loans have consumed them or property prices have escalated away from them, but it had the unmistakable ring of failure then: it was an inversion of the natural order to return to one's parental home. Inevitably, eyebrows were raised on campus. Not that my wife's absence topped the gossip list for long: relegated by the altogether more seismic revelation that Elizabeth Mullens had tried to kill herself. I rang the in-laws' house every day, but they refused to let me converse with my wife. I also contacted Liz's lodgings in a bid to establish *her* condition, but all I got was an uncooperative landlady who didn't appreciate calls after 9 p.m. and complained about overdue rent.

"Are you a fan of The Rolling Stones?" Richard Carter had asked.

"I'm familiar with them."

"Because Mick Jagger wrote a song called 'You Can't Always Get What You Want.' He might have a point."

I rebuffed him. "Humans aren't constructed that way."

"I disagree. We're capable of immense displays of selflessness, often at great personal sacrifice."

"We're selective about our altruism. It's targeted—typically at kin, in a direct bid to ensure reciprocity."

"Not so. I have a direct debit to a charity that digs wells in eastern Uganda. How does that benefit me?"

"It might enable you to sleep at night, or to highlight it to me, in so doing potentially enabling you to execute your job more efficiently."

"That's a phenomenally bleak prognosis," he said. "Altruism can be pure. There are female spiders that let their offspring eat them to improve their chances of survival. Similarly, male ones that allow the female to eat them after they've mated. Fairly one-sided relationships, wouldn't you concur?"

"Typical bloody woman." I wondered if Liz had heard about the spiders; she'd be fascinated by them.

"But we're not talking about animals or evolution," he said, "we're talking about you."

"So we *are* talking precisely about animals and evolution."

Can't recall if I expounded the full saga back then, Larry, but I was summoned in front of an academic "panel": a bloody kangaroo court, where they'd regarded me quizzically—the plaster on my forehead, the rumpled clothes—and graciously informed me that if I cooperated in preventing this "debacle" from reaching the press, they'd regard that favorably. I still had much to offer. "Something" rather than "much" might have been the actual descriptor they used; it's hard to tie down specifics.

"Could the reason you sought out an extramarital relationship be a response to you not having children?" Richard had asked.

Fliss and I hadn't entirely relinquished our parenting ambitions prior to my dalliance with Liz coming to light, but it had become ever more hypothetical: like the IRA quitting its bombing or me attaining a breakthrough in the work in which I was involved (basically a derivative offshoot of Chomsky). Liz, meanwhile, had been desperate to get married and have a family; it was the eighties—women still did. She could reel off examples of animals that mated for life—a type of antelope, black vultures, sandhill cranes, a species of fish called the convict cichlid—but she kept making bad choices, and, frankly, I was the worst.

"Do you feel responsible for what Liz did?" Richard asked.

She'd hung herself from a beam above a table in the refectory. A fascinating room, that. High ceilings, leaded-light windows, rafters from an old Tudor warship. A cleaner popped in to fetch a tub of floor polish and found her dangling, drunk, her beautiful long spider legs stretched out beneath her, the flap expiring from them.

"I can't exculpate myself of blame." I had a desire to crawl back to my office, where I knew all the rules. Imagined immersing myself in marking, like collapsing onto a soft bed. "Have you ever read Tolstoy, Richard? His contention was that happy families are all alike and unhappy ones are unhappy in their own way, but he got that wrong. Unhappiness is crushingly predictable. It's making sure one's pockets are empty before putting one's trousers in the laundry basket; it's bathing to rid oneself of an unfamiliar perfume before scuttling into one's marital bed; it's familiar faces contorted into unfamiliar shapes by pain and drink. Happiness is what's unique. The minutiae of two lives spent together: the warm and unshowy mechanics of a monogamous relationship."

"But you slept with another woman."

"Yes, because lust is a drug; it addles our brains."

"Did the pain you'd inevitably inflict not cross your mind?"

"I could anticipate it, I could rationalize it, I could hazard a guess at the magnitude of it but I couldn't *feel* it. Does that make me a psychopath?"

That night she confronted me in the kitchen, Fliss demanded I explain what this Elizabeth *tart* had that she didn't, and when I stated it wasn't like that, she said: "I feel so let down, so stupid."

"What's your wife's view, now you've both taken stock?" Richard had asked.

"She's in Lincoln."

"Ah, still Lincoln. Beautiful cathedral," he said. "Much underrated."

I'd come to expect these switches of direction. It was a device my favorite political pundit, Robin Day, was wont to use: a random catechism. "She'd probably be pleased I'm sticking with these sessions," I said. "She's always had me down as a slogger. Bless her, she means it as a compliment, but the tag rankles. Sloggers dig roads and pack boxes in factories. It's originality I've sought."

"Personally I'd take happiness over originality," my shrink declared. "I'd take an absence of pain."

"The absence of pain and happiness aren't synonymous. The former is merely that—the lower tranches of Maslow's triangle fulfilled."

"Don't knock it," he said, checking his watch. "Millions of people would kill for that."

Extract from Alice Salmon's diary,
September 3, 2011, age 25

"We should get a place," Luke said.

Going away often prompted conversations to arc off into territory beyond the norm; it was as if under the surface there was a slight rebalancing of our relationship. It wasn't until Malta—six months in—that he'd revealed how infrequently he saw his parents.

"What I mean is," he added, "I'd like to live with you and I hope you do me."

"Luke, it's a great idea. I wasn't expecting you to ask, that's all—or not today."

"We'd need to save up for a few months, but we could get a half-decent place."

"Where?"

He stabbed one of his chips with his fork and tossed it to a gull. "If this was a movie, this would be when the schmaltzy music would cut in and I'd say, 'I don't care as long as we're together.' But I'm not living in Stockwell!"

"Or New Cross."

"Ultimately I'd like to get out of London," he said. There was a new urgency about him; it was as if he'd stored this up and now couldn't contain it. "It's about time you settled down. You *are* twenty-five, after all!"

"Excuse me," I said. "Aaaarrrrgghhh!"

The gull had flapped up, wheeled in a circle and landed on the rusty railings in front of us. Luke went into his pocket and a crazy notion popped into my head that he might be about to propose, but it was his cigarettes he pulled out. He lit up, blew smoke out, and it trailed off into the bright, brittle seaside light.

"We could actually go anywhere," he said, and he was giddy, boylike. "Carpe diem and all that."

"*Go fishing?*" I quipped, one of his favorite lines from *The Inbetweeners.* Only last week, he'd joked that one of his prerequisites for choosing a flat was having sufficient space for his DVD collection, so he must have had the moving-in conversation in mind then. When we'd met in Victoria yesterday he would have done, as he would when he'd returned from the buffet car with my skinny frothy latte and his tea, or when he'd said at Faversham, after I'd finally sussed where we were headed, "Barbados has got nothing on the white sands of Margate."

"It is OK for you here, isn't it?" he asked. "I almost went for Paris, but this seemed more you."

"Luke, it's perfect." It was, too. Its faded glamour, its lack of ostentatiousness, its unpretentious approach to fun; I adored it.

"Anyway, I couldn't take you to Paris because you've had a dirty weekend there before!"

I remembered the hotel where a doorman—"the twat in the hat," Ben had dubbed him—had referred to me as "madame" and how we'd clinked glasses over a bowl of *moules marinières* and he'd said, "To us, Lissa," and I could have cried. So much for the City of Light.

"We can save Paris," Luke said.

It gave me a warm shiver: us saving stuff, having it still to do.

"Margate used to have a Victorian pier," he said. "A Eugenius Birch one. Spot the frustrated architect!"

It pained me that he might have regrets, because twenty-seven might be ancient, but it was too early for regrets. I didn't want this man to ever have regrets.

"We can do anything," he said. "If it's me and you—us against the world—we'll be unstoppable, Al."

I leant in and kissed my boyfriend.

"What was that for?"

"For bringing me here; for being you." *Tell him everything about yourself. The nights you couldn't sleep, the disastrous deliciousness of that relationship with Ben, how you'd perpetually felt thin (not thin-thin, I wish!) and insignificant, even the day in the bathroom when you let the pain out*—tell him. *Have this gorgeous man hear it from you. The tide is out, but by the time it reaches the top of the beach, I could have told him; then, when it recedes, all that crap will be washed out to sea and we can move forward together.*

"What's the one thing you'd most like to change about yourself?" he asked.

"Right now, nothing—because if I did, we might not be here. Maybe *now's* when the schmaltzy music should play!"

He bowed his head. He was welling up. Luke was actually crying. "I love you, Al Salmon," he said.

"I love you, too," I said.

He'd taken a few months to say it, but I'd blurted it out after five weeks, probably way too early.

"What about you?" I asked. "What would you change if you were the one with the magic wand?"

"I *have* got one," he said, smirking and glancing down at his lap.

Now he'd been serious, he needed to let go—it was palpable, the tension draining out of him. He was in pub mode. "You're not getting off the hook that easily," I said. "Come on, what?"

"I'd have met you when I was younger."

"Good answer!"

"Before we had baggage."

"Speak for yourself!"

"There's other stuff, too."

A kid hurtled along the prom on a scooter, flying by, having simply the *best* time, and then the conversation was back on "the flat" and the respective merits of Streatham versus Clerkenwell. I'd get to collect the slow cooker and pictures I'd deposited at Mum and Dad's, unpack the boxes of books in their loft; I might even dust down the "Best Newcomer" trophy I'd won at work and put it on the fireplace. Imagine that: a *fireplace*. Friends would pick up the trophy and turn it over when they came for dinner. It would spark conversations: jokes about its weight, how you could do someone some serious damage with it, discussions about crime and politics unfolding over the Greek salad or white chocolate and passion-fruit mousse I'd got from Nigella. "Do you know what I like about you most?" I asked.

"My killer good looks? My charming personality? My forensic wit?"

"It's what a good listener you are. Has anyone ever told you that before?"

"Probably. But I expect I wasn't listening!"

He'd get drunk tonight. I could tell. His answers, the way he was throwing chip scraps to the gulls, even the way he was smoking. And it would be nice—the two of us holed up in a pub in an out-of-the-way town. There was an illicit quality about being here: away from London, from the girls, hidden. We were going to move in together. I could hear the conversation I'd have with Meg. We'd hug and she'd hang on. "I'm not going to lose you, am I?" she'd texted randomly earlier, when I mentioned Luke had taken me on a surprise weekend away. "I couldn't cope with that, you're like a sister to me."

Luke sparked up another cigarette, gave me one and said: "When you said about giving up, you meant after we finish this packet—obviously."

This is my life, I thought. *This is where my life is happening*. In a seaside town where the color of the pebbles made me wish I could paint; on rickety trains out of Platform 2 in Victoria with conductors who still said, "Good evening"; with a man called Luke Stuart Addison who'd admitted when we'd joked about riding the carousel that he'd topped the thirteen-stone mark, which prompted me to instigate an immediate midweek curry ban. Finally, *finally,* it felt enough. "This all feels very grown-up," I said. "I need wine."

"Beer o'clock," Luke said.

Walking back to the hotel, I thought: *This is* ours *now, too.* Margate. Even the minimart we'd bought Fanta in. I'd add them to the "ours" we already had: how our "treat" restaurant was Thai House on Balham High Street, how our ideal Thursday was a movie at Clapham Picturehouse, how our favorite music venue was Brixton Academy. I felt on more of an even keel than I had for years: an equilibrium. I typically swerved the corollary (that's definitely my word of this entry) that Luke had made me happy, because none of us needs a man for that, right? But it was inescapable: I was happier since I'd met him.

And now he'd gone to buy cigarettes. Our final, *final* packet. Strange that I had once waited for another man in another hotel while *he* went out for cigarettes. I had a vision of that lovely old dear, Queenie, riding the roller coaster at Thorpe Park: hanging on for dear life with her marbly liver-spotted hands, her wrinkly face flattened with the g-force, her gummy mouth exhaling crackly screams of terror and joy. I hope she makes it there. "I translate the world in words," I'd told her. So as for my word of this entry? Bugger "corollary": that's old-school; that's one I'd have picked at eighteen when I pretentiously sought the erudite or many-syllabled. Sometimes the simplest express the most. Like "boyfriend" or "trust" or "commitment." Or even "love."

Yes, that'll do nicely. *Love.*

Blog post by Megan Parker,
April 7, 2012, 11:20 a.m.

OMG just read on the Internet that Luke's been taken in by the police. Can't believe this; he's been taken to a station in Southampton. Apparently they could charge him. There's nothing on the police's website, no statements, but Twitter's ablaze with it.

Knew there was something about him. Tried telling Alice once but she wasn't having any of it—she was always so headstrong when it came to men; she could be blind to their faults. She had a right go at me and accused me of being jealous.

Seriously, I had half a mind to blog about my suspicions that he could have been dodgy, but Jeremy said I needed to be careful what I put on here, and reckoned I could get into trouble if I bandied accusations around but, holy shit, *Luke?!*

You could see it, the way he was around Alice. He had a jealous streak and you wouldn't have wanted to get on the wrong side of him—he's built like a barn door. Alice confided in me that he had yelled at her once and I did witness him get loud in a pub—yes, it was over nothing, but he had that edge. He'd only been on the scene recently, but tried to paint me out to be some peripheral afterthought; she was my best friend not his.

Jesus, I can't believe this. I went and offered the police a second statement after that newspaper ran the story about the dead flowers, but they hadn't seemed that interested. The nice police lady heard me out, but when you're mega upset, stuff comes out wrong and then you begin to doubt yourself and that makes you sound doubly implausible. She probably had me pegged as "emotional." Course I'm emotional, wouldn't anyone be if their best friend had died? It's like half of *me* has died.

I say "died" rather than "was killed" because that's where we were at with it. If one of the scumbags she brought to justice wasn't responsible and she didn't do it herself, then we'd all come to the conclusion it was a dreadful accident—but why are they now talking to Luke? Jesus, LUKE. The police don't drag someone in without a reason and he was furious about Alice dumping him; she said he was absolutely gutted when she did the deed, and behaved like a madman. His eyes, she said, were wild. If he genuinely loved her how could he explain Prague? See, Alice and I confided in each other; girls do, best friends do. How much hate must you have in your heart to cheat on someone as trusting as Alice?

Nothing's ever as simple as it seems, Jeremy reckons, but he often talks in riddles and answers real questions with theoretical answers. "A man is not dead while his name is spoken," he keeps saying, conveniently omitting to mention it's a Terry Pratchett quote. It's like he's hoping I'll conclude *he* made it up.

He tells me I ought to be careful blogging, that I might inadvertently give a distorted impression, but that TV interview I gave turned out to be a bad move. I didn't even *look* like myself. Someone posted paraphrased chunks of what I said on to Alice's Facebook wall and a local paper reporter then recycled extracts of those (not even accurately, but I was beyond caring by that stage because the clip that went out on telly wasn't in itself representative of what I'd said) and attributed them to Megan "Harker," which prompted more people to dive headlong onto Facebook and spout off about the comments I'd purportedly given the newspaper.

Thing is, when you lose someone close to you, you get properly paranoid, you get suspicious of everyone. I'll be honest here, even Jeremy's beginning to creep me out a bit. The way he refers to his wife, it's like she's some inferior species. No way would I let a man speak about me like that, and Alice a hundred percent wouldn't; she'd have told the chauvinist it was 2012 not the flipping Stone Age.

Then the other night he invited me over to catalogue more "submissions" and meet his wife, except his wife wasn't there so he opened a bottle of wine, a Chilean red that he described as a punchy little number, and we chatted about the options for me going back to uni. He promised to write me a reference, even though he's only known me a short while. I'd get a special dispensation, he says, because of Alice. Because I got a bit drunk, I ended up staying over.

Just seen on Twitter that the reason they pulled Luke in was because he was in Southampton on the night Alice died. Holy shit, that totally contradicts his earlier story. Some lawyer on Twitter reckons they can keep him in for twenty-four hours without charging him—but that they'll be going for it with him, the full works, searching his flat and all sorts.

No smoke without fire, that's what they say.

I best ring Alice's mum. Just when you think this can't get any worse for them.

She's even got her own hashtag. Is that what it comes to, what my best friend's been reduced to? #alicesalmon

Comment left on the above blog post:

Megan, I can only apologize if you've ever had reason to feel uncomfortable in my company. Fliss and I would very much like you to come over for supper at the weekend—a perfect opportunity for the two of you to become acquainted. You have my mobile—ring me and we can discuss.

Jeremy "Silver Surfer" Cooke

Voice-mail message left by Alice Salmon for Megan Parker, *February 4, 2012, 8:43 p.m.*

Where are you, Parker? Hope you've got your Bridget Jones pants on . . . it must be freeeeeezing in the hills. Got a teensy confession . . . OK, a whopper of a teensy one but you'll go schiz, so not gonna tell you till you call me. Meg, same length of time since the end of the second year again and we'll be dirty thirty! Might have done something I haven't for ages, which might have involved a tiddly snort. Toot toot, as they say. Don't hate me, Meg, don't begrudge me a night out. S'need it. So need to get away from it all. I'm trying to not even think about that email of Mum's. Come down off your hill and call me this instant, Parker Larker!

Southampton StudentNet online forum, *April 7, 2012*

Topic: Arrest

See the boyfriend's been arrested in the Alice Salmon case. Always reckoned there was something shifty about him.

Posted by ExtremeGamer, 1:20 p.m.

Like, reckoned <u>how</u> exactly? Pal of his were you, ExtremeGamer, or that another of your crackpot theories?

Posted by Su, 1:26 p.m.

Facts speak for themselves. Arrested.

Posted by ExtremeGamer, 1:33 p.m.

According to Bookface he was at Liverpool Uni between 2003 and 2006. Must be a bit of a brainbox cos he got a first then was hired by a big building firm on a grad-training scheme.

Posted by Graeme, 1:56 p.m.

He did well to get to uni at all—was a shitty school he went to.

Posted by Lex, 2:14 p.m.

There was a lad in my sixth form, probably the brainiest kid in the school, but he liked a tear-up on a Friday night with the best of them. Because he was clever don't mean he don't talk with his fists.

Posted by Baz the driver, 2:28 p.m.

I read a "backgrounder" on him in a newspaper . . . His parents split up when he was eight. They quoted some psychiatrist who explained repressed emotions over shit like that can manifest themselves decades later as misogyny.

Posted by Fi, 2:41 p.m.

Welcome back, Fi! Why's everything boil down to misogyny in your head? Or is that a misogynistic comment? It couldn't simply be that one person lost his rag with another and drowned her?

Posted by Tom, 2:46 p.m.

Hang on, you're putting the cart in front of the horse again. People get arrested every day and aren't charged. It's the authorities saying we've got enough info to make us keen to find out more.

Posted by Jacko, 2:54 p.m.

Still convinced she jumped personally.

Posted by The Other Katniss, 2:54 p.m.

Yes good point Kat—2012 is a leap year!!!!

Posted by Smithy, 3:02 p.m.

Promising rugger player when he was younger, I heard. Had a trial as a schoolboy for Harlequins then knackered his knee, which put the kibosh on that.

Posted by Phil, 3:20 p.m.

More to the point, you seen the pictures of him? Well, HELLO!

Posted by Christi 3:31 p.m.

Will he get bail?

Posted by Not so plain jane, 3:49 p.m.

Depends. Cops have twenty-four hours to either charge you or release you. They can get an extension but it's not easy. Was watching a TV show where they did it for ninety-six hours, although they had to get permission from a magistrate.

Posted by ArtConnoisseur, 3:50 p.m.

Once again I find myself forced to inform you that I'll be taking this thread down forthwith. I should remind all contributors that this is a "live" police investigation, therefore commenting about it could be potentially legally prejudicial.

Posted by StudentNet Forum Administrator, 4:26 p.m.

But no one's actually named him if you bothered to read the thread so you're wrong.

Posted by Barley Mow, 4:26 p.m.

Email sent by Professor Jeremy Cooke, *July 23, 2012*

From: jfhcooke@gmail.com

To: Elizabeth_salmon101@hotmail.com

Subject: Tell me

My dear Liz,

I was going to email you so you heard it from me, but events have overtaken me. That note was—*is*—indeed attributable to me. My handwriting's always been spidery.

You may not believe me, but when I initiated my Alice research, I barely remembered the note. I'd been in a right imbroglio in 2004. Then Alice arrived and she reminded me so much of all the emotions I'd tried—and largely succeeded—to subjugate. *You,* basically. Then, discovering who she was, it was as if a piece of my past—a piece of me—came back to life. Once I invited her to a drinks party, the annual anthropology bash.

"That sounds like a barrel of laughs," she'd joked. "Won't it be just academic staff?"

"You get a special dispensation because your mother used to work here."

She'd hesitated.

"There'll be free refreshments," I informed her, and that was the clincher.

"You lot really know how to let your hair down," she'd said, observing us shuffling around like warmed-up cadavers. "Where's the music? Where the *booze*?"

Three hours later we were in my office. She'd pulled a joint out of her pocket, we passed it between us and it reminded me of what I'd frequently felt my uni days *should* remind me of. She said she felt woozy, came and sat on my lap and I said, "No, don't." Later she fell asleep on the sofa in the corner and I lay my sweater over her, went to pull it up around her, tuck her in, but she put her arms round my neck. "Smell nice," she said. Wasn't intending to do what came next—you've got to believe me, Liz—but my hand brushed her hair and it was like an electric shock: a jolt of you coursing up into me.

I'm drunk, Liz. Not that it's apparent. Can't even do that well: get drunk. Look at this email: even the goddamn punctuation is right. I'm going to have another drink. The lecherous lecturer is going to get pie-eyed. A sober drunk. That's an oxymoron if ever I heard one. Listen to me, *an oxymoron*. I'm even pretentious when I'm sozzled.

Fliss knows all about our affair. Finding out what I did with Alice will break her heart, but I owe her the truth. We mustn't die with secrets and frankly I'm drowning under them. I wish I'd been let in on that particular one earlier: that they corrode the soul.

You often used to refer to the here and now, Liz—well, the trouble with that is it's so bloody fleeting. Who'd have thought it, eh? The big C. A bugger of a brand, which is sufficiently rare that its evolution is impervious to predictions. It won't finish me off forthwith, but it's questionable whether I'll become a septuagenarian. I'm sorry if this is unpalatable, but illness, like age, does that: makes one less empathetic and more immune to embarrassment.

Might you have it in your heart to not completely detest me? The Liz I shared part of my life with would. The one with whom I stood on Chesil Beach, who whooped with pleasure at the Titians and Caravaggios in the National, who—aged twenty-something but little-girl-like—beamed when she learnt that the fur on a deer's antlers was called "velvet." Understanding and forgiveness: that's pretty much all there is. And justice.

We shouldn't be ashamed of us; we mustn't whitewash ourselves out of history. We had a relationship, we slept together, we fucked. We matter.

It's raining. I might sleep here tonight. It wouldn't be unprecedented for me to wake among the chaos of paperwork, my phone bleeping from missed calls from Fliss. I've put that woman through so much worry. I've been such a selfish man, but shouldn't it be how one typically behaves that dictates how one is judged? The person one is day in and day out over the long haul, rather than the best or worst thing one's done? Wouldn't that be a fairer barometer of the life you've led, the person you are?

When I wake it might be better. Tell me it will be. Tell me I'll sleep. Tell me I won't be staring at the walls in the night, concentrating on not screaming, or hugging my books or writing in the condensation on the window: JFHC RIP. Tell me I'll wake and I'll be nine again—nine, say, or fourteen or even thirty-five would do. I'd take the sharp sting of my father's belt, that evil old bastard, the schoolyard taunts, the coalescing gloom of Fliss's hospital visits and those ever more hypothetical conversations about names and nurseries and schools, or the emptying despair of middle age. I'd take any of it not to be a man who feels the black end pressing down on me.

Let me sleep a good sleep. Let me whisky. Let me go gentle.

Was it gentle for you, when you so nearly went into that good night? That day in the refectory, the black beams of Tudor warships above your head, the table smooth from the rubbing of generations of academics' elbows too far below your feet. You must have felt so utterly alone.

I saw a shrink after we split up and he was fond of one particular epigram: pain has to go somewhere. Right now mine is going to you. It's unfair, but where else is there? Where it goes after that is up to you. I'm too tired to care. Isn't this a bolt from the blue? The man who's zealously guarded his own decision making, putting his fate in the hands of another.

Have pity on me. Throw me to the lions. It's your call.

She'll come into her own after I'm gone, Fliss will; I just *know* she will. She'll make me proud. I wish I could say the same of myself.

Good night. Sleep tight. Don't let the bedbugs bite. That's what I would have said to my kids if I'd ever had them.

I'm sorry.

Love Jem

Statement issued by Hampshire Constabulary,
April 7, 2012, 5:22 p.m.

A 27-year-old man arrested on suspicion of the murder of a former Southampton resident has been released without charge.

Police have confirmed that the man has been freed from custody following questioning in relation to the February 5 death of Alice Salmon.

Police made the arrest yesterday after a new witness came forward in connection with the case, but the man from south London was released this afternoon.

Detective Superintendent Simon Ranger says: "Our investigations continue into the exact circumstances surrounding Alice's death. A postmortem has concluded that she died by drowning, but we are systematically working to establish her last movements.

"I would like to thank members of the public who have assisted thus far and stress we remain keen to talk to anyone who saw Alice that evening or witnessed any activity near the river Dane."

Alice Salmon's body was discovered at 7:15 GMT on February 5.

If you have any information that could assist the investigation, please contact the incident room or call Crimestoppers anonymously on 0800 555111.

Extract from transcript of interview at Southampton Central Police Station between Detective Superintendent Simon Ranger, Detective Julie Welbeck and Elizabeth Salmon, ***August 5, 2012, 5:45 p.m.***

ES: Do you have kids?

SR: Yes, one, a girl.

ES: How old?

SR: Seven. Why?

ES: Because they grow up and you can't protect them. You do your best to set them off on the best course you can, but you have to stand back and watch them go. Can't wrap them in cotton wool. Tuck them up or fuck them up, which is it us parents do?

SR: Was there a specific reason you called by today, Mrs. Salmon? Only we weren't expecting to see you.

ES: Came to lay flowers at . . . at . . . by the river. Water must have been so very cold.

SR: I gather you're also keen to share some new information.

ES: It's been six months. Where are my answers?

SR: I appreciate how painful this all must be.

ES: Do you? I doubt you do. Because you'll finish your shift and fill out the paperwork—what will you say about me, that I'm inconsistent, unstable, inebriated?—and tuck your daughter up in bed and I'll . . . I'll . . . I haven't the faintest clue what I'll do.

Interviewee stands up and paces around the room . . . cries again . . .

ES: I'm not stupid.

JW: No one's suggesting that. How about we get you that cup of tea now?

ES: Tea, no, no tea. He stalked her.

SR: Who?

ES: The lecturer who's writing the book about Alice; he stalked her when she was at uni . . . Took advantage of her, he did, him a middle-aged man and her a fresher, barely eighteen, her first time away from home. Makes me sick, the thought of him waiting till she was vulnerable then enticing her into his lair and pouncing. My baby, a lamb to the slaughter. I've got evidence: I've got an email from Cooke admitting it.

SR: Please, slow down, Mrs. Salmon—

ES: Like a confessional, maybe the snake's lapsed Catholicism has lapsed. It was Christmas 2004: he took her to his disgusting hovel of an office and . . . [*Interviewee rocks forwards and backwards on her seat, cries, peers upwards*] . . . You need to arrest him!

SR: It's not as simple as that.

ES: But I've got evidence, his confession: that's *proof.*

SR: I appreciate this is painful—

ES: Nothing's painful after you've lost a child. It's merely layers of numbness.

JW: Mrs. Salmon, have you been drinking?

ES: What's booze? Another layer of numbness—water running off ice. Wouldn't you, if you were me?

SR: Yes, yes, I expect I would. Are you positive we can't get you that tea?

ES: Stop offering me tea! What good will tea do? Alice is *dead.* The vicar said, "God must have needed another angel," but she wasn't God's angel to take: she was mine. You've given up on her; if it wasn't for the media keeping her in the news, you'd have moved on completely. What they say might not always be right, but at least they haven't forgotten her.

SR: Let me assure you our inquiries have been extensive and we're still very much keeping an open mind.

ES: Forget an open mind—it's Cooke you should arrest.

SR: Did your daughter mention this alleged incident to you—indeed to anyone—at the time?

ES: No "alleged" about it and, no, she didn't, at least not to me. She bottled it all up: if I'd have got wind of it, I'd have been on the phone to the police within milliseconds . . . then I'd have paid the monster a visit of my own, made him wish he'd never been born.

Interviewee hugs herself, then cries . . .

ES: All you've done is go on a wild-goose chase after Luke—most ridiculous thing I've ever heard.

SR: Arresting someone on suspicion of murder is not a step we take lightly.

ES: That boy loved my daughter and I'll always love him for that. It's Cooke you should be interrogating. *Someone* killed her and he's clearly fixated with her—then and now.

SR: What makes you so certain?

ES: It wasn't an accident and my Alice certainly wouldn't have, you know, done this herself—it came to me in a dream, too.

JW: This might be a good point to break for a few minutes.

ES: Poor boy, he's bereaved and you haul him over the coals.

SR: With respect, my job is to reveal patterns.

ES: Patterns. *Patterns?* There's one: rain on the window behind you. Alice would have liked that. Animal paw prints in snow, bubbles in lemonade, the stripes on the tabby cat she had as a kid . . . she called that cat Gandalf. She was into *Lord of the Rings* long before any of these films came along.

JW: Mrs. Salmon, I can see you're finding things difficult and that's understandable. Are you seeing your doctor?

ES: Was . . . he can't help.

SR: Are you taking any medication we should be aware of, Mrs. Salmon?

ES: They call it self-medicating!

JW: Presumably you'll go home after you leave here today?

ES: Home? Home? That's one option.

JW: Will your husband be there?

ES: He's away . . .

Interviewee cries.

ES: Be sure your sins will find you out.

SR: Mrs. Salmon?

ES: I've done something terrible. Alice saw an email that Jem—I mean Cooke—sent me on the day she died.

SR: Why did he send you an email?

ES: He's trying to put his house in order before he snuffs it and we'd once been an item.

SR: What did the email say? How did Alice react to it?

ES: We didn't speak . . . She sent plenty of texts, mind . . . said I was disgusting, a hypocrite, a liar, two-faced . . . She's so like me, that girl, flying off the handle. Do you believe in karma, Superintendent? Because I must have done some pretty awful stuff in a former life.

JW: Are you OK? Do you need to take a breather here?

ES: I'm anything but OK. I'm about as far from OK as I have been since 1982. What if he comes after me? He's got nothing to lose.

JW: Perhaps we should get in contact with your husband . . . Where might we be able to get hold of him?

ES: Your guess is as good as mine. Hope this wretched book bankrupts him, Cooke. What *is* a book, Superintendent? It's nothing. Paper, ink, vanity. A million pages aren't worth a single person's happiness.

SR: Your son—it's Robert, isn't it?—could we have him pick you up?

ES: He wouldn't. Guess what he called me last week? A lush! His own mother, charming. Can I stay here a bit?

SR: Of course. You can stay as long as you need to, but will there be someone to collect you later?

ES: Will the liaison officer be able to come to the house? Not sure I trust myself to be alone today.

Blog post by Megan Parker,
August 3, 2012, 8:24 p.m.

What Cooke's doing is sick. He promised me it was a tribute, but it's turned into a character assassination. I can't believe I ever cooperated with his grave robbing. I'm supposed to be a communications expert, for fuck's sake. I had the best intentions, but grief clouded my vision. This is it, though—I'm having no more to do with him and am urging all my and Alice's friends to do likewise.

He's worse than the gutter press—as if delving into her past wasn't enough, now he's picking over the remains of her last few hours.

He's even gone on record as backing Luke, piously asserting that we have to have confidence in the authorities, but how can you trust them when you hear about these miscarriages of justice?

I'll be honest, Cooke's not normal. I liked him at first, but he wants to talk about me more than Alice, keeps rattling on about how I should follow my dream of returning to full-time study. "You'd definitely get a place, especially if I put a word in with the powers that be," he said.

"Thank you, but it wouldn't be Southampton," I explained. "Too many ghosts."

"I wasn't necessarily referring to this august establishment. My reputation may not be what it was, but I'm not atrociously connected in academic circles. Not that you'd need a reference from me. You're intelligent, you're sensitive, you've got experience of industry, so institutions would be positively falling over themselves to get their hands on you—and if they weren't, they jolly well should be!"

Then the other night—surprise, surprise, his wife just *happened* to be out—he took a call, so I had a snoop around (Alice used to say inquisitiveness was a good trait!), and in one of his drawers he's got this file of pictures. Not like what we'd been amassing; these were extra, and stashed in the middle of them—it was all grainy, like a printout of a digital scan of an old-fashioned print—her as a KID on a beach. I was totally weirded out and then, because I was terrified of arousing his suspicion, had to sit in the dining room with him, the image of Alice in a pink polka dot bikini, water wings on her arms, burnt bright into my mind while he slavered on about the "stages of grief" like he was reciting a text. It's as if there's a bit of that man missing. Every fiber in my body was screaming: *Run . . .*

He talked about guilt, but where can I begin with that? The guilt at not being with her that weekend to take care of her, the guilt at not picking up her texts, her voice-mails, the guilt at not being a better friend? And then (we always used to argue about whether you could begin a sentence with "and," but she was unmovable on it being fine . . . it even reminds me of her when I use brackets, because she did that a lot) there's the anger. Anger at how old men get to stockpile pictures of her as a child in a swimsuit and philanderers like Luke get to go out drinking again when he's lied to the police. Chloe and Lauren reckon I shouldn't be so horrid to him, but why shouldn't I be horrid? If I let this anger go, it's like I'm letting *her* go.

I'm going to quit blogging. I figured speaking out was being true to Alice's memory, but it's not. We might need to fill in the gaps, but attaining closure for ourselves won't bring her back. This prurient preoccupation with detail, this compulsion to clasp logic when it doesn't necessarily exist—that's not how you show respect. The specifics of her final few moments—they're hers, not ours . . . they're the only secret she will be left with at this rate, especially if Cooke publishes his god-awful book.

Public opinion seems to be uniting around the theory that she was on her own at the end, so beyond that, I suppose the precise details are irrelevant. Ignore Cooke: he's a sad, discredited deviant who's fixated with intrigue and scandal where it doesn't exist. Hasn't got enough excitement or drama in his own life, that man, so he's seeking it vicariously. Whether she slipped on a muddy bank or tripped over a tree root or paused to gaze out in wonder at the shimmering blackness and crumpled. Even if she decided in her drunken state that it was, you know, time to go to sleep, let's let her keep that private at least. Her final mystery. Fitting, in a way.

She had a romantic streak, our Alice, a weakness for red roses, doomed heroines, tear-smudged ink on love letters. (Alice Palace, right now my tears are falling on to the keyboard.) So you, Alice, toppling into a river . . . If you hadn't died, it would be hysterical, a story we'd wheel out at get-togethers: Francesca's birthday is only four weeks away; you're going to miss that now, aren't you? So very *you*, missus.

Death is random, and if you fight that, the questions drive you mad.

"There'll be enough unanswered questions to fill a book," Alice's mum said to me during one of our many late-night hours-long tearful conversations.

Drunk girls do fall in rivers and drown.

Before I leave the best friend I'll ever have to sleep in peace, I need to set the record straight on one final thing. Our feted, lauded academic, who hoards pictures of children in swimming costumes—you mustn't believe a word of what he says in his book. Because he's got an agenda. There's more to him than meets the eye: he's a pervert and he assaulted me. When I made my excuses and stood up from the dining-room table, his hand, it gripped like a vise.

Publish and be damned, hey, Lissa?

Comments on the above blog post:

I've tried emailing and ringing you to no avail, so I'm left with no choice but to leave a comment here. I can appreciate you're upset, but what you are making are extremely serious—and unfounded—allegations.

If you don't delete them within twelve hours, I will take legal advice. I'm very disappointed in you, Megan.

Jeremy "Silver Surfer" Cooke

"Take legal advice"—you don't scare me, Professor Cooke. I won't be intimidated by a bully like you; Alice wouldn't have wanted that. I'm allowed an opinion. I'm quitting blogging, but not because it would suit you, and what's already here stays live out of respect for Alice, which in case you haven't noticed—you and Luke and the rest of the vultures—is a privilege my best friend never had.

Megan Parker

Megan, you're totally losing it. Can't believe you'd write this about Jeremy. He's a sound bloke and that stuff you've been posting about me, it's shite—yes, I did get taken to the station but I was let go, i.e., NOT charged. The police wouldn't have done that if they'd had the slightest suspicion about me. Alice would hate us fighting over her memory so don't get all holier than thou—yes, you were her best mate but you hadn't visited her for ages. One mention in a shitty PR mag as "one of the thirty under thirty to watch" and you turned your back on your old friends. Besides, Alice told me the last time she'd rung you, you'd had a right go at her.

Luke A

Why were the police so keen to talk to you, then, Luke, if you're innocent? They must have had a reason or they wouldn't have dragged you to Southampton, and they might have let you go, but that doesn't mean they can't subsequently charge you. I'm sick of people dissing me because in one stupid interview I dared to mention she wasn't perfect. With real friends you don't need to pretend they're perfect. I was her oldest friend, not some temporary boyfriend! Actually it's disrespectful to make out she was faultless—she liked to indulge herself, she liked a night out; it's not a crime. You of all people should know that, though I bet she didn't share the story about the weekend she was here in December, did she? When she got so drunk she fell down the stairs and knocked me flying in the process! Suppose I imagined that, did I?!

Megan Parker

Yeah, and I bet you were just as bad.

Luke A

Actually, I wasn't, so there. For the record, I wasn't drinking and it was your fault, if anyone's, she was so hammered, because it was the day after she discovered you'd been putting it around in Prague and she was upset and needed some company, so don't preach to me!

Megan Parker

Extract from transcript of interview with Jessica Barnes conducted at Southampton Central Police Station by Detective Superintendent Simon Ranger,
April 5, 2012, 5:20 p.m.

SR: Just so I'm clear, your view is that after the man in the black shirt, to reiterate your phrase, "put his arms round her, but not in a good way," she ran off. Is that correct?

JB: Yes. I explained. She got away. She legged it.

SR: This is really important Jessica—are you a hundred percent on that?

JB: Yes, she went one way and he went the other.

SR: Could either of them have been aware of you?

Interviewee shrugs her shoulders.

JB: Suppose he could have come back, but I went home. This happening, it's the crappest thing ever.

SR: How drunk was she?

JB: She wasn't, like, properly mortal, but she weren't sober. Wobbly but walking.

SR: "Wobbly but walking" in which direction?

JB: Down towards that sluice thing. It's horrible there. You hear about dogs getting sucked in. It's well dangerous—everyone knows that.

SR: Possibly not Alice Salmon.

JB: So it *was* her! I knew it was.

SR: But you're claiming the man in the black shirt, the man she'd referred to as Luke, was nowhere to be seen at this point?

JB: Yes. I mean, no.

SR: Which was it?

JB: He was gone in the other direction, headed towards the main road.

SR: You must have long since finished your cigarette by this point.

JB: I had, but that was when I got worried.

SR: Why did you get worried, Jessica?

JB: Because she started to climb onto the weir.

SR: Why might she have done that?

JB: Kids do it in the summer to swim.

SR: But this wasn't the summer, was it? It was February.

JB: That's why it was so nuts. Was like when it's hard to make out if videos on YouTube are real or made up.

SR: I can assure you this isn't YouTube, Jessica. Someone's dead.

JB: I didn't do nothing wrong. Am I being arrested?

SR: No, you're free to go at any point, but climbing onto the weir seems a curious thing to do. Maybe you called out?

JB: I did, yes, that's what I did, on my life I yelled, but she was miles away by then and in her own world. I kind of froze, too, like when you have a dream and you're bricking yourself so much you can't speak.

SR: What happened next?

JB: She stood on the grid thing, so the water must have been going under her, and then climbed over the fence, and I was, like, *Whoooa, why's she doing that?* Was it true? Was she pregnant?

SR: What did she do then?

JB: There's this platform thing that's, like, the top level, and she climbed up there. She must have been twenty feet above the river and I was, like, well freaked. Dunno why it's not properly fenced off; kids could get onto it. It reminded me of that advert on the telly where the geezer climbs the scaffolding because he's pissed and thinks he can fly, except she was kind of careful.

SR: Careful?

JB: Yes, sort of deliberate. When some people are mortal they go all manic and run around shouting the odds. Well, she was the opposite: she was all precise. It was as if she was doing stuff in slow motion. I never thought, *She's about to fall.* What I thought was *She's doing something very deliberate.* That was when it first occurred to me.

SR: What did? What occurred to you, Jessica?

JB: That she was about to jump.

PART FIVE

Not Signing Off with an X

Extract from Alice Salmon's diary,
December 9, 2011, age 25

I pretended I hadn't heard in the restaurant earlier. If I hadn't done that, I'd have exploded—seriously, I'd have lost it: burst into tears or screamed or thrown Luke's food into his fat, smug face. Plus, idiot that I am, I was still giving him the benefit of the doubt. Mum always said I flew off the handle too easily, so I was waiting for him to pipe up with a "Don't get the wrong end of the stick about that conversation between me and Adam" or "Don't pay any attention to Adam; he can be a right knob." But he didn't and I didn't mishear or misunderstand, because I might be stupid but I'm not that stupid.

No wonder he'd been so desperate to come over here after he'd got back from Prague. Talk about a guilty conscience. He'd called me the minute he got off the plane in Heathrow.

"It's Sunday," I protested, conscious I had a big day at work the next day.

"Please," he begged.

"Go on, then, twist my arm," I said, and an hour later he breezed in with his rucksack and a bouquet of flowers and one eyebrow missing (shaved off, so the story went, in some stupid bet). "What did you get up to, then? Or shouldn't I ask?"

"What goes on tour stays on tour," he'd laughed.

Clearly.

He collapsed in front of the telly: he'd managed fewer than four hours' sleep on both nights.

The two-faced liar had been on the same side of the table as me in the restaurant, three along; it had been boy-girl, boy-girl. It was his work crowd, but I wasn't going to be antisocial and bail out, even though I had Christmas shopping to do tomorrow. A guy from the bar at the front bowled past, heading to the loos, and, spotting Luke, slapped him on the shoulder, crouched beside him and started gassing. I didn't get the impression they were close-close: the handshake Luke gave him was the one he gave my work colleagues. I got snippets of the conversation. He was a friend of Charlie's from home, in London for the weekend; they'd met on the Prague weekend.

"You were downing tequila in an Irish bar when I last saw you," Luke said.

"Top weekend, wasn't it?"

The two of them chatted—"bonding," Luke would have described it as—about some altercation in a bar and drinking games and I felt a prickle of jealousy. I wanted to be part of the exchange. *What must it be like to be a boy?* I'd thought. *Would it be* very *different?*

And when we bundled out of the restaurant, after the game was up, he'd had the gall to ask: "Your place or mine?"

"Mine," I replied, needing to be on home territory when I confronted him.

So we sat together on the Tube from Leicester Square to Balham like a normal, everyday couple. Ten stops he had, to deny or admit it. Even acknowledging his exchange with Adam hadn't been a figment of my imagination would have been a start. But he sat, slouched in his seat with his legs apart, sticking out into the carriage so other passengers had to negotiate round them, and said absolutely nada. I'm such an idiot. When he'd rolled up after Prague, he'd dismissed my inquiries about the weekend with a "Bars, mostly," and I'd swallowed it. Why wouldn't I? Even when he'd added "A strip club or two, obviously," I wasn't over the moon, but it's what boys do and I liked how he *could* share that with me.

According to the sanitized version I'd got, they'd "seen" the castle, but not gone in. Debated whether to visit the Museum of Communism but never got round to it. Luke had gushed about the Charles Bridge and its baroque statues and informed me smugly it was where they filmed part of *Mission: Impossible.* "We had coffee in the Old Town Square, too—does that count as culture?" he'd joked, plumping up the cushions and stretching back on the sofa.

"For you, yes."

"Missed you," he said.

"Me too," I replied.

"I'm too old for this shit," he said. "I feel broken."

I'd watched Luke and his pal and this guy had the same easy manner as him, but wasn't anywhere near as hot. *My boyfriend,* I thought, watching him nodding and laughing. They talked about what a tragedy it was, Gary Speed hanging himself, and what Apple were going to do now Steve Jobs had died. "They're at a creative crossroads," Luke said, and I stored that one away; I'd tease him with that later. " 'Creative crossroads,' " I'd say. "Get you!" Then I largely tuned the pair of them out and joined a conversation on my left about a new exhibition at Tate Britain, a retrospective. Luke winked at me: it was a "Sorry, we can go soon," and it gave me a warm, indulgent glow: we'd been seeing each other for eighteen months.

"How much tequila did we put away on that trip?" I heard my boyfriend ask his new best mate.

"No idea," he replied, "and I doubt you did. You were sunk to the nuts most of the weekend with that girl from Dartmouth."

Article in *Student News: Hot off the Press* website, *September 9, 2012*

EXCLUSIVE: New Salmon "Romance" Link with "Father Figure" Cooke

The academic slammed for taking a sick interest in Alice Salmon has been "romantically" linked to the dead girl.

A disgusted witness says loner Jeremy Cooke, who's penning a book on the femme fatale, took an "unnatural level of attention" in her when she was a student under his care.

The onlooker claims to have spotted the childless 65-year-old, who lives in a £500,000 house, leading the tragic beauty back to his office when she was a fresher in 2004.

Speaking on condition of anonymity, the former undergraduate, now a successful Midlands-based professional, came forward yesterday to lift the lid on the behavior of the self-confessed "relic," who cycles everywhere on his trademark decrepit bicycle. She'd approached other media outlets, but *Student News: Hot off the Press* is the only website prepared to go public with it.

"I bumped into the pair of them one evening just before Christmas and she was distinctly wobbly," she said. "I offered to take her back to her room in halls but he said, 'No, she's all mine, this one,' and she was laughing, so I figured she was OK. I should have been more forthright, but he was well senior so I had no reason to be suspicious."

Only recently, reading press reports about the two individuals, has the whistle-blower come to view the incident in a different light and conclude that he and Salmon may have had a "special connection."

"I've heard it said that they hung out together when she was doing her finals. She was probably flattered by the attention, as any young girl would have been. Cooke often offered to counsel students who weren't even on his courses; he showered them—the boys and the girls—with inappropriate levels of kindness and support. Alice could have been infatuated or in awe of him. Maybe she saw him as a father figure. Yes, it could have been a kind of romance."

The former student said Cooke's interest in piecing her life together appeared to be more of a bid for fame and attention than a genuine academic endeavor. "A lot of lecturers are obsessed with recognition and legacy," she said.

A leaked student feedback form on the Gender, Language and Culture module shows the way the man, who was educated at a public school in a wealthy part of Scotland and has only worked in one academic institution, was regarded by undergraduates.

"He's like some throwback to a former era. It's like he's on autopilot or not in the room with you," one commented.

Another concluded: "Talk about clinging by your fingernails to the wreckage! Rumor has it the powers that be tried to get rid of him way back in the 1980s after some scandal but he's hung on ever since."

In an era when zero physical contact between teaching staff and students is tolerated, these allegations are bound to raise questions over the future of the ailing academic.

Student News: Hot off the Press contacted Cooke this morning, but he declined to comment.

Letter sent by Robert Salmon,
July 27, 2012

Harding, Young & Sharp
3 Bow's Yard
London EC1Y 7BZ

Mr. Cooke,

We've never met and won't, so I'll keep this brief. I am Alice Salmon's brother. My mother may or may not have deemed fit to mention in her correspondence with you that I'm a lawyer. It appears she's gone into fanciful details about everything else.

My area is corporate law, but I have consulted colleagues who specialize in publishing and wish to bring it to your attention that your "Alice book" is taking you into dangerous legal territory. Defamation is a potentially costly business. Cases centering on it are protracted and expensive, and personal bankruptcies are far from uncommon among those subject to claims. One can't defame the dead, it's true, but there are many legal avenues one could explore either to prevent publication or to seek post-publication recourse in relation to this work.

I presume my mother overlooked to request you resist putting the information she supplied—or indeed her own outpourings—into the public domain. Communication between myself and her is limited at present, but I need to remind you that, aside from any legal aspect, doing so would be highly unethical given her current state of mind. She had been coping so well, too. Her exchanges with you clearly trigger bouts of intensified unpredictability, so you must cease any contact with her forthwith.

The instant you began your pursuit of Alice, you opened a Pandora's box. You're driving a wedge through what's left of this family. By nature my father is not a jealous or violent man, but we all have our breaking point. How would you react if you heard your wife once had a relationship with the very man who is now taking such a priapic interest in your late daughter? That your wife once attempted to take her own life? That she was (I'm minded I should say "is") an alcoholic was, I gather, a fact of which he was aware; that one was a revelation solely to me. Congratulations, Professor, you've achieved what no one else has for thirty years—you've made my mother drink again.

You may surmise me contacting you is inappropriate—me sharing this information could in itself be interpreted as a breach of confidentiality—but when someone is not in their right mind it's beholden on those closest to them to make decisions on their behalf.

You need to understand that if you further jeopardize my mother's welfare, or indeed her relationship with my father, I will pursue you until you are penniless and the last copy of your squalid book has been pulped.

Yours sincerely,
Robert M. Salmon

Extract from transcript of interview with Jessica Barnes conducted at Southampton Central Police Station led by Detective Superintendent Simon Ranger,
April 5, 2012, 5:20 p.m.

SR: You said the girl on the weir was about to jump. Then what?

JB: She started singing.

SR: *Singing?*

JB: I was waving and stuff and reckoned I'd got her attention because she waved back. I could see her phone going through the air, the light of the screen, like.

SR: How did you respond?

JB: What sort of a world is it my baby's going to grow up in when a girl can die and no one notices?

SR: How did she respond when you waved, Jessica?

JB: On Facebook someone's put "She's gone to a better place," but guess what some sicko's wrote? "That rules Portsmouth out."

SR: Jessica, can you please focus? What happened next?

JB: She stopped waving and stood still on the weir and that made me calmer, because I figured if you were going to do something dreadful you'd be more careless—you wouldn't give a shit, would you? Way she'd been screaming at that fella, too, she had too much fight in her; women like that don't top themselves. Good on her, I say. No offense, like, but most men are utter wankers.

SR: So the man she'd been with—any sign of him at this point?

JB: He was long gone.

SR: But he could have returned unbeknown to you?

JB: You reckon it was him?

SR: One of our lines of inquiry is that she wasn't alone when she entered the water.

JB: My boyfriend's right: he says you lot haven't got a clue. No wonder the newspapers are giving you a kicking. They reckon she was being stalked. Was she?

SR: What did Alice do after she'd stopped waving?

JB: She was pacing around and I was all, *Shit, what do I do? What do I do?* So I yelled "*Hello,*" then grabbed my phone. I weren't sure who to ring, whether to call the police or what, but there was no signal and that was when I twigged why she was up there waving her arms. She went up there to get a signal.

SR: That seems a wee bit far-fetched.

JB: You do weird stuff when you're pissed; crazy stuff makes sense and normal stuff feels crazy. She kept putting her phone in front of her face; I could see the light from the screen. She must have been texting or picking up a message.

SR: Jessica, I'm going to ask you a very simple question and it's crucial that you answer honestly. What did Alice do next?

JB: She climbed down; swear on my kid's life, she climbed down.

SR: Would you be prepared to swear that under oath in a court of law?

JB: Yes, deffo. I did make out someone else on her side of the river a bit further up when I left—some old granddad. Must've been out walking a dog. I didn't see no dog, but why else would you have been out there? It was about minus 200.

SR: You were.

JB: I've explained that. I'd never have left her if I'd known she was going to die, would I? You can't blame me . . .

SR: You're not a suspect here.

JB: I remembered when I was on the bus coming here what song it was she was singing. It was like she was doing karaoke with no one listening.

SR: Elaborate on this "old granddad" walking a dog.

JB: Can't get the tune out of my head now. It was Example, because she sang the line about "the love kickstarts again." Says on the Internet it was one of her favorite songs. I ain't no policewoman, but if she was going to jump, she'd have done it on the weir and she wasn't so hammered that she slipped, so from where I'm sitting that leaves one thing.

SR: Which is what, Jessica?
JB: Obvious, isn't it? She was murdered.

Alice Salmon's Twitter biography,
January 4, 2012

Jackess of all trades. Neither fish nor fowl. Personal views—some borrowed, some blue (mainly blue at mo). Remember, it's not about the money, money, money . . .

Letter sent by Professor Jeremy Cooke,
July 25, 2012

Dear Larry,

You'll have to excuse my preoccupation with the past; 1982 feels remarkably *present*. I stuck with Dr. Richard Carter into the autumn. His observations remained challenging, but I'd begun to derive a nebulous satisfaction from them. When I wobbled, Fliss reminded me of our deal. She'd keep me, she'd said, as if referring to an old piece of furniture or an unpleasant pet—a dog, perhaps, that had taken to biting—as long as I persisted with the "consultations."

I'd pulled into the drive one evening after six or so weeks of her absence—don't quote me on that: time morphs and bends at the edges—and the sitting-room light was on. "You're back," I'd said.

"Don't mistake this for weakness," she replied. "Don't ever mistake this for weakness."

Communication between us was clumsy and maladroit in the period following her return. She'd been astounded when I'd initially confided where I was creeping off to on Wednesday afternoons. "My profession,"

I'd informed her with more than a hint of pretension, "is quick enough to hold up a mirror to mankind, so I figured it was appropriate I did so to myself."

Richard was suitably enervated when I articulated my contrition. My sparring partner even proffered up a few snippets of himself: he had a fiancée, an interest in arboriculture, a penchant for the Gothic. He had unconventional yet fascinating views on Jung. "Of all the careers you could have chosen, why this one?" I inquired.

"There's not a whole lot else to do on a Wednesday afternoon," he said, and we both chuckled; another watershed.

In fact, three decades on, I've half a mind to root out Dr. Richard Carter again; we'd have a whole new raft of issues to, as he might term it, "explore." But back then I was witnessing a most implausible phenomenon: progress. I felt like a new man. In November I asked Fliss if she concurred.

"It's not a new man I'm hoping for," she said, "just a slightly improved version of the old one. My dad said you might ultimately not be very nice, but I disagree. You're a fool, but you're not fundamentally bad, not at heart."

"I've been so very stupid."

"You'll not get an argument over that." She'd carried on preparing the pastry, a Delia recipe, probably; she was all the rage back then, as indeed she's become again thirty years later. "What did you see?" Fliss asked, smoothing her hair back behind her ear and inadvertently leaving a dab of flour there. "When you held up that mirror to yourself?"

"Someone who's very lucky. Someone who won't ever make the same mistake again."

I reached out and brushed the flour off her hair. I was glad she'd rumbled me. I couldn't carry the weight of my secret anymore. "Evolution is supposed to make us better, but I fear we're going backwards," I said. "We're becoming less human. I read yesterday that well over 10,000 people have been killed in this latest outbreak of war in Lebanon. Can you believe that it's 1982 and we're still killing each other over *ground*?"

She did her best to buoy me up, dubbed me a pessimistic old stick—reminded me there was plenty of good news around: *Columbia* striking out into space; the man at the university of Utah getting the world's first artificial heart; our engineers beating back the watery forces of the Thames before they engulfed London; even, she said apprehensively—aware that despite my left leanings I was skeptical of that ragtag bunch of lesbians at Greenham Common—the backlash against the arms race.

Larry, I'd never expected a Damascene conversion. Richard had warned me that there wouldn't be a lightbulb moment, but I was revitalized. That said, it would be a misrepresentation to assert I'd had some sort of personality reengineering, because I was lobbying hard behind the scenes to get that turncoat Devereux relieved of his duties, on account of the bastard's one-man campaign against my "lack of moral integrity." (Ultimately, as you'll recall, my efforts were thwarted because he was so chummy with the top brass.)

"With the benefit of hindsight, how might you describe your actions?" Richard had asked in one of our final sessions, the question reminiscent of school. I was never in trouble, so only heard it secondhand, but the fierier boys, the ones with real spunk—the ones who I'd later read in the alumni magazine had become venture capitalists or relocated to Kuala Lumpur—would recount how the headmaster, mid-admonishment, would ask how they'd describe their actions.

"Shoddy," I said. "Bad form."

Then one afternoon, clearly having concluded our relationship had moved on to a new plane, Richard let rip. "There's much I admire about you, Jeremy, but you do realize you're a tremendous hypocrite. You cite our insignificance, but at heart you believe that you're the most special creature that's ever set foot on God's earth. You can't accept the self-evident truths you preach to your students. For all your qualifications—and please spare me any more of the Oxford bullshit—you can't reconcile yourself to one fact. You're mortal. You're going to die. You won't change the world. Plus, were this a lecturer-and-student relationship, I'd feel duty-bound to remind you that you've never satisfactorily answered my initial question as to why you come here!"

"I needed some forgiving."

"That's beyond my remit," he said, inclining his head to the heavens.

I remembered my school motto, *Dulcius ex asperis.* "I wanted to be better," I said. "I wanted to stop hurting people."

"See," he said, with the faintest trace of smugness. "Altruism! It's not as if you're even referring to your kin, either."

Larry, I'd often grappled with whom "kin" constituted in my case. Both parents in the ground: one service attended, the other boycotted. No siblings; a cousin in Edinburgh I hadn't encountered in a blue moon. Fliss was the nearest I had, the woman I'd married in a small flint church in Wiltshire, the sunshine spearing through the stained-glass windows.

"How would you *love,* if you had an artificial heart?" she'd asked once, fascinated.

"One hasn't performed overly proficiently with a real one," I'd replied.

"Same time, same place next week?" Richard said in December.

"No," I said. "We're done."

"They all abandon me eventually," he chuckled.

"We've got that in common. The students do that to me. Thanks for everything. I feel better. I'm cured."

"That's not a description I tend to use. I'd view you as 'in remission.' "

I jumped in my car—the TVR I'd bought on a whim the previous summer—and played my new favorite song, "You Can't Always Get What You Want."

Doctor Richard Carter had become one of my closest friends.

Twitter activity referencing Alice Salmon,
January 29 to February 5, 2012

From @EmmaIrons7

So much for me never joining the Twitterati—I've landed! Can't wait to see u next month. Bring your dancing shoes!!

January 29, 11:39 a.m.

From @EmmaIrons7

You'll LOVE the dress I bought yesterday BTW.

January 29, 12:04 p.m.

From @EmmaIrons7

Why you not replying to my much-slaved-over tweets???

January 29, 6:31 p.m.

From @AliceSalmon1

Much soz, Ems. Been plowing thru work ahead of weekend. Party party x

January 30, 5:55 p.m.

From @Carolynstocks

Good luck with the article this week. Go knock 'em dead

January 31, 8:50 a.m.

From @AliceSalmon1

Aw thanks, Cazza. Bricking it x

January 31, 9:16 a.m.

From @NickFonzer

In your part of town tomoz and owe u dinner if u fancy grabbing bite to eat? That Italian u like?

February 1, 3:44 p.m.

From @AliceSalmon1

Be ace to see you, but will struggle this week—next week?

February 1, 3:55 p.m.

From @AliceSalmon1

Early nite tonite for this crime-busting gal ahead of big weekend in my old hood. Stay safe x

February 3, 7:37 p.m.

From @AliceSalmon1

When will I ever learn?

February 4, 8:07 p.m.

From @GeordieLauren12

You lightweight, we're never gonna let you forget this, bailing out early on a reunion!

February 4, 11:05 p.m.

From @AliceSalmon1

Say hello, wave good-bye.

February 4, 11:44 p.m.

From @Carolynstocks

Answer your flippinphone, Salmon . . .

February 5, 11:09 a.m.

From @MissMeganParker

Can't get hold of @AliceSalmon1 either. Prob nursing monster hangover somewhere!

February 5, 1:34 p.m.

From @Carolynstocks

You been kidnapped? Am sending out search party if you don't call me back soon.

February 5, 2:04 p.m.

From @MissMeganParker

Also been ringing @AliceSalmon1 with no luck—assuming her phone's dead, she never charges it!

February 5, 2:22 p.m.

Letter sent by Professor Jeremy Cooke,
August 8, 2012

Hello again, Larry,

"It's going to be bitter: Don't be late back," Fliss had instructed me, when I informed her at 4 p.m. I was nipping out for my constitutional.

At six, a text inquiring when I'd like supper. At seven, a phlegmatic "Where are you?"

But I couldn't pass up an opportunity such as this. You see, old chap, Alice was in town. A gift from the gods.

It wasn't hard to locate her. Initially via her digital trail; then, the scent picked up, I was onto her in the flesh. Like a bloodhound, I was. The melee enabled me to go unnoticed relatively easily; it merely necessitated selecting suitably distant vantage points from which to monitor her—the challenge was staying in close proximity. She soon had me puffing; ran me ragged, she did. That was to be the night, Larry. I was determined to exorcise a few ghosts, come clean about the night of the anthropology bash.

She was in a group of four, a fluid tetrad that expanded and contracted, her three friends dropping out of sight, then reappearing, others joining them, staying, melting away, breezing back. Inevitably there was a cavalcade of men vying for her attention. Not that I objected to them plying her with alcohol; it would gird her for the conversation I intended to have with her. City lads, some of them: hoodlums. "On a reunion," I heard her shout to one over the din. Others, students: boisterous and garrulous. Much frivolity.

As you'll have ascertained, I've been back over the events of that February evening in intricate detail, deconstructing Alice's movements and conversations. You see—and you'll have to bear with me on this one—but the authorities have got it wrong. My suspicion is that someone close to Alice wished her ill. You'll understand if I don't elaborate at this stage. Going public on a hunch can be a dangerous business for an academic; reputations have been ruined by less. I'm afraid this will have to be an exception to our rule: for now, a secret between us.

"Worried about you," Fliss texted me.

None of those philistines would have been alert to it, but behind the alcohol-propagated happiness, Alice wore a veil of sadness. It was so reminiscent of Liz, I had to restrain myself from tramping over and marching her out of those places. She was about the same age that her mother had been when our paths crossed. Mid-twenties. *Ripe.*

Another fellow on the scene at one point. A well-heeled sort. I'd edged closer; his hand might have been on her arm. She laughed so violently at one of his wisecracks that her head rolled backwards and the strip light made her hair look identical to her mother's. I'd been intending to explain about my association with Liz, too, when we had our discourse later, but feared that might be too much for her to hear in one go. I feared there'd be a scene.

Alice's response to him I couldn't decipher, but I did catch his. "Whoever he is, he's an idiot for letting you go."

"Tell him that," she said.

"Give me your phone and I will."

This, I thought, with a swirl of melancholy, *must be "chemistry."*

Another text from Fliss: "Are you safe?"

I actually made a record of the events of that evening upon my return home: locked myself in my study and logged them while they were fresh. Subsequently, I've repeatedly anatomized the constituent parts. One's training teaches one to amass a watertight case. Heaven knows, there have been plenty of digressions in this case: attention-grabbing deviations. Sideshows, the lot.

At one point, this boy inverted his empty pint pot on his head, then deposited it on the table and punched both arms skyward and she liked that, Alice did: she howled with laughter. I could see why; if he'd been at my school, I'd have had a crush on him: those shoulders rigid from rowing, an easy, insolent smile, intelligent but failing to fully apply himself. I'd encountered plenty of boys like that. I'd scuttle along in their slipstream, perversely grateful for their contempt and cruelty. If I had to pinpoint it, that was where my misanthropy was gestated: against a backdrop of rugger boots clicking on changing-room floors and the drilling of Latin declensions and conjugations. The abiding conviction that every last damn one of them was against me.

"Ever indulge in a dab of the old charlie?" he asked her.

"No. Or hardly ever."

"Which is it?"

"The latter, hardly ever."

"Tonight's hardly ever," he said.

Another text from Fliss. "What the hell are you playing at?"

Alice turned and it was tricky to make out if she was peering back towards her group or the chalkboard on the wall with its rainbow of lettering: 8 SHOTS, £7. "Suppose you only live once."

"Attagirl," he said. "Attagirl."

Internal memorandum among governors at Southampton University,
August 17, 1982

From: Anthony Devereux
To: Charles Whittaker
Status: Urgent and strictly confidential

Charles,

I'm unable to reach you by telephone, but we need to speak as a matter of urgency. I expect you'll be up to speed regarding the situation with the English tutor Elizabeth Mullens. You may have more information at your disposal than that to which I'm currently privy, but my understanding is that she attempted suicide earlier today. It appears one of the cleaning staff alerted the emergency services having discovered her, whereafter she was rushed to the emergency room. I gather her condition was dire. Clearly a personal tragedy, but with my professional and commercial hat on, I'm mindful of the wider implications. The press are bound to pick this up—especially given that a cleaner's involved; they're clinically incapable of discretion—so we need to thrash out a statement. Much sadness, shock, that sort of tone. Wouldn't hurt to hint at a few personal "issues," and with a fair wind they'll join the dots re her penchant for a drink. If it had been off-site it wouldn't be so damaging. Since the incident, rumors about Mullens and Cooke in anthropology have been brought to my attention. If the two of them are/were in a relationship, that will complicate matters. Cooke is older than her and married and neither of those facts will escape notice. The last thing we need is a scandal, Charles. A lecturer killed himself at one of those dreary, provincial northern polytechnics last year and the newspapers had a field day; it ended in resignations. My instinct—and I write this in confidence, because our association dates back over twenty years—is that Cooke is devoid of talent, so this could be a germane point at which to reappraise *his* future. That may also go some way to satiating the newspapers' bloodlust. It might be prudent for you to send Mullens flowers. Thank heavens the students are on vac: can you imagine the febrile environment we'd be attempting to contain were it term?

Yours as ever,
Anthony

PS: On an unrelated note, might you be free to join us on the evening of the 24th for our business-in-practice roundtable? One of the guests is an IBM director whose premise is that home computers will soon be as common as TV sets.

Alice Salmon's "Favorite Quotations" Facebook profile,
December 14, 2011

> "I will eviscerate you in fiction. Every pimple, every character flaw. I was naked for a day; you will be naked for eternity."
>
> **Geoffrey Chaucer**

"Be yourself, everyone else is already taken."

Oscar Wilde

"If you tell the truth, you don't have to remember anything."

Mark Twain

"For Sale: one heart. Horrible condition. Will take anything for it. Please."

Anon.

"In a free society, there comes a time when the truth—however hard it may be to hear, however impolitic it may seem to say—must be told."

Al Gore

Post on Truth Speakers web forum by Lone Wolf, *August 14, 2012, 11:51 p.m.*

It's not just the Iceman's head I've seen inside, I've seen inside his house and it's a mansion! I had a squiz on Google Earth, but had to wait for him and his missus, the pointy shrew-like snob, to go to Waitrose to get inside. Don't judge me, the end most def justifies the means in this case, and this is proper journalism—not that shite that Alice did, but uncovering things the establishment don't want uncovered. The Iceman needs to be exposed for the PERVERT he is.

That Megan bird who used to hang around with Alice has been gobbing off about him on her blog. Like, weird photos and stuff he's got stashed around the house, though I didn't stick around long enough to rummage them out. Anyway, I've more. I've tapped another professor for info—oh yes, some fossil in a nursing home by the name of Devereux who I heard about from one of the maintenance men at the uni and this dude worked with Iceman way back and despises him. I had to spin some line about researching an article on the great professors that this part of the world had produced for them to let me in, but don't hold that against me—it's not like I'm some *News of the World* journo hacking that murdered schoolgirl Milly Dowler's voice-mail!

I opened by stressing how fantastic it was to see him and putting on my best posh voice and he tucked into the chocolates like he hadn't been fed for a week. I had to wind him up a bit, tell him this book of the Iceman's would ensure *he'd* be the one who got remembered—like how everyone gushes about Darwin but no one recalls Wallace, a line I'd rehearsed—but he soon blabbed like a baby.

"He raped a student, that's what he did," Devereux said, bubbles of spit in the corner of his mouth. "Took her to his office and put it up her."

"Go on."

"I always had my suspicions but couldn't corroborate them—then recently read an article quoting someone who implied as much, too. She'd spotted him arm in arm with an intoxicated student. The pieces of the jigsaw fell into place then. I've calculated when it was and I bumped into him the next morning scuttling out of his office, shifty as buggery. Why would you spend a night in your office when you've got a charming old rectory of your own just a few miles away in the New Forest? Mmm?"

"Good point."

"Wasn't his usual prickly, combative self that morning, either. Yes, it rings true. He believed his own hype. 'Untouchable,' that was what he used to call himself."

Bingo! There was me half-prepared to give Icy the benefit of the doubt, let him get away with merely being a stalker, but he took her to his office by all accounts and shagged her when she was COMATOSE drunk, and now me climbing in a back window isn't such a big deal, is it?!!!

I played it cool with Devereux, pretended I already knew that, sensing that there might be more to come. Gave him my spiel about how Jeremy Frederick Harry Cooke will be claiming in his book that he had impeccable morals while others like him were shagging like rabbits.

"Rabbits," he screeched. "I'll give you *rabbits*. Cooke couldn't keep his pencil prick in his pants. He was a sex addict."

Then he told me something else. I've got much MORE information than Megan Parker and all I'm going to say now is it's mega and when you hear this you'll start taking the other stuff I say more seriously. Then my revelations will go VIRAL and his stupid book will rot in a few libraries, but my stuff will go round the world, except for countries like China where you can't even get on Facebook because the government's got this "great firewall of China" thing.

I wasn't originally intending to go public, but he's the one who went back on our deal and if he's going to play dirty then I am, too. He bangs on about evolution but I'm flexible, I'm responsive, I adapt.

I'm going in for the kill. Time for the lone wolf to howl. Pity my prey.

Extract from Alice Salmon's diary,
December 9, 2011, age 25

When you love someone, you notice stuff the rest of the world doesn't. A blink, a rigidity in their shoulders, a minuscule aberration in their intonation. I saw all those things in my boyfriend (is that now ex-boyfriend?) after Adam came out with that line in the restaurant. Then, cool as a cucumber, Luke retorted with: "What's the food like in here?" And the conversation wheeled off, diverted, precisely as he'd intended it to.

But I hadn't imagined it. *You were sunk to the nuts most of the weekend with that girl from Dartmouth.* This guy obviously hadn't realized Luke and I were an item—or he certainly hadn't twigged we had been at the time of the Prague trip. Luke briefly twisted round to me and smiled an artificial, forced smile, his whole demeanor screaming, "Did she hear?"

Yes, I heard all right.

Then he sat through the rest of the meal—even insisted on ordering a dessert—and acted as if it hadn't happened. Had coffee, still said nothing. Even a liqueur.

How many other trips away had he lied about? He'd been on loads since we'd met—with the rugby club, lads' weekends, birthday bashes, a stag do or two. Dublin, Newcastle, Brighton, Barcelona.

Then all the way home, those ten stops on the Tube, nothing. Maybe he was working on the principle that if I didn't raise it, then he'd have got away with it. There was a calm, calculated steeliness about him I'd never witnessed before.

Those ten stops on the Tube were his opportunity either to deny it or confess. The man I thought I loved wouldn't have sat for ten stops and not raised it. At Oval, he even had the balls to suggest we go to see *Tinker Tailor Soldier* Spy because there was a poster for it, but I shrugged off the suggestion; I was calculating exactly when the Prague trip had been—and concluded it must have been a good couple of months after we met, because it was definitely after Emily T's wedding.

It occurred to me that I could pretend I hadn't heard. I had that choice. It would actually be simple to pack it away at the back of my brain, ignore it. Some women go through their entire lives like that, holding the truth at bay—but bollocks to that old bollocks. He'd messed up and now we had to deal with it.

I'd been apprehensive of tempting fate, but Luke was different. Meg said I shouldn't get carried away. "There's got to be something wrong with him—he's a man!"

"If there is, I haven't found it yet," I always responded. "And I've had a pretty good look! There again, my judgment's hardly bombproof when it comes to men, is it?"

"No, but it's impeccable when it comes to friends!"

When we got back to the flat, Soph and Alex were in the lounge with friends, so we went to my bedroom and I blurted it out: "That rugby weekend you went on in Prague—did you sleep with someone?"

He denied it initially but soon changed his tune, perching awkwardly on the edge of the bed like a schoolboy who'd been caught out.

It was nothing. He was drunk. The two of us were barely an item. Blah blah blah. "I'm the same person I always was," he claimed.

"That's the problem—maybe I hadn't realized who that was."

I'd been so determined not to cry, but of course I did. It was the mini Christmas tree that set me off, the lights twinkling, and I remembered how the most random stuff used to make me upset—an old photograph, a child walking a dog, a sink full of saucepans—and I despised Luke for making me feel *that* again. "I'm not fucking stupid," I screamed, and someone in the flat next door banged on the wall.

"No one said you are."

"And don't patronize me."

He rubbed his forehead.

Maybe we'd simply never been compatible. The way he'd blathered on about that movie at Oval—how stylish it was, how classy, how clever—I'd been listening, thinking, *Yes, but probably boring,* and what kind of man rattles on about a spy film and Gary Oldman when he's slept with another woman?

I saw the picture of flowers on the wall, left behind by the previous occupant. I'd come back here because I'd needed to be on my own territory, but this flat wasn't mine; this room wasn't. We were supposed to be getting a place together. "I want us to not communicate for two months. No phoning, no texting, no nothing." And the stupidest thing came to mind—that that was a double negative.

"But we're getting a place together," he said. "It's only a fortnight to Christmas."

I so wanted a hug, to nestle my head into the crook of his neck, breathe in that smell: alcohol and smoke and the remnants of shower gel, then collapse into bed—me on the right, him on the left.

"I like being near the door," he'd said the second night he stayed. "In case I need to make a speedy getaway!"

He'd made me laugh a lot that day.

"I'm not going to let this happen. I won't, I can't," he said.

Carry on, I thought. *You keep going. You're merely digging your own grave.*

Article on *Your Place, Your People* website,
October 20, 2012

Academic Fighting to "Keep Salmon Name Alive" Is Dying

The popular professor undertaking a "touching tribute" to former student Alice Salmon is dying of terminal cancer, we can reveal today.

Professor Jeremy Cooke has been diagnosed with prostate cancer, the most common form of the disease among men in the UK.

The leading academic is believed to have privately vowed to continue living a normal life despite his illness, which became public after an anonymous post on a forum by someone referring to themselves as "Lone Wolf."

"Survival statistics for prostate cancer have been improving for thirty years, and if it's caught early, a sizable majority of patients can live for five-plus years," a retired surgeon from a Southampton hospital explained. "The outlook is far bleaker if it spreads to other parts of the body, such as the bones."

Students and staff have rallied to support the man known fondly as "Old Cookie." Former colleague Amelia Bartlett said: "He's a terrific academic with a fierce intellect. I hope he's able to apply his trademark philosophical wisdom to this awful situation."

Ex-student Carly Tinsley said: "He was a bit of a legend—happy to play squash with us or join us for a beer in the union. He consistently went the extra mile in providing mentoring and support. He even gave me vitamin tablets when I had fresher's flu. I wish the press would stop hounding him."

In a recent anonymous review-form feedback from students, one declared: "His lecture on Melanesia was amazing. It's made me totally determined to visit that part of the world—that's got to be about the ultimate accolade for an anthropologist."

Another said: "At school the teachers parroted what they'd

read in other books, but at least he's been there done that. His knowledge on sociolinguistics is second to none."

A long-term resident of Hampshire, Cooke first came to public prominence in 2000 when he featured in the popular BBC documentary *How We Made Ourselves.*

The recipient of a clutch of high-profile awards, including the coveted Merton Harvey Award for "Inspiring Young People in the Field of Anthropology," he's well-known for his strong environmental views.

Educated at the respected Glenhart School near Edinburgh, and a stalwart supporter of several local charities, he famously vowed in a BBC radio interview five years ago to "ditch the bloody car and cycle wherever the bloody hell I can."

Letter sent by Professor Jeremy Cooke,
August 21, 2012

Dear Larry,

Alice slung the contents of the glass into my face and screamed: "You pervert."

I dabbed at my eyes with my handkerchief; the place was so busy, no one gave us a second glance. In the din we stood stiffly, but one of us had to speak, so ridiculously I inquired: "How's your reunion going?"

"Shit, that's how, the worst day of my life. Any more stupid questions?"

"Gosh."

"Actually, it's the second worst day of my life. You'll remember the first, you were there—you made it the worst, you *creep*!"

You'll never guess what she did next, Larry. By golly, she slapped my face.

"There. That's for what you did when I was eighteen."

The last person to have hit me was my father, five-plus decades ago, and her contact had the same blunt, mechanical quality. Bizarrely, in the commotion, no one noticed. "I deserved that," I said. "If it's any consolation, I regret what I did with every fiber of my being."

"Very poetic, but no, it's not."

"I haven't come to hurt you. I'm here to explain."

Her look reminded me of a near-dead weasel I'd once encountered in a snare.

"There's no need to be frightened."

"Not. Not frightened of any man."

"Should I get you some water?"

"Water?" she replied, as if I'd suggested we book a restaurant. "It's alcohol I need."

I scuttled across to the bar and bought her a drink—opted for a gin and tonic, because that was her mother's tipple, a double—and when I returned she was struggling to breathe, puffing as if fresh from a bout of exercise.

"Just go," she said. "If you go now, I can tell myself this is a coincidence."

"But it isn't. I knew you were here from Twitter."

"You followed me?"

"The over-sixties *can* use the Internet."

"Yes, clearly—to email my mum! What the fuck—"

"About 2004," I interrupted. "You need to hear."

"No, you need to get out of my face."

But it was bravado. Not dissimilar to how I'd repeat the mantra: I'm not scared of dying. A sense of exigency pressed in on me. "I owe you an enormous debt of gratitude. For your discretion. My life could have panned out very differently."

"I didn't do it for you. Is that what you think? You stupid old fuck! I kept quiet because I didn't have a clue what went on. I wasn't confident enough to do anything else. If it was now, I'd have you strung up."

No lies, Larry, we said no lies, and I'm aware I've never told you exactly what did occur that night. It was 2004: the anthropology community had been ablaze with chatter about the discovery of fossilized hominid remains in Indonesia, *Homo floresiensis*. It dominated conversation at our little bash: how this hobbitesque species could have existed as recently as 12,000 years ago, their skeletons like Homo erectus, but their bodies and brains tiny. I've never told you how afterwards, safely ensconced in my office, Alice had virtually collapsed into me.

"You could barely walk," I said.

She shivered, a look of horror passing across her face.

Yes, I may have locked the door—not for any malign reason, but because she'd made a spectacle of herself at the function and I was anxious to prevent anyone else witnessing her in that state. The inalienable fact remains, however, that no student—regardless of gender—should have been alone with a member of the faculty while that intoxicated. Certainly not for an entire night. Even disregarding the Liz component, it was a gargantuan transgression.

"I put you to bed," I said, but she didn't hear, so I repeated it more loudly, and my declaration had the same bizarre ring as it might were I to have proclaimed: I live on the moon.

She went to turn away but clearly couldn't. "How?"

"There was an element of manhandling."

"When I woke up I was . . . I didn't have all my clothes on."

"Your top was covered in wine, Alice; it was drenched. You wouldn't have been able to sleep in it."

"So you took it off?"

"I helped *you* remove it."

She shuddered and peered over my shoulder at the throng of Saturday-night revelers. *That's where you want to be, isn't it, sweetheart?* I thought. *Out there in the middle of all that untarnished and optimistic life.*

"I made sure you were comfy," I said. "I tended to you."

"You could have got a female colleague to do that."

"Indeed, and with hindsight, that's what I should have done. The student-staff relationship is predicated on trust and I violated that."

But, Larry, I didn't engineer events to unfold as they did. I didn't choose to see her slim, pale body or the shaded pinch of her navel or the startling bright purple of her underwear.

I should have left the pub then, but it would be the last opportunity I ever had to speak with her; I wasn't intending to leave her with questions. "It was the same with your skirt," I said. "You were snatching at it, complaining you wouldn't be able to sleep in it. I assisted you out of it."

"You slimeball, you should have been fired."

I'd come to make amends, but it was running away from me, my carefully crafted lines swept aside by her momentum. "We have a code and I breached it. I acted unethically."

"I should have gone to the authorities. I could have had you prosecuted."

"For what exactly? I acted irresponsibly, immorally, but legally my conduct was unimpeachable. I transgressed one boundary, but there are others I would never cross."

I didn't elect to smell her sugary breath or feel her limp limbs concertina against me or have to stand back and stare detached and abstractedly at the unadulterated Liz-like gorgeousness of the woman prostrate in my office.

"You're disgusting; you're virtually a pedophile."

"No, that's not on, I won't have that." My right eye twitched; a vein in my right temple pulsed. I rarely lose my temper—three or four times in the last two decades—but when I blow, I really blow. Once, after a hospital visit, we'd gone to the park—to "decompress," as Fliss had put it, because the news hadn't been good—and I'd banged a bench until my hands had bled. What's weird is how I recall so little of that day now. Exorcised from my mind. One's memory—one's brain—works in astounding ways; it's an artful, self-regulating self-defense mechanism, bolting out the bad. "I looked after you," I said. "I took care of you."

She'd been out for the count, so I'd draped my sweater over her and she'd emitted little animal noises: my snuffling blind kitten, my harvest mouse. I'd flicked the wireless on and leant in and got the close, uninterrupted look, the examination, I'd so long coveted: black whorls of hair on her neck, a tiny mole on the side of her head, the faintest dusting of hair on her face, like down.

"I watched over you while you slept," I said.

I'd sat beside her all night—her tiny body, my tiny brain—and held her hand and outside a dark breeze had brushed the branches of the elm tree against the window. I did think about sex, I very much did—but it was how ultimately inadequate it was. Not much to wreck a marriage over, is it? A stranger putting one part of their body against yours and moving it a bit. Wet against wet, that's all.

"You could have done anything," she said.

"But, Alice, it would have been an abomination."

"Are you lying?"

"No," I said.

She glanced around for her friends, a shot of loneliness connecting us. "You wouldn't believe how often I've *nearly* confronted you about that night," she said. "Always chickened out."

"I've always had a soft spot for you. Even when you were a fresher, I felt protective towards you because of your mother. You're so like her."

"I saw your email—earlier today, I read it. Is *Jem* what she called you? The pair of you are gross!"

"Bless you, Alice. We weren't born old."

"My dad's more of a man than you'll ever be."

"That I don't doubt." She was driving us off on a tangent, but I had to make my peace, so blundered on. "Thing is—thing was—the concern I had for *you* manifested itself speciously. There is the night to which we've been referring, plus you may recollect receiving an anonymous note during freshers' week. I'm rather afraid that was from me."

"You bastard."

I'd damped my handkerchief and periodically wiped her brow and held water to her mouth and pulled back her hair when she flopped sideways to be sick. I'd fought sleep—I had to ensure she didn't choke on her own vomit—and a monotonic presenter had chatted to a procession of callers about the city's recycling policy and the menace of urban foxes, and daylight had filtered between the drawn blinds and I'd seen her faded brown skirt on the floor, twisted and rumpled like a rope, and I'd thought: *Is this all it is to be a man? All those millions—billions—of years of evolution and this is all it's made us?*

"I'm here to say sorry."

"Sorry's not good enough."

"It's a start," I said. "And it's all I've got. I am profoundly sorry."

She stared down at the pub table, traced the lines of the wood with her finger. Always amazed me as a boy how you could age a tree by the rings in the wood, one of the first occasions upon which I appreciated the power of science to yield answers. Other revelations circled in my head—Liz's drinking, the attempt she made on her own life—but they weren't mine to share.

"The truth can never be an entirely bad thing," I said.

"Why did you email her?"

"Alice, learning you were in the city brought back lots of emotions. They say the death of an old man can never be a complete tragedy, but, damn it, I'm not quite old. I don't feel it, at any rate." Fear slithered in at me. "Prostate cancer. I have prostate cancer."

"That supposed to make me feel sorry for you?"

"It's not supposed to make you feel anything. It is what it is. One of your mother's favorite expressions used to be 'Look at your monsters.' You've done that tonight. I'm proud of you."

We were barely three feet apart, but it could have been a mile; it was as if she was regarding me through a body of water. I felt a curious release: letting go.

"I left my mum a message after I read your email—not a nice one."

"Why don't you call her, put her mind at rest? One should never let the sun go down on an argument."

"Can't, too late, it'll come out wrong. I'll ring her in the morning. Not that it's any of your business."

"Promise me one thing," I implored her. "Don't do anything tonight you'll regret forever."

"Fuck forever."

She sniffled a bit then, on the verge of tears, and I felt an ache in my gut, my balls, a twinge, muscle memory. Time, Larry, I was running out of the wretched stuff. I'd had sixty-five years to be a better person; how could I have wasted that opportunity? The police have been onto me, too, can you believe it? *Me.* Apparently Liz burst into the station—drunk, from what I could infer—and leveled a mélange of allegations against me. It wasn't onerous to run rings round that bunch of incompetent buffoons, though. I intend to release information on my terms, at a time of my choosing.

"You're not going to do anything stupid, are you?"

"That's rich coming from you."

She had a point. I was debating whether to get behind the wheel of my car loaded up on Scotch. I felt myself in a new, altered space: a Zen-like calm bordering on the existential. It was done. "That quote you've got on your Facebook page—I'm rather taken with that: how the truth hurts for a little while but lies hurt forever."

In the morning, Larry, I'd stood to leave, but she'd looked so defenseless, I'd bent down and kissed her lightly on the forehead. "Good-bye, Alice," I whispered. "Good-bye, my darling." She'd woken in a panic, flustered and mystified, then fled from my office and never once spoke of that night during her three-year tenure at the university. Fate largely conspired to keep us apart, allowing us only a handful of on-her-part-painful chance encounters.

"This isn't the end of this," she said.

A song that I wasn't familiar with stopped, and another one started.

"Bet you got a right buzz out of manhandling me like that, didn't you?"

I could feel ire and antagonism burgeoning inside me. Of course I wasn't expecting gratitude or thanks, but what would she have preferred—that I throw her to the wolves? I decided to take a stroll to clear my head. The river would be nice: quiet, bracing, invigorating. As I departed, she seized my arm, spun me round.

"Asked you a question, Professor Pervert. How did it feel when you were touching me?"

"Heaven, Alice. It felt like heaven."

Post on Truth Speakers web forum by Lone Wolf,
August 20, 2012, 11:02 p.m.

I'd practiced my posh accent, learnt a few new words and bish bash bosh it was soon flooding out of the old boy Devereux. He was lonely and itching to talk. I'd told him Cooke was billing himself in his book as the university's top academic and predictably he took the bait and said he was a shit.

This was my third visit. The second had been a right balls-up: he hadn't slept the previous night because an ambulance had come to take one of them from the home and he had been dopey and nice, and that was no use to me. Today he was wound up and perfect.

"He's not in your league," I said, rattling off the list of prizes this old turd had won—he even had his own Wikipedia page, and how vain is that? I might have "slipped" into the conversation that the word Cooke would use to describe him was "limited."

"'Cock,' we called him," he announced, gob gathering round his mouth. "'Jeremy Cock.'"

I've got a gift for seeing inside people and there was more here, I just needed to scratch the scab, so I concocted some story about how Cooke had been spreading it around the university that he was a cabbage.

"He slept with the girl's mother back in the 1980s, too."

I didn't respond. Alice told me in Caledonian Road how journalists use silence because we're all frightened of it and so tend to fill gaps.

"Mullens," he said. "Elizabeth Mullens."

Well, well, so the Iceman boned Alice Salmon's mum like he did her. Result! I pictured myself back in my room on the third floor posting this info and waited for more silence to do its work, except there was a long wail from another room and someone crying, "Nooooo."

"She tried to kill herself when he ended it. He should have lost his job."

"He might yet," I laughed. "He might yet."

Pointless was on the telly and I came out with some rubbish about how Mullens must have hated the world to attempt the old hara-kiri.

"Suicides hate themselves first and foremost," Devereux answered, "though expediting the end goes against God's plan. Ah, God's plan. Another bone of contention between Cock and me."

"You're well smart, aren't you?"

"The body might be frail, but the spirit is still willing."

They'd have you believe they're better than the rest of us, these professor types, but they're like kids. His and Iceman's feud began with a petty dispute over departmental budgets apparently and rumbled on for three decades: squabbles over research grants, politics, offices, teaching methods—you name it, the pair were at each other's throats over it.

"He's still at it, the shagging," I said randomly, in a bid to coax out more.

One of the orderlies came in and announced that it would be dinner soon: roast lamb.

"His misdeeds weren't limited to the bedroom. Plagiarism is not an accusation I level lightly. Budgets were also questioned; money went unaccounted for. Naturally, it may have been innocuous."

"Your memory—it's friggin' amazing," I said, buttering him up.

If you're reading this, don't judge me. We've been over this ground before—about ends justifying means and professors shagging students and Icemen who kill salmon.

"It wasn't solely the anthropology party itself that was a great tradition," he said. "Cock taking a drunk victim back to his office afterwards was, too."

"Let's destroy him," I whispered.

He stared at *Pointless* and there was a smell that reminded me of piss.

"The Mullens girl nearly died and he still couldn't leave her alone. They were at it again years later, you know. When she was married. Convinced they kept it quiet, they were, but I was onto him. It was three years after their affair."

I did the maths. It would have been the year before Alice was born.

Reading by Megan Parker at Alice Salmon's funeral service,
February 13, 2012

What is dying?
I am standing on the seashore.
A ship sails to the morning breeze and starts for the ocean.
She is an object and I stand watching her
Till at last she fades from the horizon,
And someone at my side says, "She is gone!" Gone where?
Gone from my sight, that is all;
She is just as large in the masts, hull and spars as she was when I saw her,
And just as able to bear her load of living freight to its destination.
The diminished size and total loss of sight is in me, not in her;
And just at the moment when someone at my side says, "She is gone,"
There are others who are watching her coming
And other voices take a glad shout,
"There she comes."
And that is dying.

Extract from Alice Salmon's diary,
December 9, 2011, age 25

Mustn't stop writing . . . need to occupy my mind . . . have to keep the demons at bay . . .

I presume Luke went home, but he might be sleeping on a bench in Balham station for all I care.

"There'll be no trains," he'd whinged when I'd booted him out. "It's late."

"Walk, then, or get a cab—it's not my problem."

He'd quibbled about the cost of a taxi, but he always had plenty of cash for lads' nights out or excursions with the boys to expensive European cities.

I rang Meg as soon as I'd slammed the door on him. "Ring me, babes," I pleaded into her voice-mail. "Desperately need to talk."

I sat on my bed and the texts arrived—Sorry, can't live without you, I'll change, never do it again, love you more than anyone, blah blah blah. "Which bit of no contact do you *not* understand?" I typed, and it felt peculiar, not signing off with an x, but I deleted it before sending.

The bastard, how could he?

I lay on my bed and flicked through the photos on my phone. So many of *him*. Was there no part of my life he hadn't infiltrated? One by one, I hit the dustbin icon. Then I pulled up his number and deleted that, too.

Outlandish notions of how I could get back at him boomeranged around the room.

Music from the flat upstairs. A door slamming, a toilet flushing, muffled conversations in Alex and Soph's rooms, them and their partners. *Don't go to bed,* I thought. *Don't leave me the only person awake.*

Tried Meg again. Voice-mail. Why isn't she answering? "What's happened *now*?" she might inquire, exasperated. "Never trust a man, Salmonette," she used to say, and before Luke I'd always agreed. Now I hated him for proving her right. "Forget the fellas—it's friends who last forever," she declared once, finding me on her doorstep after some drama with Ben. She'd taken me in, put *Hollyoaks* on, and said, "They're bastards, each and every one of them, ruled by their dicks," then she poured some wine and the hurt seeped away.

Ben had been in touch out of the blue a few weeks ago: an innocuous enough text inquiring, "What's occurring, Fish Face?" I'd ignored it, conscious of where exchanges like that could lead, but now I take up my phone, my hands shaking, and stab in a short message to him.

Luke, you complete and utter bastard, how *could* you? We had enough cash saved for a deposit and our first month's rent. Had put it into our joint bank account—Miss A. L. Salmon and Mr. L. S. Addison—periodically totting up the tally, its rising total a springboard to conversations about "the flat"—an increasingly real concept as we'd traipsed around Wandsworth and Lambeth and out into the badlands of Denmark Hill and even into pretty Pimlico to see how the other half lived, settling on Tooting Bec, which we'd decided was affordable but on the up ("It's the next Shoreditch," one agent optimistically assured us). We hoped to get two rooms but could cope with one. Fancied purpose-built rather than a conversion. Preferred no one above us to avoid noise. Maisonettes were a no-no. A garden would be a bonus, but the absence of one wouldn't be a deal breaker. There was only one deal breaker here. Luke.

Only one heartbreaker.

I could go to Australia, the prospect a brief fluorescent light of positivity. *I* am *only twenty-five.* I'd known it was a mistake, settling down at twenty-five; that's what thirty-year-olds do! But the brightness dimmed as swiftly. What fun would it be without Luke?

Needed air, space. I'd walk. Often, when I was out on the common, I'd go on Facebook or Twitter and trace friends' friends or followers' followers outwards in concentric circles until they were perfect strangers, then message them, saying, "Hey, how are you?"; or in case they thought it was spam, I'd send a personalized one like "How was the theater?" or "I like that dress in your profile picture." One night some randomer asked, "Where are you?" and I replied, "Standing by the pond on Clapham Common, staring into the water," and that was the end of that conversation. Meg says it's weird conversing with people I don't know, but living in a city's weird, cooped up like battery hens, sleeping inches from strangers, emailing colleagues when they only sit a few feet from you.

Why aren't you calling me, Megan?

"They'll never have what we've got," she'd said once when we were teenagers. "Whoever we meet, whoever we marry, they'll never have what we've got."

The traffic died away and I didn't ring him and I didn't text him. I hung on to that crumb of control. I opened my laptop and made myself type. Did what Luke often did, summing up situations in tabloidese.

The girl threw the miniature Christmas tree out of the window.

The girl felt an old, familiar detachment, almost as if she was floating.

The girl lay awake wondering where the fox she'd once been friends with had gone.

I will not let him wreck Christmas. Was so looking forward to it, too—seeing my folks, Mum's food, playing Aunty Alice. When I was eighteen, I couldn't wait to get away from the burbs, but when I'm stressed now it can exert a near-magnetic pull on me—*home home.* The bedroom where me and Meg ("It's 'Meg and I,' " Mum would insist) would spend lazy, stretched Sunday afternoons, bikes zigzagging along the street, the smell of barbecues, recorders being badly blown, figures at computer screens and families framed by alcoves in the evenings, cats on doorsteps and dewy lawns in the mornings waiting for the jangle of keys, kids shouting demandingly and lovingly: "*Muuuuuuum.*" What will Mum and Dad make of this? They like Luke. Won't when I fill them in on the real Luke, his aversion to hard work, his indecisiveness about his career, his boy-like vulnerability, his temper. Well, we can add his pathological inability to be faithful to the list.

How could I have been so foolish? Stupid, stupid, stupid me.

"Tosser!" I shouted, and when I hadn't typed for a few minutes the screen saver appeared: a picture of Luke with sunglasses on taken from a low-down angle. It infuriated me, that it was him there. Delete.

Eventually I gave up even reading the texts from him. I slid my finger across the screen so the red Delete tab appeared, then they were gone.

So that was it, was it? Eighteen months. A Greek restaurant in Dean Street. A friend of a friend of his. One misjudged line by a man I'd never met and probably wouldn't ever again.

I wasn't going to ring him and I wasn't going to text him and I wasn't going to cry and I wasn't going to let *IT* sneak back in.

I managed the first two.

I make myself type and the dry irony buffets me. I'd deleted every picture of him from my phone and here I am, putting him back into my laptop. I make myself carry on, although my hands are deadweights—fat, pale, blotchy lumps of meat.

Clichés. All clichés.

The twenty-five-year-old hates herself, but hates Luke Addison more.

Eventually the noise of the traffic stops and I don't ring him and I don't text him.

I thump the keys with my gross hands and the whirling, jagged sentiments in my head become type on the page. The room spins. I'm not drunk but I have that in reserve.

Keep writing, Alice . . . don't stop.

Need to focus on the good stuff. Christmas—and then there's the February reunion in the Hampton, too. Is this how unhappiness is, how the second half of your twenties is going to be? Clutching at milestones to get you through.

A text from Ben. "Waaaaaas up? When we hooking up?"

When I was a kid, I used to visualize romantic crises: I figured I couldn't be a woman without having experienced them. I composed poems about them, loaded with airy, theoretical claptrap. But this is the reality—not having the faintest idea whether hate trumps love and, beyond that, the messy, practical details, not knowing whether to leave my phone on or turn it off, and what I'll say if a colleague asks after Luke at work, and what to do about our theater tickets for next Thursday.

Luke Addison is a liar.

That's my word for this entry. "Liar." Or "bastard." Or "Prague." Or "unfaithful." Or "naive." Plenty of choice.

This will be my last diary entry for a while.

I wish he was dead. I wish *I* was dead.

Meg still hasn't called back.

"In your neck of woods first week of Feb x," I reply to Ben, the self-satisfied feeling of getting one over Luke promptly overtaken by a hesitant guilt.

Outside, quiet—or the near quiet you briefly get in a city in the night. "Hello, old friends," I find myself saying to the night and the near quiet and the gritty exhaustion behind my eyes, because I can't face writing it.

I'll write one last line here: *I'll make Luke regret this if it kills me.*

Letter sent by Professor Jeremy Cooke,
September 7, 2012

Larry,

It didn't come to me in a dream or a burst of frenzied late-night concentration. It wasn't accompanied by a thunderclap or the renderings of a celestial choir. There was no grand romantic canvas, merely a woodland walk with the dog. An understated backdrop for such a potentially grand epiphany. A murder.

You see, I know what happened to Alice. It was one of those unanticipated yet electrifying leaps. I expect it had shades of how you felt when stumbling (I do you a disservice, sir, yours was no stumble, instead the product of years of thorough, systematic work) upon Gutenberg's theorem. A flash of—and forgive me for using the term in connection with myself—inspiration. It was the nearest I've come to a eureka moment.

It can't be, I told myself. It simply *couldn't.* But what is the job of us so-called intellectuals if not to think the unthinkable? Even if only for argument's sake, I postulated: *What if?*

Thing is, once you've had a seminal thought, the doors of the imagination open. Everything is filtered through that prism. Like dominoes falling. How, after the human genome was mapped, a raft of opportunity became attainable—even deciphering our predisposition to illness. Too late for me, that little marvel of discovery, but what monumental steps our descendants might take.

Everyone's an amateur sleuth these days, but the police have been approaching it from the wrong angle. It's analogous to when one hunts a room for a specific item: one's eyes can't *not* be part closed to everything else. The logical, plausible way in which they set about the task—constructing theories, then setting about proving or disproving them—was contingent on one of those theories actually being correct. Science frees us to look—indeed, it dictates we must look—at situations from obtuse angles.

Discussing the merits of my work, the mechanics of "Project Alice," this person had made a mistake, one injudicious utterance, and, hallelujah, it was like a mist lifting. "We can make Alice whoever we want her to be," they'd carelessly said. "We can invent a person and reinvent ourselves in the process."

Larry, I was keen to rush off a short missive to you straightaway, but there's work to be done. I've been shot down previously over an inadequately prepared hypothesis. There's evidence to be collected, arguments to be marshaled. I need to make it bombproof. I am convinced, however. As with all the most seemingly obtuse and impenetrable problems, the solution is blindingly obvious.

Fliss and I are heading out this evening: a well-received *Tempest* at the Mayflower. I've always been rather drawn to that most enigmatic of protagonists, Prospero—god-like, childlike, master of his universe, ex-communicated, crippled by love and a lack of it, flawed yet capable of forgiveness. But don't worry, my old friend, I won't be swayed by his display of benevolence. Justice must prevail.

Mahler's Fifth, a cup of Earl Grey, the draft of my resignation letter (one I've begun on so many occasions before) in front of me. It's not a bad life, this. Notes for the structure of my book, the Alice book, scattered pell-mell across my desk. After this afternoon's woodland walk, I rather suspect it may have an unexpected ending.

Text messages sent by Alice Salmon,
February 4, 2012, between 11:47 p.m. and 11:59 p.m.

To Ben Finch:

You're right we're something passing stopped . . . you there? Fancy meeting me at our fave spot???

To Megan Parker:

Soz for being a rubbish friend. Love you missus x

To Luke Addison:

That didn't go how I intended—I'm such a fuckup. No wonder you hate me :-(

To Elizabeth Salmon:

How could you? How could you?

To Luke Addison:

Not waving but drowning

PART SIX

The Things That Make You ***You***

Blog post by Megan Parker,
October 26, 2012, 5:15 p.m.

I read on Twitter this morning that I'm insane.

It made me laugh out loud. Seriously. You have to laugh, otherwise you'd cry. Otherwise this stuff would drag you under.

After we lost Alice, her family were first in the media's spotlight. Then it was any man she'd ever as much as spoken to—depending on the publication, they were either "exes," "romantic liaisons," "love interests" or "conquests." Then friends joined the list of legitimate targets and I was top of the pile. I was a sitting duck.

There was a spell when I couldn't leave the flat—a tight, chummy huddle of journalists camped outside, bringing each other Starbucks and greeting me whenever I opened the door with a shutter-clicking hail of "Megan, Megan, how are you feeling today, Megan?"

A dead adult never ignites quite the coverage a case involving a child does, but one editor went as far as claiming our story had a "tragic Shakespearian quality—two almost-sisters torn apart by death."

Funny how they're such experts on me. I never realized I had "the classic, suburban upbringing," that I was "a typical Libran," that my sadness was proving "an unbearable millstone."

Grief counselors have been wheeled out, articles illustrated with colorful drawings and infographics. *Coping with loss. What to expect when your best friend dies. Celebrities who've lost their besties.*

I tried cooperating—forced myself to look into their cameras, responded to their questions, because, like wasps in a jar, I feared antagonizing them. When that backfired, I refused to engage, but it made no difference: they'd decided on their angle anyway.

Having rinsed me, one website ran a photo of my mum and dad on "a break from supporting me," the snide subtext, as evidenced by the "Parker parents enjoy a beach stroll in Devon" caption, presumably being that they weren't allowed a weekend away for their anniversary. It was far from the sole such case. Stuff about parenthood, friendship, how our city centers have become Friday- and Saturday-night no-go zones—they're all fair game, if Alice is the "hook." Spotting a bandwagon, one broadsheet jumped aboard with a feature headlined "Salmon Story Highlights Press Ethics Enquiry's Impotence." Apparently I raise some interesting questions.

I forget what I have—and haven't—said. I'm utterly worn-out by it, yet still they circle jackal-like for another bite of the corpse, another twist, an encore, a sequel.

There's been interpretation, extrapolation and exaggeration (Alice would have said that reminded her of the *Just a Minute* catchphrase); leaps of logic and faith; two and two added together in a credible way to make five. Why let the facts get in the way of a good story?

I read somewhere that I quit my job not because of my wish to return to full-time education but because I was left incapable of working. Fellow employees—unnamed—had witnessed me become "a shadow of my former self" and "in danger of buckling under the blunt force of bereavement." There have been a lot of unnamed sources.

Only this week, one blog broke the "news," sandwiched between stuff about Jay-Z and Jim Davidson, that Alice and I "regularly smoked weed." Well, hello. Since when has three or four times in the last ten years constituted "regularly"? The justification? Half a line from a mutual friend. (Don't worry, Nik, I don't hold it against you; you were a lamb to the slaughter.)

Among the pop-up ads for fifty-percent-off shoes, the personal injury claims, the guarantees to lose seven pounds in seven days, I've been given the wrong surname, the incorrect age, and had my home town transplanted to Cambridgeshire. For what it's worth, my dad wasn't a manager in a furniture store; it was an upholstery firm. It was a semidetached house I grew up in. The holiday I had with Alice's family when I was eleven was in Greece, not Turkey. Even the nice stuff they say is tainted. It wasn't a "picture-postcard" childhood we had; it was a typical, normal one and it's disingenuous to recast it.

I've been called a religious fanatic, a party girl, a PR drudge, a run-of-the-mill twenty-something. What's happening to me has parallels to what's happened to Alice. I should count my blessings, though. I'm here to read it.

A few sites—presumably because they feel the angle would strike a chord with their readers—have called on the public to leave me alone. "How much more should this woman have to take?" they asked.

I can see why the never-ending nature of news intermittently wore Alice out. "It never sleeps," she told me once. "Like me!"

For every individual who decrees me nice, there's another who protests the opposite—who pitches in when I'm debated in chat rooms like the double-dip recession or the cleanliness of tablecloths on TripAdvisor; suggestions of "brave" countered by "broken," "loyal" parried by "false," "normal" by "weird."

I've come to see why celebs and politicians employ spin doctors. It's never been my bag, that brand of PR, the sneaky and furtive dealings that pushed names into—and kept names out of—the media, the backroom trades for which Max Clifford was so famed before the media beast he'd tamed turned on him. Serves him right: that's what you get if you swim with sharks.

They must have had enough of me by now? Surely they'll soon move on, locust-like, to their next victim? Haven't they had their pound of flesh? Please leave me alone now.

Naively, I thought it would be helpful to blog, but it's merely fanned the flames, so this is definitely my last post. Besides, here's what they *ought* to be focusing on. How Cooke is capitalizing on a calamity. "A unique perspective on the Alice Salmon case," the advance publicity for his book is promising. "An explosive insider's account of the case that's got the country talking."

Smelling a best seller, the publishers announced it could be on the shelves as early as next summer or even spring. They should be ashamed. Him, too, and his self-satisfied, self-deprecating creepiness: sucking his glasses and informing interviewers there'll be another chapter in this whole sorry saga.

PR teaches you to stick to the script, but sometimes you have to speak from the heart. "Spit it out," Alice used to say, and I will, I will.

I'm sorry if my grief isn't enough for you, if it isn't the right kind of grief—but please leave me alone now. No one knows how much I've lost.

Comments have been disabled on this blog post.

Letter sent by Robert Salmon,
September 3, 2012

Harding, Young & Sharp
3 Bow's Yard
London EC1Y 7BZ

Mr. Cooke,

The task has fallen to me to write to you on behalf of my family.

For the record, I wish to state that we in no way sanction, approve or applaud the contents of your book. That's one word you won't get to use on the cover: authorized.

My mother's going on and on about one description of it she spotted: "hybrid of page-turner and social science." "Grave robbing, more like," she says. Peculiar way to spend a life, she reckons, digging up the dead.

You bastard, Cooke. I'm enclosing a printout of an email Alice drafted, but apparently never sent, on December 10, 2004. Bet you won't include this in your so-called all-inclusive book. Yes, you carp on about truth—well, publish this, then your claims might have less of a hollow ring.

I caught the tail end of a Radio 4 show recently on which you were pontificating about "righting wrongs" and your ultimate faith in the law. Well, the law hasn't delivered us answers yet, so perhaps it is an ass, after all.

I've discharged my filial duty by informing you of our position on the book. What my parents didn't request I inform you—but I will—is that Mum hasn't gone near a drink for some weeks now and has vowed to never do so again. We're incredibly proud of her.

Listen to me, I'm doing what I vowed not to—entering a dialogue, conversing, elaborating. It's true what they say: you do draw people in. But don't let your famous ego run away with you. Mum says you mean less to her than one single mote of dust. Her words.

As for my father and me, we know a dirty old man when we see one; we actually feel pity for you. Contain any temptations to self-aggrandizement or any inflated sense of grandeur, Professor—hearing of your assignation with Mum was actually a relatively minor blow, given the tragedy we've experienced.

I began this fully intending to compose a legal missive, but it appears to be transmogrifying. Alice used to say I was a stuffed-shirt solicitor. "Take a risk every now and then, Robster," she'd say. "It'll do you good." So I will. I have a confession: I left you a voice-mail on May 24, which I shouldn't have. For that, I apologize.

Regardless of that, do keep uppermost in your mind our warning about leaving this family alone, because I won't elaborate here on what my father has vowed to do should you ignore that request.

Even if you do attempt to bother them, they'll be gone. They're having a fresh start, moving, changing their contact details, wiping the slate clean. You won't find them, Professor, and Mum says you can put that in your pipe and smoke it. She says you, like the rest of the world, can go hang. She says Alice—the *real* Alice—will live on longer in her heart than she will in any book. And you can put that somewhere else, she says, somewhere the sun don't shine.

Incidentally, none of us have the slightest intention of reading your book.

Yours,
Robert Salmon

Email sent by Alice Salmon,
February 3, 2012

From: Alicethefish7@gmail.com

To: Lukea504@gmail.com

Subject: US

Attachment: Lemmings.jpg

Hey Mr. L,

Been thinking about us—been thinking about v little else, in fact, for the past two months and I've come to a conclusion. I'm not going to lie, I've gone round in circles and I'll never not hate what you did, but I don't hate you. I can't. I love you. I love you and the rest is detail. I need more time before we talk, but it's important you know now. That's all.

You made a huge, selfish mistake, but I'm no paragon (look it up!) of virtue and I'm not prepared to let my pride derail our future. Don't panic, I'm not getting all heavy—let's take a chill pill before we even reconsider moving in together—but that's what we could have together here—a *future*.

Remember the day we went up on the Eye? I want more days like that. That was the best. Up in the sky, flying; London, *our* London, spread out beneath us. I pretended to be gazing at the river and

Parliament and the South Bank, but it was you I was fixated by—you—and I was consumed by a sugar rush of awareness: *Some girls spend a lifetime waiting for this.*

I've been in a trance these past two months—going to work and the gym and seeing the girls; it's not as if I haven't been busy, but it's been black-and-white, vanilla, nothing's sparkled or sung or stood out. I feel very alive when I'm with you and when I remember that my decision seemed phenomenally simple. Here's the thing, Mr. L, I want us to be together, not because I'm afraid of the alternative—I'd cope, I'd be just fine, we both would, but who wants to cope? Who wants to be just fine? Bollocks to that old bollocks. I deserve more than that. We both do.

I'll have to go in a mo; the boss is chasing me for a story. I'll ring this man who apparently came home from work last night to find double yellow lines painted across the entrance to his drive and I'll document the words he uses: ones, I expect, like "shocked" and "fuming" and "bureaucracy gone mad." And you call me a high-flyer! Have just tapped your number up on my phone keypad—I might have deleted it from the contacts list, but it's etched onto my brain—and nearly called you. It's so hard *not* to. I can hear how you'd sound when you pick up: the tone of your voice, your cadence (look that up too!). But I need more time and space to get my head round what's happened—let's not skate around it, what *you've done*—and you need to respect that. Can you do that for me, please? Our two months will be up next week and there would be a certain appeal to us meeting then, a symmetry, but you mustn't push me, Luke. Besides, part of me likes the notion of saving talking to you—having it to look forward to. I'll keep it in my head all weekend when I'm trailing round the Hampton (it's going to be a messy one!); it'll be my secret—our secret. Does that make me sound bat-shit crazy? Well, aren't we all a little bit? Especially when we're in love. Because have I mentioned that? I LOVE YOU.

Ax

PS: This is all assuming you want to carry on dating me, of course, because you might have met someone far smarter and far prettier in the last eight weeks. There again, you'd need more than eight weeks to find someone who'd put up with your incessant carping on about films and shirt-ironing OCD!

PPS: If you ever pull a stunt like this again I'll cut your knackers off!

PPPS: I love you.

Email sent by Elizabeth Salmon,
October 8, 2012

From: Elizabeth_salmon101@hotmail.com
To: jfhcooke@gmail.com
Subject: Her

Dear Jem,

Bet you didn't expect to hear from me again, did you? I never expected to be back in contact. I never expected any of this. Well, don't fret, I'll be out of your hair soon. But having chatted to Meg, I feel obliged to email. I appreciate the two of you no longer see eye to eye, but you need to put aside your silly prejudices. She's opened my eyes.

"Sorry for not being in touch recently," she said. "Sometimes it's easier to avoid reminders. The longer I left it, the harder it got."

"Sweetheart, come here," I said. She tumbled into my arms and I inhaled deeply: a smell that reminded me of a smell that reminded me of Alice.

I visited under the pretext of returning the Kazuo Ishiguro book. Bless her, clearly unable to face knocking, she'd left it on my doorstep one night, but I figured if Alice gave it to her, it meant she'd have wanted her to have it.

"I still miss her every single day, Auntie Liz."

It must have been well over ten years since she'd called me that: the "auntie" unshowily dropped at exactly the point Alice abandoned calling this girl's mum "Auntie Pam."

"They say you don't get better, that you never get over it. You learn a new reality, you learn to adapt," I said. On the table, cigarettes, a brown bottle of tablets, leftover weekend papers, headlines about President Obama's debate with Mitt Romney, a ferry collision in Hong Kong, a Georgian woman who'd purportedly died age 132. Her new reality. "It's nothing to be ashamed of, bearing the scars—it makes us who we are."

Meg's presence was making Alice's absence more real, her aliveness throwing my daughter's deadness into sharper focus: giving color and depth to her distance. I recollected their voices upstairs, squeals of laughter, whispers, plotting, singing, saving up for Rollerblades. Later, getting ready for nights out, hours in front of the mirror: excited, fearless girls. "Some parents name stars after their dead children," I said. "Next time it's a clear night, Meg, gaze up. There's a whole galaxy of our kids up there." We wiped the tears from each other's cheeks; skin Alice had touched. "One day, love, you'll have beautiful babies and they'll bring you as much joy as Alice did me, as Alice does me."

"Why did she do it, Auntie Liz?"

I carried on running my thumb across her face, like I was trying to erase an invisible smudge.

"Why did she choose *this* way? She didn't have to . . ."

It took me a few seconds to twig what she was alluding to; a lever in me recalibrated itself. "Love, it was an accident."

"I'm sorry, Auntie Liz, but we can't help each other unless we're honest."

"Alice would have never done that."

"But she did."

"No, you mustn't say that."

"I'm sorry it's me who has to, but we won't be able to move forward until we face this. You mustn't be ashamed. People kill . . . I mean, they take their own lives for a million reasons. It's too horrid to fathom, but ultimately it was a choice she made."

"My daughter wasn't like that."

"It's not about what she was like; there isn't a template. Anyone could get to that point."

The breathy panic constricted around me: I'm never going to see Alice again.

"She told me about what you did when you were in Southampton. How you'd . . . you know . . . how . . . She confided in me that her grampy had let it slip."

"That was thirty years ago."

Jem, they reckon there are no secrets in this Internet age, but there are. I received a text from Alice.

Cell site analysis, the family liaison officer called it. Forensic data recovery. Alice's texts, her calls, even her Internet browsing history percolated into the public domain—released by investigators or guessed or leaked or shared by those she'd been communicating with. Amid the swooshing untruths, from the iPhone she so loved that they fished from the river, facts from fiction, matter from myth. But not all her texts came to light. Most did, but one didn't. One she sent me on her final night.

See, secrets.

What am I going to do, Jem?

Yours,

Liz

Reading by Elizabeth Salmon at Alice Salmon's funeral service, *February 13, 2012*

Death is nothing at all.
I have only slipped away to the next room.
I am I, and you are you.
Whatever we were to each other,
That, we still are.

Call me by my old familiar name.
Speak to me in the easy way
Which you always used.
Put no difference into your tone.
Wear no forced air of solemnity or sorrow.

Laugh as we always laughed
At the little jokes we enjoyed together.
Play, smile, think of me. Pray for me.
Let my name be ever the household word
That it always was.
Let it be spoken without effect.
Without the trace of a shadow on it.

Life means all that it ever meant.
It is the same that it ever was;
There is absolute unbroken continuity.
Why should I be out of mind
Because I am out of sight?

I am but waiting for you.
For an interval.
Somewhere. Very near.
Just around the corner.

All is well.

Letter sent by Professor Jeremy Cooke,
October 10, 2012

Larry, she's been here. No appointment, no warning; merely a knock on the door and there she was.

She's still beautiful. Scruffily dressed and a touch scatty; a hint of the Redgrave or Hepburn. Presumably it's politically incorrect to compare a woman with a fine wine, but she's matured impressively. "Where are your answers, then?" she demanded.

"Liz. How are you?"

She took a seat, perched on the edge. "Come on, Dr. Death. All this research you've been doing—where are the conclusions?"

So much for pleasantries or small talk. As regards tone, we'd taken up exactly where we'd left off three decades previously.

"If you're such an intellectual heavyweight, you explain—what happened to my daughter? Come on, I'm *waiting*."

There was a waft of booze, but it wasn't emanating from her, it was the glass of red on my desk. A memory filtered back at me: watery and indiscreet.

"What if it's true? What if she did kill herself?"

"She didn't."

"Megan's convinced."

"I'd take anything Ms. Parker says with a pinch of salt," I replied.

"You need to get over your ridiculous dislike of her. The way you've been so publicly critical of her, accusing her of being a 'fantasist'—it's not helpful. It's infantile."

I went to recount what Fliss had said, how Meg clearly had a thing about me, but halted myself. It felt wrong, mentioning my wife to her—as it would later, were I to communicate this encounter to Fliss.

"Megan was her best friend."

I was in a quandary, Larry. I'd had a run-in with Alice on her last night, remember, and she was indignant, but her behavior most definitely wasn't that of someone on the brink of suicide (not that I was ready to furnish Liz at that stage with that scrap of information; to her and the world at large, our exchange had never happened). Plus, when you spend hundreds of hours trawling through the minutiae of a life, you get a handle on a person's personality. The notion that she might have killed herself—it simply won't wash. "Liz," I said and almost reached out.

"The one thing I had, that I hung on to, was that it wasn't *that*—and now it feels like everyone's saying it is."

"No, she was strong."

"Jem, you utter moron, you don't need to be *weak* to take your own life. Suicide's like depression: it's a disease *of* the strong."

We sat and she scrutinized my office, the empty in-tray, the box files, the stone paperweight she'd bought me a lifetime ago. I recalled hotels, motorway services, fights, the elastic stretch of her bra.

"What if I have been wrong all along?" she said. "Suicide's the one outcome I couldn't take, simply couldn't—that my baby girl might have felt that bad. I've spent the last eight months denying it, but maybe you can't deny the undeniable."

Shadows around her eyes; a fellow insomniac. Us at a concert, eating mackerel in a wood-paneled room, a boardinghouse in a provincial seaside town long prior to it going upmarket, the leather and fabric seats of my TR7, tan-colored and sticky. One memory prompting another—layers of them, accretions, like strata in rock.

"There was the text, too."

"The text?"

"She sent it at twenty-one minutes past midnight, but I didn't see it until the Sunday morning."

"The text?"

"Wasn't fazed by it initially—Alice was forever late-night texting—but by about ten I was in a proper tizz at her not returning my call. Then the knock on the door—a policeman and a policewoman. I knew it was bad because they don't come to your house unless it's bad." She dabbed at a mark on the arm of the chair. "It was still an ordinary Sunday morning when I read that text, the last ever ordinary Sunday morning."

"Liz, talk to me. What text?"

"It was Plath. That *fucking* woman. The line about lying in the grass—it's a suicide line."

She licked her finger and had another go at the mark on the chair more frantically, chipping at it with her nail. "Won't come off," she said, and compassion gripped me like a vise. "The press got everything else, but they never got that. I haven't been able to face it until now, but it *can* only mean one thing. I couldn't bear those to be her last words, so I've never mentioned it to a soul—I couldn't—not even David."

"But the police—"

"Not the ones who came to the door but the ones afterwards; they're up to speed on it, but no one else is. It's one of the few pieces of Alice that isn't public property. It's no one else's business."

We sat and there was a brittle, taut atmosphere, like the aftermath of an argument we'd never actually had.

"I guessed she'd been at the wine, because she'd mangled the quote, and my Alice was a stickler for getting quotes right." She sniffled, half smiled, but that fell away. "You're never short of an opinion: What do you make of this, then?"

It could have been thirty years before, her spitting: "You're never going to leave your wife, are you?" Back then, my desire for her had been feverish: the inescapable apogee of it, her unraveling. Now, her dismantled, that desire had transmogrified into only one wish: to ameliorate pain.

"I think due process will eventually prevail. But for now, I don't think you should be here. Can I give you a lift anywhere—home, for example?"

"It's miles."

"I'd do that—you know I'd do that for you."

"And I'd avoid my husband if I were you."

I poured myself a top-up and an image of Liz presented itself: red wine on her teeth. Guilt chafed at me, but I'd done nothing wrong, Larry. I'd depart this rendezvous in a few minutes and head home to another woman with similarly graying hair: a man in his sixties who suffers from heartburn and strains to read train departure boards, when thirty years ago I'd done likewise, except I was someone who'd bored along green lanes in a sparkling sports car and gone five games on the squash court, then jumped on my Raleigh Europa, and was cancer-free.

"Does David know you're here?"

"What do you think?"

As in 1982, questions engendering questions.

"Dave and Robbie are convinced I'm still vulnerable; they're babying me. I'm no baby."

"You're strong."

"I'm not strong, Jem. Who'd be strong?" She crossed her arms, rubbing herself as if she was cold. Her *shell*. Beside us, the sofa that her daughter had slept on drunk eight years ago.

She said: "You need to know, Jem, that I love my husband very much."

"Sandhill cranes, eh?"

"Sandhill cranes. I presume you picked up on the flurry of puerile speculation you were Alice's father."

"Mocksy," I said, "stoked up by Devereux. My nemeses."

"I'd never cheat on a man as good as David."

Alice used to remind me of her, but at that instant it was the other way round: it was she who reminded me of Alice.

"You ought to read Fanthorpe's 'Atlas,'" she said. "That sums marriage up perfectly."

I wiped the lenses of my glasses; it used to be prescient to have a stock of tissues on standby to dispense when freshers bared their souls, but latterly they only visited to assert their rights and demand a re-mark. I've got my own theory, Larry. More than a theory, a *fact*. It doesn't involve suicide, either.

"Are you going to be OK?" I asked.

"The blue of police uniforms isn't how it is on the telly when you see it in the flesh."

"Liz, are you going to be OK?"

What I was about to do might mean she'd never be OK ever again.

Transcript of live phone-in on Martin "The Morning Man" Clark's show on Dane Radio,
September 2, 2012

MC: Later we'll be getting political and hearing your views on opening up our borders, but first it's serendipity and when you've experienced it . . . We're after the lowdown on your most splendidly bizarre encounters, and to kick us off we've got Ellie on the line from Southampton. Ellie, a big fat breakfast show welcome, what's on your mind?

EE: I'm ringing about the serendipity stuff. I had it with that dead girl who was all over the news.

MC: Right, OK. What dead girl in particular is this?

EE: Alice Salmon. I chatted to her on the day she died.

MC: This is . . . a little . . . off-piste, but let's go with it . . .

EE: I was seven months pregnant and she gave me her seat on a bus. "You look like you could do with taking the weight off," she goes, then asked if I was having twins, and when I said no she said she really had to learn to engage brain before gob, but I said it was an easy mistake to make because I was like a barge and she said she was, too, but without the excuse! She said I was glowing. A woman I work with had been going on about this book called *Random Acts of Kindness* and that's what that was, because no one normally talks on buses.

MC: You're bringing a much-needed element of culture to this show, Ellie—we even give listeners reading recommendations! But we were all profoundly touched by that incident, and your take on it sounds heartbreaking and profound . . . Fill us in on the details.

EE: It was only a few days later I twigged she was the girl who was plastered over the news.

MC: Yes, we're sadly familiar with Alice's tragic tale. We had guests in the studio in the aftermath to discuss it. Your anecdote—it's touching, but if I was being devil's advocate. I'd say more *sad* than serendipitous, Ellie.

EE: Was going on to that. See, my husband texted me out of the blue while I was on the bus, suggesting 'Alice' as a name for our baby. "That's *my* name," the lady said when I told her.

MC: Thanks, Ellie, and join in, south coast, have you got a serendipitous story that can beat this one? The killer coincidence, the roll of the dice, the hand of fate . . . get involved in all the usual ways: details on the website.

EE: She said she was going to get right royally blotto and I said I wished I could. She looked at my tummy and said it must be exhausting lugging that around and then that we don't make it easy for mums, do we? But they always stand by us and sometimes in the end we have to stand by them.

MC: That's a lovely point, Ellie, thanks for calling . . . I nearly forgot to ask, what *did* you call your baby in the end?

EE: Alice. We called her Alice.

MC: We're going to have some music and go to the traffic then we'll be right back with more of your stories of serendipity . . .

Extract from letter sent by Professor Jeremy Cooke,
November 6, 2012

"You asked to see me," she said. "Here I am."

"So you are, young Megan. Please, come in."

She did as instructed, unraveled her scarf, then declared: "You're a bit old to be creeping around leaving notes, aren't you?"

Larry, if she'd responded to my correspondence, I wouldn't have needed to resort to the old note-under-the-door trick. "I wish to make amends for my actions," I'd scribbled, confident that would flush her out. "Drop by; it could be the most lucrative hour you ever spend." She was wearing boots and black tights and had opted for a short skirt despite the inclement weather. "You look well," I lied.

She slipped out of her coat and draped it over the arm of a chair. "It's like a dungeon in here; there's no air."

I passed her the wine I'd kept on hand for her arrival. White, very chilled: how she preferred it. "Make yourself at home. Sit."

She did, then asked: "So, this offer?"

I'd alluded in my missive to securing her a couple of museum accounts for her new PR firm, her intention to reenter the world of academia seemingly abandoned. Our relationship had degenerated, but I suspected her greed for business would outweigh any misgivings on her part about visiting. Now, reeling from some not-so-good news from my specialist, I had a brash, confrontational edge. "Why did you claim I touched you?"

"If the cap fits."

"But it's not true."

She took a big disdainful glug of the wine. "What is this stuff?"

"Gagnard-Delagrange. It's phenomenally good."

"Rarely drink these days," she said. "After what happened to Alice, it scares me. When I see girls trolleyed, I get the urge to lecture them on the dangers of alcohol. Must be getting old!"

"I'm becoming more impulsive as I get older," I said absentmindedly. "In the next life, I'll be positively reckless."

"Alice is one big game to you, isn't she?"

"I'd hardly deem her that."

"I read that interview where you claimed to be an 'inveterate observer of human nature,' but you're only interested in people if they're dead or in some tribe on another continent. It's like reading—it's avoiding real life because dead people and faraway people can't hurt you."

I tried to place that phrase from a book, "faraway people," but my memory isn't what it was. "Finished with the character assassination?"

"No, not yet. What about us, the living? Don't we deserve the same duty of care? What about the right to privacy? The media have ridden roughshod over that. Some of the stuff they've written about Alice and I, it's pure fantasy."

" 'Alice and me,' " I said. "It's 'Alice and me,' not 'Alice and I.' "

She held out her empty glass, like a supplicant, so I obliged.

"Today's news, tomorrow's chip paper—that's what I remind myself, but it doesn't help."

She plays the privacy card, but hasn't missed an opportunity to thrust herself into the limelight, give her hard-done-by coquettish smile—there's something of the Diana in her—then take a deep breath and eulogize about her best friend.

"It's all right for you," she added, "you're Teflon-coated. But doesn't it wear you out, everyone having an opinion on you?"

"One becomes accustomed to it." So many of my associations had gone that way, Larry: my father, my contemporaries from school, university peers, colleagues. Last I heard of Devereux, he'd been farmed out to some nursing home, hunched in a corner, deluded and spouting vitriol. I cut to the chase. "Why did you try to frame me?"

"Sometimes people get arrested for stuff they don't do. They get convicted of the wrong offense and it might not be for what they did but they've done something equally bad. Is that a miscarriage of justice?"

"Technically," I said.

"Screw *technically*. It all rolls into one. It's justice. I decided you needed it."

"Justice isn't yours to dispense," I said.

"It's not yours, either." She was knocking back the wine as if it was water; it would hit her presently. "I've learnt one thing. The public much prefer a simple lie to a complex truth."

I saw the winter sun, weak and watery. "The truth travels in straight lines, Megan. Like light."

"Stop speaking in riddles—and what's this offer? Or was it another one of your lies? If it was, I'm leaving."

"There are no free cars or holidays to be had here."

She snorted. "Pah. One paper said it was up to me now to write my own future."

"*The Magic Faraway Tree,*" I replied, recalling the misplaced phrase. "That was it. The Enid Blyton book."

"You're a wack job."

"Is it that you're jealous? Is it that it's not *you* in the spotlight?"

"That's the craziest, creepiest thing you've said, and you've said plenty."

"I can give you compliments, if it's attention you're craving."

The radiator clicked, water moving, warmth. "I've spoken to Liz in recent weeks. She informs me you're now adamant it was suicide. I'd be interested to hear on what basis."

"That bridge is like Beachy Head. Hurl themselves off it like lemmings, they do."

I'm not unaware of the structure's reputation. I regularly used to stroll alongside it; it's one of the few spots in this city one could court solitude. "Wrong answer. Have another go."

"I shouldn't be here; you'd get into trouble if it got out."

You'll not get out, I thought, discreetly eyeing my desk for the door key. "Come on, why did she kill herself?"

"They reckon I'm a bad friend, but I didn't have a crystal ball. When Alice got drunk, she could be stupendously unpredictable—factor in the drugs and that made her so Alice-like, it hurt to watch. She'd talked about suicide before."

I was back to scribe, Larry, a reversion to the role I'd so comfortably slotted into: archivist, analyst, investigator. Evidence gatherer. "Had she? When?"

"Before. She must have run out of the will to live."

"You don't need will *to* live, Megan. That's our default position. What you need will for is to *stop* living, to take your own life."

"I don't have all the answers. I'm not God." She sank back in the armchair, fanned her face. "Mistake," she said. "It was a mistake coming here. Should be going. Was supposed to be babysitting this evening. Stop writing stuff down, too!"

I discreetly gathered up the key, shuffled behind her, pretended to replace a book on a shelf and, temporarily out of her sight line, locked the door. She was going nowhere, this one.

"Who are you to judge me and my opinions?"

Larry, I wasn't unqualified to have a view; I'd become jolly well acquainted with this young lady—numerous evenings, my wife at bridge or the U3A, side by side at my dining-room table for our "Project Alice" sessions. A curious, claustrophobic coupling, sifting through those reams of material, a ghoulish exercise, an exhumation of sorts. "How did Alice kill herself, Megan?"

"None of your questions can bring her back—she's gone." She lunged for a pile of papers, tore out a page. "This isn't her and it isn't me . . . We're more than this."

Outside, a light was flickering; I made a mental note to ring Facilities tomorrow.

"I used to be impressed by you," she said, her voice raised, "but there's nothing to you. You're words, wind, hot air . . . You're a"—and she let out a derisive laugh, a LOL, she'd once informed me it was termed—"a complete tool!"

One by one, the lights had gone off in adjoining offices, my colleagues drifting away. I bombarded Megan with questions, compliments, questions. Opened a second bottle. She became slightly woozy; it was in her eyes, how she crossed and uncrossed her legs clumsily. She checked her watch at a couple of points, agitated, but she was losing focus. And I willed her whispered words into my head, logged them, because detail increasingly isn't a strong point of mine (the other day I called Fliss "Liz"—mercifully an oversight she failed to hear).

"Describe the last occasion upon which you saw Alice," I instructed her semiformally.

"Snow," she replied dreamily. "There was snow."

It had only snowed once last winter: the night of February 4.

"It was by the river, wasn't it, Megan? You were there, weren't you? You were in Southampton."

Letter sent by Professor Jeremy Cooke,
April 20, 2013

Dear Larry,

"Is it normal to be this obsessed by women?" he asked last night. "By sex?"

"They say sex is like oxygen," I told him. "You only miss it when you haven't got it."

I'm fascinated by the sharp roughness of him, the markings on his body. And yes, before you admonish me, Larry, I'm well aware I should hand the bugger over to the police, but he who is without sin and all that.

"Alice was my oxygen."

Mocksy, he calls himself, but his real name's Gavin.

"Did collecting her stuff help?" I asked.

"Not really. All it was was her stuff; it's not as if it was *her*."

On the floor, gathered for safe return to the Salmons: a set of bangles, playing cards, a printout of an assignment on Maya Angelou, postcards, pens, a beer mat with a kangaroo on it, a dried rose, a toothbrush, notes for a gig review, a sweatshirt with "LAUGH LOVE LIVE" embossed on the front.

"Only thing I haven't handed over to you is the book by the man with the Japanese name, and I dumped that on her mum's doorstep," he said.

"My closest friend died recently," I replied.

"I still hate a lot of stuff about you."

"He was my best friend and I never met him."

"Still hate Alice, too."

"Be careful of hate, Gavin. It stains you—you take on its color if you harbor it for too long."

It's a dazzling new concept: trying not to see the worst in someone. A small confession is apposite at this point: I haven't been unreservedly candid with Fliss about these "meetings." Not that there's anything untoward to admit, but she wouldn't approve and that's perfectly understandable given what the lad did, particularly breaking into our home. He's self-evidently capable of great malevolence, but underneath—and is that not the job of the academic, to see underneath?—he's not exclusively bad. No one is. He assures me he wishes to wipe the slate clean, to have a fresh start. A tabula rasa, as we might term it.

"Will I be in this book of yours?" he asked.

"You already are."

"You better not slag me off."

"I'll display you the same amount of respect as you did me on those forums!"

"That was only the Internet; a book's different. They won't take my posts down, if that's what you're angling for. It's policy not to."

"I've had worse things said about me. Besides, they're part of this."

"I've quit them forums—no more of that lone wolf crap. All that stuff I posted, no one gives a shit about that. Your book's more likely to make me famous—even if it will be bollocks."

I like his contempt; it reminds me of my exchanges with that shrink, Carter. Another confession: I've tracked that bugger down.

"I could read the whole thing. Could be your editor!"

"I'm of the view that no one who's featured ought to catch advance sight of it."

"You have! You don't trust me to keep my gob shut about the ending, do you?"

The boy went and stood by the window. What a pair we must have made: two creatures from incommensurable continents. Exhibits A and B. He fiddled with his right ear, one of those hole-in-the-lobe piercings that's currently fashionable, and it gave me a jab of pity that he could mutilate himself in this manner.

"This office, this university, this town—they're *your* forums, aren't they?" he said. "They let you carry on unchallenged."

Curiously, he's more articulate in the flesh, less intimidating. The Internet bent him out of shape, his words detached, disembodied, devoid of nonverbal communication—a real-time bar brawl in which the lowest common denominator prevails.

"She was too strong for both of us, wasn't she, Alice was."

"Desire," I said, "is hardwired into us. The choice we have is how to respond to it." Briefly, I summoned the sequestered complexion of lust—the metallic meatiness of another human tongue, the ancient, uncompromising smell of sex—but it vanished, flitting into faintness as when one recollects scenery from a long-ago holiday, the hills on Skye, say, or the Italian Dolomites. A sex maniac, he'd referred to me as in one of his online rants; an anachronistic term, straight out of some long-defunct sitcom or a *Carry On* movie. Is this how I'll be remembered? A remotely comical figure, in his youth shambolically propelled by testosterone and selfishness, dressed up as intellectualism or, more likely, eccentricity?

"Gavin, learn from my mistakes," I said. "You defuse situations by making it so your secrets are no longer secrets."

"I suppose I loved her," he said. "Alice. Sort of. My new missus, Zoe, she's an actual girlfriend—I might love her as well."

"I love Fliss. More, in fact, than I do myself."

"Jeez, that much! I reckon women make us better."

"Amen to that. But worse, too. They have that in common with religion. I rather wish I could rediscover my faith. In the meantime, I'll put it in the potential of humans, the power of us."

"Do you believe in all that, Iceman? Love and stuff?"

Silence as I, inarticulate and inexpressive, recalled an avenue of research I'd toyed with exploring decades ago, and luxuriated in the recollection of my definition: my wife shooing me from the sink in the kitchen to the utility room, the click of her pruning shears, the squeeze of the "World's Best Chef" apron she bought me for my sixtieth, a tea room in a market town, a secondhand bookshop. "Yes, I do. Very much so. It's what remains after everything else. It's what Alice gave out every day and now she's gone it's what she left."

I went and stood beside him and rested my hand on his shoulder—small yet surprisingly muscled.

"I'm not gay, Iceman, just so you know."

I returned to my seat. "Me neither," I said. "Just so *you* know. Trouble with standing back from the herd, young man, is that sometimes we need the herd. Protection, concealment, company, love—we're social animals."

We're not so different, Larry, myself and that boy: our compulsion to be heard, preoccupied with recording our stories, capturing the legacy of our lives, him in a rainbow of colors on his arms, me in this book, just as our forebears had on the cave walls at Lascaux.

"Do you really reckon we can change?" he asked.

"Yes, I do. It's what being a human is, to have that possibility. Every day we choose who to be. What clothes to wear, what to say, what to eat, how to behave, what pictures to put on our arms—it's through this myriad of small decisions that cumulatively we become who we are."

"I've got a confession for *you*. That Devereux geezer never claimed you were knocking off Alice's mum the year before she was born. That was one of my flourishes!"

It's so hard not to hate, Larry, but I'm having a stab at it. I repositioned myself in my chair—the usual stiffness, but an atypical twinge of pain, too, which made me wince.

"What's it like, Iceman? Cancer? My gran reckoned it was like being eaten up from the inside out."

That's not what it's like for me. It's not the medical procedures or the piecemeal disintegration of one's physical capabilities; it's the fluid dread I get at the concept of me not existing yet it all damn well carrying on. We academics spend billions of pounds and invest immense reserves of intellectual energy in pursuit of the most nebulous goals when we haven't even scratched the surface of how to keep ourselves alive. "I shall see justice done before I pass. For Alice."

"Hope her mum didn't read that book I left on her doorstep," he said. "It's about people bred to be broken up and used as spares—harvested, donors, clones. All that stuff about living to more than a hundred or dying young, that completion malarkey, that would have been well grim for her to read. Suppose it's only a story ultimately—like, made up."

He scratched his arm, a nervous habit and, over the war paint, eczema. I intended to say, "You shouldn't have those, you're a child," but it came out as: "Does it hurt, getting tattooed?"

"A bit. It's worth it, though."

Yes, give us a few thousand more years and we'll put it all together, this gargantuan jigsaw puzzle. We scientists. We anthropologists. My tribe.

"Thing is with tats," he said, "they stay with you; they mark you."

"So does life, son. So does life."

Extract from letter sent by Professor Jeremy Cooke,
November 6, 2012

"You were there, weren't you?" I repeated. "You were in Southampton?"

Larry, she grappled with the consequences of her utterance, struggling, lunging mentally for a response. The alcohol had definitely begun to take its toll: her features were pinched, strands of hair wayward. Bloody pricey, this wine, but worth every penny at this rate.

I pulled my chair towards hers so we were closer. "You were there, Megan, weren't you? Admit it."

She was furious, terrified—a compound I'd scarcely witnessed before. Only once, in fact: Liz. She muttered half a line.

"Again," I demanded. "Louder." Larry, my voice was raised. For an impotent man, I had a savagely charged focus. I may have been on the verge of physical aggression. "Again," I repeated. "We'll stay here all night if need be."

She screwed up her face—calculations, computations, formulations—but the Gagnard-Delagrange, that exquisite white, elegant and energizing and full of grace, had worked its magic, twisting the machinery of her mind out of shape.

I said: "It'll be preferable if you volunteer this up. Here. Now. To me. It'll be better for you."

"Only went because she was so drunk."

"So you *were* there?"

Her sight line wandered up to the ceiling and erratically followed the coving around. "Yes, but not with her, not near her."

"Why?"

"Suicide," she said.

"No."

"Yes."

"No."

"Yes." Her attention rolled off the garish Victorian rose bowl on to the patch of mold that had recently grown from tennis-ball to dinner-plate size. "She'd talked about it before. How much more evidence do you need?"

"Some. I'd like some."

"There's plenty."

"There's none."

She hiccoughed, squirmed in her seat. I poured her the remainder of the bottle. Not the first girl to have been in this office in this condition. There was Alice, and others. Yes, others.

"We're making progress now, Megan." I took hold of my letter opener, an old-fashioned slender stainless-steel knife. Tapped it with my right hand in the palm of my left. "It wasn't suicide, was it?"

"Stop denying it. There's proof."

"There's not a shred."

"The text!" she shouted. "That's proof!"

We locked eyes and I shivered. "What text, Megan?"

She hesitated, then blundered on: "The suicide text."

"Suicide text?"

"That Plath quote she sent to Liz just before she did it. You can't get more conclusive than that—a suicide text!"

Liz's secret permeated back to me: *They got everything else, but they never got that.* "Where did you hear about that?"

"Read about it."

"You can't have."

"Did . . . was in the paper."

"Which paper?"

"*A* paper. Don't have to put up with this," she said, hauling herself up.

I put my hand on her shoulder, applied pressure. "Surely, you can illuminate me as to which paper, because there sure as hell hasn't been any reference to a suicide text in anything I've seen, and Alice is the one subject on which I'd confidently claim to be better read than anyone."

"Yes, you freak."

"That's right. I've got box files full of cuttings. We can go through them if you like. Come on, let's do it together."

"Actually, Mr. Kleptomaniac, it was on a website; yes, that's it, on a website."

"Pop yourself round here, then, and I'll pull up every single online piece about her that's ever been written—I've got them bookmarked—and you point it out."

"Haven't got a photographic memory, have I? All I can remember is that it was on the web: her texting the thing about death being beautiful and lying in the soft brown earth."

"For someone who claims to have an imperfect memory, you seem remarkably well acquainted with that line."

"Feel peculiar," she said.

"It's time, Megan. No more lies."

She made a jagged, zigzagging movement with her hand. "Doesn't always travel in straight lines," she said, then lost her thread.

I've never mentioned the text to a soul . . . not even David—that's what Liz had said. "It ends tonight."

"She fell."

"So you saw it happen?"

"Yes. No."

"Which was it?"

"That weir, it's so high."

"Why mention the weir, Megan?"

"Was a long way away."

"But you did see her go in the water?"

"She jumped."

"How can you be positive if you were a long way away?"

She put her head in her hands; I prayed she didn't descend into gobbledygook or pass out. "I tried to save her."

"Oh, you tried to save her now, did you?"

"Over the last twenty-five years, I mean. Spent my whole life saving her from herself. She was an accident waiting to happen."

I stared at the mold on the ceiling. No point getting that treated now; a task for the next incumbent of this office. "Beyond the police force, only three people in the world know about that text: Liz, me and the person who sent it."

"Tried to get her away from the edge, but she'd got the madness. She got it from her mum; she couldn't help herself."

She went to stand, but I forced her down. Her stare darted to the door. Locked.

"She ran away from me. She slipped."

"But you said she jumped."

"Can't you just leave me alone? Please. I can't do this."

"What did it sound like, Megan? When she entered the water?"

"Why are you doing this to me?"

"Because no one knows we're here. Because I can. What did the splash that Alice made sound like?"

"I tried to save her after she'd fallen in; she was howling out for help and I tried; I've never tried to do anything harder in my whole life . . ."

Larry, she'd been exuberant when news broke that Luke had been arrested. *Too* exuberant. Then, when he was released, she needed a new focus, a new target. Coldly and calculatingly attempting to shift the finger of suspicion towards a new suspect: *Me.*

I said: "She wouldn't have been able to cry out for help because her mouth would have been full of water. She wouldn't have been able to get the air to shout out."

"Stop it," she said.

"She'd have tried to cough it back up, but water would have flooded her stomach."

"No," she said.

"She'd have been struggling, flailing, flapping, crying; she'd have tried to roll onto her back; she'd have been hyperventilating."

"Hate it," she said. "Hate you. Hate her."

"She would have held her breath, but you can't hold your breath forever; we have a breathing reflex because we have to get rid of the carbon dioxide in us. Within a minute or so she'd have gone under—sunk, sunk like a lump of lead."

I recalled how, her options constricting, Megan had dubbed me a liar, a pervert, a *monster*. She knew I was onto her. Her throwaway line about reinventing Alice and us reinventing ourselves in the process had been the giveaway. "Why would we wish to do that?" I'd asked and her hand had crept across my knee. Of course we enter contested waters here—those of recall, interpretation and description (it's been an enduring source of curiosity to my wife and me that we have diverging views on what actually constitutes "pink"). But of Megan's actions, even though the incident in question was some weeks ago, I have no doubt. Her hand had twitched and moved a fraction higher. "How would you like that?" she'd asked. "Us having a secret? You'd like that very much, wouldn't you? They wouldn't understand, but we do. It can be our secret—one of our secrets."

"Get out of my house," I'd commanded her.

Subsequently, evidently wise to my percipience, a raft of blog posts making all manner of fallacious claims.

"Alice's brain wouldn't have had oxygen," I said now. Me, the puppet master. Whipping her grief and shame and fury towards some inexorable climax. "Starved of oxygen."

"No," she wailed.

Nearly there, I thought, and was back at her, punching on, pushing, surges of power racking my frail body, virile, primal, immortal, grabbing for the luminescent insight, like a Navajo after peyote or a Guahibo after ayahuasca. "She would have been convulsing; she would have frothed at the mouth."

A long, ghostly scream. I did that, I made Megan Parker cry and I kept it up as I hove in on the breakthrough, my own ultra-pure revelation: truth. Truth for me and for Alice.

"It would have been pitch-black. Alice would have sunk into the blackness."

She put her hands over her ears, banged her feet on the floor. "What gives you the right to torture me like this?"

"Being at death's door. Touching mortality, that's what does. But mostly, knowing." Apologies, Larry, for not sharing my theory with you earlier, but putting one's head above the parapet can be a dangerous occupation. "It was you, wasn't it? You killed her, didn't you?"

She blinked and let out a kittenish mewl, and I went to her and stroked her hair and she angled her head up at me, doe-eyed and hunted, and her mouth made the words: "She killed my baby."

Notes by Luke Addison on his laptop,
June 30, 2013

Three weeks after you died, it was, when I discovered your email. Subject field: *US*. That was almost eighteen months ago, but it still grates. Of all the places you didn't deserve to end up, Al—in my junk folder. It got shunted in there because of the attachment: the photo of a card you'd scanned, a picture of two lemmings peering over a cliff, one saying, "You go first," the other, "No, you go first," and underneath you'd put *Sometimes in life you have to make a leap of faith.*

When I'd seen it, it was like a hammerblow. So that was what you'd meant by the river when you'd referred to lemmings—the email you'd sent me a day before you died explaining you wanted us to get back together but needed more time. The email you never had a reply to. No wonder you were furious I turned up.

Didn't share the email with anyone initially; figured it would only support those stupid suicide theories that were doing the rounds. But the brain-dead dolts who were suggesting that hadn't been with us in Margate, had they? They hadn't been there when we were planning getting a place together, hadn't heard you say it was all very grown-up and scary, but sometimes in life you have to make a leap of faith. Like so much of their information, it was secondhand. Then Cooke got in contact about his project. He said he'd understand if I'd rather not share any of our communications—or that I could do so "off the record" and he'd only use them for background—but you'd have been quite taken with his book idea. Came to the same conclusion about the stuff I jotted on my laptop immediately after we lost you. My gut reaction was to delete it—some I have—but transparency's what's called for. "It's not good to bottle stuff up," you used to say, bugging me, so there's one life lesson I *have* taken from you.

"Have it," I told him, handing him a memory stick. "Take it. You'll struggle to make head or tail of it. It's nonsense."

Fact is, we're part of each other's stories. Being your boyfriend, Al, that was a privilege, an honor. I can hear you calling me an old sop bag, but it's important to put that on the record. Cos in the unlikely event of anyone ever actually reading his book—it's no Dan Brown, is it?—that's what I'd like them to view me as, *your boyfriend*. Can't get my head round why a woman as wonderful as you ever dated a bloke like me, but being open feels like being respectful to who you were ("paying homage," you might have said, what with your arty Radio 4 talk!). I've got a sneaky suspicion you'd like the notion of the pair of us in a book together, too. Stories need balance, you used to say. They need context. They have to hear from all sides.

I suppose we all dealt—are dealing—with what happened differently and I can appreciate why some people have stayed schtum. We're damned if we do and damned if we don't, but opening up felt right for me. I had to get that stuff off my chest. I might be a mug, but I trust Cooke.

"Don't make your mind up about me conclusively yet," he's urging me. "When it's actually published, you might take a dimmer view."

Sounds like he's got one or two ghosts of his own to exorcise, but it seems such an act of respect, worship almost, the care and passion he's put into researching you and getting answers.

"My volume," he cautioned, "there'll be parts that you'll find difficult."

"You've heard about my reading abilities, then!" I joked.

Hope you don't mind, Al, but I do laugh at times. You wouldn't want me never laughing, would you? Is it bad, but nowadays I can go nearly whole days without thinking about you? Then you'll rush in at me? This afternoon I was in a tedious meeting at work—I'm still there, but am going to take your advice and retrain as an architect—and I discreetly pulled up your email. You felt very alive when you were with me. You loved me.

Cooke's right, it is a crime to forget, and that's happening. Not among those who were close to you and cared for you and loved you (although we've obviously had to reappraise who falls into this category), but more widely. Alice Salmon, people will say. The one who was kidnapped? No, she was the Christmas one. No, the one who drowned, attacked by her boyfriend. No, he was let off, positive he was. Didn't she have a complicated love life? Didn't that professor man work it out in the end . . . ?

Hope you don't mind, Al, but I've seen a couple of other girls. Nothing serious and neither's worked out, so I'm having a break from dating. It's not fair on anyone. Maybe there'll come a point when I am ready. Is that OK? Whoever she is, she's going to have a tough act to follow.

After you died I might have gone a bit nuts, because I used to reply to the lemming email (I most definitely haven't shown those to Cooke), but now I'd like to laugh a bit more again, if that's OK. Your mum tells me—we meet in Starbucks; your dad won't have me in the house—that I can't torture myself forever. "Live," she says. "You have to live."

"But *how*?" I used to not infrequently ask her.

"One day at a time," she'd reply, "one day at a time."

You know some people do that air quotes thing with their fingers when they mention the word "relationship"; well, when I think of our relationship, Al, it's not in air quotes. It's in the million tiny reminders. Anyone sitting cross-legged, big glasses, skater skirts, Margate on the telly, Prague, seeing someone read a text on a train and smile, fluffy earmuffs, a tiny tattoo. It's the stuff that anyone who'd never met you would say was silly, but to me they're the things that make you *you*.

It's music, especially. Used to hate hearing songs you loved, but I like it now, so I've done you a playlist of what you'd have been listening to this summer. Haven't gone for any soppy, sentimental shite: I've picked tracks that would have prompted you to spring up from the sofa and scream, "I *love* this song," or reach across and crank up the car radio, or send you charging headlong out onto the dance floor at Clapham Grand, then smile back at me, then keep on dancing.

I'm going to put on my iPod now, Al, turn up the volume and walk—walk into the night on the common as you used to, and listen to your voice . . .

Pompeii	**Bastille**
Wake Me Up	**Avicii**
Locked Out of Heaven	**Bruno Mars**
Ho Hey	**The Lumineers**
Wrecking Ball	**Miley Cyrus**
Drinking from the Bottle	**Calvin Harris (featuring Tinie Tempah)**
I Need Your Love	**Calvin Harris (featuring Ellie Goulding)**
I Love It	**Icona Pop**
Play Hard	**David Guetta**
You and Me Song	**The Wannadies**
Get Lucky	**Daft Punk**
We Are Young	**Fun (featuring Janelle Monáe)**

Extract from letter sent by Professor Jeremy Cooke,
November 6, 2012

"She killed my baby," Megan screeched.

I recoiled, but she grabbed for my waist.

"That was why I went to Southampton. She had to know what she'd done—went there to tell her."

I extricated myself from her grasp and her hands dropped clumsily onto her stomach and she started to cry then, Larry.

"Night after she discovered Luke had done the dirty on her, she turned up at my place and got mortal. She wouldn't go to bed. I got us up the stairs, but she slipped."

The tree outside my office whooshed. More tears. Big, snotty gulps.

"If she hadn't hung on to me, it would have been all right, but then we were at the bottom of the stairs and she was on top of me and she was laughing; she was fucking *laughing*."

Pity flooded me, commingled with a fast, glittering fury. The window, a slab of glass against the blackness.

"For once it was going to be about me, not Alice, but she couldn't even let me have that could she—a baby? Flushed away part born and dead, flushed away . . ."

"My God," I said.

"The press say *I've* got a screw loose, but Alice was nuts. She opened up her wrist once when she was thirteen like she was peeling back the ring-pull on a Diet Coke can, but Alice, your precious Alice, even managed to make that sound rational."

"She's not mine," I said. "For the record, she's not that."

"Those threats she got," she said, a string of snot hanging from her nose, "that stuff on Twitter, those letters—they were all me. I'm Freeman. Even the dead flowers, me."

"You pushed her into the water, didn't you?"

"Went there to show her the damage she'd done, because me, *I* was the damage she'd done."

"You pushed her into the water, didn't you?"

"Don't hurt me," she whimpered. "Please don't hurt me." Then: "They won't believe you."

"You pushed her and then you sent that text to make it look as if she'd taken her own life."

"They don't trust you. If you were a brand, you'd be toxic."

"But we're not brands."

"We're all brands."

The wind whipped through the branches of the elm, *my* elm.

"Used to worship that woman, I idolized her. Would pretend I was her sister to strangers, her twin."

I'm ignorant to much, Larry, but obsession is territory with which I'm well acquainted. Its coarse rub, its barbed spike, its musty spoiled sourness. The line between love and hate is paper-thin, and when you love someone and it turns to hate, there's an inverse relationship between the two. What I asked next was cruelty in extremis given her disclosure, but I had no choice. "Boy or girl?"

"Too early," she said. "Too soon." She stood up; I let her, and she sneaked into a corner before crumpling to the floor. "Tried to explain I was pregnant when she was at my place, but blind to it she was, too drunk. Blind blind blind. She was supposed to be my oldest friend."

No witnesses, no CCTV footage. Two girls and one of those in a graveyard in a village near Corby, a Brontë inscription on her headstone: *I am no bird; and no net ensnares me.*

"I'll be dead soon," I said. "At least give me the consolation prize of closure."

"What have I done?"

"Lied."

"Once you cross a line, you can't turn back."

"You can, you always can." I recalled an adage of my mother's: A lie's halfway round the world before the truth's got its boots on. "Being honest isn't hard; it's lying that's hard."

Larry, I deliberated whether to force her into my car—dragoon her to a police station or coerce her to repeat her confession so it would be on the record. "You won't get away with this."

"I'm good at secrets."

"I am, too. But I'm better at truths."

"PR's a story," she said.

Yes, a story. She'd have turned up the collar on her coat or wrapped her scarf round her face—it was snowing, it wouldn't have attracted any attention—and headed back to the car, driven to the Lake District, then the next day she'd have rung Liz and Dave, having left it until the news had broken, and been a tower of support. She'd filled that role well, as for years she had the one of best friend. "No wonder you turned on me so abruptly."

"Had no choice. Luke was in the clear, the suicide theory was getting sidelined—you were the next best suspect."

So my hypothesis was correct. Chameleonlike, she'd backed whatever the prevailing premise was, then, when it became expedient, fixed her crosshairs on me.

An impartial observer may decree that I myself have an agenda here. Clearly, a book such as mine—*What She Left* is the title we've opted for—could benefit from a revelation such as this. A twist. But it's the truth and one can't be partly truthful, any more than one can be partly blind, or partly dead, or partly pregnant.

I stared out at the night. I'd be out there soon. The fact blackjacked me: I'm dying. "You don't deserve to be a mother. If you had a child, you'd destroy it."

"I pushed her and I heard her screaming and I walked away and I'm glad I did." Her head lolled sideways. "Feel sick," she said. "Didn't even want a baby; I'm too young to have a kid. Just my luck: a one-night stand with some douchebag from work and I end up pregnant! But once I realized, it felt so right." She hugged her knees, buried her face in her hands. "Priest I should be talking to, not a has-been lecturer. How can you miss something you never had?"

"Easy. It's called imagination. You've had ours running ten to the dozen." We sat and in the eerie quiet I thought: *After tonight, I'm never going to make anyone cry ever again.* "That text, the line about death being beautiful; it was Wilde originally. Plath appropriated it."

"Me too." Then after a pause, she added: "Her phone was on the ground. After she went in the water—jumped, slipped, *you pick*—after it had gone quiet, I grabbed it and, bingo, off the text went to Mummy. Far as Liz was concerned, I was Alice. I was Alice saying good-bye."

It was that effortless—the press of a few buttons, a couple of exclamation marks, an emoticon or two. That's all it takes to say good-bye. That's all it takes to die.

"Crocodile tears," I said. "All crocodile tears."

"An eye for an eye. A tooth for a tooth. She was a murderer."

The little vixen may be confident she's got away with it, but I shall bring her in front of the courts. I shall put my head above the parapet, I shall stand on the ramparts and shout, and she will not escape the long arm of the law. I, too, shall "publish and be damned" and this iniquity will not stand. Larry, I was shedding a tear or two myself. It felt warmly cathartic. I could cry—I could.

"You can't touch me," she said.

"I can," I said, crabbing towards her, raising my hand. "And I shall."
She looked up and there was more than fear in her eyes.

Email sent by Professor Jeremy Cooke,
August 25, 2013

From: jfhcooke@gmail.com

To: marlenegutenberg@gmail.com

Subject: Departure

Dear Marlene,

I have a little time on my hands ahead of tomorrow's flight so will take this opportunity to pen slightly more than my rushed-off, phlegmatic dispatch of yesterday.

My most recent specialist appointment didn't go well. Three years is his current best guess, five at a push. So much for a bloody book making you immortal, eh?

I'm reasonably reconciled to my fate. Ironically, the news often elucidates more vexation among those with whom I share it. I haven't perfected the language of such exchanges yet. A *Guardian* crossword compositor I'm fond of latterly announced his terminal illness through his clues: a sign of growth (6) and a food transporter heard to gradually reduce an endless effusion (10). "Cancer of the esophagus," it dawned on me as I filled in the boxes in the faculty room.

There shall be no more hanging on, limpet-like, for redundancy. I am to retire. I'd prefer to slip away, but they're planning a bash. So, a warm glass of mediocre wine, some canapés and a few words from my leader (take the tie off him and he could pass as a student himself), inevitably referring to my "contribution" and "unique" methodology, then after that brief bout of bonhomie I'll pack away my office, wipe clean the desk, click the door shut behind me and head home to Fliss and the dog.

My wife is reacting to the circus that's building around the forthcoming publication with characteristic fortitude and grace. Dutifully, she plowed through a proof in one sitting before wheeling round to an apprehensive me and declaring, "Well, well." I may not give a fig about the critics' response, but my wife's I most definitely do. "I'm not proud of what you did, but I'm proud of you for getting to the truth" is her official line. Behind the scenes, off-camera, there have been tears and smashed kitchenware: the lightning bolt that Liz's maiden name was Mullens a notably distressing one.

She jokes about me becoming a media luvvie because of my TV and radio appearances. Inscrutably honest (I'm hardly in a position to self-censor now, am I?), unintimidated by controversy, prepared to vault from a discussion on contemporary cocaine usage to ethnography, I'm arraigned on panels with genial presenters who grapple with how to pitch me: "tireless pursuer of justice" or "old lech."

Hitherto, I've zealously resisted disclosing my final revelation, deflecting such hungry demands with the riposte that my principal wish is to bring the guilty party to justice and that necessitates imparting an unabbreviated story. It's also, of course, the book's denouement and spoilers hit sales.

Perhaps I should have gone public with my theory as soon as it dawned on me, but I've learnt the dangers of going off half-cocked. Instead, I redoubled my efforts, prompting Megan to do likewise. Surreal, with hindsight, those research sessions we shared: an elaborate chess game, Alice's past the pieces, moves and countermoves, my suspicions blooming, her attempts to influence my conclusions becoming more craven, her ever more desperate bid to create her own narrative, the one she'd have written, the past she would have wished, the future she sought. I was onto her long before her one ill-advised reference to the text she'd sent from Alice's phone, but that was the clinching corroboration. Fiction aficionados refer to "the lie that reveals the truth." Well, so it was for me—the lie that revealed the truth in this case an electronic message about lying in the grass and having no yesterday or tomorrow, and being at peace.

I am not blind to the fact that claiming publicly someone murdered their best friend is potentially libelous. Even intimating one didn't do all one could in that situation could be construed as defamatory. But the truth is an indefatigable defense against libel. Plus, there is a precedent. Media scholars will be familiar with a *Daily Mail* front page from 1997. Under the headline "Murderers," it published photographs of five men, so convinced was it they were responsible for Stephen Lawrence's death. "If we are wrong, let them sue us," it said.

Come on, Megan. If I'm wrong, if I'm lying, sue me.

As for Alice herself, I'll never claim my volume is encyclopedic. One merely has to recall coverage of the Joanna Yeates case (Fliss berated me for taking an "unhealthy" interest in it) to be reminded of this. Her Wikipedia page proffers her alma mater, her height, the pub in which she was last spotted—it even apprises you of the last CCTV footage of her, buying a pizza—but, ultimately, such *paucity* of detail. It may give you the grid reference where her body was found, but it doesn't give the coordinates of her heart.

No doubt readers drawn to its novelistic qualities will also castigate me for partly giving away the finale at the beginning (our heroine dies in chapter one). But that's how life is; it's not as if one's unaware at the start what's going to happen at the end.

Fliss teases me that it's destined for the remaindered pile, but success is a lottery. Coincidences, luck, assumptions, misunderstandings—these are the primary drivers of fate. If Liz hadn't mistakenly assumed the book deposited on her doorstep was put there by Megan, rather than Gavin, she may have never visited her and, in turn, might never have arrived, waif-like, on my doorstep—which, in turn, would have meant I'd have never summoned Megan. It was one of Alice's favorite books, *Never Let Me Go.*

I can't wait until the morning; I've planned it down to the nth degree. Fliss has always dreamed of visiting California, and tomorrow I'll make that dream come true. All those holidays traipsing around the Valley of the Kings and the Panathenaic Stadium and the Ades Synagogue were utterly spellbinding, but this will be two weeks of unashamed *fun*. We'll lap up the sunshine and eat cardiac-inducing servings and drive too fast in our 1970 Chevy—hideously impractical, of course, and an atrocious gas guzzler, but to hell with the bicycle for a fortnight: it's one of my bucket-list items. I wonder when exactly the penny will drop with Fliss—when I announce she'll be missing night school, when I inform her we need to drop Harley off at the kennels, when she sees her passport? That's one of the things I'm most looking forward to: a smile breaking on my wife's face. Because she's got the most beautiful smile.

Marlene, I'd be a liar if I claimed it hadn't crossed my mind that you and I take up corresponding. But I won't be writing again, for similar reasons to why I've drawn a halt to my tête-à-têtes with young Gavin. We'd hate anyone to get the wrong idea, now, wouldn't we? Whatever might they say? He's an odd one, that Old Cookie. You've got to watch him. Let's leave it at this, eh? At "Yours sincerely."

Let me instead dream often of visiting your great country. Arriving unannounced on your doorstep, your husband bowling out to greet me. "Well, I'll be jiggered," he'd say. We'd take a dram together and put the world to rights and reminisce and head out on day trips, two old buddies, two brilliant minds, two old rogues, driving along Route 1 or Route 11 and visiting Fredericton and Moncton, specks against the mountains. The great Larry Gutenberg and I.

Now I shall return to my packing. First, though, I shall go to the condensation-covered window and, with a flicker of déjà vu, draw the outline of a heart and in it write my and my wife's initials. That's enough. For now at least, that's more than enough.

Yours sincerely,
Jeremy Cooke

Mother's Day card sent by Alice Salmon, *2011*

Dear Mum,

Keep Sunday free, you're getting taken out for lunch—mine and Robbie's treat. I know I've driven you nuts at times, but you've always been an inspiration to me and pretty much everything you've ever said has been right, even if it's taken me a decade or so to realize in some cases. I even like asparagus these days! Thank you for being there and for being you. I really did win the lottery when it came to mums. You're a totally, totally amazing woman.

Hugs and kisses,
Ax
PS: Wear a posh frock!

Letter written by Professor Jeremy Cooke,
6 November 2013

My dearest Fliss,

I read somewhere that a marriage is like a dance—you have to find a tempo that works for both of you, but each of you has your own steps. I rather agree with that.

If I could have another go at this whole business, a second stab where I got things exclusively right, I'd want you again. In this second life, as a better man, as one who didn't make mistakes, I'd treat you how I should have in this first one.

Darling, I could fill a book with all the things I would wish to thank you for but, as you often observe, the world doesn't need another book.

Too often I bemoan man's inhumanity to man and evolution's inability to improve us—it's 2013 and we're still dropping bombs on children—but sometimes life has a phenomenal capacity to surprise you with its goodness. Here we are in our sixties swapping love letters—tiny shards of our history, our footprints in the sand, our echoes in the cave, our vapor trails.

Thank you for being part of my story. For making it my story. Our story. Thank you for making me feel blessed upon this earth. You were the lightbulb moment, Fliss. You were the Eureka moment.

I love you.
J.

EPILOGUE

Letter written by Alice Salmon,
September 8, 2011

Dear Me,

You're probably wondering why I'm writing to you. A twenty-five-year-old journalist living in south London. Don't worry, you're not in trouble. I'm not about to do some awful exposé on you, either. That's not my style.

It's because I'm reading this fantastic book called *Dear Me,* full of letters people have written offering words of wisdom to their sixteen-year-old selves. I'm going to use the idea at work and would like to launch it with mine. With *yours.*

You need to go with the flow a bit more, young lady. Lying awake stressing in the middle of the night doesn't achieve anything. As a boss you haven't yet met will be fond of saying when there's a cock-up: Ultimately no one's died.

It's OK to be scared. It's fine. What's important is that you don't let fear hold you back. Sometimes you've just got to throw yourself in at the deep end.

Stop beating yourself up about how you look, too. You haven't got giant's feet or weightlifter's shoulders. You're unique. It might take a while to find out exactly who that is, but it'll be worth the wait, because as your dad—my dad, *our* dad—used to say, there's only one you, Ace Salmon.

I hope reading this doesn't embarrass you. If it's any consolation, the *Advertiser* (that's the paper you'll go on to work for) has only got a circulation of about eighty-one, so it's hardly going to go viral (I'll obviously edit this line out before the boss sees this, ditto the swear-words). Either that, or I'll publish and be damned. I'll publish and be "out there," but that in itself is part of who we are: products of the Internet generation.

I doubt you'll listen to me, because to you I'll be past it, middle-aged, virtually dead, and I can't blame you, because right now *I* wouldn't pay any attention to my thirty-something-year-old self if she was banging on about pension plans and school catchment areas. But can I at least suggest a few don'ts? Don't do drugs, don't drink so much, don't get in debt, don't spend as much time online, don't lose sleep over what people think (this is beginning to sound like that "Sunscreen" song from the 1990s), don't worry about men and certainly don't hate yourself. Then again, don't entirely *don't* because, as a seedy scumbag of a professor will one day inform you (*said in my best posh voice*), you tend to regret the things you don't do, not the things you do. He was wrong. Sometimes you regret the things you *do,* too. I know that. He should as well. Him more than anyone.

Try to be nicer to your mum as well. She hasn't had it easy and has secrets of her own, secrets she couldn't admit to you at sixteen, that she still can't to me at twenty-five. One day she'll share them and I'll be here to listen. Fact is, there was a her before me, just as there'll be a me after her. Remember how you were convinced that turning into your mum would be a fate worse than death? Well, you'll get to a stage when sometimes you positively can't wait. When it feels like it would be a privilege.

Be nicer to the Robster as well. You might have stopped pinching him by sixteen, but you weren't the easiest teenager to live with and he always had your back: his kid sister who obsessively wrote it all down, then was so desperate to get away from what she saw that she burnt her diaries in a fit of disgusted rage.

Well done, incidentally, on winning that "What's in a Name?" writing competition. I'm not sure I've ever congratulated you. As a go-getting journalist (Caitlin Moran, watch out), I have to point out it had too many brackets and exclamation marks (as if this doesn't!) and didn't exactly answer the question (what's changed?). Plus, you only used 996 of the 1,000 allowed words. But the fact is, you won. Still strikes me as strange nearly a decade on. You—*I, we*—won.

What, of course, you didn't know as you were writing those 996 words is that you'd soon come to think fondly of the town you were so desperate to get away from; that Southampton would be the uni you'd head to (smart move turning Oxford down BTW); and that you'd get over your Leonardo DiCaprio crush within about twelve seconds of hitting the Send button. You didn't know any of this any more than you knew that the track you'd be playing on your iPod ten years later as you write this, "Iris" by the Goo Goo Dolls, would have become your favorite song *ever,* that you'd meet a man called Luke in a bar in Covent Garden or, for that matter, that the very day after you'd heard you'd won the competition, the Twin Towers would come down and the world would spend the next decade looking for the man who was responsible, only to find him a few months ago in Pakistan, the first inkling of his death permeating via the web, a neighbor tweeting about the noise of American helicopters overhead.

You'd like Luke. You used to say the word "boyfriend" secretly out loud, didn't you? Enjoying its lush round shapes, the way pronouncing it made your mouth move, its hypothetical possibilities. You'll learn it's a complicated word, one with many sides and interpretations and degrees of definitiveness. But Luke's my boyfriend and it feels right.

A few more Alices have become famous since you listed some, like Alice Cullen, who shot to fame as a character in *Twilight,* and Alice Munro, who was actually always famous but you only discovered her recently. Our name clearly does a good line in writers. I've come to adore Alice Walker's *The Color Purple* since I was you, even if I did have to look up "epistolary." Who knows, if my music reviewing takes off, I could even join the roll call. Imagine. Immortalized like some romantic heroine. Me. This Alice. Alice Salmon.

For now, though, I'll be the slightly-too-tall one who's grown into my body, who's learnt to live with it, who gets a fizzying zip of joy at being among her friends, who still loves a box set of *Dawson's Creek,* even if she occasionally finds herself listening to those teenagers' wise proclamations and muttering quietly: *Yeah, right.* Because life's not all beach parties and autumn-hued landscapes. It's complicated and doesn't necessarily have a happy ending. It's not all days when everyone's on your side, when everyone's Team Alice. But it's like in *Finding Nemo* (I'm as bad as my other half Luke, quoting films) when the fish says if life gets you down you've got to just keep on swimming. That's what I'll do: keep on swimming.

Yes, take heart, because in ten years you'll feel like you're where you're supposed to be. You'll have even stopped wishing the time away, and you were always prey to that, weren't you? Wanting it to be the *next* thing.

Ultimately, all you can do is get on with it, this thing we call "life." No one gets through entirely unblemished, but it's our scars that show who we are, where we've been, how we've fought on, how we've won. When you slide down a snake, climb straight back up a ladder. Remember, it's like Scrabble: Use your good letters as soon as you get them.

And as for those missing four words? What they would have been, what they *are*? That's easy.

I am Alice Salmon.

ACKNOWLEDGMENTS

I'd like to thank everyone at Simon & Schuster, particularly my editors, Sarah Knight, who was a constant source of fabulous ideas and a great champion of this book from its early stages, and Karyn Marcus, who has been at the helm to steer it so skillfully to publication.

In the UK, massive thanks as well to my amazing agent Hellie Ogden of Janklow & Nesbit, plus the team at Michael Joseph/Penguin—particularly my editor, the brilliant Rowland White.

ABOUT THE AUTHOR

T. R. Richmond is an award-winning author and journalist living in London.